STOLEN PASSION

Kyle lay sound asleep—until the sound of the door opening and the vision of a cloaked figure passing before him alerted his senses. From the slight build of the would-be thief, Kyle could tell it was a woman, and he had a good idea of who it was—Paige DuPree. He waited until she approached the bed and grabbed her neck in a vice-like grip.

"Please, Captain Brenner! Please don't hurt me," Paige cried, the fright in her voice penetrating the stillness.

Kyle swore furiously. "If it's money you want, Miss DuPree, why didn't you say so? Then, all of this would not be necessary."

Fully realizing the Captain's intentions, Paige commenced a desperate struggle. But soon, with a muffled groan, the Captain found her full, sensuous lips. And Paige, to her own horror, found herself responding to this rugged man's penetrating warmth.

There were many things Paige had done in the name of the South. Now she would add Captain Kyle Brenner to that list. . . .

HISTORICAL ROMANCE IN THE MAKING!

ECSTASY'S TREASURE

JEAN HAUGHT

ZEBRA BOOKS
KENSINGTON PUBLISHING CORP.

*To Jim . . . my love . . . my life. Also to
a dear friend, Judy Sallee, who once walked
with me to yesterday.*

ZEBRA BOOKS

are published by

KENSINGTON PUBLISHING CORP.
475 Park Avenue South
New York, N.Y. 10016

Chapter One

The Potomac River churned into white foam as an endless line of black clouds came charging over the horizon. Squat, ugly gunboats lining the water's edge tossed at the storm's mercy. The trees whipped with an unyielding fury. Lightning flashed and crackled through the sky. Thunder rolled with a noise so loud, it sounded like a mighty battle of cannons. Then the heavens opened and torrents of rain and hail beat ferociously down on the city. Ultimately, the storm abated, leaving a grayish fog behind that was so murky, it was difficult for the war-weary soldiers who were marching through the muddy streets to even breathe.

It was late in the evening before Kyle slipped unseen through the back gates of the White House. He had spent the entire afternoon with the president's secretary, studying the tedious, grueling details involved in his upcoming mission. It was hard for Kyle to believe that President Lincoln had entrusted him with such an important undertaking. Everything had happened so quickly. Atlanta had been secured for only a few days when he received top secret orders instructing him to come to Washington for a personal audience with the great man himself. After Kyle arrived, so much charisma and respect surrounded President Lincoln, he accepted the assignment without any doubts of its success. But many more hours of briefing still lay ahead of him. Then too, he had to return to Atlanta and convince his two most trusted friends and compadres to join him before heading for the piney woods of East Texas.

Kyle headed for his hotel but the deep rumblings in his belly demanded attention. He turned the corner into the frigid north wind and to his delight, a delicious aroma drifted out into the night air. He ambled slowly into the restaurant, found a table in a quiet corner and ordered a meal at his leisure. After finishing an enormous steak, a hefty portion of quartered, deep-fried potatoes and a mouth watering slab of apple pie, he leaned back in his chair and enjoyed a steaming cup of black coffee the waitress had brought him. His pleasant mood was spoiled when he heard a loud disturbance. Kyle looked abruptly around to see a Union soldier struggling with a young woman who apparently had been mopping the floor.

"Take your Yankee hands off me!" the girl shouted, her voice heavy with the soft drawl of the south.

"Listen here, you little Johnny-Reb bitch," the man thundered, "it's bad enough that we're having to fight this war because of the likes of you, but by God, I sure as hell don't have to take my supper in the same room with one of you, especially after what I caught you trying to do!" He shoved the girl roughly to the floor.

Leaping to his feet, Kyle scraped his chair against the floor and hurried to the girl's aid. "Mister!" he snapped, addressing the soldier. "We do not wage war on defenseless women. I think you ought to apologize to the lady before you disgrace your uniform further!"

The soldier started to reply angrily, but his eyes caught the captain's bars on Kyle's sleeve. He snapped to attention quickly. "Yes, sir! But, sir, I caught her trying to put something in my food. I thought she was trying to poison me or something." Kyle looked at the woman questioningly when he heard what the soldier had to say.

The woman spoke in a rage-tremored voice. "I appreciate your coming to my rescue, sir. But, as far as you're concerned," she said, glaring at the soldier, "the lady who is waiting tables got behind with her orders and the cook asked me to bring your food to you. I was simply sprinkling some sugar on the cobbler and you jumped to conclusions. But," she added haughtily, "if I had any poison and had thought about it, I certainly would have put it in your food!"

The manager had been in the back of the restaurant. He now came scurrying out front to see what was taking place. "What is going on here?" he demanded.

Kyle spoke up. "Nothing of any importance. There was just a little misunderstanding between this man and your employee. But I believe it's settled now."

The manager turned to the young woman with a thunderous expression on his face. "I warned you when you were hired, if you caused any trouble around here, I wouldn't be able to keep you. This is Union country, full of Union soldiers. and I can't afford to have trouble and lose business simply because I have a southerner working for me. I think the best thing you could do is gather your belongings and leave."

"But . . . but . . . Mr. Griffin," she pleaded. "I really need this job."

"That makes no difference to me. I can't have you ruining my business. I'm sorry, but that is how it'll have to stand."

The girl's face went white with rage as she snapped, "All right! I don't want your job. You Yankees have swept across our lands, burning our plantations and destroying our farmlands, and tearing down all we've built up in the past. Now you make it impossible for a person to earn an honest wage." She shook her head defiantly. "I have asked my last favor from a Yankee. The one thing you'll never do, is break my spirit or strip me of my pride. You, sir," she said, thrusting the mop in Griffin's face, "can take this and go straight to your Yankee hell!" She turned and stomped off into the kitchen then returned shortly with a small bag and a cloak. She then whisked determinedly through the front doors, leaving Griffin sputtering his indignation.

Kyle glared at the men, threw some money on the table and hurried after the girl. "Ma'am," he called upon reaching the street. "Wait a moment."

She turned, placing her hands on her small hips and with fire flying from her eyes, she started lashing him unmercifully with a sharp tongue. "Why are you following me? Haven't you done enough? Do you think I'm a deadly Confederate spy and you're protecting life and country by keeping me under surveillance?" She did not give him a chance to answer; instead, she continued with her verbal assault. "Well, I'll have you know, if they would accept me as a spy, I'd volunteer as one tomorrow!"

Kyle tipped his hat. "I understand why you're upset, ma'am, and you have every reason to be. You were mistreated back there. I . . . only wanted to apologize for the way the soldier treated you, and his making you lose your job. What happened between you and your boss . . . well, I guess that was entirely your business. But when a man is wearing the same uniform I am, and he disgraces it, then that's my business."

"You don't have to apologize. You didn't do anything to me."

Kyle stood for a moment, his eyes searching hers, seeing the hurt, pain and heartache, yet the bite of courage and determination. Nothing else was in his sight, only her eyes. Big dark green emeralds flecked with tiny bits of golden hues. It was as though he was being drawn deeper and deeper into the dark pools, when suddenly, the spell was broken as the young woman started crying. "I'm sorry, ma'am," he stammered. "I didn't mean to make you cry."

11

"You didn't make me cry," she sobbed as she glared angrily at the tall officer. "It's just . . . just . . ." she collapsed once again, this time into hard, jerking tears.

"There, there," Kyle soothed awkwardly. "Let's go into this little cafe and see if a glass of wine will help calm you down some."

Paige felt herself being led into a warm building and seated beside a roaring fireplace. She did not even acknowledge the stranger's presence as he placed the order for wine. She could only sit trance-like, staring at the flames disappearing up the chimney flue. It was apparent to her that her life was heading in the same futile direction.

An uneasy feeling swept over Kyle as he studied her. She had delicate features which hinted at so many discrepancies: Woman! Child! Fragile! Yet strong! But not strong enough to prevent a man from loving her and for her to return the love with a passion. She was of average height but that was where all normalcy ended. He had never seen a more beautiful woman in his life. Her raven colored hair had come uncoiled and was drifting down her back like ripples of waves flowing on a turbulent sea. Her cheeks were flushed rosy from the warmth of the fire, which only served to enhance her beauty. Kyle felt himself being drawn to her full, sensuous lips that curved upward, reminding him of a cupid's bow. Her skin was so fair and lovely, her entire appearance made Kyle's breath catch deep in his throat. But she was a puzzle to him. Why was a southern lady with obviously good breeding, scrubbing floors here in the Union capital?

His inquisitive mood was interrupted by the waiter bringing their wine. Kyle poured her a glass then watched as she slowly sipped the white wine. "Are you feeling better now?" he asked when the glass was empty.

"Yes, thank you," she said, helping herself to another glass full. "My papa always said, it only took two glasses of good wine to cure whatever ailed them; now, I believe him."

"I'll be honest," Kyle said. "You have aroused my curiosity."

"What do you mean, Mister . . . ?" Her voice trailed off.

"Brenner, ma'am. Captain Kyle Brenner. May I ask, what is your name?"

"My name is Paige DuPree." She paused then smiled hesitantly. "I do want to properly thank you for doing what you did back there."

"That's all right, Miss DuPree," Kyle replied off-handedly. "The soldier was mistreating you. Sometimes a war will make a man act the way he did." He looked at her strangely. "I don't know why it's suddenly important to me for you to realize all the people on the side of the Union are not like him." Kyle cleared his throat, obviously feeling ill at ease for saying what he had been thinking. "Let's change the subject. I can't help but wonder why you are all by yourself? Here, of all places."

Paige started to snap that it was none of his business but the words caught in her throat. Finally, she was able to mutter, "I guess you could say I am

13

one of the misfortunes of this damnable war.''

A hush settled over the couple as each was deep in his own thoughts. Paige sat back and studied the tall, Yankee soldier who somehow seemed different from the others she had chanced to meet. He was a big, broad shouldered man who showed signs of weariness. Not necessarily physically, but a weariness stemming from the steady but gradual decay of war. Underneath it all, his eyes revealed a warmth that could only come from laughter. She could not help but admire how his black curly hair and neatly trimmed beard complimented his ruggedly handsome features. Paige choked back a gasp. She was clearly shocked to find she could have such amicable thoughts about a Yankee! She had every reason in the world to hate them.

Her parents were not wealthy, but her papa worked for a kind-hearted plantation owner who was cut from a different cloth than most. Silas Anderson never allowed his money to come between the friendship he shared with Paige's father. Daniel DuPree earned an honest and comfortable living by working as overseer for Silas on his plantation.

After the battle of Fort Sumter in April of 1861 and the beginning of the Civil War, Silas sent his daughter, Susanne, and Paige to a school in Boston. He and Daniel had discussed the matter about Paige, and both decided since there were so many Federal soldiers in the general area, both girls would be safer where there was no fighting. Years passed by, and then the unhappy day came; Susanne and Paige received word that their parents had been killed during an advance of the Union soldiers. The Anderson's plantation had been confiscated by the Federalists, which left Susanne with only a small trust fund, and Paige was left penniless. The head mistress of the school carried Paige for the remainder of the semester and through the summer, but when the school reopened in the fall, she had to dismiss Paige.

A distant relative of Susanne's came to her rescue, recommending Paige for a governess' job located in the Union capital. Passage by train was provided by her new employer. But that soon proved to be a disaster. The children's mother was insanely jealous of the lovely governess and soon invented a reason to dismiss her, leaving Paige once again penniless and in a strange city all alone. Faintly recalling her papa's brother, Paige remembered her parents talking about him and his farm located in far away East Texas. She decided to stay where she was until she could find a job, and make enough money to try and reach him. She had just gone to work at the restaurant, only to be fired almost immediately. Yankees? She had nothing but hatred for them. They caused her to lose everything she had ever held dear to her and stripped all forms of security from her life.

Kyle sat quietly while Paige took her walk back through the past. He could tell she was recalling many painful memories by the stricken expression in her eyes. Pity for her filled him. He knew how alone and desperate she must be feeling. He could not help but wonder how she truly felt about the people who were on opposite sides of the Confederate cause. Unfortunately, war was never pretty and this war had pitted brother against brother, father against son, and families against families. The innocent were suffering right along with the guilty, if . . . one could be labeled guilty during a time of war. Kyle waited a moment longer then spoke softly, "You've had it pretty rough, haven't you?"

"Don't you dare pity me!" Paige snapped. Then she ducked her head sheepishly, realizing this person was the only one who had even showed her a scrap of human kindness. "I'm sorry. It was terribly rude of me to talk to you that way. I didn't mean to sound so cross. To answer your question, yes. I suppose I have had it bad, but, there are many others who have suffered much more than I have."

Admiration gripped Kyle. Never had he encountered such a woman! Here was a person who had every reason in the world to hate with a passionate bitterness, but she appeared to have very little animosity. Except for the episode back at the restaurant, it would have been difficult to tell which side she was on.

The clock above the mantel chimed nine o'clock, catching Kyle's attention. He hurriedly stood, hating to leave her company, but also knowing he had to return to the White House early the next morning. Suddenly, an idea formed in his mind. "Miss DuPree, if you would allow me, I'd be happy to see you to your room. There are so many soldiers garrisoned here, it would be dangerous for you to be out on the streets alone at this time of night."

Paige lowered her head and admitted, "I don't . . . have a room."

"Well, come on and I'll help you find one," Kyle offered.

"Captain Brenner," Paige said, squaring her shoulders independently, "I can take care of myself, although, I do appreciate your offer."

"I figure you're just about broke," Kyle growled before he thought about how his tone of voice sounded. "So how in the world are you gonna find a room?"

Paige held her tongue, not with acquiescense, but since she was determined not to get too deeply involved with a Yankee, it was best to remain silent. Finally, when his manner demanded a response, she shrugged flippantly. "There is absolutely no need for you to trouble yourself. Besides, I feel as though I am in your debt deeply enough."

Kyle sighed impatiently. "Look, Miss DuPree, be reasonable. You are alone in a strange city, broke, and I guess I'm the only person you know. I don't think *now* is the time for foolish pride to stand in the way."

"Captain Brenner, I'll have you to know, I do not have any so-called foolish pride. You may find it strange that some people were raised to believe nice ladies do not accept favors from strangers!" She threw her wrap around her shoulders and added with forced politeness. "I must be on my way. I thank you for the wine. *Good night, Mister Brenner.*"

Kyle swore under his breath. He had made the mistake in judging her to be downtrodden. Miss

DuPree was apparently the epitome of the stubborn, prideful South, one of the most loyal breed of humanity. He figured she was bested by circumstances for the moment, yet, she seemed little daunted. Still, underneath all her fire and spirit, she displayed none of the underlying viciousness he had encountered with other southern women. He found himself neither discouraged nor repulsed by her actions, perhaps a small amount of anger though, because of her lack of personal fear. "Damn it, woman, I certainly didn't mean anything improper by my offer. Hell, I'm only concerned about your safety!"

Paige tossed her raven hair. "Captain Brenner, I find your manners fresh and insolent. I have already told you, I can take care of myself. It is rude of you to insist on escorting me when it should be quite clear I am tired of your company!" She glared at him then marched determinedly to the door, smugly satisfied that she was not obligated to anyone.

"All right!" Kyle shouted after her. "Be stubborn, but don't say later I didn't warn you." He looked around to see a waiter staring at him openmouthed. "Do you have anything stronger than this?" he asked, indicating the wine.

"Yes sir," the waiter sputtered.

"Then bring me a drink and I don't want any of that watered down booze you usually push off on the soldiers coming in here."

The waiter spun on his heel, muttering under his breath. In a few moments he was back with a partially filled glass. Slamming it down on the table, he snapped, "I suggest you hurry up and drink it, 'cause we close in a few minutes."

Kyle nursed his drink slowly, proving his defiance to the closing time. He knew he ought to feel ashamed of himself for snapping at the waiter; after all, he was an old man, when in truth it was the young woman who deserved his anger. He stared moodily into the glowing coals of the fireplace. Suddenly a weary feeling slipped over him. It had been far too long since he had had a decent night's sleep. He quickly downed the remainder of his drink so he could go to his hotel.

The blast of the cold night air made Kyle hurry his steps. He turned a corner, paused, then continued on. Was he so tired that he was now hearing imaginary sounds? He thought he had heard a scream. Slowing his steps once again and listening carefully, Kyle cautiously removed his gun from his holster. This time, he was certain. Screams were coming from the small alley running along the side of his hotel. Kyle slipped into the dark, narrow street, not knowing what he would find.

In the shadows, a young woman was struggling for her life as two men tried to force themselves on her. Paige could slowly feel her strength ebbing away. "God!" she whispered aloud. Why hadn't she accepted Captain Brenner's offer.

One of the men pinned her arms behind her while the other ripped her blouse, exposing her firm, jutting breasts. Paige shut her eyes tightly and blocked out the noise of the man's heavy breathing as she prayed for the darkness that did not come. Instead, the memory of his avid, grue-some expression burned permanently into her mind. The odor of their unwashed bodies pene-trated her nostrils as her attacker pressed her against the cold, hard ground. She gritted her teeth and braced herself for the coming assault, when suddenly the man cried out and his body weight slumped heavily against her.

"You certainly have a hell of a way of taking care of yourself," Kyle snarled when he recognized Paige. He pulled the unconscious man away from her. "Did he hurt you?" he asked anxiously.

"No . . . I . . . don't think so." Paige gasped, tears running freely down her face as she tried to pull her torn blouse back into place. "Oh! There was another man somewhere!" she warned. Then her eyes widened when she saw him slumped in the middle of the alley. Paige sank back onto the ground, crying so hard, her shoulders were shaking uncontrollably.

Kyle awkwardly took her in his arms and tried to comfort her. When it was apparent she had calmed some, Kyle asked her, "Now, will you let me get you a room?"

Paige nodded gratefully and hurried to arrange the cloak around her shoulders so the torn blouse would not show.

Paige walked close beside Kyle as they entered the hotel lobby.

"I'd like to get a room for this lady," Kyle stated plainly.

The desk clerk gave Kyle a wink and knowing smile as he replied. "Sorry sir. There's no more rooms left. Re'kon the lady would mind sharing yours?"

"Listen you," Kyle snapped. "Miss DuPree happens to be a lady and I resent like hell your implying otherwise. I asked you for a room. Do you have one or not?"

"Well . . . ," the man drawled. "Yeah, I suppose so. I just thought . . ."

"I know what you thought and you are mistaken. One more mistake like that and I'll have this place labeled off-limits to every soldier in town!" Kyle grabbed the pen, swung the register around and signed Paige's name on it before the desk clerk could change his mind. After snatching the key to her room off the counter, he took Paige by the arm and led her to the stairs. "I guess you know," Kyle spoke when they were out of hearing range from the lobby, "that man had the wrong impression about you."

Paige blushed. "I think so. But," she protested, "you could have explained what happened outside, and perhaps he wouldn't have thought what he did."

"Yeah, I probably could have explained, but after thinking about it, I believe this hotel caters to a certain kind of trade. Those men out there more than likely thought you worked here or something."

"You mean they thought I was a trollop!" Paige gasped.

Kyle laughed aloud at her innocence. By this time, they had reached the door to her room. He stood quietly for a moment, just staring at her;

then he tipped his hat and said, "It's been a pleasure knowing you, Miss DuPree. I'll probably be gone in the morning . . . but I know you will need some help. Would it offend you if I offered you a little money just to tide you over until you can find a job?"

"Oh no, Captain Brenner. You've done too much as it is. I assure you, I will be fine. Thank you for being so kind to me. Maybe . . . next time we meet it will be under more favorable conditions."

"Those are my feelings exactly, Miss DuPree." Kyle figured there was no use arguing with her. He simply took her hand, pressed it to his lips and turned and quickly disappeared down the hall.

Later that night, Paige lay tossing and turning, unable to sleep. Try as she would, she could not rid her mind of the handsome captain who had come to her rescue twice that day. In her mind's eye, she could see him as he walked, moving like an animal stalking its prey. She could see the gentleness he showed, also the virility and strength. Why was there such an emptiness about her when she thought of him? He was a Yankee! He was the hated enemy! The likes of him were the cause of her parents and other loved ones lying in their graves. Surely she was a traitor for even having such amicable thoughts about him. Sighing deeply, Paige pushed the memory of his face from her mind and turned to the desperate problem facing her.

Somehow, she had to raise money in order to be

able to reach her uncle. He was her last link to family, but the only thing she could recall about him was where he lived. She had no idea how much money it would take to reach him, and even if she could secure passage through the war-torn south, would he still be living in the same place? The only thing for certain, tonight proved just how desperately she needed a home again. Just the thought of a little house in a faraway place, seemed like a safe haven against a raging storm.

Somehow, someway, she had to lay her hands on some money, and the sooner the better. She had to get away from here! A faint glimmer of an idea came to her, but she felt horrified at the thoughts she was thinking. Paige quickly pushed it from her mind but it came slowly creeping back. The longer she lay there, the greater her desperation came to be. She knew what had to be done. Regardless of the atrocity she was contemplating and the possible hardships she could be bringing on others, survival must come first. After all, she reasoned, a Yankee wouldn't have second thoughts if it was a southerner.

Kyle lay sound asleep. He was so tired and weary, he almost didn't hear the door open and see the cloaked figure steal quietly into his room. His eyes flew wide open as he listened, suddenly alert for any danger. His hand edged silently under his pillow, and grasped the gun firmly, preparing to spring into action at any moment. Kyle allowed his eyes to adjust to the darkness, then watched as the figure walked lightly around the bed to where

23

his clothes were scattered on the floor. From the slight build of the would be thief, Kyle could tell it was not a man. It was definitely a woman and he had a good idea who she was. He waited until she approached the bed before grabbing her. In a flash his arms were around her neck in a vice like grip.

"Please, Captain Brenner! Please don't hurt me!" Paige cried, the fright in her voice piercing the stillness.

"'Is this the thanks I get for helping you?" Kyle snarled roughly. Then a light of realization flashed over his features. "I'm beginning to see it all now." He pulled her down on the bed then pinned her body with his own. "I've been played for a fool before, but not by an innocent-acting woman like you." He spat bitterly, "How many times have you pulled this little game?" Laughing sardonically, Kyle continued, "I guess it's a pretty good sham you've got going . . . getting someone to help you, then robbing the poor man blind!" Anger infested him for having been played the fool.

"Oh no! Please believe me, Captain Brenner," she cried. "It's not like that at all."

Kyle swore furiously. "Like hell it's not! Woman, I know when I've been had." He was suddenly aware of her warmth penetrating through the thin chemise and threadbare robe she wore under her cloak which was now hanging loose. "Listen, Frenchie, if it was money you were after, then why in the hell didn't you say so in the first place? Then, all of this would have been unneces- sary." His breath came in short, rapid, gasps.

Although Paige was very innocent she fully realized what the captain meant. "Oh no!" She gasped. "I didn't mean . . . I won't ever . . . I promise never to do this again, just please let me go!"

"Sure you promise, honey," Kyle said mockingly. "You promise never to do this again . . . that is, until the next time you have a chance. I'll teach you a lesson, then, maybe there won't be a next time!" Kyle felt his maleness grow rigid with desire. The harder she struggled, the more his desire for her increased. It had been such a long time since he had had a woman; especially one so beautiful, desirable, and firm-loined. It did not matter that she was a treacherous Confederate wench.

With a muffled groan, Kyle sought her full sensuous lips, probing with his mouth, seeking . . . searching . . . He had grown to his fullest height with a swiftness he didn't think possible. The woman desperately tried to free herself but Kyle's strength overpowered her until she was quite helpless in his arms. His lips searched until they found her breasts. He plied each firm mound until he could no longer contain himself. Grasping both wrists in one large hand, he was free to scoop her hips up to meet his forward thrust. Paige cried out as the pain of him filled her. A look of stunned surprise flashed across Kyle's face when he penetrated the restraining barrier. He swore softly under his breath. "Well, I'll be . . . A damn virgin!"

For a moment all motion was stilled and the

only noise was Paige's violent sobs. Kyle's thoughts raced. There was no way he could undo what he had taken from her. He also knew it would be next to impossible to stop what he had started. His lips found hers again. Gently kissing her sweet tasting mouth, his lips trailed to the delicate hollow of her throat. He had no desire to rape her, he had actually thought her innocent act was nothing but "put-on" to deceive the men she was attempting to rob. But, since she was indeed a virgin, he knew he must do something to try and make her respond to his lovemaking or she would probably hate men forever. He cradled her neck in his hands, all the while stroking and gently caressing until her resistance began to ease. Not able to wait any longer, Kyle lifted her to meet him completely. After months of being without a woman, it was only a matter of moments until his passion was satisfied although he realized her need did not match his desire.

Afterwards, he tasted the salty tears as he kissed her. Not releasing his hold, he muttered tenderly, "I didn't know you were a virgin."

"What difference would it have made?" Paige spat bitterly. "Let me go! You've used and defiled me and should be very happy to add my name to your conquests."

"Listen," Kyle interrupted. "I think you should remember that it was you who came to my bedroom."

"That may be true, but I didn't come in here for you to rape me!"

"Probably not, Frenchie," Kyle mocked. "You

did come in here to rob me though."

Tears welled up behind Paige's eyes. "No, not really. I was only going to take enough money to try and reach my uncle's home, nothing more." She glared at him furiously. "I'll never forgive you or forget what you've done to me."

"Look, I said I was sorry. I didn't know you were a virgin. I thought . . ."

"I know what you thought. I read you right the first time I saw you. Tell me, are Yankee women such pigs you can't wait to get your hands on a real woman?" She rushed on, not giving him time to answer. "I demand to be released this instant!" she shrieked. "You've taken what was precious to me. Now you can sit around the campfire and tell your men another sordid, despicable tale!"

The muscles in Kyle's cheek worked furiously. "I'll not let you go yet. Regardless of what you think. I'm not a defiler of women and I do not boast of my sex life." He chuckled easily, "In fact, some women would be honored to share my bed."

She glared at him. "I feel no honor. Only disgust!"

Kyle smirked, "That's what I thought. Because of what happened between us, you think men and sex are dirty and bad. No, Frenchie, I don't think I ought to let you go. I think I should show you just how wonderful sex can be between two people."

Horror swept over Paige as she felt Kyle's maleness grow rigid. "Oh no!" she gasped. "Please don't do that horrible thing to me again."

"That's where you're wrong, darling. It's not horrible. Relax and I'll show you."

"Please, captain, no."

Kyle chuckled deeply. "I think we can be on a first name basis, Paige. You should call me Kyle."

She moaned, fear strangling her when she felt the hardness probing at her tight, resisting flesh. Paige bit her lip until she tasted blood, while unheeded tears trickled down her face. Then his hungering lips searched out her mouth and he kissed her with such leisurely thoroughness, the ache of his invasion began to subside. This time, he did not rush but seemed to savor each pleasurable moment. A feeling foreign to Paige began to pound through her breasts. It was a feeling she could not deny. His slow movements began to attack her senses; the throbbing heat of him warmed her and she started to respond slowly to his ardent kisses. She silently cursed her body for betraying her and was startled to hear deep moans coming from her throat. But it suddenly seemed as though she was possessed by something she could not explain. Her desire increased until she was completely consumed by it. Kyle breathed heavily and moved with an increasing crescendo but her own ecstasy was building at even a faster rate. She was about to explode but she did not care, even if it blasted her throughout the universe. Kyle sensed the urgency and he allowed his passion to meet hers. When it finally happened, it was the most uninhibited feeling that had ever captivated her. It was as though her soul had fled her body and was searching the heavens.

Paige felt as though she had been awakened from a long, deep sleep. She cradled Kyle's head against her breasts, knowing but not caring she was under his spell. Paige melted in his arms and delighted in the ecstasy which swept over her. This time, it was she who brazenly searched for his lips and tasted the ardor of his love. . . .

Much later, everything drifted back into place. As dawn cast her sleepy eyes through the window, Kyle awoke fresh and alert. He carefully eased out of bed taking pains not to disturb the lovely lady. After dressing, he paused by her bedside and with no malice in his heart or mind, he placed a generous amount of gold coins under her pillow. He stared wistfully at her for a brief moment then shook his head sadly. Kyle, then turned, walked to the door and disappeared down the hallway.

It was hours before Paige awoke. She stretched lazily then as the memory of the preceding night came flooding back, a rose colored hue swept across her face. Raising up, she was immediately thankful she was alone. Not because she did not want to face Kyle, she simply wanted a moment to collect her thoughts. She revelled in the memory of his arms around her. Never would she have believed she could feel this way toward any man, especially one who was on opposite sides of all her beliefs. What spell had he cast over her to make her forget all the teachings and decency that had been instilled in her since childhood? Paige turned and gasped horrified, when the sunlight caught the glimmer of the coins. They appeared so sinister! With trembling hands she clasped them to her breasts, then flung them across the room before dissolving into a pool of helpless tears.

Chapter Two

The wheels of the locomotive chugged along singing a tuneless song. The shrill wail of the whistle pierced through the night stillness as if it was a mother calling . . . crying for her lost child.

Paige pressed her face close to the window, feeling very thankful that the train was moving again. It seemed they could only travel ten or fifteen miles before the train was stopped and searched time after time by Union soldiers. They were everywhere!

She could feel tears brimming behind her eyes at the thought of so many Union soldiers with such a pitiful few Confederate ones remaining. A bitter feeling swept over her as she realized the reports she had been hearing were true. Soon, the South would fall. It was only a matter of a few months, possibly a few weeks. What would happen to them then?

She shook the unpleasant thoughts from her mind and took her handkerchief and tried to wipe some of the sooty grime away from the windows. With the train having to stop for inspection, repairing mangled tracks, and the engineer trying to coax another mile from the tired old locomotive, it would take them forever to reach Shreveport.

Ah, Shreveport! Just the idea of being in a home again, surrounded and protected by loved ones, was enough to send shivers of anticipation rippling up and down her spine. She could only hope and pray her Uncle Oscar had received the wire she had sent earlier. But . . . if he hadn't, then she would cross that bridge when she got to it.

It was turning very cold and the pot-bellied stove standing in the rear of the passenger car did not provide the warmth required to heat the entire area. Paige gratefully removed her fur lined cloak from her traveling bag, thankful she had purchased it in Boston where the winters were fierce and people prepared more thoroughly for the cold. She had just snuggled down under its protective warmth when she saw a woman not much older than herself bundling a small child with a threadbare coverlet. The baby whimpered, sounding as though he didn't have the strength to cry a lusty wail. Paige noticed tears of frustration slip quietly down the young mother's face. She knew the child had to be suffering not only from the cold but from hunger as well. Gathering her wits firmly together, Paige removed some biscuits and sausages from her bag. After taking a deep breath, she marched determinedly over to the woman.

"Would you object to my joining you?" Paige asked in a small but friendly voice.

"Oh no, ma'am. Please do," the woman said as

she moved over, obviously happy for a friendly face for a change.

"My name is Paige DuPree. I'm so tired of sitting by myself and eating alone. I thought perhaps . . . if you haven't had your supper yet, you might join me?"

"Oh, thank you for the invitation but you go right on ahead. Me and William will get us something to eat when we get to the next town. I didn't have a chance to buy us anything to carry along . . ." Her voice trailed off proudly.

"Now this is utter nonsense," Paige stated firmly. "You and your son are more than welcome to join me. Why, there is no telling how long it will take to reach the next town as slow as this train is going. Besides, this food could ruin if it's not eaten soon, and heaven knows how hard it is to come by at times. I think," she added, fishing around in her bag, "yes, I'm sure I even have a tin of marmalade. I think that William's little digestion could handle biscuits and marmalade, don't you?"

The woman stared at Paige for a moment then she started to cry, silently at first only to break into deep, rasping sobs. "I'm sorry. But I can't take anything. You see, I wasn't really going to buy me anything to eat, just William, 'cause I spent almost all my money for this train ticket. But . . . if you wouldn't mind sparing a little bit of bread for my son, I'd certainly be obliged."

"Now don't be foolish!" Paige snapped, turning her face so the woman couldn't see the tears welling up behind her eyes. "I invited you both to have supper with me and I will not take no for an answer. Now that everything is settled, what did you say your name was?"

"I didn't say, but it's Lynna, Lynna Johnston." She revealed a beautiful but rare smile as she continued. "Ma'am, me and William would be pleased to join you for supper. I really don't know hardly what to say though because it's not often that I meet someone as gracious as you."

"I'm not gracious," Paige said as embarrassment swept over her. "I merely believe it is about time we women stood together for a change."

Paige watched as Lynna carefully spread the jam on the bread, giving William his fill before one morsel of food entered her own mouth. A warm glow filled Paige while she watched Lynna eat. Not a crumb of food was left when they finished.

Paige started to move back to her own seat when her eyes caught the pitifully thin comforter which was wrapped around the child. "I know!" she exclaimed. "Instead of my going back over there, why don't I stay here with you? We could all wrap up together and be a lot warmer than if we sit alone."

"I do declare, I think you are an angel of mercy God sent to see me and William through to our destination."

Paige laughed. "You are the first one to ever call me that." Her manner turned to a more serious note. "Where are you going?"

"To join my husband. He's on duty at Camp Ford. That is a prison camp in East Texas, near

33

Tyler, I think."

"Have you been apart long?"

Lynna sighed. "It seems like years but actually it has only been six months since I saw him last. He got shot up pretty bad at Shiloh back in '62. They let him come home to recover from his wounds. He was just getting our little farm back on its feet when his old captain got in touch with him. It seems they needed some men to guard this prison and William volunteered. I guess it was about a month ago now, that the Yankees burnt their way through and our little house got in their way. Luckily they didn't bother our livestock none. I managed to sell it and raised enough money for the train fare. And just as soon as the war is over we are gonna head west and start our life all over again."

Paige reached over and patted Lynna's hand. "You are a very brave woman and I wish you all the happiness in the world."

"Thank you. But what about you? How come a nice, refined woman such as yourself is traveling all alone?"

Paige explained what had happened, being careful not to mention certain experiences. After awhile, Lynna was lulled by the music of the train wheels, to a resting and peaceful sleep. Paige sat wide eyed as she thought remorsefully, "I wonder if you would be sitting here beside me if you knew it was a whore's money that bought passage for this seat and provided the money for the food we just ate?" She pensively remembered the night she spent with Kyle Brenner. How could she have lain in his arms and actually enjoyed the sinful wicked-

34

ness? In her mind's eye she could recall every detail of Kyle's body and the feel of his hands on her. She shook her head and tried to calm the pounding of her heart. Why did she still care? Somehow she had to rid her memory of him. After all, he had defiled her! She also knew it should be hatred in her heart but somehow that seemed impossible, although deep inside she realized the day would come, probably the day she went to her husband's bed and he discovered she was not a virgin.

The following morning, some of the passengers were standing and stretching, trying to rid the ache from their muscles caused by the hard, wooden benches which served as seats when suddenly, the train came to an abrupt halt.

"Everyone keep to your seats," the conductor bellowed as several of the passengers tried to lower windows to see what had happened.

For a moment the people sat in a muted silence then the silence turned to screams and shouts of terror when sounds of gunfire echoed throughout other cars. The door of the car that Paige was in flew open and a man dressed in a Confederate uniform appeared, brandishing an evil looking gun.

"Everybody just stay calm," he ordered, "and there will be no cause for me to use this." Then he walked over to the stove and ordered everyone to leave the train one at a time.

A man in the back of the car shouted. "Wait a minute! It's real cold outside. Us men can take it, but what about the women and children?"

"I'm sorry, but it can't be helped. Since we're acting on behalf of the Confederacy and we are needing this train badly, nothing else can inter-fere, not even women and children." He glanced down at the firewood. "I will let you take some of this dry wood with you so you can build a fire until some help comes along."

While the soldier was talking, the conductor eased his hand inside his coat and pulled out a small pistol. The soldier saw him just as the con-ductor fired, and he dodged but not quick enough to avoid the bullet hitting his leg. The soldier's gun barked an answer and when the gunfire died away, the conductor lay in a crumpled heap.

"I told you all not to try anything funny!" he shouted. "You," he pointed to a man standing nearby, "see if anything can be done for him."

"No sir. He's dead. You killed him."

The soldier's eyes darted back and forth. "I didn't want anyone to get hurt. I'm sorry he had to die but it was either him or me. From now on," he added menacingly, "I'd suggest you folks do exactly as I say and perhaps there won't be any more bloodshed. Before you people leave the train, I want to say just one more thing. I realize this will cause hardships to some of you and for that, I'm sorry. But remember, it's for the Confederacy."

In a few moments, the passenger car was emp-tied and all the people were lined up close to the shallow ravine which ran alongside the tracks. Another soldier came riding up quickly. "Cap'n! Cap'n! Scout says there is a whole troop of Union soldiers ridin' hell fer leather and they're comin' this way!"

"Get the men together and get 'em out of here!"

the captain shouted. He turned and eyed the passengers warily. "You, ma'am, come with me," he ordered after a moment's decision. "You can either come peacefully or I'll force you . . . the choice is yours to make."

Paige felt a surge of horror rush over her as she realized he was talking to her.

"All right, folks, I know I've made some of you really mad at me, especially since I had to shoot that man, but let me give you fair warning, if you don't want this woman's life on your shoulders, then I'd suggest you tell the Yankees we've gone in a different direction. My horse is tied over there in that stand of trees. Don't anybody play hero and try to stop us either, or she'll still be dead!" The captain took off running as fast as he could on his wounded leg, pulling Paige along behind him. They were well out of sight of the train when he tripped over an unseen stump and went sprawling on the ground. "Oh! God-damn!" he moaned in agony. "My leg, I think it's broken!"

Paige stood back, her eyes wide with fear. She knew this was her chance for escape, but if she ran, the Union soldiers would capture this man and possibly hang him for the murder of the conductor.

"Go on! Don't stand there looking at me like that. You've got your chance to run for it, so take it," the soldier whispered harshly.

"No! If I leave you, you'll be captured."

The man looked at her in bewilderment, but an expression of hope flashed over his face.

Paige looked around quickly. "Where is your

37

horse tied? I don't approve of what happened back there but if that man had listened to you, he probably would be alive right now. My folks were murdered by Yankees and there is no way I'm going to turn you over to them. I'll get your horse, help you mount him, then I'll go back to the train and tell them I escaped and you rode off in a different direction than you actually did. Hurry, tell me, where's your horse?"

"It's . . . it's over there," he said, indicating some trees to the left.

Paige ran for the horse and wordlessly helped him on it. Even though he was suffering a great deal of pain, he took Paige's hand and pressed it to his lips when he was mounted. "Thank you for my life, ma'am. Perhaps one of these days, we'll meet again and I can repay the favor." With those words, he whirled his horse about and disappeared into the thick underbrush.

Four days later, they finally reached Shreveport. As Paige left the train, she pressed a few of her remaining coins into Lynna's hand, explaining that Lynna still had some distance to travel and since she had already reached her destination, it would make her happy if her newfound friend accepted what pitiful amount she had to share.

Later, after good-byes were said and the train had left the station, Paige walked determinedly down the street. Her head was held high and proud as she ignored the soldiers' and other men's piercing eyes slide over her slim and attractive figure. Although she was silently pleased with their admiring glances, she couldn't help but feel thankful that Shreveport was held by the Confederacy. If not, the streets would not have been safe for a decent woman to walk them.

She made her way to the town marshal's office, hoping her uncle had been in and possibly inquired about her.

"Yep," the marshal said as he scratched his head. "He's in town but I don't know where he's at though. I sho' hope I don't disappoint you none, but he wasn't asking 'bout any relative. I guess you could try Roxanne's saloon. That's about the only place he goes whenever he's in town."

Cold fingers of fear gripped at Paige for a brief instant. "Could . . . you tell me where this saloon is?" she stammered.

"Yep. Sho' can. Fact is, I s'pect anyone in town could tell you where Roxanne's is at. Just go down that street there," he said, pointing, "and turn left at the next corner. Before you know it, you'll be standing right in front of her place." He leaned over and spit carelessly into a soiled spittoon. After wiping his mouth on the sleeve of his dirty shirt, he asked, "Would you be planning on going to work for her? She's always looking for new girls."

Paige blushed at his suggestion, knowing what kind of women worked in saloons. "No, sir. I am only looking for my uncle. I imagine when I find him, we'll be leaving for his farm."

The marshal laughed crudely. "Well, good luck, honey. I got a hunch you're gonna be needing it."

Paige hurried from the horrible man's office,

fear clutching at her heart. She simply was not used to being around such an unsavory character. After finally finding the saloon, Paige took a deep breath to muster her courage and entered the saloon. She bravely walked over to where an enormous woman was sitting. "Ma'am, may I see Miss Roxanne, please?"

The woman looked at the young woman through squinted eyes. "I'm Roxanne. What do you want?"

"I was told you could possibly direct me to my uncle," Paige answered in a small voice.

Roxanne leaned forward and grunted then fanned the air behind her. "Good Gawd! That sure stunk." She glanced back up at Paige and laughed when she saw the girl blushing at her unladylike act. "Perhaps I could be some help to you if I knew who your uncle was?" she said when she had finished laughing.

Paige stammered. "Oscar DuPree."

"Oh my Gawd!" Roxanne roared once again in laughter. "Here I was a-thinking that you were really looking for someone!" You came in here a-prancing with your hoity-toity airs and come to find out, you're looking for that frigging bastard. Hey Amos," she hollered as she turned around to the barkeeper. "Did you hear that?"

"Sho' did, Miz Roxanne," the man said.

Paige was so shocked, she could only look help-lessly back and forth between the fat woman and the barkeeper.

Roxanne's chair shuddered and creaked when her huge belly jiggled in laughter. "Hell, honey, I sure don't know what you could want with him! But you sure don't fool me none. Huh! Uncle my ass! Anyway, I guess that's your business. If you want him, I re'kon he's where I chunked him a while ago. He was drunker than a pole cat when he staggered in here wanting like hell to hump me, only he calls it pleasuring me. Ha! Why that lazy bastard couldn't get up a hard if he had to, so I tossed him and his green pecker out the back door."

Paige swallowed hard trying to fight back the tears. "Thank you," was all she could mumble as she took faltering steps toward the door. Roxanne's harsh, crackling laughter filled the entire saloon and rang in Paige's ears when she stumbled because of her anxiety to be gone from this horrible place.

Chapter Three

The afternoon sun was streaming through the windows before the man finally awoke. "What . . . where am I?" he asked in mumbled confusion. He squinted one eye at the girl sitting quietly in the room's only chair. "Who in the hell are you?"

"Before I answer, I have to ask you a question. Did you have a brother by the name of Daniel DuPree?"

"Yeah, what's it to you?" he asked warily.

"He was my father," she said simply.

Ignoring the pain which pierced his head when he swung his feet to the floor, Oscar took a closer look at the girl. He raised one eyebrow in surprise. "Well, I'll be . . . you certainly favor Daniel." Then what she had said dawned on him. "What did you mean, he *was* your father? What's wrong? What's happened to him?"

"Mama and Papa were both killed during an advance by Union soldiers. They used to talk about you quite a bit, so when I was left all alone I decided to try and find you. I believe I was fortunate because I didn't have much trouble."

"Imagine that! My only brother dead." Oscar dropped his head into his hands for a few moments, then raised sorrowful eyes. "How long ago did it happen?" he asked quietly.

"It's been a long time now, or at least it seems like a long time . . . perhaps a lifetime." Paige went on to explain how she had been at school when they were murdered. "I didn't know where else to turn." She brushed tears from her eyes. "Do you think I could live with you for a while until I can decide what I can do?"

Oscar ran his hand through his thinning hair. "Yeah, I suppose you can. Lord only knows though where we're gonna put you. I'm married to a grass widow and she's got four young'uns. We don't have much room but I guess I can show more Christian charity than my brother did to me."

"Why, Uncle Oscar," she gasped. "What do you mean?"

"You probably know how our grandfather came over here from France. At one time he had a lot of money but he liked the ladies and his liquor. When our papa grew up and became a man, he had a way with cards . . . only thing . . . his was a losing way. By the time me and Daniel grew up, Papa didn't have a dime to his name. Dan went to work for that big land owner, Silas Anderson. I couldn't see working all my life for someone else so I knocked around for a while." His eyes grew cold and hard. "I remember the time I came to Dan and asked him for a job. Now, mind you, I didn't ask for a handout but he wouldn't put me to work. He told me Mr. Anderson didn't need any more hands, but I really think he was ashamed for me to work alongside his field niggers." Oscar had a smug look on his face when he added, "In '49, I went out to California during the gold rush and found me a little gold. It was enough for me to come back here and buy me a little farm. I recall the letter I wrote to your pa. It gave me a lot of satisfaction to be able to tell him how his worthless brother now owned some land. I also told him if he ever needed a job, I'd try and make room at my farm for him."

"Uncle Oscar," Paige injected, "You sound so bitter. I'm sure you don't realize how proud he was of you. I remember how he boasted about you to all of his friends. At night," her voice took on a wistful tone, "we'd sit around the fireplace and Papa would talk about coming to Texas to join you. But, somehow . . . we never did. Perhaps if we had come, they would be alive today." She took a deep breath. "Back to the pressing subject. I don't want to be a burden to you or your family. If I could only stay the winter, maybe I could find work somewhere in the spring. I promise to be helpful to your wife. I know how to cook and care for a home just like a married woman . . . and I really don't eat very much." She was surprised to find herself pleading, she was so afraid her uncle would turn her away.

"Now, don't fret, girlie. I already said you could stay with us for a while. Only . . . I have to convince Sadie that you'll be a help to her. I'll tell you right now, you are going to have to work hard, 'cause after all my hard work on my farm and me raking and scraping enough money to buy me a field nigger, the sorry so and so ran off soon as he heard he was free. I owe a bunch of thanks to that son-of-a-bitch in Washington. I just hope they are around to teach them heathens how to take care of themselves when this war is over." Paige was obviously frightened. She had never seen a man rant and carry on so much. She bit back a reply as Oscar continued. "Don't just stand there," he ordered as he pulled on his worn boots. "Get your things together. We have a long way to go and Sadie is going to be madder than a wet hen as it is. By the way," he asked worriedly, "do you know how I got in this room?"

"Yes, sir. I had a small amount of money left when I arrived here and found you. You . . . were in no condition to . . . I rented the room so you could rest until you started feeling better."

"You might as well learn right now that I'm not a rich man and times are real hard now. You might ought to give me what you have left. It will help pay your keep for a while. Lord only knows how we're going to make it anyway."

Paige was surprised at the shabbiness of the wagon Oscar drove up in front of the hotel. To make matters worse, apparently some of his drinking buddies were standing around sneaking sly looks in their direction. A crimson blush spread over her face when one of his friends called out.

"Hey, Oscar. That sure is a pretty young woman you have in your wagon. Didn't think you would have it in you to catch a looker like that!"

Oscar snarled, "Shut up, you stupid fool. She happens to be my dead brother's daughter. I'm taking her home to stay with me and Sadie."

"Woowee, that sure sounds like one of your tall tales to me." The man turned and spoke to the group of men standing behind him. "Wonder what ole Sadie will have to say about all of this?" He turned back to Oscar. "Where are you gonna put her . . . in with all those young'uns or are you gonna let her bed with you and Sadie?"

Oscar grinned as he took his hand and wiped away the tobacco juice dribbling down his chin. "Awwww, come off it boys. You're embarrassing my niece here. After all, she's what you would call a refined lady and you might hurt her ears with all your bullshit." Paige ducked her head, her face blazing with shame. Oscar flicked his whip and in a few moments the mules had the wagon a safe distance away from the men who had been taunting them.

After they had been traveling for a while, Paige took her first chance to thoroughly study her uncle. He was a small wiry man. His appearance indicated he had lived a hard life. His face had a leathery, weathered look; his clothes were unwashed and stained. It was obvious that Oscar had not bathed in a long time. Paige wrinkled her nose in disgust. She could not help but wonder what situation she had gotten herself into. Paige also compared this man to her father. Actually there was no comparison. Her father was the complete opposite of Oscar. The vision of Roxanne flashed through her memory. She knew men called on women with loose morals, but how could her uncle have anything to do with that horrid creature she met in the saloon? Oscar was definitely not the man she thought he would be.

When all traces of the day disappeared, Oscar brought the mules to a stop. Paige looked around in bewilderment. "Where are we going to spend the night?" she asked anxiously.

Oscar guffawed. "You can sure tell that you ain't been out in the wilds very much. Our beds will be wherever we lay our heads and there is some hard-tack under the seat of the wagon. When I travel, I travel light and don't need a fancy bed-roll or no fancy meal. The only thing I have to have, is a hot cup of fresh coffee." He climbed out of the wagon. "I'll gather up some firewood and you can go down to that stream and get some water."

The lump in Paige's throat grew larger as she did what Oscar requested. Later, she sat across from him on the ground eating a cold biscuit and trying to force down the stringy beef jerky. She had never sampled fare such as this and it was quite an experience for her. The expression on her uncle's face frightened her. He looked as though he was remembering the jeering taunts those men in town gave them. Suddenly, she felt unclean and naked under his piercing, penetrating examination of her.

Oscar turned up his coffee mug, wiped his mouth with the back of his hand and said. "Guess we had better turn in for the night. You can bunch up some of that pine straw to sleep on. But first, you can give your Uncle Oscar a goodnight kiss."

Paige's bottom lip trembled defiantly. "No sir, I don't believe I shall."

"What do you mean? You ain't going to kiss me goodnight or you ain't going to sleep on the pine straw?"

"I'm not going to kiss you goodnight, nor will I sleep on the ground. I will make my bed in the back of the wagon."

Oscar shrugged. "Suit yourself. But, I would suggest you forget about some of your uppity ways. You might think that sleeping on the ground is too good for you, but the truth is, it's going to get mighty cold before morning and the pine straw helps to keep you warm. So you go ahead and sleep in the wagon. See if I care." With those words, Oscar scooped up some of the straw and made a bed. Paige sat there with her mouth agape while he spread his blanket over the piling and laid down. Soon, he was snoring.

Paige lay in the back of the wagon, being very careful how she moved for fear of getting splinters from the rough wood. Her nose curled in disgust. The blanket she had curled up in smelled of unwashed bodies. Even though she was exhausted, it was almost impossible to slip into a much needed sleep. She had no idea people like her uncle existed. Even the slaves on the plantation took more pride in themselves than her uncle appeared to have. Surely when they reached Oscar's home, things would be different. Paige couldn't help but wonder what his wife would be like. If she would be in the same class as Oscar or more or less trapped into a helpless situation. Her eyelids finally became heavy and a drowsiness swept over her, sending the tired young woman into the slumberland of pleasant dreams. For a moment she was transported back to a time when problems were non-existent. She dreamt of fantastic mental images of her father, mother, and unencumbered times. Then her sleep was clouded by the presence of a tall dark stranger with foreboding eyes. She could feel his arms go around her and seek out her lips. The kisses became more and more demanding. Something in her sleep fogged mind demanded that she awake. Her eyes flew open with a start and to her horror, she discovered Oscar fumbling with the buttons on her blouse. "Get away from me . . . you horrible man!" she screamed.

"Now, there ain't no need in you getting riled up," Oscar stammered. "I heard you mumbling in your sleep and thought you was having a bad dream or something."

"No you wasn't, you were . . . trying to take liberties with me. It was deliberate!"

"Wasn't either!" Oscar bantered. "Like I said, I thought you were having a bad dream and I was only trying to comfort you some."

Paige felt his heavy breath on her skin and saw the truth shining from his eyes. "Don't you dare try to touch me again." she threatened fiercely.

"Awww shit!" Oscar jerked his hand sideways in a futile gesture. "There ain't no use trying to reason with you tonight. I'm going back to sleep," he announced in a blustering voice.

Paige bit back a retort when she saw he was

49

actually going to leave her alone. She settled back in her makeshift bed, but did not allow her eyes to close. Paige knew if she had not wakened when she did, she would not have been able to stop Oscar from doing what he had planned. She refused to give in to her tears of frustration while she waited for the coming dawn.

The morning broke clear and crisp with the false promise of beautiful weather. Dew glimmered and glistened on the treetops and birds sang but Paige did not see the beauty. All she could see and feel was the heartbreak deep inside her breast. She climbed stiffly out of the wagon, walked silently over to where he was sitting, drinking his coffee. She poured herself a cup of the bitter liquid and was almost finished before she gained enough courage to ask, "How long will it take us to reach your farm?"

"We ought to get there before nightfall." He looked her squarely in the eye. "I want to make one thing clear right now," he warned. "I don't want you telling your Aunt Sadie a pack of lies about what happened last night. Like I told you before, I thought I heard you crying and that's all there was to it."

Paige ducked her head. She knew it would be useless to argue with him even though it was a shameless lie. "All . . . right, Uncle Oscar. I won't say anything."

The rest of the day passed uneventfully as they pressed onward, deeper and deeper into the forest, far from any signs of civilization. By midday the sun had disappeared and the sky turned gray and crusty, and later on in the day, Paige felt the ominous drops of rain fall on her shoulders. Old man winter was definitely showing his face when Oscar coaxed the tired mules into his yard. Leaves, withered and brown were scattered about in a colored profusion. But, all beauty ended there. Oscar's much talked about farm consisted of a run-down shanty and scraggily farm land. She looked in dismay at the house. The front door was barely hanging on its hinges and only one of the windows had any glass, the rest were covered in soiled dirty canvas. The rough wood seemed never to have been whitewashed and the front porch was sagging so badly, it was beyond Paige's compre-hension as to how it was even standing. The barn where the animals were kept appeared to be in much better condition than the living quarters. Trash and all sorts of debris was scattered all about the yard. Even the out-house had no door on it for privacy!

A large slovenly woman came rushing down the front steps while four pitifully thin children crowded the front door to see who had arrived.

Sadie started to rant, "It's 'bout time you got your sorry carcass home. I'll bet you forgot to get what I wanted from the general store." Her voice trailed off when she saw the attractive young woman sitting beside Oscar. "Land sakes. Who do we have here? Shame on you, Oscar," she chided. "If I had any idea you were bringing home com-pany, I would have fixed myself up a bit." She self-consciously smoothed back a stray wisp of hair.

"Ain't no use in getting all worked up over

nothing. This girl is just poor relation coming to stay with us for a while." He turned to Paige. "Don't just sit there, get down and carry your bag into the house and see if there's anything you can do to help your Aunt Sadie."

Paige desperately hoped the inside of the house was in better repair than the outside, but she was disappointed. Oscar's house consisted of two drafty rooms. The largest room served as a bedroom for all, while the kitchen was a smaller room. She had not expected much, but this was nothing more than a hovel. Her nose crinkled in disgust at the filth. Clumsy attempts had been made at straightening it up, but one glance told her it had been done by the children and not Sadie. She was shocked to see flies circling the table and settling on the food which remained on it.

Sadie entered the kitchen and planted her hands firmly on her buxom hips. "Oscar explained how you showed up in Shreveport with nothing but the clothes on your back." She sighed deeply. "I guess it's my Christian duty to take you in but it sure will cause a hardship on this family." She gave a sweep of her hand. "I was feeling poorly today so I didn't get to do much cleaning. I guess you can roll up your sleeves and help me clean up this mess before I have to start cooking some supper."

It was hard to ignore the raging argument going on in the other room while Paige tried to put some order to the kitchen. "Why did you have to bring home another mouth to feed? Heaven knows we just barely get by as it is," Sadie raved.

"Now, Sadie, I couldn't turn my back on my

own brother's daughter. Besides, I kind of figured she would be able to give you a hand around here. And you know yourself, we can always use some extra help with the rest of the cotton that still needs to be picked."

"Huh! We wouldn't have to be worrying about the cotton if you hadn't beat that field nigger you picked up." Sadie wavered, "I suppose we can use another pair of hands around here though. But let me tell you one thing, Oscar DuPree, I can tell she has had better than what we can provide, so I won't put up with any of her uppity ways."

Oscar laughed. "I don't imagine she'll have too many fine ways left after she hits that cotton patch. After the cotton is in though, I plan on taking her into town and maybe hiring her out to one of those rich families. I heard the war isn't going too good for us and I figure it'll all be over with before too much longer. Those Northerners will be flocking in here like flies as soon as the war is over. And who knows . . . we may even be able to marry her off to one of those wealthy Yankees."

Sadie frowned. "All right. But I still want you to know that I'm not overly fond of the idea."

It was all Paige could do to keep from bolting toward the door and freedom. But common sense told her it would be useless. She would have to endure this horrible place until the time came when she would be able to leave.

That night, the evening meal consisted of a thin watery gruel for her and the children but Sadie and Oscar had a nice portion of ham and fresh eggs. Paige realized why the children looked so undernourished and thin. She judged them between the ages of five to twelve. Each one would steal a glance at her every so often, revealing soft but wistful brown eyes. None had spoken to her but she was not offended, she simply felt they were too shy and in time, they could all be friends. Pity for the children filled her. Each one had such a hopeless look about them as if they knew their lives would not change and they were resigned to that fact.

Oscar pushed his plate back and belched loudly. "Girl, clean up the dishes then you had better go to bed and try to get a little rest. We still got cotton in the fields and you're going to have to help us pick it."

"Yes, sir." she mumbled. Oh how she hated it already. Not because of the hard work that was expected of her, but because the poverty and the helplessness that stemmed from ignorance and lack of self help. Sighing loudly, Paige busied herself cleaning the kitchen. She thought she would never finish but finally the room was in order and she stumbled to the pallet which Sadie had prepared for her. The last thought she had before sleep overtook her was how lonely and afraid she felt.

Rough hands brought Paige back from the land of pleasant memories as Oscar shook her violently. "Wake up, we don't stay in bed until all hours of the day around here. There's work to be done and the sooner we get to it, the sooner we'll all be through."

Paige sat up, rubbing her eyes. It seemed as

though she had just gone to bed. The only light in the room was coming from the fireplace. It wasn't even dawn yet. She pulled at her chemise, searching for the cameo watch which had been her mother's.

Oscar called once again. "I said, get up. You can help Sadie fix some breakfast."

Paige leaped to her feet, pulling on her well worn robe, trying to hide the revealing curves hidden underneath. But she had not been quick enough for Oscar had seen her swollen bosom and the expression on his face frightened her badly.

That morning, she and the children had the same thin watery gruel while Sadie and Oscar had a hearty breakfast. Paige could almost taste the delicious food but too much pride prevented her from asking for any. With her mouth stuffed with food, Sadie rolled her eyes at Oscar. "Honey," she whined, "I feel poorly this morning. Since Paige is here, do you think she could take my place in the fields today?"

"All right. But you know how bad we need to get it picked before the weather gets to it too bad."

Paige shrugged her shoulders indifferently. She knew field work was extremely hard but anything would be better than having to listen to Sadie whine all day long.

Oscar nodded to the oldest boy. "You show her what she is suppose to do, and I don't want any tomfoolery now. I mean a whole lot of cotton had better get picked today," he added threateningly.

Paige noticed the frightened expressions which flashed over the children's faces as they scrambled out the door. She managed to toss Oscar a hateful glare before she followed them outside. Walking briskly behind the children, Paige shook her head, not in pity, but in admiration at how they marched proudly along in their rag-tag clothes. Matthew, the eldest, was the clear leader when it came to guiding the other children, Mark, Luke and little Jessie. Sadie must have been on the brink of insanity when she named the little blonde headed girl, Jezebelle! Thank goodness it had been shortened to a nickname in her few short years.

After they reached the field, Matthew showed Paige how to pick the silky cotton from its boll and place it in the reed basket. He explained how to take the filled basket up to the wagon which had been placed in the middle of the field. All of them, even Jessie, started on rows of their own. Even though Paige worked as quickly as possible, it wasn't long before the children were far ahead of her and had even emptied their baskets into the wagon several times. Finally, Matthew came back to where Paige was struggling with her half filled basket. He watched her for a moment before he spoke. "You're going about it the hard way. Put your fingers in the boll like this and pluck it out. The way you're doing it leaves half the cotton."

Paige glanced back over her shoulder and was surprised to see the row still white. "Oh no! But . . . I'm doing the best I can!"

"I know you are," he said patiently. "I also know you shouldn't be out here, doing this. You ought to be in some fine house with people waiting on you!"

"Thank you, Matthew, but I really don't mind helping, but I do object to Oscar pushing all this work off onto you children when he should be helping with the work."

Matthew shook his head. "Aw, Paige, we don't mind the hard work. I guess you could say, we're used to it by now. Besides, somebody has to pick that cotton or we sure will have a hungry winter." He turned and shouted to the other children. "Mark, Luke, Jessie, come on back here and help Paige get caught up." Soon, the row Paige was working on was as clean as the children's, and they kept her up with them. Whenever she would fall behind, either Matthew or Mark would turn and work on her row until they were all working side by side.

By midmorning, Paige felt as though her back was breaking. Also, the thorny stems which held the cotton scratched and pricked her arms and hands, causing them to bleed. She desperately wanted to rest for a while, but she was afraid if she did, Oscar would come up and take his anger out on the children. Besides, pride prevented Paige from sitting down and resting. She figured if the children could do the work and not complain, so could she. Poor little Jessie, Paige thought, glancing over at the little girl. Her tiny fingers flew at a pace that could only have been credited to fear of the threatened strap and whipping. Paige's thoughts drifted to how much her life had changed in a few short months. She tried not to remember her papa's hearty laughter nor the softness of her mother's breast when Paige needed to be comforted. She glanced up to see Oscar leaning against a tree, closely watching them. Slamming her basket to the ground, Paige stomped over to where Oscar was standing. "How do you expect a person who has never done this type of work and four children to do all this by ourselves?" she asked, making a sweeping motion with her hand.

"You listen to me, girlie. Don't start that fresh mouthing at me! After I've given you a good home and warm food to go in your belly when no one else would take you in. The best thing for you to do is get back over there and help those kids get the work done instead of being over here, smarting off at me!"

Paige stood for a moment so angry her fists clenched in tight balls. She wanted nothing more than to fly into Oscar in a rage. Then the realization dawned on her that if she defied Oscar, he would take his spite out on the children. She turned slowly and marched back to where the children were still working.

"Paige," Matthew said shyly, "don't worry about us. We're used to this type of work and we can do it without any trouble. But, we're mighty worried about you. We all know that you are a refined lady and you shouldn't be here, working like this. If you don't stop and rest for a while, you probably won't be able to make it the rest of the day."

Paige smiled and touched Matthew's cheek. "Thank you, but I'm not as frail as I appear. I am very familiar with hard work. True, not field labor, but I'll make it just fine. If I do get too tired,

I promise to stop and rest a while."

The sun had almost set before Oscar called them out of the field. For the past few hours Matthew and Luke had begged Paige to take a short rest, but she had doggedly refused. She knew if she ever sat down she would never have the strength to will her tired and weary body back to the tedious work.

Matthew walked tall and proud beside Paige as they trudged their way home. He offered his shoulder for support to the faltering young woman. Paige was grateful. She doubted if she could have made it alone. When they finally reached the house, Paige's eyes brimmed in tears because Sadie was standing in the doorway. She had somehow squeezed her mammoth body into Paige's best dress. In fact, it had been the last dress her mother had made for her before going to school. It was so small on Sadie, most of the delicate stitches in the bodice stretched past their endurance and a large ugly stain spilled down the front.

Sadie flashed a toothy smile revealing chipped, browned snuff-stained teeth. "I saw this old thing and figured it was so old you wouldn't be wanting it any longer. Besides," she added, "it looks better on me anyhow because the color is more my shade."

The pain which racked Paige's heart was much worse than the pain coursing through her body. She could only cringe at the woman. She mumbled something about the dress looking nice and turned her face so Sadie wouldn't see the tears.

Supper was a mindless blur. Paige ate the food

set before her, not tasting or even caring how it was cooked. After the first few bites, she pushed the plate away, ignoring Oscar's comment about not wasting food. She was simply too tired and weary to eat any more. She walked out on the porch and stared up at the star-filled sky. Determination filled her. Somehow, someway, she would get away from this horrible place and away from the terrible people inside.

The next day was repetitious of the day before, and the next was the same as yesterday, until finally, the last boll of cotton was picked and safely on the wagon, waiting for Oscar to take it to Shreveport the following day.

The food that night tasted bland and unseasoned, but Paige didn't mind. She was too proud of the fact that they wouldn't have to go back to the fields the following day. After the dishes were done, Sadie handed a basket to Paige. "Take this out to your Uncle Oscar. I decided to fix it tonight instead of waiting until morning. He had some harness to mend, so you can tell him to go ahead and put it under the wagon seat." She shook her head worriedly. "He has to get that cotton to market before it weathers on it anymore."

"All right," Paige said, wishing she had enough nerve to insist he take her with him. But these past few days had only served to heighten her fear of the man. He watched her with such a strange expression on his face, she was actually afraid to be alone with him. Besides, what could she do in town? From what she had observed on her way here, people were not hiring any domestic help and schools had practically become non-existent since the war began raging in the south. She decided the best thing to do was to try and tough it out until spring. Perhaps the war would be winding down by then and she could find employment in the city. Paige took the basket of food after draping her cloak around her shoulders.

The night had a definite frost in it as she started for the barn. "Well," Oscar drawled when he saw the basket, "I was wondering if Sadie was going to pack me a lunch."

Paige was frightened. The smell of whiskey was overpowering. When he reached for her arm, she pulled away, shouting, "Leave me alone!"

"Now, girlie, I ain't going to hurt you. I just think it's time you started showing some gratitude; after all, I've done a lot for you." He laughed as he pushed her back onto the hay which had fallen carelessly out of the crib.

"Leave me alone, you horrible man!" Paige screamed, trying to free herself from his grasp.

"Girlie, you ain't showing the proper amount of respect," Oscar panted as he tried to press his foul smelling mouth to her lips. He yanked savagely at her bodice. "Oh my God!" he muttered when he saw her full, ripe breasts. Passion flowed through his veins. "Quit fighting me, girl. I mean to have you and have you I will!"

The scream of protest froze in Paige's throat. This could not be happening to her! Her own blood uncle was trying to rape her and there was nothing she could do to stop him! Still, she struggled, but his strength was overpowering.

With one mighty tug, Oscar finished tearing the dress from her young and tempting body. Suddenly, his body stiffened. He leaped to his feet to face a thunderous looking Sadie.

"Now ain't this a pretty sight," she sneered.

Paige breathed a sigh of relief then to her horror, Sadie yanked her to her feet.

"You little tramp," Sadie screamed, slapping Paige hard across the face. "You think I ain't noticed how you've come into my house and twisted that fancy butt around, trying to entice my man! You little slut, it won't work at all!"

"But Sadie . . . I didn't . . . I", Paige stammered.

"Like hell you didn't! I saw those sly looks you've been giving him. You must have the morals of an animal to lust after your own God given uncle! You ought to be ashamed, you little bitch, but you probably don't know what the word shame means!"

Oscar sided in with his wife. "That's exactly how it was, Sadie. She . . . she has been trying to get me to bed her ever since she came here. I tried to resist her . . . but a man can only take so much before he gives in to temptation!"

"Shut up!" Sadie screamed at him. "You worthless scum, you're as bad as she is for giving in like you did." Sadie's face was white with rage. Then she saw the harness Oscar had been working on. "I guess I'll just have to beat the old devil out of you," she said to Paige. She wrapped the ends of the leather strap around her hand for a better grip, then started beating the girl. Paige twisted from her grasp, but Oscar rushed to assist Sadie. He held

had turned against his own family to follow his convictions, which were to support the north and freedom of mankind. He was very tall and lanky. His blond hair always seemed to be in need of a trim, but it framed a very handsome face. He had a slow, easy going manner. But if you crossed him, he could show a fiery temperament. Blinn, on the other hand, was just the opposite. He had been left an orphan at an early age and had no family ties. He was a short stocky man, dark and very rugged in feature. He was muscular and strong as an ox. Prescience flowed between them very easily. Many times, when they had been in battle, they acted as though they were one. Standing back to back, they saved each other's lives countless times.

Blinn poured him and Seth another cup of coffee then spoke in a slow deliberate speech. "The way I see it, if we accept this assignment, we'd be working without the benefit of our uniforms. And, if we're caught, we'd all be hung as spies. Kyle," he turned to his friend, "what would happen if we were to wait until the war is over? There would be no need in all this secrecy then."

Kyle shook his head. "It just wouldn't work, Blinn. If we waited until the war is over, we might be too late. The South, and I mainly speak about Kansas and Texas, will be flooded with a lot of unscrupulous people who will swoop down on this land like vultures. They will tear and pull apart the South until nothing is left of her dignity. No," he said, shaking his head thoughtfully, "if we are going to do any good, we will have to start now."

Seth spoke up. "I think I understand what you are getting at, Kyle, but how in the hell are the three of us going to help matters?"

Kyle removed his hat and ran his fingers through his hair. "That's just the point. It is not just the three of us. There are a lot of men doing what we've been asked to do. The way it was explained to me is this; each state has been divided into regions. Take Texas for instance. There will be over fifty men here. I was told that this state is the key to the entire operation. Sure, a few battles have been fought here, but damn few. Nothing like the ruination the other states have suffered." Kyle's voice trembled with emotion as he continued. "Texas is like a virgin bride on her wedding night. She's anticipating, but frightened about what is going to happen. Her land and wealth is virtually untouched. The fields have not been torched and there are vast forests just sitting, waiting for the axe and saws. Hell, cattle are almost for the taking, there are so many. And I mean cattle without brands on them. Seth, Blinn," he paused. "Do you have any idea what will happen to the North and South alike if the big money machines come down here and buy up all the available cattle, lumber, and cotton? I'll tell you what will happen. The prices on everything will shoot so high it will remind one of California during the big gold rush back in '49. The only ones who will be able to buy food for their bellies and clothes for their backs will be the rich ones. Then where will that leave the poor old soldier boys coming home from the war? Like I said before, I'm talking about the North and South alike. Men," he said solemnly, "if I can keep a little baby from crying itself to sleep at night because of an empty belly, then damn it, I'll do it!"

Seth looked over at Blinn and winked slyly. In a very serious tone, he said, "I thought Kyle was called to Washington to talk with the president. I sure as hell didn't know he would come back as a preacher!"

Blinn bantered back with a wink. "I know what you mean," he said in a mock tone of voice. "In fact, I wonder if this was his first sermon?"

Kyle leaned back astonished. He wondered why they were taking the subject so lightly. When he realized they were only kidding, he broke into laughter.

Kyle flipped backwards in the snow. By the time he got to his feet, two huge snowballs were in each hand. "I'll teach you to make fun of me when I am serious about something. Prepare to defend yourselves, you yellow bellied skunks!" Kyle shouted good-naturedly.

Blinn yelled, "Get him, Seth."

Seth and Blinn grabbed Kyle as he unleashed the snowballs at them. For the next half hour or so, the men played like school boys frolicking in the snow. First, Seth and Blinn would team up against Kyle then it would be reversed to where Blinn and then Seth would be the object of the attack. Finally, the men dropped from exhaustion. Their frosty breaths reflected like white daggers dueling in the cold night air while their hearts slowed from their rapid poundings. Blinn laid on his back and started chuckling quietly. Soon, the other men joined in with him, laughing as though they didn't have a care in the entire world.

Seth looked over at Kyle, still laughing, and said, "I know we will probably kick ourselves later, but you can count us in on this mission."

"Good! I knew I could rely on the both of you." Kyle stood and brushed away the snow which clung determinedly to his trousers. "Let's build that fire up again and put on some more coffee. We have a lot of things to go over before we can leave."

Soon the carefree scuffle was forgotten as Kyle told them of his plans.

"The most important thing is to have a good enough cover story that won't throw suspicion on any of us. The final decision is up to you, Seth, but here is my idea. I thought it would be a good idea if you were to buy a little plot of land on the river bottom. People around here ship a lot of their goods up on the Big Cypress Bayou to Jefferson. Perhaps you could build a ferry and do a little transporting of your own. Plus, it wouldn't hurt a bit to have access to the local people's comings and goings. Do you think something like this would suit you, or would you rather do something else?"

Seth grinned. "Hell yes! It will be fine with me. You know as well as I how much I love the river and the swampy land that goes with it."

Kyle flashed a smile showing his appreciation of Seth's approval. "We have to situate in and around Marshall and Jefferson. Blinn, I have given you a lot of thought. Of course, this plan would have to have your approval too. I know you used to work as a smith before the war. I've looked into the matter and there is only one blacksmith shop in this area. It is connected with the military. Reckon you would like to settle down in Marshall?" he asked.

"Kyle, if I didn't know any better, I would swear that you was some kind of a magic genie. You know damn good and well you just granted Seth's and my fondest wishes. But how in the world are we going to swing all of this?"

"That is a good question, Blinn." Kyle walked over to his horse and removed a large leather pouch from his saddle bags. "Mr. Lincoln provided more than enough to get us started. He even threw in an extra incentive. Soon as we have completed our mission, the cover we have set up will be ours to keep."

"You mean the blacksmith shop and Seth's ferry will be ours to keep?" Blinn asked incredibly.

Kyle nodded. "That's right."

Seth spoke up. "Since it is settled about what me and Blinn is going to do, what do you intend on doing, Kyle?"

He looked thoughtful for a moment before speaking. "You both know I don't have a home to go back to either. With Papa dead, there is no desire to return to whatever is left of our ranch. I thought after the war is over, I would head out to California and start all over out there. So," he said slowly, "there is no need for me to set up anything too elaborate. I figure I'll drift around, keep my

69

eyes open and maybe do a little gambling. I think I can hold my own doing that."

Seth flashed a curious glance at Blinn. They both knew the reason why Kyle didn't want to return to his ranch out in West Texas. Right before the war started, Comanches raided it, kidnapped his fiancee and murdered his pa, leaving Kyle with no real ties to the past, only memories. Seth, knowing how moody Kyle became whenever he remembered the past, quickly changed the subject. "It's a shame ole Kyle can't charm the men like he does the women. If he could, then we'd have no problems at all."

Blinn piped up. "If the truth was known, I'd bet a month's pay on why we beat him here by a week. He probably met up with some pretty young lady somewhere."

For a brief instant, a pang of regret swept over Kyle. He well remembered the raven-haired beauty in Washington. He shrugged his shoulders. What was past, was past. "All right, men, let's get back to our business." After he split the gold, he said, "It will probably be about a month or so before you hear from me. So . . . we'll set the middle of January as a target date to meet in Jefferson." He frowned as he added, "It goes without saying, if any of us gets into trouble, he is on his own unless the others can help without revealing themselves and their cover. Agreed?"

Seth and Blinn both nodded. For a brief moment they stood in silence, each reflecting in his own thoughts.

After dousing the campfire, the three men

mounted their horses and rode off, none giving a backward glance.

In a few hours time, the wind started to blow, erasing all signs of the men's presence. The wind howled through the trees, the owls and night birds called in the night and the snow filled the boot prints.

Chapter Five

For the next few days, battling the cold and the snow, Kyle rode around the area getting the feel of the land and of the general surrounding countryside. He was amazed at the beauty of the land. Even though he was well traveled and had been in similar types of terrain, it was as though his eyes had been opened for the first time and he was seeing the beauty about him. Even in the dead of winter, something was always green. Oh, there were plenty of trees without leaves and not much grass forced its way through the ground but the pine and cedar trees were magnificent! The pines dotting the rolling hills towered over him. Sometimes the underbrush was so thick, he would have to ride for miles to skirt it. He had even heard of a place further south and east, where the thicket was so thick, man could not even make his way through it on foot. He was fortunate enough to find shelter against the inclement weather as each night fell. Sometimes, it was only a cave hidden in a small ravine or gully, or a shack that had long since been deserted.

Kyle discovered a shabby but warm cabin on Christmas Eve. Someone had left a generous supply of firewood ricked up beside the house. He made good use of it that night because a fierce storm blew in. And almost as quickly as it had started, the storm abated, leaving Christmas day dawning clear and bright. The branches of the pines hung low under the heavy burden of fresh snow. Kyle watched in awe as the sunlight created tiny prisms of light, reflecting through the icicles and dancing on the walls of the cabin. He absent-mindedly walked out on the small porch, tore off an icicle hanging from one of the rafters on the porch and began sucking on it. The cold dripped down his throat and his mind raced back through a period of time. A time to where there was laughter, love, and thoughts and plans of a new tomorrow. His memory was so stark . . . so realistic, he could almost smell a wild turkey roasting over the fireplace and a mince and pumpkin pie cooling on the kitchen safe.

And then there was Caroline . . . sweet, lovely Caroline. A lost love that time had pushed back into the dark corners of his memory. Sometimes, a rush of a woman's petticoats or a soft fragrance drifting across a crowded room would cause him pain, but always in his mind's eye, he would see Caroline as he saw her last.

The Comanches had raided their ranch one day when he had been out, rounding up stray cattle. Terror filled him when he crested the small rise above his and his father's ranch. The acrid smell of burned flesh penetrated his nostrils. He rushed down the small hill with no thought of his own safety. Leaping off his horse, he ran to the almost lifeless body of his father. Although the old man had been scalped, he had hung on to a faint glimmer of life, praying that his son would return before death laid its cold hand on his shoulder. How he had been tortured was almost indescribable. Countless knife wounds had pierced his skin, not deep enough to kill, but enough to cause horrible agony. His scalp dropped over pain-blurred eyes. A heartless Comanche had sliced the old man's lips from his mouth . . . but still, he lived long enough to tell Kyle what had happened to Caroline. She had ridden over to bake him a birthday cake. It had just come out of the oven when the savage heathens swooped down on them. They rained terror, savagely killing the two hired men, torturing him, then carrying Caroline off with them. When his purpose to live the pain-wracked hours was over, the old man peacefully breathed his last breath and passed into the loving hands of his Maker.

Kyle's agony had just begun. He scoured the countryside, looking, searching for the woman he loved. But his efforts were in vain. It was nearly a year later that he stumbled over a newly deserted Indian camp. He wearily climbed down from his horse to search for some signs as to what tribe the Indians were from, only to find a body of a young woman. He could not tell if she had been white, Mexican, or an Indian. Kyle could tell she had suffered greatly. Her nose had been cut off her face and apparently it had been done for some period of time because the scars had healed. She had been dead for too long of a time to tell much more about her features. He prepared a grave for the woman and as he was lowering the body into it, his breath caught in his throat. Around the woman's neck was a rawhide strap, and it held a ring. The ring he had given Caroline when they became engaged. Kyle did not remember the journey back to the remains of his ranch. It still stood, like a skeleton jutting out against the West Texas sunset. He walked up to the hilltop where his parents were buried, said his final farewell, mounted his horse and slowly rode away. . . .

Kyle's thoughts came rushing back to the present. To his amazement, tears were falling effortlessly down his face. This was the first time he had been able to shed any tears of grief. He looked up into the heavens and spoke aloud. "God, all these years I have blamed you for what happened. I never stopped to give thanks for the time you allowed me to spend with them. I know I have a lot of sins against my soul, but you know, God, for the first time in a long while, I actually want to see the ending of tomorrow, and the beginning of the next day." He tipped his hat and added sincerely, "Thank you, Lord."

Kyle gathered his few belongings together and started to tie them to the back of his saddle. On a sudden impulse, he removed most of the gold from the saddle bags. He walked behind the cabin, scraped away the snow and hacked a small hole in the ground with his knife. After burying the gold, Kyle covered the spot with a stone then sprinkled snow around it to make it look as if it was undisturbed.

Kyle cinched up the saddle on his horse in a leisurely manner. He knew he should be in a hurry to leave the cabin and surrounding area since his supplies were almost depleted, but everything was so peaceful, he hated to break the spell the land had cast over him. His memory also flashed back to the woman he had met in Washington with the French sounding name. Ahhh, Paige DuPree, a beautiful, yet inexperienced woman, who would one day make some man a good wife. Her image, as it did the day he met with Blinn and Seth, flashed through his mind like a picture. Kyle shook his head almost angrily. There was no use in recalling a woman whose path he would never cross again.

Chapter Six

The rest of the day found Kyle making his way slowly southwestward. It was nearing sundown when he saw a cabin. Noticing the steady stream of smoke coming from the chimney, Kyle decided he had put off meeting with civilization long enough. Now would be the time to test out his undercover agent's role. He hoped the occupants of the cabin were not too inquisitive about who he was or where he was heading.

A half starved dog came out from underneath the porch, growling ferociously at him as he dismounted from his horse. "Easy dog," Kyle said in a calm, soothing voice. "I won't hurt you or your master."

The dog cautiously advanced on Kyle, eyeing him menacingly. Kyle continued to utter soothing words to him, all the while, edging closer and closer to the animal. When Kyle was close enough to touch the dog, he eased his hand down slowly and placed it on the animal's head. The dog flinched and ran back to the safety of the porch. This time when Kyle stepped forward, the dog did not growl, but he did inch back out from underneath the porch and followed every step Kyle made with watchful, wary eyes. The front door flew open and out stepped a small, wiry man brandishing a shotgun.

"Howdy, stranger. Can I help you any?" When he saw the dog, he kicked at him, sending the animal yelping from the yard. "Damn strays," he muttered. "Folks move off and leave their dogs to run wild. Then they get hungry—hungry enough to rip open a cow's throat if'n it was to catch it alone in the open."

Kyle stated firmly, "I agree. It is a shame for people to abandon good animals like that."

The man turned his attention to Kyle. "What can I help you with? You got some business around these parts?"

Kyle replied quickly, slipping into an easy southern drawl. "I don't mean you any harm. I was just passing through and am running awfully low on supplies. I thought if you had any extra beans and bacon, and maybe some grain for my horse, I'd be rightly obliged. Naturally, I'd be willing to pay a fair price for it."

"What do you mean by 'jest passing through'? You ain't one of them deserters or a Yankee, are you?"

Kyle stiffened slightly. His mind raced furiously. "No sir! I ain't no deserter and I sure as hell ain't no damn Yankee! I am recovering from the wounds I received at the battle of Vicksburg." He decided to take a gamble. "It's true, the war is still going on—for how much longer, I don't rightly

78

know. Up until a week or so ago, I wasn't in good enough shape physically to go back to the battle field, then, I got to thinking. Don't mind serving my time or doing my duty for the south, but ain't no use in getting my head shot off just so the war can last another month or so. To be really honest with you, I thought the best thing I could do was to start rebuilding my life the best way I could."

The man lowered his gun. "Well, I guess we could spare a little bit. Me and the missus has too many young'ns to put you up in the house, but if you want to spend the night, you'll be welcome to sleep out in the barn. At least it's warm out there and it will keep you out of the night air."

Kyle touched his hat. "That is right friendly of you," he said as he started for his horse.

"Wait a minute, Mister," the man said as he moved a few steps closer to Kyle. "You said you'd be willing to pay for the vittles. I figure a dollar would be a fair price, and since I've been beaten out of money before, you can go ahead and pay me in advance."

Kyle reached into his shirt pocket, removed a dollar, and tossed it to the man. He said, "All right. Here is your money."

After glancing casually at the money, the man replied, "For a minute there, I thought maybe you would try to pay me with Confederate money. Don't reckon they will be worth too much 'fore long."

Kyle nodded in agreement. "I guess you are right about that," he said as he turned to lead his horse to the barn.

"Wait a minute, stranger." The man nudged at the arm of a young boy who had ventured out to stand beside him. "Go tell your ma to fix up a plate and send it out to the barn. Then, you can stable this man's horse for him."

"That's all right about stabling my horse. He tends to act a bit skittish around strangers and I wouldn't want a fine looking lad like him to get hurt." He grinned down at the boy who was grinning shyly up at him. "But I sure could use some hot food for a change though."

Kyle was unsaddling his horse when he caught movement out of the corner of his eye. His reflexes being what they were, and knowing the people had not had time to send any food out yet, he whirled around with his gun drawn. He was obviously relieved to see the old stray dog. "Why, hello fellow. Did you figure I needed some company tonight, or were you just trying to get out of the cold?"

The dog crept low on his haunches, a mourning whine came from deep in his throat, as he ventured closer to Kyle. He was frightened, yet appearing to want some scrap of human kindness. Kyle pulled the last of his beef jerky from his saddle bags and tossed a small piece at a time over to the hungry animal. It only took a small amount of coaxing to get the animal to eat from his hand. He was kneeling down and petting his newly found friend when he heard a soft, feminine voice.

"My aunt instructed me to bring this food to you, sir."

Kyle spun around, startled by the interruption.

Paige was so surprised to see Kyle kneeling in their barn, she dropped the plate of food.

"Oh my God!" she mumbled. "What . . . wha . . . what are you doing here?"

Kyle's mind raced. Never in his wildest dreams did he expect to see Paige, here of all places! Then a cold stark realism swept over him. She knew he was an officer in the union army. She had the power to reveal his true identity, and she also had the reason to want to do him harm. Somehow, he had to convince her he had a legitimate excuse to be here and persuade her to keep his secret. "Well, I must say, you certainly took me by surprise. I see you made it home without too much difficulty."

Shame flushed Paige's face. Her memory ran rampant. How the captain had rightly accused her of being a thief then took her by force. How she had shamelessly thrown away her pride and responded to his lovemaking with a wild, wanton abandonment. How the following morning she had felt like a common whore! And how she had prostituted herself for the few dollars it took to reach this hell she now called home. Paige bent down to pick up the plate, grateful for the reason to tear her eyes from Kyle's and the memory of what happened between them. Finally she spoke. "Yes, sir, I guess you could say I made it home." A sob caught in her throat over the word home.

Kyle misunderstood her unshed tears as he rushed to her side. "Paige, please don't feel embarrassed about what happened back there in Washington. I'm . . . I'm sorry about the way things turned out. I don't go around defiling young women. It was . . . you caught me off guard. I had been without proper rest for weeks and it had been days since I had had any sleep to speak of. I guess . . . I wasn't thinking very clearly, and then when you suddenly appeared in my room, how could I think anything else but what I did?" He silently cursed himself for stammering so foolishly. Somehow, this feminine, dainty creature seemed to cast an instant spell over him, making him feel and act like an idiot.

She raised her eyes and stared defiantly into his face. "As far as I'm concerned, nothing—absolutely nothing happened in Washington. You are a stranger who rescued me from two men in a dark alley. That was all! Understand?"

Kyle looked at her strangely. She acted almost hysterical. He nodded slowly. "Yeah, I think I understand everything perfectly." It was obvious she wanted to dismiss the episode entirely. "But I am happy to see everything worked out all right for you and you were able to reach home safely."

A frantic expression crossed Paige's face. "Oh, I made it here just fine." Then her voice broke, her endurance coming to an end. "I made it home just fine . . . if you can call it that!" She collapsed into tears.

Kyle rushed to her side and took her in his arms. His concern was apparent. "Paige, what is the matter?"

"Oh, captain," Paige cried, resting her head briefly on his broad shoulder. "Everything here is wrong! I've never had to live like this in my life. Oscar and Sadie are horrible people. He is nothing like my father. They are cruel and heartless!" She pulled away, ashamed that her emotions had gotten out of control. "I'm sorry, I must sound totally ungrateful. Only . . . the entire story cannot be told." She tried to smile. "Forgive me. I've been a little upset lately. I guess it is a touch of the flu or something."

"That's all right," Kyle said, patting her awkwardly. "Everyone has to get things off their chests once in a while. I was afraid you were still angry at me for what happened between us."

Paige stiffened and pulled away from his touch as if afraid of the power there. "What happened between us would best be forgotten, captain," she said icily. "You have your life to live and I have mine. I refuse to let one foolish mistake haunt me for the rest of my life. There is one thing, though," she added haughtily. "I would like to have the address where you will be stationed. As soon as I am employed, I want to send you the money to repay what you left on the pillow."

Kyle waved the suggestion away with a wave of his hand. "That isn't necessary. Let's call it a gift."

Paige replied with vehemence. "Oh, no! We shall not call it a gift. Gifts are usually exchanged. I did not give freely what you took from me. Regardless of what you think, I have my pride and I have my dignity, although I no longer have my innocence. So, I will repay you!"

Kyle scowled darkly. "Look, I am not going to argue with you. It is as simple as this, I have no idea where I am going or what I will be doing, so there is no way I can leave you an address. As I said before, there is no debt."

Paige started to answer when suddenly, the barn door flew open and Oscar stood, staring at them. "What in the hell is going on out here?"

Color drained from Paige's face. "There is nothing going on," she snapped. "I simply dropped the plate of food."

"You dropped the food!" Oscar shouted. "Don't you know how scarce food is around here? You clumsy . . ."

"Wait a minute," Kyle interrupted angrily. He had no intention of standing by and letting Paige take all the blame for a simple accident. "There is no need in talking to her that way. When she brought the food out, I startled her and she dropped the plate. Here," he said, digging into his pocket. "I'll pay the same price again."

Oscar looked from one to the other, a sly grin breaking across his face. "Well, now, it looks like something else was going on out here. . . ." his voice trailed off. Turning to Paige, he snapped sharply. "Go tell Sadie to fix another plate, and this time, have Matthew bring it out. He is worthless too, but at least he ain't as clumsy." Oscar glanced toward Kyle. "All right, where's my other dollar?"

Paige's mouth settled into a thin white line. "You can't be serious. A dollar is too much money for a plate of beans."

"Shut your mouth, girl. It appears to me that you're mighty generous with my belongings. Just because I had enough goodness in my heart to take you in and keep you, ain't no sign I'm going to feed every stranger that comes along." Kyle started to protest but Oscar interrupted him. "Look, stranger, it seems to me you are interfering in my own personal business. This girl here is my charge and I'd thank you not to butt in on family matters."

Kyle watched as Oscar took Paige roughly by the arm and led her from the barn. She paused at the door, yanked her arm away, and marched stormily into the house. Oscar stood with a suspicious gleam in his eye.

Later that night Kyle made a comfortable bed in the loft where the hay was piled high. For a long time, he found sleep impossible. Paige had certainly made a lasting impression on him. An impression that was foreign to him. His first thoughts, when she intimated how awful the situation was, were that her imagination or the near poverty she was forced to live in had bested her. But now, he wasn't so sure. He knew he should saddle his horse and ride away as fast as the animal could carry him, but, somehow he couldn't shake the feeling that he was responsible. In the back of his mind was the memory of Paige's warm, passionate arms and her ability to make him feel wanted and needed. She always seemed to be in need. Finally, after forcing the entire matter from his mind, Kyle slipped into a fretful sleep.

A door creaked softly in the night. A crunching sound of feet rustling the hay which had fallen from the loft awoke Kyle. He lay there for a moment trying to reason where he was and what had disturbed him. Shaking the sleep from his fogged mind, he crept tward the edge of the loft, silently inching his way forward to see who was stealing into the barn.

Paige stood for a moment trying to adjust to the dim light. She squared her shoulders determinedly and made her way to where Kyle's horse was stabled. "Whoa, boy," she whispered, trying to soothe the big black steed.

Anger raged through Kyle as he watched her attempt to steal his horse. He waited until she had the horse saddled and her foot in the stirrup before he pursed his lip and let out a soft, yet piercing whistle, which his horse, Satchel, was bound to recognize. Chaos erupted immediately. Paige flung herself away from the horse when he reared on his hind legs. Getting away from the crushing hooves was imperative. Kyle leaped from the hay loft and grabbed Paige, pulling her out of danger, although, he handled her none too gently. "Damn it woman! This is the second time you have tried to steal me blind. Don't you know horse thieves are hung in Texas?" he thundered.

Paige withered in agony. But her agony came mostly from shame. "I'm sorry. But . . . but . . . I couldn't spend another night in that house. I saw my chance. I had to take it," she added defiantly.

Kyle was so angry, he yanked her roughly by the arm as he took long, furious steps toward the door.

Paige tried to pull free from his grasp. "Where are you taking me?" she asked fearfully.

"I'm taking you to your uncle. Perhaps he will whale the tar out of you and teach you not to go around attempting to steal other people's property!

86

Maybe . . . just maybe . . . he will be able to teach you some kind of lesson!"

In her terror, Paige wrenched free of Kyle. "No! I won't go in there. I won't let you tell him! I won't! I won't!" She started pounding his chest in desperation.

Kyle seized her fists with his hands. Where they were standing, the moon reflected on the remaining snow on the ground, enabling Kyle to get a closer look at Paige. His mouth flew open in astonishment. She had a large bruise on her cheek. He could tell it was swollen red, and purple. "My God! What happened? Did Satchel do that to you?"

"No!" she spat. "The man you were taking me to, to teach me a lesson, has already taught me one. I don't believe I want any more of them."

"Good Lord, why?"

"I'll tell you why," she screeched, still hysterical. "Because I dropped the plate of food. At least that was the excuse he used. But he didn't need any excuse because he is just mean!" She looked up at Kyle, imploring him with her eyes. "It shames me, but there are more reasons why I am afraid of him."

"What are they?" Kyle asked coldly, his rage starting to rise.

"I'm afraid Oscar will try . . . will try . . . to rape me," she said in a small voice.

"His own niece?" Kyle asked incredibly.

Paige nodded. "Now you know why I must escape from this horrible place and go to any means to do so."

Kyle looked thoughtful. "I don't believe a slap on your cheek would have caused you to act this way. It must have happened before."

"Yes it has. My back still isn't healed completely from the first beating I received at their hands. Oscar tried to attack me one night and Sadie walked in and caught us. She claimed that I was enticing Oscar. I got a beating for it."

Kyle's brow was furrowed in concern. "Would you mind showing me what they did to you?" he asked in a quiet voice. Paige laid her cloak over a cask, then unbuttoned enough buttons of her dress to enable her to slip it off her shoulders. Kyle struck a match to get a better look. He flinched when he saw the scars and unhealed marks on her back. A cold fury raged through him. "That sorry . . . no good . . . ! He needs to be taught a thing or two."

"Oh no, Kyle," Paige gasped, clutching his arm. "You'll only make it worse." Again, she started crying. Kyle wrapped her in his arms and began stroking her long hair, soothing her as best he could.

"Well now," Oscar cackled sarcastically. "If this isn't a pretty sight!"

Kyle and Paige both spun around to see Oscar standing in the doorway with a shotgun in his hands.

"It would appear to me that I broke up your little love nest," he glowered at Kyle. "Here I have opened up my home and larder to a perfect stranger, and what happens? He repays me by enticing my niece out to the hayloft." He motioned the shotgun toward Kyle dangerously. "I think you ought to take that hip gun you're wearing and drop it real slow and easy like, to the ground."

Kyle knew the man had the drop on him. Even though he hated to part with his gun, he had no other choice. With slow and deliberate movements, Kyle unbuckled his gunbelt and let it slide easily to the ground. His mind was racing. He had to get the upper hand and the advantage over Oscar. "I wouldn't try anything too hasty, my friend," Kyle said, being extra careful not to make any sudden movement. "I've got some men camped nearby and if I'm not back soon, they will be swarming your place."

Oscar drew back, his eyes dancing craftily. "What do you mean?"

"Exactly what I said. We've had a report that you have been sheltering enemy soldiers and I was sent to investigate. I left orders with my men to come in with their guns smoking if I wasn't back in a reasonable length of time."

Oscar shook his head. This time, he looked worried. "That don't matter none. I ain't been hiding no Yankees and you don't have the right to come in here and bed my niece."

"Hell, man, I didn't touch your niece."

"Shit, that's what you say. When I came in here, her dress was undone and you had your hands all over her body." He was nervous. He had intended on murdering the stranger, taking his horse and money and disposing of the body in the woods.

Now, with the threat of soldiers camped nearby, he would have to change his plans. He motioned for Paige to step closer to him. "Did this man bed you, girlie?"

"Oh, Oscar! You are simply disgusting. Of course he didn't touch me."

"Hummmph. Figured you would say that. Knew it was a waste of time to ask. I reckon the only way to prove for sure is to have Sadie check you and see if you've been busted. If she's been spoiled, mister, then you are a dead son-of-a-bitch!"

Paige tried to stifle her cry of consternation. Oscar glanced at her and laughed coldly. "Guess that answers my question, girlie." Oscar stared at Kyle. "It appears to me that we got two choices. One, I can either blast your guts all over the barn, or two, since this girl ain't innocent no more, Sadie is liable to think I did it to her. She is most probably knocked up by your little romp in the hay, so we can take a ride over to the parson's house. I don't need another snotty nosed brat running around here. I got enough mouths to feed."

"That is a hell of a choice you are saddling me with. I can either be shot or be married, and I really don't hanker to do either." A cloud of doubt began to form in his mind. Everything had worked out too conveniently. Could Paige and her uncle have plotted to trap him? The entire matter was very suspicious.

"Hurry up and make up your mind, stranger,"

Oscar threatened. "I ain't got all night." He motioned with his shotgun. "Make it light on yourself. I figured to get a nice-sized dowry out of her. After all, she's a right handsome woman. So, while you are making up your mind, you can empty your pockets."

Kyle looked over at Paige. He felt so much hatred, he didn't notice the trapped, helpless expression on her face. "All right, I know when I'm bested. I'll marry her, but I damn sure don't like the idea."

"I don't give a shit whether you like it or not. I just can't take the chance of having more young'ns running around here."

Paige could not stand them haggling over her like she had no say in the matter. "Stop it! Stop it right now! This is insane. I'm not going to marry this man."

"All right," Oscar mumbled slowly. "I'll just splatter his guts then." He pulled the hammer back on the shotgun.

"No! No! You can't kill him."

Kyle flashed Paige a cold look. "Leave it be, Paige. I know when I'm licked. I don't have much choice with that gun in my belly, so I am not going to argue with him. But, I will say this, something ain't right here, and if I ever find out all this was simply a sham," he shook his finger in Paige's face, "then you'll have hell to pay."

Paige did not answer his accusations. She could only watch as Oscar marched Kyle over to saddle bags and removed the money from it. Oscar searched it thoroughly before he was satisfied he had it all. Kyle stood with his arms folded over his chest. His lips were pressed into a thin white line as he glared at Paige. Finally, he muttered through clenched teeth, "Well, well, one bride, bought and paid for!"

Chapter Seven

As long as she lived, Paige would never forget the terrible humiliation she suffered when Oscar marched her into the cabin to gather the few belongings that remained, since Sadie had taken most of her things for herself. The children clustered in the kitchen, watching Paige with knowing, yet understanding eyes.

"I guess you young'ns are going to repay me the same way this tramp has!" Oscar shouted. "I want you to all take a good look at what happens when someone gets caught doing something they shouldn't. I caught her out in the barn a'dallying with that stranger. This was after I had the decency to take her in my home and provide for her." He nodded in Paige's direction. "Hurry up and get your things together. I have to go back outside and make sure that stranger ain't going no where."

Paige snapped, "How in the world can he escape? After all, you tied him up."

"Don't give me any more of your sass, girl. I couldn't take the chance of him running off while we were in here. I don't want him leaving you with

93

a bastard in your belly and me left holding the bag on feeding it and you!" He turned and sauntered out the door, obviously pleased with getting the upper hand over the girl who had resisted him.

Paige looked at the children, her eyes pleading for them to believe the truth. "I wasn't doing anything wrong."

"We know you wouldn't do anything wrong," Matthew said. "I guess why we're so sad is, we just hate to see you leave." He rushed on to add, "Oh, we all know how unhappy you have been here, and for that reason we're glad . . . but that's the only reason."

Paige ran to the children and gathered them into her arms. "I'm going to miss all of you, too. Listen," she said, gazing intently at Matthew, "somehow, I'll get word to you and let you know how to reach me. And if you ever need help, I'll find a way to return."

Jessie wound her arms around Paige's neck. "I don't want you to leave. You are the onliest one that treats me good, 'sides my brothers. Mama and Papa Oscar don't whup us as much since you've been here."

"Oh Jessie, sweet Jessie!" Page soothed as she rocked the child to and fro in her arms. "I have to leave. Oscar is making me go, but like I said before, if any of you children need me real badly, I'll come to you or perhaps, you can come to me."

Matthew touched Paige on the shoulder. "Maybe you ought to get your things together. Oscar will be back in a few minutes and if you aren't ready, he'll start rantin' and ravin' again."

Paige nodded. "I know. But I had to tell you what happened, that I wasn't doing anything wrong." She touched Matthew's cheek, "I'll miss you all, terribly."

Sadie came into the kitchen. Her laughter cackled throughout the room. "Little Miss High and Mighty got herself in trouble. Your innocent act didn't fool me none. First man came on the place, and you're rolling in the hay barn with him. I'm just lucky I stopped you from pestering Oscar before it was too late." A cruel expression crossed her face. "Since you haven't been carrying your weight around here with all the chores the kids have done for you, I'll take that fancy timepiece and cloak you've been flauntin' in my face ever since you came here."

"Oh no! Not my mother's watch!" Paige gasped.

"Yep, your Ma's watch," Sadie repeated. "But since I've got Christian charity in my heart, I'll give you my cloth cloak. I wouldn't want it on my soul if you were to freeze."

Paige reluctantly handed the watch to Sadie, took a deep ragged breath, picked up her bag and slowly walked to the door. She turned and faced the children who were lined against the wall. "I'm not going to say goodbye, because, I know we'll see each other again." She turned quickly to keep the children from seeing the tears welling up behind her eyes. Finally, without another backward glance, Paige rushed outside to the fate which lay in store.

What a sight the wedding party made as they

rode through the night. Oscar, who was driving the team of mules, had his shotgun across his lap while Paige sat stiffly beside him. Kyle stood on his knees behind the seat with his hands tightly bound to the side-boards of the wagon. The reins of Satchel's bridle were also tied to the wagon and the horse trotted alongside the rig. Tension hung over them like a gloomy fog. The weather did nothing to lift their spirits. The clouds hung low and heavy, threatening snow, but instead of a cleansing beauty, it now seemed foreboding, almost sinister and evil. They pushed on, no one saying a word except for Oscar occasionally cursing at the mules while snapping the whip over their heads.

When they finally reached the parsonage, Oscar stopped the wagon and jumped to the ground. "There ain't no sense in staying out here and freezing to death."

Kyle snapped, "It's sort of hard to hurry since you have me trussed up like a Christmas turkey!"

"You hush that smart mouth." Oscar nodded toward Paige, "If you want a husband instead of a corpse lying at your feet, I'd suggest you untie him."

Paige slid behind the seat of the wagon. In a few moments she had the ropes untied. "I'm sorry," she whispered under her breath, "I never meant anything like this to happen."

Kyle studied her closely while clenching and unclenching his wrists, trying to get the circulation going through them again. "I guess the best thing we can do is go through this charade—

especially since I'm not particularly anxious to be a dead man." He took a deep breath and muttered to himself. "Looks as if I'll have a wife before too much time passes, and there's not a damn thing I can do about it."

Oscar threatened his shotgun toward Kyle. "I have already told you once to get a move on it, and I don't intend on having to say it again!"

The door of the parsonage was opened only after Oscar's insistent pounding. The parson stood in the doorway with a candle flickering in the wind. The light caught the shimmer of his gray beard and white hair. When he recognized Oscar, he exclaimed, "My oh my! Oscar DuPree!" He cleared his throat, stalling for time to get over his shock. "It's certainly been a long time since I've seen you." His brow creased into a frown. "The only time folks come calling this time of night, usually means there has been a death in the family. Sadie and the kids all right?"

"Oh, Sadie and the young'ns are fine. But, I do have a bit of trouble and you're the only man who can help me out. You see, I took my dead brother's daughter into my home a-while back and she repays me by carrying on with the first stranger who happens by. I'm afraid she is spoiled now and no God-fearing man would want her after some other man has . . . er . . . er . . . taken special privileges," he stuttered. "I believe the proper thing for us to do is marry these two up. One thing for certain, it would save me from wondering if I was going to have another mouth to feed in 'bout nine more months." He turned and pushed Paige and Kyle through the front door, past the preacher who was standing by that time, with his mouth wide open in surprise.

The parson ushered them all into the house. He paced back and forth in front of the fireplace, stroking his beard while he thought. His long nightshirt almost dragged the floor and the tassel on his nightcap reminded Paige of the character Dickens had so clearly described. Parson Jones came to an abrupt halt in front of Kyle.

"Son," he paused, "I have to be sure we're not doing you an injustice. I believe marriage should not be entered into lightly, but, what you have been accused of is quite serious. Can you in all honesty lay your hand on the Holy Bible and swear that you've never laid a hand on this young lady in a manner that would cause her any shame?"

Kyle looked at Paige and then back to the parson. In a clear voice he said, "No, sir. I couldn't honestly swear to that."

Parson Jones cleared his throat once more. He scratched the back of his head. "Well, at least it appears that you are an honest man. But, you have left me no choice. Since this young woman's uncle is demanding satisfaction, and since you have committed a sin against God and his teachings, I am going to have to marry you. I . . . I . . . just hope the good Lord in all his wisdom will choose to bless this union, and I might add, both of you ought to do a little knee bending, asking for his forgiveness!"

A white haired, matronly woman came bustling up to them. "Now, Joshua," she scolded in a soft voice, "I'm sure this sweet couple didn't mean any harm. With this awful war raging, they were probably trying to grab at some happiness. I'm sure what they did won't keep them out of heaven, 'specially since they are going to right the wrong they committed by getting married. Come on children," she said as she ushered them toward the parlor, "let's go into the sitting room. It's much nicer than in here. Besides," she smiled, "my pianie is in there."

Paige chanced a glance in Kyle's direction. He had a stony expression on his face but he offered no resistance. Instead, he took Paige by the elbow and marched staunchly toward the parlor. Mrs. Jones started playing "Oh Promise Me," on her battered but apparently cherished piano. The parson took his place and started with the ceremony. His words came in a rush as Paige fought to retain control of her emotions. She had always supposed she would cry at her wedding but, for far different reasons. Somehow, she managed to mutter the correct words. All she could think of was that at last she had regained her freedom from her uncle, but for what price? What would this husband expect of her? She had a sinking feeling she would continue to pay for this night. It seemed she was doomed to exchange one form of prison for another.

Chapter Eight

Paige's arms felt as though they were about to be pulled from their sockets. She was weary. They had been riding double on Kyle's horse, Satchel, for what seemed like hours. Paige sat behind Kyle with her arms around his middle until she was completely numb. Still, she did not complain. She was determined not to slow him down, nor, be a burden, but they would have to stop soon or she would fall off from complete frozen exhaustion. Not once since they left the parson's house had he even acknowledged her presence. Oh, how he must hate her! Paige was frightened and she had every reason to be. She had no idea when or if Kyle would decide to leave her alone. It was certain he didn't owe her any moral obligations. True, they were man and wife, but still it had no bearing on anything since they were forced at gunpoint to exchange their vows. The one thing which allowed Paige to have a faint glimmer of hope was the fact this captain was an honest man. He could have denied he had had any relations with her, for that, she was grateful.

Paige squeezed her eyes tightly shut, vowing to herself never to beg or plead with Kyle. If he wanted a divorce from her, then she would allow him to obtain one even though it was highly unheard of during these times. But if he wanted her to remain his wife, then she would try her best to be a good wife everywhere except in his bed.

How different the wedding ceremony had been than the one she had dreamed of for so long. Back at school she and the other girls had voiced their dreams and wishes about a virle handsome man gazing lovingly into their eyes throughout eternity. There was no doubt Kyle was a handsome man, but the expression she had last seen on his face could not resemble a look of love. In fact, if she thought he would cherish her like their wedding vows had said, she was afraid she would be sadly mistaken.

At long last Kyle slowed the demanding pace he was putting his mount through. He pulled slowly back on the reins and stopped in front of a tumble-down shanty. He glanced over his shoulder and barked a command. "Slide down. We can spend what is left of the night here. Both of us need some rest." He gripped his hand tightly around the upper part of her arm and lowered her none too gently to the ground.

"Ouch!" Paige snapped. "You do not have to be so rough."

"Well, excuse me!" Kyle growled sarcastically. "Since I've been in this saddle all day yesterday and much of tonight and I happen to be damned tired!" He threw one leg over the saddle and slid off the horse. "You ought to be proud I even helped you down."

Paige tossed her long black hair and bounced toward the cabin, only to turn hesitantly at the door. She was reluctant to ask, but she knew she must. "I suppose we are going to stay in the cabin or do you intend for me to sleep outside?"

"Don't go putting ideas in my head," Kyle thundered. "The thought really hadn't crossed my mind, but come to think of it, it sounds like a damn good idea!"

Paige stamped her foot showing her indignation. She knew he was angry and she was ready for a counter-attack. "Listen to me, Mr. Kyle Brenner, don't take that holier than thou attitude. I know you have been looking for the chance to shout at me. I did not ask you to marry me and if you had denied having relations with me to the parson, I would have backed your story up. Since you were so damnably honest, it's certainly not my fault you had to marry me. In fact, from the way you have acted, you, sir, are the last person on earth I want to be married to!"

"Little miss high and mighty wife of mine, did you ever stop and consider that I simply could not bring myself to lie to a man of the cloth. I dislike the idea of being married to you as much as you abhor being married to me!" Kyle stormed back in response.

Each one stood staring hatefully at one another, neither wanting to budge an inch in their stubbornness. Finally, Paige spoke. "I'm hungry. Do you have any food in your saddle bags, or, are we going to have to wait until we reach where your men are camped . . . ?" Her voice trailed off as she suddenly realized Kyle's story did not fit together. "Wait a minute," she said slowly, "something is not right. You told Oscar that you had men camped near by, and . . . that would be impossible since you are in the Union army . . . unless you have advanced on this area already, or, unless you are planning on invading . . . ?" She looked sharply at him. "What are you doing out of uniform?"

Kyle swore softly. He had hoped Paige would have failed to remember the conversation that went on back at her uncle's home. "Hell, Paige, I thought you had enough sense to figure out how I was trying to bargain for my life. There aren't any men camped around here, at least not any of mine. That crazy fool was going to kill me for sure. I had to think fast. As far as me being out of uniform," he took a deep breath and continued, "I happen to be damn tired of all this infernal fighting. It was one day not long after I first met you, I took my Union blues off and I haven't regretted it yet. I was hunting for a place to start all over again when I met that thieving uncle of yours."

Paige gasped involuntarily. "You mean you deserted your men and country in time of war? Why . . . why . . . that makes you nothing but a coward and a traitor."

Kyle grabbed her instantly. He caught himself just before striking her. His eyes were blazing and a murderous expression gripped his face. "You are the first person to call me a name like that and lived. I'll tell you now," he threatened, "don't ever do it again!" He shoved her roughly from him. "If people such as you would learn to find out a few more details before rushing headlong into running your mouth, then everyone would be a lot better off."

"But . . . but . . . I didn't mean . . ."

Kyle interrupted. "Paige, right now the only thing I know for sure is the fact that I've been pushed into a marriage which I have no desire to be in, I've been threatened with loss of life, been called a coward and a traitor, and I have been pushed about as far as I intend to go. Would you please just go on in the cabin and do as you're told?"

Paige fought back the tears threatening to spill from her eyes. In a small trembling voice she asked, "Would you please hand me your saddle bags?"

He stepped wearily back to his horse and tossed the saddle bags to her. He then removed the rifle from his scabbard. "I'll be back as soon as I find something."

"What do you mean?"

"You said you were hungry," he said simply. "Thought I would try to scare up a rabbit or something."

Paige waited until he had disappeared from sight, then she turned and pushed open the door to the cabin. Blanking all thoughts from her mind, Paige went about the task of starting a fire. Soon, she had one roaring in the fireplace. Rummaging in the saddle bags, she discovered some coffee. She went outside and gathered snow into a blackened pot she had found. After putting the coffee on to brew, Paige sat down at the rickety table and surveyed the dismal surroundings. The fireplace had been built with red clay bricks which she knew had been made locally. The interior walls were rough and obviously hand milled. Over by the door was a small but sturdy wash stand. In the far corner was a narrow bed. She walked over to it; finding the mattress stuffed with straw pleased her. She knew if it had been filled with cotton, no telling what would be crawling through it. A terrible thought crossed her mind. There was only one bed. What if Kyle expected her to sleep with him? Would he demand his husbandly rights? Surely the way they were at each other's throats he wouldn't expect her to be intimate with him. She knew he had said earlier that he wouldn't bother her, but with Kyle Brenner she had learned not to be too careful. She pushed these thoughts from her mind as she recalled what had happened earlier that night. She realized she had overstepped her bounds when she accused Kyle of being a coward. He had proved his bravery. But still, there was something about his story she couldn't quite believe. One thing was for certain, she would never be able to believe he had deserted his men. Her impression was that he was much too loyal for that. If she was given the chance, she would find out why he had left his post in Washington.

Finally, the cabin door flew open and Kyle walked in, stomping the snow off his boots. He placed a freshly skinned rabbit on the table and walked over to warm his hands by the fire. He sniffed the air and for the first time that night, smiled at Paige. "The coffee smells good." He pointed at the rabbit. "It's not much, in fact, its sort of skinny, but it was all I could do on such notice." He skewered the rabbit and before long, it was a golden toasty brown.

Paige savored each bite. Even if the rabbit was a little tough and stringy, it was the first fresh meat she had tasted in a long time. It could have been the most exclusive item on a menu and she couldn't have told the difference. While Kyle was eating, he looked around the room appraisingly. Apparently, Paige had been busy while he had been out hunting. The floor had been swept with a stump of a broom that had been left by the cabin's former owners. He couldn't help but notice how the bed had been freshly made with his bedroll. Clearing his throat, he said, "There is only about two or three hours left before daylight, but we will be able to get a little sleep if we turn in now."

Paige looked at him expectantly. "Where are you going to sleep?"

Kyle laughed. "Well," he drawled, "I would imagine in the bed. Why?"

"Hummmph! That is just about what I figured!" Paige snorted.

"Now what do you mean by that smart remark?" Kyle asked, his temper starting to rise.

"You certainly don't expect me to sleep with you?"

"Lady, sleeping with you is really the furthest thing from my mind. Would you mind telling me where I am supposed to sleep?"

"Well . . . you could sleep in the chair," Paige stammered. "It would be the gentlemanly thing to do."

"Oh no," Kyle said shaking his head. "I don't think I care to sleep in the chair. I happen to be cold, and tired." He made a wide, sweeping gesture with his arm. "If you don't want to share my bed, then you can sleep in the chair or on top of the table if you've a mind to. But me? I'm gonna stretch out in comfort." He nodded toward the wood box. "But, there is one thing you ought to think about, Mrs. Brenner. I would imagine you will get pretty cold before morning. There is only enough wood to get one good fire started, and since I'm not gonna cut wood this time of night, and then too, you noticed I only have two blankets when you made the bed, so, I would think you'll probably be one big chunk of ice by morning."

Paige sputtered her indignation. "You mean you'd let me freeze?"

"No, I won't let you freeze. There's a bed over there. I realize it is small, but I believe if we cuddled real close, neither one of us would have to be cold."

Paige shook her head stubbornly. "No! I'll sit up in that chair, but I will take one of the blankets to keep warm by."

Kyle stared at her long and hard, his aggravation obvious. "If you want to act like a fool, I'll not stop you. But I'll make one thing clear right now, I don't intend freezing my butt off just to satisfy some crazy whim of yours. That fire is going out in a few minutes and it is gonna get mighty cold in here. And, I don't think it would serve any purpose for both of us to freeze so the blankets will stay right where they are." He made a gallant bow and sauntered over to the candle. "As for me, I'm tired and I'm going to bed," he said as he blew out the light.

Paige knew Kyle was right. The cabin was already cooling and she had no desire to sit in a hard chair all night. Neither did she want to share a bed with this man who was nothing but a stranger, yet, he was so much more than a stranger, he was actually her husband! That fact was almost too much for her to accept. She stared in Kyle's direction. The glimmering light of the snow shone through the windows combined with the soft glow of the dying embers from the fireplace cast a mellow light in the room. She gasped when Kyle started removing his trousers. Paige sputtered embarrassingly, "You could have said you were removing your clothes! Besides, if it is all that cold, you could sleep with your clothes on."

Kyle grinned, clearly enjoying teasing Paige. He also knew what light there was in the cabin showed the muscular outline of his body. "Frenchie, ever since this damn war started, I've had to go weeks at a time without even taking my clothes off. Now that I'm out of it, there is no way I intend sleeping uncomfortable."

Paige could see the smile that was toying on Kyle's lips. There was just enough light in the cabin to throw shadows across his face, making him appear sinister and diabolical looking. Suddenly, she was very scared. She felt completely at his mercy.

Kyle yawned and stretched. "Well, goodnight. I'm going to bed." He turned on an afterthought. "By the way, when it gets too cold for you to stay up, please take off your dress before you join me."

Paige's eyes widened in anger. "I will not!" she exclaimed.

"Oh, hell!" Kyle muttered. "Don't misunderstand me. If you'll notice the hem of your dress, you'll find it to be damp. I felt of it with my foot while we were eating. I wouldn't want you to lie down beside me with that thing on." After the self-satisfying remark, Kyle eased down on the bed and breathed an exaggerated sigh of comfort.

Paige stood fuming in anger. The nerve of him! Expecting her to sleep in the chair while he enjoyed the comforts of the only bed, however small it was. She rubbed her arms with her hands, trying to stir some warmth back into them. The fire had finally died down and it wouldn't be long before it was reduced to ashes. Paige sighed and accepted the inevitable. She hesitantly started unbuttoning the dress and slipped it over her head, as Kyle had requested. Then, she lay down beside him, knowing all along the bed would be too small for the both of them. Their bodies were so close, it was hard for Paige to relax. Suddenly, Kyle flinched and jerked away from her, swearing rapidly. Paige sat up in the bed and glared at him. "I simply do not understand you. You insist upon my sharing this bed, and when I do lie down, you jump away from me like I have some kind of disease. There is no pleasing you, Kyle Brenner!"

"You are beginning to irritate me, Frenchie," Kyle muttered through clenched teeth. "Your feet feel like two chunks of ice and when you touched them to me, I jumped. It is as simple as that!" He snuggled his feet over hers. "There, that ought to feel better."

Paige protested very loudly as she struggled to be released.

"Oh hell!" Kyle swore. "Be still and go to sleep. Would you please think for a moment. If I wanted to claim you as my wife, I could. I already know what pleasures you hide beneath your petticoats. If I wanted, I could have your thighs parted and be working between them right now, so I strongly suggest you shut your mouth before you give me any more encouraging ideas and I forget how tired I am!"

Paige was frightened. While tears streamed quietly down her cheeks, she listened as Kyle's breathing leveled off to a steady sound. She was so afraid he would awaken and demand his husbandly rights, she lay welded to one place, even though his maleness jutted into her side. Finally, Paige could not hold her eyes open any longer. Without realizing it, she had drifted off into a misty dreamland.

Kyle awoke as soon as the sun streamed through the window. He dressed and slipped outside without disturbing Paige, who was sound asleep. After gathering firewood and starting a fire, Kyle removed his damp clothes and slipped back into the bed while waiting for the cabin to warm. The sudden chill of his body brought Paige instantly awake. She started to get out of bed, but Kyle encircled her waist with his strong hands. "There's no use in getting up yet because the cabin's not warm. Let's just lie here and wait a few minutes."

For a moment Paige lay perfectly still. She was very conscious of Kyle's body so near. To her dismay, he started to stroke her cheek with his large hand.

"You said...you...would...not...demand your ... husbandly rights ..." she stammered.

Kyle chuckled mischievously. "But, darling," he chided, "Last night I was very tired." Kyle took a deep breath as he became more and more aware of her warm, beautiful body. "You have to admit, I behaved very admirably last night," he said as he pulled her even closer to him.

She tried to pull away but Kyle's strength was far greater than hers. Paige looked at him accusingly. "You know you are stronger than I am. If you are bound and determined to have me, there is nothing I can do, but it will be against my will."

"Now, Frenchie, don't be like that. You don't have to pretend with me. This is Kyle, remember? I know how much desire there is in you. I well recall how you responded to me ... after ..."

Paige was quick to reply. "Yes, and that night has haunted me ever since."

"But this time we have a right," Kyle was quick to answer. "After all, we are married now. You know," he said slowly, "it may not be too bad—my having a wife. I slept pretty darn comfortable last night. In fact, you could even say it was the best night I've spent in a long time." With a slow and deliberate motion he pulled her lips to his, tasting, seeking, delighting in the softness of her feminine, sensuous mouth. His kisses trailed to the hollow of her throat. The aroma of her soft yet firm pulsating breasts was driving him to the state of readiness. "Come on, Frenchie," he whispered tenderly, "respond to me, loosen up, I won't hurt you."

Paige's answer came in a gasping sob. "I will not resist you, Kyle. I know a man's needs and desires are much stronger than a woman's. I also realize I am your wife and you have every right to use my body as you see fit. I will endure your advances but I do not have to enjoy them. I made a vow last night. I decided to stand by you and be a wife to you, so I will submit to your needs." She sat up in the bed, pulled the petticoat over her head and tossed it onto the floor. She lay back against the straw mattress, her raven hair fanned over the striped denim covering. She took a deep breath, trying to build her courage to continue. "Go ahead and take me, I'll offer no resistance."

Kyle was astounded. His emotions went from surprise to rage. He bellowed, "What in the hell do you think I am? Or who do you think I am? Regardless of what you think, I am not a damn rutting boar that's wanting to mate like an animal in the barnyard!" He grabbed her shoulders and shook her. All sense of reasoning had departed his thinking. It was as though Paige's body taunted him like a red matador's cape enraged a bull.

112

"What are you trying to do to me?" he ranted. "One minute you act like you can't stand the sight of me, the next, you throw yourself at me with as much emotion as a bag of salt. Just what do you want of me?"

Paige was trembling. She was scared. She knew Kyle had been pushed and taunted to the edge of madness by her actions. She managed to stammer, "Kyle . . . I didn't mean. I . . . only wanted to let you know it was all right . . . and if you wanted . . ."

"You're damn right it's all right for me to take you if I want to!" Kyle shouted. "Or do I need to remind you," he slurred, "that I didn't ask for your hand in marriage. If I remember right, there was a damned shotgun rammed in between my shoulder blades, so don't you dare tell me what I have a right to do or what I don't. I'll tell you right now, if I want to take you, I will, whether you give your permission or not!"

Before Paige knew what was happening, Kyle had thrown her back against the bed. Like a crazed demon suddenly gone berserk, Kyle had her thighs parted and had thrown himself between them. An involuntary scream of pain escaped Paige's lips as her unyielding body accepted Kyle. Her face contorted in pain and tears began to fall down her cheeks. After the first shock of the assault was over, she began to beat upon his chest with her hand.

"You animal! You horrible, horrible animal!" she cried.

Suddenly, Kyle stopped. A look of pure astonishment crossed his face. "My God!" he muttered. "What am I doing?" Then, with an expression of bewilderment mixed with hatred, Kyle raised himself from her unconquered body. He stumbled to where his clothes lay in a crumpled heap, dressed quickly, then walked over to the table and plopped down in the chair. He rested his brow on his hand, rubbing it while trying to get his emotions under control.

Paige lay in a trembling terror. Her hands shakily pulled the blankets up under her chin. She spat, "I knew you were nothing but a sadistic fiend!"

Kyle glared at her. In a voice filled with venom he spoke. "Paige, that tongue of yours is equipped with too damn many barbs. Would you please shut up before you push me too far." Then in a surprisingly calm voice he added, "We are married in the eyes of God and in the eyes of the law. In our vows we exchanged, we promised to hold each other for better or worse." He laughed ruefully. "So far, it's been for the worse. This I promise though, there will be no repetition of what just happened between us." Paige started to interrupt but Kyle snapped, "Will you please shut up and let me finish what I was trying to say?"

She nodded.

"Never in my life," Kyle continued, "have I treated a woman the way I just treated you. For my actions I have to apologize." He took a deep breath. "Even though we were forced into this marriage, the promise we made was before God and I will not go back on my word if I can help it. I will be a good husband to you."

"You mean I am supposed to forgive and forget

about what happened, just because you feel ashamed and remorseful?" She glared at him with hatred flaring from her eyes.

"I don't care if you forgive me or not!" Kyle snapped. "I've apologized and that is all I can do." He ran his fingers through his hair. "I don't know what you do to me. I will say this," he looked at her honestly, "I've never treated a woman the way I have treated you."

"And I suppose that is my fault? The way you talk, I am to blame for you mistreating me so badly."

"No, I'm not trying to blame you. I didn't mean it that way. But I will say, sometimes you act like you can push me into a corner and I've never had a woman treat me like that before. I've never had a woman who makes me feel the way you do," he added truthfully. He pulled on his boots and reached for his gun. "I'm going out to see if I can find us something to eat. While I am gone, I would suggest you try and make up your mind what you want to do. But let me add this, as soon as the war is over, it is going to be even more difficult for a decent woman to get along by herself—especially a beautiful decent woman. In fact, and you can believe me or not, women who have had families, a husband and children, have been forced to take to the streets in the world's oldest profession just to provide food for their children. I'm afraid after the war is over, it will be a while before the situation improves any. So . . . Frenchie, the choice is yours. You can make up your mind and I will abide by your decision."

Tears clouded Paige's vision. She knew Kyle was speaking the truth but at that moment she hated him so much, it was hard to even comprehend the thought of sharing Kyle's life at the present. The silence in the room was overpowering before she finally managed to stammer, "That's certainly a fine choice you leave me with. I can stay with you and be faced with constant abuse or I can turn to the streets and be faced with other men doing the same. Frankly, it's hard to make a choice."

The muscles worked furiously in Kyle's cheek. "I guess I deserved such a remark, Paige. But, from now on, you'll have no worry on my part. I'll not lay a hand on you in that manner again. If there is ever to be anything between us, then it will be you who comes to me."

"This decision you say I must make is very important." She rubbed her brow. "I must have time to think."

Kyle walked toward the door. "Like I said before, I have some things to do outside; while I'm gone, you can make up your mind." Kyle stomped outside. He stood staring for a moment at the sky as he tried to sort out the feelings that were stampeding through his mind. He was so angry and furious at himself for the way he had acted, and yes, he was furious because Paige attracted him so much. It had been a long time since a woman made his pulse quicken the way Paige did. He kicked the hitching post in frustration. He had only meant to tease and play with Paige. He certainly didn't mean for things to get out of hand the

116

way they did. So, it appeared she was having a difficult time in choosing what she wanted to do. Kyle kicked the post once more then stomped off muttering under his breath that before it was all over with, Paige would be begging for him to take care of her.

Kyle pushed the heavy feeling from his mind. He walked behind the cabin and dug up some of the gold he had buried earlier. After hiding it in a secret compartment in his saddle, Kyle picked up his rifle and went off to find a squirrel or rabbit for breakfast.

Paige paced the floor relentlessly. She worried about Kyle's return, yet, she was afraid she would hear his horse ride away, leaving her alone. She knew she had acted foolishly. She had acted like a Christian about to be thrown to the lions and now she regretted it. She could have discouraged Kyle's amorous feelings in a different manner. Instead, she had helped to drive a wedge between them, causing problems that might never be solved. True, Kyle had acted like a beast, but still, deep down, Paige knew she had to share the blame. Now, she was powerless to change her rash actions. A thought crossed her mind and she ran to the window and pulled the tattered curtain aside. She breathed a sigh of relief. At least Kyle had not ridden off and deserted her. For an instant, she had had visions of him silently leading the horse away, and then riding off forever. She dropped the curtain determinedly, turned and walked over to the fireplace and put some coffee on to boil.

A short time later, Kyle pushed the door open.

He was obviously surprised to smell the aroma of freshly brewed coffee and to see his bedroll rolled into a tight little bundle. He looked expectantly at Paige.

She noticed the grim expression set on his face. After saying a short silent prayer, she said, "Don't look so surprised. After all, a wife is supposed to cook her man breakfast, isn't she?"

Kyle raised his eyebrow warily, nodded slowly, then tossed the fresh skinned squirrel on the table. "A husband is also supposed to provide the breakfast. It isn't much, but I will do a lot better in the future."

Paige ducked her head shyly then raised her eyes boldly to meet Kyle's questioning gaze. "I was wrong. I realize I have to share some of the blame, if there is any blame, of what happened between us this morning. However," she added determinedly, "I will accept your conditions—all of your conditions," she stressed. "But, if we are going to be living together, I would at least like for us to act civilized." She extended her hand and asked, "Friends?"

Kyle stared at her, obviously puzzled, yet relieved. He shrugged his shoulders, took her extended hand and said, "All right, it is agreed—friends."

After an awkward moment, Paige pulled her hand from his and said, "I guess if we are going to be on our way, I had best get this squirrel on to cook."

After they had eaten, Kyle went outside to secure the bedroll on the saddle. As he walked to the edge of the porch he stopped suddenly. Lying on the bottom step was the old dog that had been at Paige's uncle's house. Apparently he had followed their trail. "Paige," Kyle called. "Paige, come here and see who we have for company."

"Well, I'll be!" Paige declared surprised. "Imagine, him following us. Wonder why he did that, and what are you going to do with him?"

Kyle laughed. "I don't reckon I'll do anything with him. I would imagine he has a mind of his own. He probably took a shine to me back there at the barn. It looks like we have adopted us a dog whether we wanted one or not." The dog panted happily and wagged his tail.

"Yes, but will we be able to care for him?" Paige asked very concernedly.

Kyle said matter-of-factly, "Well, I would think he'll get damn sight better care from me than he was getting at Oscar's house."

"I guess you are right about that," Paige said slowly.

Kyle mounted Satchel, then he helped Paige on behind him. The sun flirted in and out of the clouds as they started off. Paige glanced back over her shoulder and smiled slightly as the dog trotted eagerly behind them.

Chapter Nine

It was midafternoon before Kyle and Paige reached the outskirts of the thriving riverport town of Jefferson, Texas.

"I guess Jefferson is just about the most important town in the state of Texas right now," Kyle explained to Paige. "It was about fifteen years ago that an industrious riverboat captain managed to steer his ship over from Shreveport. When he proved it could be done, they invested the money to clear the sloughs and bayous, dredging them, and making it possible for the big steamers from the Ohio and Mississippi Rivers to navigate. Then Jefferson became more and more important as the war progressed. When the forts below New Orleans fell to the Union, as many as possible of the Confederate ships fled to the safety of this friendly port and the Federal government has not been able to establish any kind of foothold in this area."

"Oh, I see," Paige said breathlessly as excitement danced in her eyes. In the distance she could see the tall, majestic stacks of the mighty steamships which lined the port of the Big Cypress River. Paige jumped, startled by the unexpected sound of a shrill whistle cutting through the lazy afternoon as one of the ships began maneuvering in the turn-basin. Kyle chuckled but didn't say anything.

As they rode on into town Paige was caught up in the bustling activity. She failed to notice how tense Kyle became when they passed a company of Confederate soldiers marching down the street.

She felt a surge of relief when they made their way through the rough, bawdy part of town without stopping. Kyle finally brought his mount to a stop in front of a beautifully luxurious hotel called The Irvine.

"Ooooh, how charming!" Paige exclaimed in delight as she saw the fancy wrought-iron chairs which lined the spotlessly clean front porch. She craned her head upward to look at the ornate iron works which made up the decoration of the balcony. "Why . . . this place is simply captivating," she said in amazement. Then she gave Kyle a hard look. "You can certainly tell the war hasn't touched here."

Kyle's arm stiffened angrily as he helped her slide down from the horse. He hissed through clenched teeth. "Frenchie, would you please stop making those cutting remarks about the war! I think you ought to have some history lessons about why this war came to be instead of blaming it all on the North!"

Paige's eyes widened at Kyle's outburst. His remarks only served to heighten her determination to find the true reason why Kyle had suddenly left the service of the Union army. Somehow, she would find out what he was actually up to.

Even though the decor was very different from the Washington hotel, repetitious memories came flooding back as Paige followed Kyle through the lobby. She self-consciously ducked her head to avoid the curious stares she received, feeling everyone in the building was staring at her bruised and blackened eye, and shabby, soiled dress.

The elderly gentleman sitting behind the desk quickly appraised the couple standing before him. He cleared his throat, leaned forward over the desk and in a kindly voice, said, "Sir, I don't want to sound presumptuous, and I sure don't want to embarrass you any, but the rates at this hotel might just be a little bit more than you can afford. I can give you the name of a place that is a whole lot cheaper . . . yet it is a clean and decent place to stay."

Kyle looked at the man rather sharply then chuckled in his rich voice. "I appreciate your concern, sir," he drawled. "But, I believe I can manage your rates all right." He tossed a couple of double eagles on the counter and started to sign the register. "I want the largest room you have here on the ground floor." He motioned outside with a nod of his head. "I noticed a mercantile down the street when we rode in. Is it a place where we can buy some decent clothes?"

"Oh yes, sir, it is!" The desk clerk ducked his head sheepishly. "I'm sorry . . . I . . . didn't mean . . ." he stammered.

Kyle laughed aloud. "That's all right. I realize we look a little seedy right now, but we've been traveling and ran into a little trouble down the road. Also, if you'd please, I would appreciate it if you would have my horse stabled for me at the livery next door."

"Immediately, sir." The clerk snapped his fingers at a small negro lad sitting on the other side of the lobby.

Kyle said to the boy, "My horse is the big black, tied out front. Make sure he gets plenty of oats and a good rub-down."

The deskman rang a bell and a stately old black gentleman hurried over. "Alfred, would you please show," he paused as he swung the register around and read the name, "Mr. and Mrs. Brenner to suite 103?"

Alfred picked up Kyle's saddle bag and asked, "Dis be all yo're baggage, suh?" His eyes widened when he saw the bruises on the woman's face, but quickly averted his glance as not to appear questioning.

Kyle caught a glimpse of Paige's crimsoned face and chuckled, "Yeah, that's all there is. But I would also like plenty of hot water brought in as soon as possible."

Paige mustered as much dignity as she possibly could as they followed the bellman. She ignored the sudden chatter and fluttering of the ladies' fans as she passed by. The bellman escorted Kyle and Paige down the hallway, past a small foyer to a suite of rooms at the end of the building. The suite consisted of two rooms. The rooms were separated

123

by an entrance hall decorated with gilt cherubs flying effortlessly around a tall brass mirror, a comfortable love seat, and a marble candelabra sat on a tiny parson's table.

The bathing room to the left consisted of a beautiful oak chiffioner, a gleaming copper-colored brass Sitz bathtub, a marble-topped vanity with a matching wrought iron chair. In the corner was a silk oriental dressing screen.

The bedroom was large and roomy, and very tastefully furnished. As they entered the doorway, Paige noticed a little nook containing a small French table. Over the table was a delicately tinted mirror. The table supported a floral etched pitcher and basin. The heavy claw legged bed was covered with a Battenburg lace spread and the huge oak bureau was adorned with the same designed Battenburg lace doily.

Paige stood in the middle of the room, fully appreciating the smell of beeswax and the crisp, freshly laundered curtains hanging on the spotlessly clean window. She watched, fascinated as Alfred started a fire in the miniature marble fireplace.

Alfred turned to Kyle when he had finished lighting the fire. "Is dere anything else I can do for you, suh?"

Kyle pressed a coin into his hand, "No, Alfred. I guess that will be all until the bath water is ready."

The old man flashed a toothy smile as he flipped the coin into the air and pocketed the money. "Yes, suh! Thank you, suh! By the time you goes down to the mercantile, d'ey'll be 'nough hot water fer you to swim in if'n you wants to!"

As soon as they were alone, Paige turned to Kyle. Her hands were planted firmly on her hips and her eyes were snapping in anger. "I suppose I'm the little bit of trouble you ran into back down the road?"

"Oh hell!" Kyle swore violently. "I had to tell the man something! After all, we came into one of the nicest hotels in Jefferson looking like a couple of waifs. But on second thought, I guess you called it right. You were the trouble I ran into down the road . . . the road all the way back to Washington!"

"You know as well as I do, that wasn't my fault, so don't blame me." Her lips pinched together as she looked around the room. "My, my, aren't we playing the big shot. But what else can you expect from a Yankee?"

"What do you mean by that remark?"

She flung her arms in a sweep of the room. "What do you call all of this? It seems to me that you are throwing money around very unnecessarily. In fact, you are acting almost vulgar by renting a room this expensive."

Instant rage churned through Kyle. "It damn sure isn't any of your business what I do with my money, Frenchie."

"Well! If that is how you feel about it, then I can leave!"

Kyle rolled his eyes upward in aggravation. "I think we have been through a similar scene before back in Washington. Remember? And you can certainly recall what happened then." He slitted his eyes at her. "I'm not going to argue with you anymore. I've got things to attend to!" He crammed his hat on his head and stomped out of the room leaving Paige to fume in her own anger.

Suddenly, Paige felt alone. Not merely alone in the room but isolated in mind and body. She stepped over to the window and stared out of it with unseeing eyes until finally she became aware of someone knocking on the door.

A buxom negro woman came rushing in with a steaming kettle of water, followed by two little boys who were miniature copies of their mother. They struggled with a foot tub filled to the brim with sloshing hot water. As soon as the sitz tub was filled, the woman shooed the boys from the room after instructing them to bring more as soon as possible. The woman stood in the middle of the room staring boldly at the woman she was to serve. Her skin gleamed a shiny ebony. Her eyes flashed with the pride of her past heritage of chieftains who roamed the dark continent. A few wisps of curly hair crept out from under the bright red bandanna she wore around her head. All in all, she presented a very striking figure.

"My name be Della. Mr. Norton 'structed me to help with your bath. But first, I think I ought to stoke up this fire and get your head washed so it can be drying 'fore supper." She picked up the poker and prodded the fire until it crackled and popped, throwing out much more warmth.

Paige could only stand helplessly by while the maid took control and busied herself around the room. "Please," Paige said hesitantly, "I can do this myself."

"Oh no, Ma'am," Della's eyes grew large. "This be what Mr. Norton is payin' me fo'. You see, he done went and give me my freedom papers and the papers fo' my young'ns a long time ago . . . even before the war started. So . . . I cain't disappoint him now by not takin' care of de hotel and de guests. You come on over here, Missy," she motioned with her hand, "and let me get started on your pretty hair before the water cools off too much."

Paige obeyed meekly, feeling as though she had no other choice in the matter.

The woman rattled on. "I reckon by the time we get your hair and body washed, your man will be back with some more clothes. Alfred done already told me that y'all didn't have any kind of baggage and you had one hum-dinger of a black eye! Tis a shame that decent folks cain't go nowhere without thieves jumpin' them and robbing the clothes off their back! We've sho' been having a bunch of thieving going on around here, lately." She leaned her head down and peered questioningly at Paige. "Dat is how you got that shiner, ain't it?"

Paige nodded as she bit back a reply. She certainly didn't want anyone to know the circumstances how she came to be at the hotel. Paige's brow creased into a frown. She was curious at Della's speech. From the short time Della had spoken, Paige had the feeling something was wrong. Della's speech was almost perfect at times, then it seemed she made an effort to throw in the slang that was so common in the south. She decided to keep silent, and perhaps she could figure it out later. Finally her hair was squeaky clean, but Della had to rinse it once more before she was thoroughly satisfied with her task. She pulled one of the rocking chairs closer to the fire and had Paige sit on it. Then she began toweling the long black curly locks before brushing them until they gleamed.

By this time, Della's sons had brought in several more tubs of hot water to the bathing room. Their laughter could be heard echoing up and down the hallway as they scampered out to play. When Della tried to help the young woman undress for her bath, that's where Paige drew the line.

"No!" Paige stated adamantly. "I can take my own bath." The last thing she wanted was for the gossipy maid to discover the welts on her back that remained from the beating she had received.

Della took Paige's reluctance for shyness, so she waited until she heard water splashing before she stuck her head around the corner. "You go right ahead and enjoy yourself, child. I'll get on back to de kitchen and make sho' your man will have some hot water fo' his bath when he comes back."

Paige smiled to herself when she heard the front door close softly behind Della. At last she was alone to linger and enjoy her bath. For an instant, her eyes misted when she recalled memories of long ago and a woman similar to Della cared for her family. She quickly brushed them aside, knowing if she dwelled in the past, she would become depressed. Paige laid her head back, relishing the feel of the hot water as it started soaking away the tiredness and soothing muscles sore from riding spraddle-legged behind Kyle for so long. Before Paige realized it, she had slipped into a semi-state of sleep, only to be awakened by Kyle's and Della's voices as they entered the entrance hall dividing the bath and bedroom.

"Yes, suh! Your lady should be 'bout ready to come out now. I left her soaking while I went to check on your water. It will be ready fo' you in jest a tad bit."

"Thank you," Kyle said politely. "I have bought Mrs. Brenner some more clothes. I would appreciate it if you would unpack them and take the pretty dressing gown in to her. I sure hope they fit. Since we haven't been married too long, I had to guess at what size she wore."

Della's face lit up in a pleasing smile. "You mean that the two of you are newly married?"

Kyle grinned at the maid's excitement. "I guess you could say that. We were married last night and just rode straight through so we wouldn't have to spend another night out on the trail. Well . . . I said we rode straight through, we actually stopped for a little while, but didn't get much rest."

Della's chuckling laughter filled the room. "Lawsey, lawsey, and I can imagine why you didn't rest much! I sho' didn't know that you two were jest freshly married, but I should have guessed when the missy was so shy acting about herself." Her eyes gleamed mischievously. "Let me hurry and unpack the clothes so I can git my black carcass out of here so you can be alone with your pretty little wife." Della hurriedly unwrapped the clothes and placed them on hangers.

129

When she reached the bottom of the bundle, her eyes widened and she broke into chuckles. "Well, lawsey me, would you look a-here. Dis robe be plumb fancy!" She held up a scarlet chiffon robe that plunged deeply at the neckline. It was trimmed with black ostrich feathers. "My, my," she exclaimed, smacking her lips in a clucking sound. "Dis will be right handsome on that pretty wife of yours; but," her voice lowered to a whisper, "I thinks you made a mistake. I thinks this is what the loose women wears to please a man. It not be the kind a man buys fo' his wife."

Kyle's eyes widened at his mistake. "Really? I didn't know . . . I had no idea . . ."

Della nodded her head as if in understanding how Kyle felt. "It's pretty enough. Missy will most probably know what you meant."

Paige called out, "Della, I heard Kyle come in. If he bought me a dressing gown, would you bring it to me, please?"

Kyle glanced at Della. He said in a lowered voice, "Go ahead and take it to her. It is too late now to go back for a different one."

Della went to the bathroom clutching the robe tightly in her hands. Paige instructed her to leave the wrap and to leave the room before she would get out of the tub. Kyle and Della both waited, feeling apprehensive until finally Paige came into the bedroom. Even if the robe was too flamboyant, Paige was beautiful. Her raven hair had dried into tiny ringlets cascading down her back. The winter wind had burned her cheeks giving them a blushing glow, and her eyes had an excited look about them making her appear extremely exotic.

Kyle could only stare open-mouthed at her. It had been a long time since he had seen anyone as beautiful as the woman who was now his wife.

Paige gave an embarrassed laugh. "Really Kyle, don't you think this is a little daring?"

He nodded sheepishly. "Della told me what kind of robe it was, or rather, what kind of woman usually wore a gown like that." He looked at her helplessly. "I'm sorry, I simply thought it was pretty."

Paige had been slightly angered when she had first seen the robe and had intended to scold Kyle for buying it for her, but when she saw the stricken expression on his face, she held her tongue, realizing Kyle had no malice, only good intentions. She managed to stammer, "It is perfectly fine, Kyle. The robe is still pretty and I would imagine you will be the only one to see me in it besides Della."

Della clucked in her southern drawl. "My, my, I see right now how pretty your babies are gonna be, and the sooner I gits my work done, the sooner you can get started on them." She chuckled again as she started picking up the wrappers.

Kyle was clearly amused over Della's suggestion. It was hard for him to understand why he enjoyed Paige's discomfort over the maid's remark. He knew it didn't matter one way or the other. Paige was simply going to add a degree of truth to his undercover role. But, the only thorn in the bush was Paige's beauty. It was going to be hard to share his bed with her and not give in to his desires. Desires which came naturally to a man. But he had

131

given his word and he knew it would be impossible for him to go back on it. He pushed the thoughts aside while he shaved, trimming back a scraggly growth on his beard. Della bustled in saying his bath water was ready. Kyle declined her offer to help him remove his boots.

"Lawsey!" Della exclaimed in a huffy tone of voice. "Ain't never seen the likes of such independent folks! Won't even let me earn my honest wage!"

"Now, Della," Kyle admonished before leaving for the bathroom. "Mrs. Brenner and I appreciate your help. We are just tired and not used to having such good help around." Della's brown face broke into a huge grin at Kyle's compliment.

Only a few moments passed before Kyle called out to Paige. "Paige? Paige, would you do me a favor, please?"

"What do you want?"

"I need you to come in and wash my back."

"Why . . . why . . . I can't come in there, you are probably in the bathtub by now."

"I am in the tub," he bellowed. "That's why I need you to wash my back."

Paige looked helplessly at Della. "Would you do it for me?"

"Land-o-sakes, no, Missy. That man in there is your husband, and the only way he is gonna be satisfied is fo' you to do it. He sho' ain't gonna be happy if'n I traipse myself in there." She grinned broadly. "Since it is getting late, I'll just have y'all's supper served in here. I'll also make sure there is a good bottle of wine on the tray." She winked at Paige as she left.

"Paige," Kyle called again when he heard the front door close. "I'm not going to call you again. I need you now!"

Paige took a deep breath; Kyle was trying to establish who was the boss in this marriage by ordering her to do as he wished. He clearly had her facing a dilemma. He thought that she would not want to suffer the embarrassment of people knowing their marriage was a farce, even if the people involved were the hotel's hired help. He was right. She couldn't suffer that kind of humiliation. But she would refuse to let him see how much it bothered her. She decided to do as he requested, but first she leaned over to experiment on how much of her bosom would be exposed. It looked as though her breasts would fall out at any moment, however they were in no danger of doing so. It was her body and no need to be embarrassed by it. She would be uncomfortable only if she let her husband make her conscious of herself.

"Paige?"

"I am coming," she answered, quickly going to the door before she changed her mind. When she reached the doorway of the bathroom, it was all she could do to keep from breaking out in gales of laughter. There, Kyle sat, in the deep bottomed, but tiny around, high, oval backed sitz tub, like an oversized king. His legs were almost folded double and his knees were practically touching his chin.

"What in the hell is so funny?" he snarled.

Paige laughed heartily. "Do you have any idea how ridiculous you look?"

"I don't give a damn how ridiculous I look. This is the first chance I have had to take a bath in a long time . . . and I mean a *real* bath and I damn sure intend on taking full advantage of it. Now you see why I've been calling you to come in here and help me."

She stood back, her expression mocking. "I can see how your back would be difficult to reach, but if you expect me to wash your back, you'll have to lean forward some." She teased further, "Are you sure there will be room for this tiny bar of soap?"

For a moment Kyle didn't say a word, he just glowered darkly at her. Then he snapped, "If that is your feeble excuse for humor, frankly I fail to see it."

Paige stifled a snicker. The more she said, the funnier it became, and the angrier Kyle got. Ignoring his stiff resistance, she raised her gown past her knees, knelt down and started sudsing away at his back. The more she washed, the more aware of the rippling shoulder muscles, the broad tanned shoulders and the animal sleekness of his body she became. Even though she had known him intimately, this was the first time she had seen him in this light. He *was* very handsome. And she had discovered one more thing. He was quite helpless. She had the distinct impression he had called her in to merely tease her, but he had truly needed her help.

Finally Kyle said. "Heaven forbid that you think I'm trying to get fresh or make a suggestion you might consider out of the way, but if I stayed in this water any longer, I would probably turn into a fish. I'm going to have to stand up to rinse off. Would you get that pitcher of water and pour it over me when I stand?"

"You mean . . . you are going . . . to stand up in front of me, naked?" Paige asked and recoiled in horror.

"Well, I damn sure don't take a bath with my clothes on, Frenchie."

Paige was terrified! When Kyle stood abruptly, she leaped to her feet. She could feel her face blazing bright crimson. She had never seen the frontal view of a naked man before. Kyle stood with his hands on his hips, obviously enjoying Paige's embarrassment. Paige rushed to the small table, picked up the pitcher of water and stumbled back to the bathtub. Kyle laughed out loud at Paige. She stretched upwards and began pouring the water over him, all the while shielding her eyes with her free hand. With a teasing, devilish tone of voice, Kyle pulled her to him and said, "Would you like for me to retract what I said earlier?"

"What . . . do . . . you . . . mean . . . ?" Paige stammered.

"You know very well what I mean," he said huskily as desire swept over him. His voice became tender and he continued. "I gave you my word this morning and I fully intend to live up to it, but if you would like to release me from my vow . . ."

"No! Never! You promised, Kyle!" Paige said, jerking away from his grasp.

Kyle's jovial mood changed instantly. "That's right!" he shouted bitterly. "And it is one promise I intend to keep." He shook his finger in her face.

135

"This is the second time you have rebuffed me, and by God, it will damn sure be the last!" He snatched a towel draped across the chair, wrapped it around his middle and stomped off into the bedroom, muttering under his breath.

Holding the pitcher in mid-air, Paige whirled around and slammed it down on the table. The nerve of that man! Acting like some kind of biblical king, expecting her to jump at his every whim, thinking she would hasten to sleep with him. He knew the details of their bargain and should not have put her in the position he did. "Why do I feel such animosity toward him? Why does the thought of a marriage bed scare me to death?" she thought. "I know Kyle would be very good to me. Regardless of what has happened between us, he is kind and I believe a basically honest man, and he is certainly attractive enough. So why am I afraid of the thought of his putting his hands on me? Could it be that I am afraid of my inner feelings? Is it possible there is something wrong with me that prevents me from having an honest relationship with a man?" She walked into the bedroom to find Kyle dressed and staring moodily out the window. "I'm sorry, Kyle," she said softly. "You may not believe this, but I do wish I could respond to you." She flung her arms in anger and frustration. "Oh! I'm so mixed up I don't even know what I'm doing or saying! Perhaps I had too many fanciful ideas about falling in love with a man and him with me." She walked over to where he was standing and placed her hand on his shoulder. "I believe I know why the things happened between us in Washington. I understand. I also shudder to think what would have become of me if you had not been such a decent person."

Kyle looked at her; bewilderment crossed his features. "What are you trying to say?" he interrupted. "It sounds as though you are willing to give this marriage a chance." He shook his head. "Let me get this straight. You want to be married to me, but you do not want the physical side of marriage. Is this right?"

A pained expression flashed across Paige's face. "Yes, I suppose that is what I am trying to say. If . . . if we had a chance to get to know each other, who knows? We may even eventually fall in love."

Kyle reached over and took a lock of Paige's hair and twined it between his fingers. "So . . . you want to wait and see if we can fall in love with each other without having to worry about my making love to you."

"Yes."

"I thought that was what we had decided in the cabin. I realize things got way out of hand out there. But what you just said sounds reasonable. We can give this marriage say . . . six months or even a year and if it isn't working out, then either one of us would be free to walk out the door and not look back. But I think you need to understand one thing. I am a man with a man's desires and needs. I can imagine how difficult it will be. After all, you are a beautiful and desirable woman . . . So, don't back me into a corner too far."

Paige smiled and extended her hand. "All right,

Kyle, we have a deal. I certainly hope it works out for the best." A knock at the door interrupted the conversation. Paige looked questioningly at Kyle, then she opened the door. Mr. Norton, the hotel manager, entered the room carrying an ice bucket and a bottle of wine. He was followed by Alfred who was carrying a tray heavily laden with food.

Alfred smiled with a flash of white teeth. "Della told me that you was freshly married and would probably be wantin' your supper in your room. I brought you somethin' to eat."

"Hush your silly titterings, Alfred," Mr. Norton said kindly. He nodded to the newly wedded couple. "Mister and Mrs. Brenner, on behalf of the management, I would like to offer this wine with the management's heartiest congratulations and also our sincere apology for the misunderstanding this afternoon."

"Why thank you, Mister Norton," Kyle smiled warmly as he took the wine. "We accept this with pleasure. And . . . no apology is necessary. I can imagine why you got the impression you did. So, think no more about it."

Mister Norton smiled. "Thank you for your understanding and we certainly hope your stay will be a pleasant one." Alfred busied himself with the small drop-leaf table he had brought in while they had been talking. After placing the food on it, he flashed another toothy smile and backed graciously from the room with the hotel manager following close behind. The delicious aroma which filled the room was overpowering. Paige and Kyle were reminded it had been a long time since they had eaten anything. The food was tempting enough to have pleased even the most particular palate. Tiny gulf shrimp lay in a rich, succulent sauce, to be served over a bed of fluffy white rice. Green beans had been simmered and seasoned to perfection, and cabbage had been finely chopped and topped with a sweet-sour sauce. Corn meal had been subtly seasoned and deep-fried as only a cajun cook could have done. The delicious meal was finished with a delicate pastried apple cobbler smothered in heavy cream and steaming cups of black, chicory coffee. After they had eaten their fill, Kyle pushed back his chair, patted his well rounded stomach, and said, "When you are finished, you might want to try on the clothes I brought in a little while ago. As I told Della, I had to use my judgment about what size you wore, but if some of the garments don't fit, you can have them altered later."

Paige's eyes lit up with excitement. "Oh! You mean you bought me more than this?" she said, fingering the beautiful red robe.

"Sure, you can't go around wearing that all the time."

She ducked her head shyly as she admitted, "I have never had an honest to goodness store bought dress before. Mama always made my clothes. I guess . . . the only ready made garment I owned was my cloak . . . that Sadie kept."

Kyle watched as she tore into the neatly folded stack of clothes. He had only purchased the necessities he figured she would need until she was able to do some shopping. But at that, the stack of clothing was quite ample. It contained two modest dresses, undergarments, stockings, and a high necked flannel night gown.

With a wry smile curving her lips, Paige stroked the flannel gown with one hand and fingered the flamboyant ostrich feathers with the other. "I must say, you certainly have varied tastes." Kyle nodded sheepishly as Paige continued. "I don't know why you said I could do more shopping later. There seems to be more than enough here."

Kyle's face shadowed and a frown drew deep between his eyes. "Those clothes are not what I want for you. I don't want you to have to make do with any old rag you can find. I have plans and they do not include having a wife dressing like she just left a share-cropper's cabin." Kyle's manner did not invite comment so Paige sat back and watched him as he abruptly turned and poured a large glass of wine. He clearly indicated the subject was closed.

He stared moodily into the flickering firelight oblivious to anything or anyone around him. "Hell," he thought to himself, "Why are you feeling like such a snake-in-the-grass? She is the one who said she wanted to give the marriage a trial run. Can you help it that it was so convenient to make your cover story more plausible. Face it, Kyle. No one will be suspicious of a newly married man being a Union spy! But why do I feel so guilty about involving Paige? Why do I suddenly feel as though I am betraying her?"

The sun had just set when Paige stretched, yawned and glanced at Kyle sleepily. "I am completely exhausted. If you don't mind, I think I will go on to bed and get a good night's rest."

"It won't be long before I'll be doing the same. First, I want to run down to the livery stable and make sure Satchel is bedded down all right." He left the suite of rooms, ambled down the hallway, nodded to some ladies sitting in the foyer, and walked on outside. The brisk night air almost took his breath away, it was so cold and sharp. He looked up and down the street, studying the people as they hurried toward their homes. He stepped off the porch and to his surprise, the dog which had followed them was still patiently waiting at the bottom of the steps. "Well, I'll just be damned!" he muttered aloud. Kyle spun on his heel, marched back inside the hotel and made his way to the kitchen where he talked the cook out of some meat scraps. He promptly took the scraps out to the dog and watched while the animal ate. When the dog had finished, it was clear that Kyle had made a friend for life. Kyle whistled for the dog to follow as he walked over to the stables. After he was satisfied that Satchel was being well cared for, he called the boy who was in charge of the stables over. "Would you see to it that this dog is fed every morning and night? I'll make arrangements with the hotel to supply the food."

"I reckon so, suh," the boy said, scratching his head.

Kyle chuckled when the dog trotted into the same stall where his horse was stabled. "If that don't beat all. . . ." He pressed a coin into the boy's hand and said, "Now, I expect you to take real

141

good care of both of them, understand?''

"Yes, suh! I sho' do, suh. I'll take care of them like they were my own," the boy said as he fingered the coin.

Kyle started back toward the hotel, but on a whim, he walked to the end of the street, turned left and before he knew it, was standing in front of a noisy saloon.

What a difference a few blocks made in a water-front town. Although the Irvine Hotel was only a few blocks away from the saloons dotting the river, their differences made them seem to be in different worlds. All sorts of characters were leaning against saloons and buildings. Most were dressed in tattered Confederate uniforms, soldiers who had apparently given the best years of their lives to the war cause. Some had missing limbs and some were whole in body, but almost all had a hopeless look about them.

Kyle walked into McGarrity's Saloon, sauntered up to the bar and ordered a cold beer. Slowly and carefully, he gave the saloon and its occupants the once-over. A toothless old man played the piano with gusto. It was at the back of the building beneath a make-shift stage. Three scantily dressed women kicked their feet high in the air to the beat of the music. There were several poker tables scattered around but only one had any serious gaming at it. Kyle turned back to the bar and was enjoying his drink when he heard a scuffle break out at the active poker table. Quick as a flash, the barkeeper had a sawed-off double barreled shotgun in his hands.

"All right!" he shouted. "That is enough! You all know I don't go fer none of that shit in my place. Which ever one of you started the ruckus can head fer the door, right now."

A man dressed in civilian clothes mouthed back at the barkeeper in a drunken snarl, "But . . . but . . . Zeke, Captain Ryan, here, has pulled the last six . . . seven pots."

"That's all right, Bill," Zeke replied, anger in his voice. "You know as well as I do that Cap'n Ryan don't do no cheating, where everybody here knows how loose you play your cards when you've had a tad too much to drink. You also know my rules. If you cain't afford to lose, then don't sit down at one of the tables. Ain't no one who plays at my tables cheats, and I don't cotton to your suggestion that Cap'n Ryan has been doing it. You've just had a bad spell of luck. Go on home and sleep it off." Bill started to protest once more but Zeke interrupted by leveling the shotgun straight at his belly. "I done already tol' you I don't want none of your lip. And I won't tell you again to go home and sleep it off."

Bill turned a sickly shade of white as he looked at the hog iron pointing at him. He watched as Zeke pulled back both hammers of the deadly gun. "All right, all right. I guess I have had too much to drink," he mumbled as he picked up his hat and headed for the front door.

Within moments the music was being pounded out again and the din of noise picked back up as the incident was forgotten. The man referred to as Cap'n Ryan gave Kyle the once-over. He pushed

143

back his chair and walked slowly over to where the stranger was standing, leaning against the bar. "Howdy, stranger. Haven't seen you around these parts before."

Kyle took another sip of his brew before answering. "No, haven't been here too long. In fact, just got in a little while ago."

"Going to be here long?" Ryan asked curiously.

"Oh, could be, I guess. Depends on how much action there is around here." Kyle nodded interestedly toward the poker tables.

Ryan gestured toward the table. "There is an open spot over there. You are more than welcome to join us. We can always use new blood so to speak, that is . . . if you are game."

Kyle laughed easily. "Nope, don't believe so. Not tonight. Like I said, I just got into town a little while ago and I'm kind of tired. Besides," he added, remembering he was supposed to be a newly wedded man, "I plan on being extra busy tonight." He wanted to say something to make the man remember the conversation. He would never know when and where and under what circumstances he might meet with this man called Captain Ryan again. If he wanted his story to ring true, he would have to act out his part as if he were actually living it. "If there is a game going on tomorrow evening, I may come over and join you, though."

"I would imagine I'll be here." He hit his leg deliberately. "Since I got this, I haven't been doing much of anything 'cept sitting around the tables." He gave Kyle a scrutinizing look. "Since you don't particularly have a southern accent, and you certainly don't have a Yankee brogue; what part of the country would you be from?''

Kyle lifted his brow and answered him in a hard voice. "Well, I'll tell you," he said slowly. "I come from a place where men mind their own business."

The friendly gleam disappeared from Ryan's eye. "I wasn't being nosy, just trying to be friendly. Besides," he added coldly, "I was wondering why an able bodied man like you wasn't out helping to win this war."

Kyle replied, "I knew what you were driving at when you asked me the first question. That's why I answered the way I did." He took another pull of his beer. "You see, I learned a long time ago to let other people have their opinions and I would keep mine. I figured out some time ago that if the north wanted to push their politics down the south's throat, and if the south wants to get its prime young men killed off on the pretense of keeping their slaves and to salvage too many prideful ways, then more power to both of them. I ain't about to make it any of my business." Kyle knew he had taken a huge gamble in declaring his neutrality in a Confederate stronghold, especially to a man who had been wounded and apparently lost a lot in the course of the war. A great wave of relief passed over him when Ryan broke out in a hearty laugh.

"I like your courage, friend," he said slapping Kyle on the back. "It took a lot of guts to stand up and tell me that." He called Zeke over to the counter. "Give him another drink on me."

Zeke eagerly poured the beer, greatly relieved

that the two men had passed off what could have been serious trouble.

Kyle accepted the beer and after a few sips, he said to Ryan. "My name's Brenner. Kyle Brenner. Thank you for the brew, and if I'm free tomorrow night, and if the invitation is still here, I may take you up on the offer to sit in on a few games."

Ryan saluted with his glass and nodded his head. "Anytime, friend, anytime."

After the stranger disappeared through the doors and into the night, Ryan looked thoughtful a brief moment before motioning to one of his friends who had been waiting expectantly at another table. "Follow him and see if he is on the level." A short time later, the man came back and reported to Ryan.

"From what I overheard of your conversation, it would appear the man was telling the truth. At least he went over to that big hotel on the next street. And his horse and dog is stabled at their livery stable."

Ryan assumed a grave expression. He took a long drink from his glass and said, "I think we need to keep a watchful eye on Mr. Brenner. He came swaggering in here, picked out the boss of the place and made me back down some. It don't appear that he made me back down, but he knows I did, and I know I did. Something don't ring quite right about him. Watch him!" he snorted angrily before turning and stomping outside.

Chapter Ten

Kyle tiptoed quietly into the hotel room in order not to disturb Paige. He was very surprised to find her awake. She had pulled one of the rocking chairs up to the small fireplace. She raised her head to see who had entered, then giggled, raising an amber filled glass.

"Have you ever been so tired you couldn't sleep?" she asked, her voice slurring from the liquor. "I tried to lie down for a while but could not sleep. I only tossed and turned. Luckily, Della came down to check on me before she went to bed. She told me she had seen you leave." Her tongue tripped over the words as she found it more and more difficult to speak coherently. Paige continued, "I told her how horrible I felt so she sent one of her little boys back with a hot toddy. Then he brought another one and another one. . . ." She giggled again. "I have to admit, this stuff sure makes you feel good."

The amusement in his voice was plain. "From the way you are acting, I would say you have never drunk any of that hard stuff before, have you?"

"No, I haven't. I guess the only thing I have ever drunk has been apricot brandy or a small glass of wine."

Kyle sat heavily in the other rocker. The beer and wine he had drunk, along with his weariness, was taking its toll. He knew they would both probably suffer from the after-effects of the liquor the following morning. It didn't usually affect him this way, but it had been a long time since he had partaken of spirits. Kyle stood and stretched. "I think I'll go to bed," he said, yawning.

Paige leaped to her feet. "All right, sit down here first," she commanded.

"But . . . why . . . ?"

Placing her hands on her hips impatiently, Paige said, "To show you how much I appreciate what you've done for me. You took me away from that hell. Besides," she touched him lightly on his chest, "don't most wives pull off their husband's boots?"

A grin flirted around Kyle's mouth. "Well . . . I guess some women do . . ."

After Paige had tugged off his boots, she marched unsteadily over to the door with boots in hand. "Della told me if I would set them outside she would have Alfred or one of her boys shine them."

Kyle started to unbutton his shirt. Paige noticed and gasped as she said, "What in the world are you doing?" Her words rang through the room like the last hollow notes of church bells on a Sunday afternoon.

"What does it look like I'm doing? If you don't

want to see me strip down to nothing, you can either close your eyes or blow out the lamp."

"I'll blow out the lamp!" she snipped.

The room grew very quiet. The only sound was the squeak of Paige's rocking chair and every so often the fire would pop and a bright spark of flame would go shooting upward. Kyle lay on his back, his feet crossed, and his hands were underneath his head. He watched Paige's darkened outline fade in and out against the flickering firelight. He groaned inwardly to himself, cursing softly that he had made such a foolish vow. "Damn!" he thought. "I wonder why I am so attracted to her? She seems so feminine . . . yet so strong at times." Suddenly fire surged through his loins as desire for her filled him. Although it took a lot of willpower, he finally forced his eyes away from the slight figure and reasoned to himself. 'I know it's best if I don't become too involved with her. True, I have to face the hard facts that I am planning on using her. But I didn't ask for any of this to happen. I am going to have to keep reminding myself Paige is going to help me seal my cover story and that is all. I will have to push any emotions aside because my mission is the most important thing right now.' Kyle pushed the tormenting thoughts from his mind and forced his eyes to close but the burning memory of Paige and her hidden pleasures were almost more than he could bear.

Paige downed the remains of her drink, smoothed the blazing crimson robe over her waist and hips, placed the empty glass on the nearby table and tried to stand. The unaccustomed liquor and her overwhelming fatigue seemed to drain away all her sense of balance. She giggled, then lurched forward, falling headlong toward the bed. Quick as a flash, Kyle leaped from the bed and steadied her on her feet. When her legs failed to respond, he scooped her easily into his arms and tenderly laid her down.

"You'll have to take it easy. I think you had a little too much to drink."

"But . . . but . . ." she protested. "I only had a few tiny little drops."

Kyle started to reply but smiled to himself when he realized she was already fast asleep. He pulled the heavy comforter up and tucked it snugly around her shoulders then lay down beside her. Later that night, Kyle awoke to find Paige snuggled close to him. Her head was lying on his outstretched arm and her hand was entwined in the dark curly hair on his chest. He brought his hand up and traced the outline of her face. Desire for her grew with each passing moment. His mouth wanted to seek the sweetness of her lips, his hands wanting to cup the fullness of each lovely breast. They ached to slide down over her belly, to test the muscles of her abdomen, wanting them to tense in passion and in anticipation. He wanted to feel the warmth of her thighs, to clasp the soft swell of her hips. He could feel the hot molten pleasure her body could bring, but then, in his mind's eye, he could see her soft, trusting eyes, and Kyle knew his desire for her could not be fulfilled. He could not betray her trust in him. He groaned in torment. There was no way he could take advantage of her in this condition. He took a deep breath and determinedly pulled the heavy quilt back up over her shoulders. It was a long time before he was able to drift off into a troubled and restless sleep.

Paige awoke with a start! Her eyes flew open in horror when she realized how close she had slept to Kyle. She tried to ease from his arms without disturbing him. Suddenly, all cause for quietness disappeared when she leaped from the bed and ran gagging toward the chamber pot. She was deathly sick. When she had finished, Paige was surprised but grateful to see Kyle standing beside her with a cool wet washcloth in his hand.

"Oh thank you," she muttered before bathing her face. "I don't know why I am so sick!"

"I would guess it is because you had too much to drink last night," Kyle said, trying to hold back a grin.

Paige sank gratefully onto a nearby chair. "I didn't think I had *that* much to drink. After all, it was only a couple of toddies."

"Yep," Kyle said, slipping on his clothes. "A couple of toddies, a few glasses of wine with dinner and heaven only knows how strong Della made your drinks. But it was probably mixing the two together that did the damage."

Paige stammered, "Speaking of damage . . . I hope . . . nothing happened between us last night. At least I don't remember anything happening," she stated questioningly.

A devilish grin touched Kyle's lips. "Nope. Nothing happened. You were the perfect lady and

151

my honor has remained intact."

"Frankly, captain," she snapped, "it wasn't your honor I was worried about. It was mine!"

Kyle whirled about, a scowl darkening his face. "Don't ever call me that again!"

"What ... wha ..." Paige stammered obviously confused.

"You called me captain! Do you realize if you called me by that name and the wrong person heard you it could be very dangerous for me? We are in the middle of a Confederate stronghold and someone could very easily get the wrong idea."

Paige had never thought about such a problem before. She had not given any more thought to Kyle being an officer in the Union army until he had shouted at her for calling him captain. For the time being, she quickly decided it would be best to go along with his request. But with what he had just said, her interest heightened in the mystery that surrounded the man she was married to. "I'm sorry, Kyle. It was a slip of the tongue and I promise that it will never happen again."

His eyes raked her, then as he realized she was sincere in what she had said, a slow tantalizing smile crossed his lips. A sharp reply had been on the tip of his tongue, but it had softened instantly. "All right." He changed the subject peering at her still slightly swollen face. "I think with a little bit of powder we could hide the remains of that black eye. Then you could go ahead and buy you some more new clothes."

Her frown lifted and delight flashed across her face. "Oh, that would be wonderful!" Then her expression fell. "But I don't have any powder and I certainly can't be seen in town trying to buy some. That is . . . unless you could . . . ?"

"Oh no!" Kyle stated firmly. "That is one thing I simply refuse to shop for. Perhaps Della could run to the store for you later this morning. But first things first. I am going down to the front desk and have some ham and eggs sent in."

At the mention of food, Paige blanched and ran once again gagging and heaving toward the chamber pot. "Oh my goodness," Paige muttered when the nausea had subsided. "I don't know what in the world is the matter with me."

Kyle gathered her in his arms and placed her carefully on the bed. "You are a sick lady, Frenchie. You must have caught some kind of a bug or something." He looked at her asking for understanding with his eyes. "I'm very hungry, but I can't see torturing you by having food sent in. I'll just go to the dining room to eat. Would you like for me to bring you some hot tea? Perhaps it would help to settle your stomach."

"Thank you, Kyle. Yes, it would be best if you didn't bring food in here right now. I know you are hungry so just ask Della to bring me some tea. I believe you are right. It may help to settle my stomach. Also, if I don't get to feeling better, I think we should postpone our shopping trip to another day."

Kyle nodded. "Whatever," he said, shrugging his broad shoulders. "I'll look in on you after I've eaten and checked at the stables."

Paige could only manage a limp nod while Kyle

walked briskly through the doorway. To a small extent, she felt enraged at the way Kyle had clucked over her then walked away as if he didn't have a care in the world. She felt very ashamed of her poisonous thoughts though, when in a few minutes, Della came rushing into the room head-long.

"Lord-a-mercy, child!" Della exclaimed, planting her hands on the massive hips which spread behind her. "What in the world is de matter with you this morning? Mister Brenner done told me that you was feeling right poorly. Re'kon it was something you et?"

"I don't know Della. I really haven't been feeling very good for the past few weeks. I laid it off to a touch of the flu but I am sure the reason my stomach is so upset is because of what I drank last night."

Della's broad face wrinkled into a frown as she looked Paige over from head to toe. "Here you go, Missy. I already put some lemon in it. I didn't sweeten it none 'cause that wouldn't be good for what is ailing you. Just as soon as I help the cook serve breakfast, I'll bring you some more. Then I'll get one of my lazy young'uns to run over to the mercantile and fetch some powder for your face. I figure after you have a few cups of my tea, you'll be up and junein' around in no time flat." She handed a fresh wet cloth to Paige, then fluffed the pillows on the bed. "Is there anything else I can get you before I leave?"

Paige smiled fondly at Della. "No, thank you. I will be fine in a little while. In fact, I feel much better after only a few sips of this tea."

Della's high forehead drew into another frown. She acted as if she wanted to say something else, but changed her mind.

"What is it, Della?" Paige asked. "Is something the matter?"

"Oh no, Missy," Della replied, backing away suddenly as if she was frightened. "I done learned a long time ago not to sass or question white folks."

"Why!" Paige gasped. "Whatever do you mean? Kyle didn't say anything hateful to you, did he?"

"Oh no, ma'am. You or your man has told me nothing. This old black woman can just tell that you are a real good woman, fact is, you ain't nothing but a snip of a girl. I can tell too, that you have had a real proper type upbringing."

"That may be," Paige answered slowly, intrigued by the change in Della's attitude. "All of a sudden something is the matter and I want to know what is wrong."

Della cut her eyes up at Paige. "Does I has to answer that question?" Her voice slipped into a deep brogue.

"Yes, you surely do!"

A large teardrop fell down Della's cheek. "Is you sho' I won't get in no kind of trouble?"

"I'm positive, Della. That is, if you go ahead and tell me!" Paige snapped, her voice on edge.

Della took a deep breath. "I sho' don't mean no disrespect but something just ain't right. Least ways since you told me that you and the mister just got hitched. Old Della has been birthing babies for nigh on to twenty years now, and I can tell." She

155

mumbled again, "I can just tell."

"Tell me what, Della?" Paige asked, all traces of color draining from her already pale and ashen face.

Della stared at the floor. "I'd druther not say, ma'am."

Paige gripped the arms of the chair. "Della! I demand you tell me what you are implying!"

Della was very hesitant, yet defiant in answering. "I done already told you it wasn't any of my business."

This time Paige shouted angrily, "I demand to know . . . immediately!"

The large black woman nervously wrung her hands together. "Awright! I'll answer you. It looks to me that you already have a baby in your belly!"

Paige gasped as her hands flew to her stomach. "Oh no! That can't be! Please . . . God, no!"

"Now don't go getting yourself in a tizzy!" Della rushed over to Paige and patted her hand. "I didn't mean no harm in saying what I did. You made me say it. Besides, I never meant for you to think that I thought you was a bad woman. When you said you had been feeling so poorly for so long, I just pieced it together. Specially since you have that look about you."

Paige waved her hand as she spoke in a calmer, but numb voice. "No . . . I didn't mean it that way." She looked pleadingly up at the black woman hovering over her. "Do you really think I can be carrying a child?"

Della tried to hold back the smile which was playing on her lips. "Only you can know if you are

156

expectin'. I've seen a whole lot in my day and there is a bunch of white folks who seem to have babes just a few months after they have been hitched."

Paige looked blindly around the room, her mind racing to what Kyle would say and do about a child, and to what a child would do to them, their agreement, and their future. She forced Della to look her face to face. "You have to promise not to tell my husband about this conversation."

A strange expression flashed across Della's face. An expression that told Paige Della thought the reason she wanted to keep it a secret was that the baby could possibly belong to someone else.

Della mumbled, "I done already told you it wasn't none of my business bunches of times. If you say for me to keep my mouth shut, then this old black nigger won't breathe a word of it to nobody!"

"Wait just a minute!" Paige tried to inject the proper sting to her voice, but it was difficult under the situation. "I am going to tell you two things. First, I never want to hear you call yourself a nigger again. That word is very demeaning and there is nothing demeaning about you. Second, I realize I don't owe you any explanation about my private life, but I saw the look on your face when I cautioned you not to mention a baby to Kyle."

Defiance flew from Della with vehemence. "I am only a *colored* maid who works in a hotel emptying bed chambers. You don't owe me a thing, certainly not an explanation!"

"I realize I don't, Della." Paige placed her hand on the woman's shoulder very gently. "But I saw what you were thinking when I cautioned you not to say anything to Kyle." She took a deep breath and continued. "If I am carrying a child, it belongs to the man I am married to. Kyle is the only man I have ever known in that manner and there is no way possible a baby could belong to anyone else. And yes, it is possible I am carrying a child. If so, Kyle is under too many pressures to concern himself with the thought of a baby right now. That is the *only* reason I asked you to keep it a secret." She silently prayed for forgiveness for the white lie she had told.

A slow grin spread across Della's face and tears filled her eyes. "Oh, thank the good Lord! I didn't know what to think when you wanted me to keep it a secret, Missy. The moment I saw you, you captured this old woman's heart, and it almost broke when . . . I . . . you . . ." She grabbed Paige and hugged her to her breast. "I promise not to tell your man, Missy."

Paige looked at her slyly. "And you can rest assured that I will keep your secret, too."

"What do you mean by . . . that?" Della asked slowly.

"Your grammar and your manners." Paige said simply. "I figure you are a fairly highly educated woman for your race. Whenever you drop your guard, your English and grammar are almost as good as mine. And for you to have this knowledge, I'm sure you know how to read and write." She looked at Della very matter-of-factly. "You do know how to read and write, don't you?"

Fear shone from Della's face. "It is against the

law for a negro to know how to do that."

"I know, at least it used to be against the law. But you have nothing to worry about, Della. Your secret is safe with me."

"Thank you, Missy. You have no idea how hard it is to act ignorant sometimes. Missus Norton, God rest her soul, taught me my book learning years ago. I thought I had kept it fairly well hid. Even Mister Norton does not have any idea what his wife did for me."

A stab of sorrow broke Paige's voice. "It must be very difficult to go through all these pretenses."

"No, not really. I have a happy life now. Oh, but I have had my share of bad times. Back on the plantation, everyone thought I was barren, but the old master kept me because I was an excellent cook. Then, he died and all of his slaves had to be sold to pay off his debts. My man was sold off three days before I went on the auction block. Since I was almost past my prime, I sold real cheap." Her eyes took on a far away look as she remembered the past. "If the old master had know I was carrying twins in my belly, he would have rolled in his grave. I was lucky that Mister Norton bought me for his missus. Others didn't have it as good. At least I got to keep my babies, and eventually we received our freedom papers." She waved her arms in the air. "Oh my goodness! Here I have been rattling away and I've chores to do." It was clear she didn't like to walk through the ragged memories of her mind. "You take it easy, Missy and I'll have you some more tea sent in, in just a little while."

Paige brushed away a tear that had crept into her eyes. She realized Della wanted to end the conversation, a conversation that was extremely painful to her.

After Della left, Paige sank into the rocking chair, her mind spinning, having learned what she had about Della. She forced the Negro maid from her mind and dwelled on the problem that was looming in the near future.

"What if I am pregnant? What will I do then? A baby will only complicate matters further. Will Kyle feel forced to stay married to me? Will we both have to endure a loveless marriage?" A cold and clammy hand gripped at her heart as she realized what Della had said was probably true. It had been three months since she had had her cycle. The troubles she had encountered had prevented her from realizing this before. She was carrying Kyle Brenner's child!

Chapter Eleven

Kyle was thoroughly enjoying his huge breakfast of smoked Virginia ham, three eggs, light fluffy biscuits, buttered grits, and steaming hot coffee when he was interrupted by a man pulling out a chair and sitting down at the table with him.

In just a loud enough voice to attract a small amount of attention, Seth asked: "Do you mind if I share your table, stranger?"

"No, go ahead and have a seat," Kyle said between bites. "Always have hated to eat alone."

"Haven't seen you around these parts before, just come in or what?"

Kyle smiled slowly. "Now I said I hated to eat alone, but I didn't say a word about people trying to pry into my business."

Seth had to consciously refrain from smiling as he replied, "I ain't never figured to be the nosy sort. I always laid it off to being downright friendly."

Kyle laughed and conceded he had been outwitted. "All right, I guess I was a little rude. Yes, in answer to your question, I am a stranger here."

161

Kyle wiped his mouth with a napkin, knowing what he was about to say would completely shock his long time friend. "In fact, me and my wife rode in yesterday." Kyle watched Seth's reaction very carefully. He had just raised his coffee cup to take a drink. When he realized what Kyle had said, coffee went spewing in every direction.

"Your what?" Seth asked in open-mouthed astonishment, as soon as he was able speak.

Kyle teetered back in his chair obviously enjoying his friend's bewilderment. "Yep. I'm married," he stated firmly. "She was feeling poorly this morning and didn't join me for breakfast. I guess the trip was rougher on her than she would care to admit. By the way, my name is Kyle Brenner," he said extending his hand across the table.

As the men shook hands, Seth introduced himself for the restaurant patron's benefit. "My name is Seth Poteet. I reckon you could say I am a stranger around here too. I've only been here 'bout a month myself. I bought a little parcel of land up the river a ways and have been busy building a ferry and clearing brush for a landing. You wouldn't by chance be looking for work?"

"No, appreciate the offer though." Kyle said matter-of-factly. "I am looking for a place to put down some roots, but I want to look the town over first. If we like it here, I might open up some kind of little business. But for now, I'm in no hurry."

"Well," Seth drawled easily, "it sure didn't hurt to ask. Good help is hard to find, 'specially with the war going the way it is. So far, all I've been able to talk to about work is the soldiers who have been wounded too bad to keep on fighting, and the few cowpokes who are back from the gold fields; of course, there are the dandies who follow the river boats, but I don't want any part of them. All they know how to do is deal a hand of cards and most of them do double dealing from the bottom of the deck. You looked like the type who isn't afraid of an honest day's work is the reason I brought the subject up."

"I appreciate the offer, but like I said, I want to look around before doing anything definite."

Seth drained the last drop from his coffee cup. "I guess I've wasted enough time in town today. Time to get back to work. Seriously though, if you see anybody lookin', send them down my way. I'm located 'bout two miles down river." Seth tipped the hat he had placed on his head. "Be seeing you." He then walked briskly through the dining room and out into the lobby.

Kyle lingered over his coffee for a while. Every now and then a smile would tease his lips as he recalled the expression on Seth's face when he found out about the surprise wife. Later on, Kyle knew he would have some tall explaining to do. Finally, he shoved back his plate and ambled slowly out to the porch where he greeted each and every passerby.

It was mid-morning before he made it back to the hotel. Paige was anxiously awaiting his return. She had applied the powder to her face, dressed in the new malachite green dress; her hair cascaded in tiny curls down her back. Kyle's breath caught in his throat when he entered their room and saw what a striking figure his wife made. She had such a sly look about her, with a small amount of imagination, Kyle could see a cat ready to pounce on its unsuspecting prey.

"You certainly look a lot better than the last time I saw you," Kyle said, quickly regaining his composure.

"I am feeling much better. Della brought me some hot tea and I guess it was exactly what I needed." She leaned her head back to where Kyle could get a better look at her face. "Do you think the powder hides the bruises well enough for me to go out and face all the good citizens of Jefferson?"

Kyle tilted his chin sidewise and closely examined the eye. "It looks all right to me. But was that a note of sarcasm I heard in your voice?"

"Why no. Did it sound like it?"

Kyle shook his head. "I don't know," he said off-handedly. "I guess I am a little too touchy here lately."

Paige cast a sidewise glance in his direction before putting on her tattered cloak. "I am ready to go if you are."

Kyle shook his head. "No, I'm not ready to go yet, and you're not either. At least if you are planning to wear that rag," he said, indicating the cloak draping over her shoulders.

Paige stopped short. She was dumbfounded. "But . . . it is all I have to wear. You want me to freeze?"

Turning to go back in the hall, a devilish grin lit up Kyle's face. "Don't move," he ordered. "I have something for you and I want to see it on you in exactly this light." Paige was somewhat confused but did as he asked. In a moment he reappeared with a stunning dark green velvet wrap. "I thought this would look lovely on you, with your coloring and all."

"Kyle! It is beautiful!" Paige squealed, running her slender fingers over the elegant material. "It is about the prettiest thing I have ever seen!"

Kyle chuckled warmly. "I thought you would like it." He draped it carefully around her shoulders and buttoned it very slowly, his hands lingering on the top button. "There," he said finally. "I'll have to admit, it certainly makes your eyes look like bright green emeralds. But to be completely honest, the beauty of the cloak is nothing compared to the loveliness of the lady wearing it."

Paige blushed graciously. "Why, thank you very much. But you certainly didn't have to go to this much expense. A cloth cloak would have served as good a purpose."

"Maybe so, but it wouldn't have been as pretty," Kyle said, suddenly feeling very awkward.

Paige looked him squarely in the eyes. "You are really something, Kyle. You are extremely difficult to try to figure out."

"Ha! I'm hard to figure out?" Kyle stared at her for a long moment. "I think you have it backward. One minute I'm almost afraid to turn my back to you and the next minute you act almost affectionate." He pressed closer to her, acutely aware of the animal-like attraction he felt for her. The attraction he swore earlier would not betray him or his emotions. His mood changed instantly as he pulled away from her. "If you would look at me as I really am, instead of the monster you have made me in your mind, you would see that I am a kind and generous man. You have had your head too high in the clouds for too long, and filling it with an awful lot of fancy daydreams about a prince charming. If you would open your eyes you could see a mortal man made of flesh and blood, and needs and wants and desires. You could also see what kind of personal hell you are putting me through!"

A long moment passed; Paige stared at him unbelievingly. Then as the words he spoke sank in, anger raced through her like a whirlwind on a rampage. "So! That is why you were so kind and generous! You thought I would be so grateful for this present, I would throw myself on the bed with my thighs parted eagerly for you. You are insane if you think you can buy me for any price!" She took the cloak and flung it on the bed. "Here, take it back. I don't need or want it and I refuse to pay the price you ask for it!" She turned to the window to keep Kyle from seeing the tears brimming behind her eyes.

Kyle stared at the floor, ashamed of what had just happened. But when he had fastened the cloak around her shoulders, he had seen the look in her eyes and had felt the quickening pace of his heart. At that moment he had felt Paige could not have a place in his future. His mission was far too important for love to get in the way. He blinked, startled by his own thoughts, the emotion he had refused to even acknowledge until now, the emotion he had called *love!* But he also knew he had to do or say something to calm her anger. Regardless of his wanting to avoid an emotional entanglement with Paige, she was sorely needed for this undercover role he had to live. "What in the hell did I say to cause that outburst?" He figured to act innocent and perhaps soothe her injured pride.

Paige whirled around, her veiled lashes almost concealing her vivid anger. "What do you mean?" she hissed through clenched teeth. "How dare you blame me for your obnoxious attitude?"

"I think you misunderstood what I was trying to say, Paige. I was merely trying to make a point of your being so difficult for me to understand. I did not expect such a bitter tirade from you. Did you ever stop to consider that I was thinking of you and your feelings when I bought that cloak for you?"

"No!" she shouted hotly. "And I doubt if those are the reasons."

"Well, they were the reasons," Kyle recountered.

Paige sniffed a reply, her pride demanding she not give in so easily. "If you weren't trying to buy my affections, then you must have bought the cloak because you were ashamed of me."

"No, Paige, I am not ashamed of you or how you look. In fact, I would be proud to stand beside you anywhere, dressed in any fashion. I only want you to look nice because you are an attractive woman, and because I figured you would like the cloak. I'm not without means and there is no sense in your having to go around looking like a slave who has just been set free." He grabbed her by the arm and pulled her roughly to him. "You place a lot of value on what is between your legs . . . well, my little hot-headed, Frenchie, let me tell you one thing. If I had wanted to buy me a woman, I could have had one for a hell of a lot less than that damn cloak cost." He grabbed the cloak from the bed and threw it around her shoulders. "You just looked out the window. Did you see how heavily it was snowing? Can you get it through your thick head that I bought the wrap so you wouldn't freeze your frigid butt off the moment we stepped outside?"

Paige realized what Kyle said was the truth. Instantly, and wordlessly she fastened the cloak around her neck. Remorse settled over her as she thought, "Good heavens above! Why can't I control my sharp tongue? Papa always said I would drive a man away with it if he wasn't someone very special. He said I would have to have someone to tame my temper. This man is the father of the baby I am carrying beneath my heart. I will have to make a special attempt to get along with him . . . at least for the sake of this innocent baby." She breathed a silent prayer. "Please, God. Let this man grow to love me and let me grow to love this man. A child should not grow up without a father to love him also." With as much dignity as she could muster, she turned to Kyle and said, "If you still want to take me shopping, I am ready to go now."

· The next few hours were spent in a haze of chiffon, velvet, ribbons, lace, pins, and yards upon yards of fine material as Paige was turned, measured, and probed while being fitted with all the finery Jefferson had to offer. But it was she who insisted upon a few cotton gowns to wear in the confines of their room. She knew since she was pregnant, the beautiful clothes would be practically useless in a few months' time. Finally she collapsed wearily on the couch.

"I simply can not stand on my feet another moment. I am tired!" Paige declared stubbornly.

"But, madam," the French dressmaker protested. "I am nearly finished with your fitting. Your husband . . . you should have much pride in him. He has such *bon vivant ton.*"

"Yes, I'll certainly have to agree with you. He has excellent tastes, but I happen to have an excellent backache and I am too tired for any more fittings today."

"*Oui,* madam. I understand fully. But you should realize how very lucky you are for him to tell me, *coute que coute.*"

Paige laughed cheerfully, happy to hear the French language again. "I know Kyle is a very generous man and I appreciate the fact, but, I haven't had a thing to eat all day long and have only had some tea to drink, and I am hungry."

The couturier nodded wisely. "*Oui,* and it is not good to do without eating. Since you have to nourish two, it is best for you to take proper care of yourself, especially in these early stages."

Paige stared at her, horror-stricken. "Whatever do you mean?"

The woman flung up her hands in mock surprise. "Why, madam, surely you know about the baby?" Upon seeing the startled expression on her customer's face, the woman laughed and said. *"Chere amie!* You must still be a babe yourself not to realize the stirrings of life beneath your heart." Then she added, recognizing the possible loss of a large clothing order, "But do not worry. I am making several allowances in your gowns and designing a few so you will be able to wear them longer than normal."

"But . . . but . . . how can you tell?"

Mrs. Roget laughed heartily. "I have been sewing for too many years not to notice the slight swelling of the breasts and the rounding fullness of the belly. You have not realized this, no?"

Paige hardly knew what to say. She was grateful for the fact that Kyle had gone back to the hotel instead of staying through all the fittings. Finally, she managed to stammer. "Please don't mention this to my husband. I want to be the one to tell him."

"Certainly, *chere amie.* It should be you who tell him he is to be a papa." She frowned then spoke hesitantly. "There is one thing this meddling old woman has to say."

Paige looked at her expectantly.

"You are very young and in time you will learn. A man does not like a harsh spoken woman. It makes him feel . . . neglected, and he could possibly seek out a woman's company who acts as though she appreciates him more. Your husband," she groped for the right words, "is a very good man and they are extremely difficult to find in these days."

Paige managed to mutter something that apparently pleased the woman. She dressed hurriedly, wanting to be rid of the inquisitive woman and her silly prattlings. But Paige was concerned. Was her hostility so plain that a common stranger noticed it? Was it so obvious she had little affection for her husband, the man she had married only a few nights ago?

Paige stumbled against the driving wind and snow, anxious to reach the warmth of the hotel. She knew this weather was very harsh for this climate and looked forward to a time when it would be more pleasant. Perhaps by that time, her dilemma with Kyle would be solved. Two people had already guessed she was pregnant. How long would she be able to keep the secret from Kyle? Paige knew she needed at least a couple of months in order for her to try to make up her mind as to what she wanted to do. Much to her relief, she finally reached the hotel and was able to push the worry from her mind for a few moments. Kyle had asked her to meet him in the dining room when she finished and they would share a leisurely lunch. She did not want the worry about the baby on her mind when they met. It would be just like her to blurt out the truth and the time was not yet right for that.

Chapter Twelve

It was well past two o'clock before Paige found herself being seated in the dining room of the Irvine Hotel. She looked anxiously around for Kyle to see if he was there and if he had waited this long. She didn't see him so she summoned a waitress and placed her order. While her food was being prepared, her curiosity was piqued by the other womens' fashions as they paraded back and forth across the room. It had been so long since she had been in a place where women dressed well, it gave her an exhilarating feeling. She soon became aware of a soft, tinkling laughter drifting from behind her. Paige's interest grew; she turned to see what was so amusing, and definitely did not like what she saw.

Kyle was sitting in a dark corner so close to a beautiful vivacious red-headed woman, their cheeks were almost touching. Paige was so astonished she could only watch dumbfoundedly when Kyle raised his glass to the lady in what appeared to be a toast. Even though the woman was sitting, Paige could tell she was very tiny and petite, probably not over five feet tall. And her complexion! She was a beauty! Not even a mole much less the usual freckles which accompanied red-headed people marred her magnificent radiance. Her eyes were the most vivid blue Paige had ever seen. Even the length of the woman's hair was amazing. She had simply brushed it back and tied it with a ribbon. Even tied up, it still fell to the small of her back. She was wearing a lovely mint gown, dipping seductively to show more than ample cleavage. "One thing for certain," Paige deduced, "the woman knows how to unleash and use her charms to hold and captivate the attention of her newly found conquest."

Paige could not quite understand the emotions which raged through her. If she had not known better, she could have sworn she was jealous. Unable to stand it any longer, she marched haughtily over to the table where Kyle and the woman were sitting. "Kyle, darling," she purred, "I'm so sorry to be this late. But time escaped me. I hope you went ahead and had lunch." She fluttered her eyelashes as seductively as possible.

Kyle, remembering his manners, leaped to his feet to introduce the women. He managed to look rather sheepish as he said. "Rosalyn Ledbetter, this is my wife, Paige DuPree Brenner." He pulled out a chair for Paige. "Sit down and join us."

The women exchanged pleasantries. Paige could immediately sense the lurking dangers of trouble the woman could cause when she spoke in a soft southern drawl.

"I hope you don't mind my taking up your

handsome husband's time, this afternoon, Mrs. Brenner. Why I do declare I don't know when I've met such a charmin' gentleman!" she said, graciously fluttering her hand fan.

Paige raised one eyebrow slightly. "Oh, I know exactly how charming this scoundrel can be when he wants to. I do appreciate how you've kept him entertained while I have been at the dressmaker's." She glanced at Kyle icily. "It has been an extremely tiring day, so if you will excuse me, I believe I will retire to our room. It has been a pleasure, Miss Ledbetter." She stood to leave, and with second thought, she turned back and said, "Please don't keep him too long, darling. I have some very important matters to discuss with him. Good day." It was all Paige could do to keep from storming through the dining room. She could feel Rosalyn's mocking stare follow her all the way to the lobby. Imagine! The nerve of Kyle, acting like a rutting Yankee dandy the moment her back was turned. He actually allowed himself to be enticed by a wench who probably made her living by seducing wayward males! Paige stopped short. In her haste to leave, she had forgotten about her food order. She marched determinedly on to her room, not wanting to humiliate herself by returning for it. She would just have to wait for the evening meal.

Paige sat by the crackling fire, her mood anything but pleasant. She dreaded to admit, to acknowledge the newly discovered feelings she experienced. Why did she feel so possessive about a man she cared nothing about? Could the baby she was carrying have something to do with it? Only a day ago, she would have felt relief that Kyle was directing his attentions in some other direction. But now, she was acting like a jealous fishwife! Her pensive mood was interrupted when Kyle came into the room. Her temper flared as he moved about with an unconcerned ease. She quickly decided to hold her tongue for once.

"I figured you changed your mind about getting anything to eat the way you stormed out of the dining room," Kyle said, glancing at her expectantly. "You're not angry with me, are you?"

"Why no, Kyle," she replied in a sugary voice. "Whatever gave you that idea?"

Kyle scratched his head. "The way you left in such a huff, I figured I would have hell to pay."

Paige forced herself to laugh off his accusation and show an air of gaiety she did not feel. "I surely don't know why you would say that. Apparently you have no idea how exhausting it is to stand for two hours being turned and prodded to get the proper fit of new clothing." Paige decided to go a step further. "I do want you to know how sorry I am for being so cross this morning. I said some very hateful things, and I am sorry."

Kyle stared at her apprehensively. He was hesitant to accept what she had just said, but since he had been caught flirting with another woman, it would be best to accept her apology and forget the matter entirely. "All right, Paige. I think we have both been under a strain lately. Let's forget the whole thing." He slumped into a chair. "I'm tired. I reckon all this fast living has caught up with me.

I think I'll lie down a while because there are some things I have to take care of this afternoon and later tonight."

After Kyle had tugged off his boots, Paige turned the covers back on the bed. When she was plumping up the pillows, someone knocked on the door. Paige went to see who was calling on them, and in a short while, she came back with a small package.

"I hope you don't mind," she said, pulling some yarn, needles and material out of the wrapper, "but I ordered some extra items from the dressmaker."

"Why was that necessary? Isn't she making you everything you'll be needing?" He saw the hurt look flash across Paige's face and quickly added, "Of course, not that I mind. You can buy anything you want."

"I didn't think you would mind. And yes, Mrs. Roget is making everything for me, but I needed something to help occupy my time. I imagine it will get pretty lonely in this room, especially with the weather so bad I can't go for walks, and no chores to do. I don't want to sound boastful," she added, "But I am a fair hand with a needle myself and I do enjoy sewing."

"That's one thing I want to caution you about, Paige, please watch where you go in this town. Most of it is very respectable, but it is a waterfront town and all sorts of trash hangs around. But, something you said gives me an idea. I don't want to give you too much money because it is dangerous; you could be robbed. So, I'll go down to the mercantile, give them some money, and have them

176

set you up with an account. That way, if I am called away unexpectedly, you won't have to do without."

"Oh? Do you think you'll have to go somewhere?" Paige asked, tension breaking her voice. Somehow, she was frightened over the prospect of being left alone.

"No, I don't anticipate having to leave, but I want to look this area over really good, and who knows? I may hear about a business deal that could call me away for a week or two." Kyle leaned back on the bed and spoke, almost to himself. "In fact, I've been thinking . . . it might be better if we rented us a house."

Paige stared at him, a delighted grin spreading across her face. "Really? she squealed in excitement. "That sounds exactly like heaven to me! Do you really think we could find one?"

"I'll ask around in the next few days and see what I can find out." He sighed deeply and turned over, snuggling up to the pillow, "In the meantime, I'm going to take a little nap."

Paige reclined in her chair, rocking contentedly while he slept. She savored the idea of living in a home again. The thought of being able to try her hand at cooking and taking care of a house intrigued her. She was so engrossed about the idea, Kyle's flirtation completely slipped her mind. She even dared to think a home might possibly eliminate the hostile feelings that were threatening to explode like a powder keg.

It was late in the afternoon; the sun had set but darkness had not yet fallen before Kyle awoke.

Much to Paige's relief, they went immediately to the dining room and ate. They smiled politely at one another, and to the other guests, but neither went out of their way to carry on a conversation. Later, Kyle took Paige back to their suite of rooms and left without telling her where he was going or when he would be back.

For the next week, each day settled into the sameness of the one that had just passed. Paige was dismayed at Kyle for not mentioning anything else about a house, but since they were at least being civil to one another, she hated to say anything for fear he would think she was nagging. She did question him as to where he had been going at night, but he would only smile and offer some sort of a feeble excuse. Deep down inside, Paige was afraid he had been seeing Rosalyn Ledbetter, but some nights he would return, late, and mud would be all over his clothes. She did not think he had been seeing another woman in that condition, because he was entirely too neat about his appearance. Paige had no way of knowing Kyle had been investigating unusually large cotton and cattle shipments. Also, checking on rumors of former slaves being burned from their homes, a large number of robberies, and an influx of Confederate soldiers suddenly appearing close to Jefferson.

At long last, the morning came when Kyle awoke and mentioned to Paige that he was ready to go house hunting.

"Oh, good!" Paige cried; she leaped out of bed and hurriedly dressed.

Kyle laughed at her enthusiasm. "I figured you

thought I had forgotten about getting a house."

"No, I knew you hadn't forgotten. I only figured you had been too busy to look for one."

"Yes, I have been too busy, but then too, the weather has been so bad, I hated to drag you out to go looking."

After a quick breakfast, Kyle went to the stables and rented a horse and buggy for the day. He stopped and inquired about several places before someone finally told him about a little house on the northwest side of town. He and Paige were told the house belonged to an elderly lady who was recently widowed. Her husband had been a riverboat captain, and had just completely remodeled the house before his death. The woman's health had deteriorated so rapidly, she had been forced to move in with her daughter.

When Kyle pulled the buggy up in front of the little house, Paige breathed a silent prayer they would be able to acquire it. The cottage was simply charming; small yes, but the rooms proved to be larger than they looked. The kitchen was bright and cheerful. It had the look and feel about it that Kyle and Paige knew many happy hours had been spent there. The parlor was furnished in beautiful Victorian furniture, and the bedrooms were graced with comfortable, sturdy oak. To their disbelief, they were able to secure a lease on the house for a very small price. After Kyle had paid the woman, she showed Paige around the kitchen with tears brimming from her eyes.

"I hope you and your husband will be able to share a small amount of the happiness Paul and I had here. If so, you'll be the happiest bride in the world. You see, my dear," her faded eyes going back in the past, "this was the first real home Paul and I ever knew. He sailed the tall ships of the sea for many a year, visiting every corner of the world. Sometimes, I was able to go with him before we started having our family. But once the children started coming, I stayed at home. It is a very lonely wind that blows when a woman is separated from the man she loves." She shook her head and laughed. "Listen to me rattle needlessly. Sometimes, I guess I get carried away by my memories. Here I am, probably boring a young thing like you."

"Oh no!" Paige said. "You sound as if you have been very happy in this home."

"Yes, I was. That's why I rented it to you and your husband," she said very honestly. "I've had several chances to rent it before, but . . . it always seemed as though the other people wouldn't appreciate the happiness that is available here in this house." She patted Paige on her cheek. "I'm sure you'll enjoy living here as much as I did." She pointed to the tiny house in the back. "If you want to hire some help, I'm sure you could find a slave who has been set free or some young girl who is anxious to get away from her papa's farm. Times are hard right now, so you could get help for a mere pittance."

"Oh no," Paige said flatly. "I have been wanting a home of my own for so long, I don't want to have to share it with another woman. That is . . . if Kyle doesn't object. He is peculiar about some things and fairly set in his ways."

The elderly woman chuckled. "I would imagine you can get your man to do about anything you want him to. I declare, I haven't seen such devotion in a man's eyes in so long I had just about forgotten what it looked like."

Paige's eyebrows arched in surprise. That's strange she should say that, Paige thought. Especially when Kyle and I are barely on speaking terms. Then she turned her head so Mrs. Sanders could not see the expression she knew she could not conceal. Kyle was up to something she thought. He acted so cold and indifferent when they were alone, but the moment someone else appeared, he presented an altogether different picture. He acted like a devoted husband and respectable citizen, when Paige was certain he was something else entirely. He had to be up to something! He just had to be! Paige ran nervous fingers through her hair, as if trying to push the unpleasant thoughts away. She had to snap out of this mood. If she allowed it, her runaway imagination would ruin the entire day for her.

By night time, they had checked out of the hotel, purchased supplies and had things placed in order. Mrs. Sanders had graciously consented to leaving Paige and Kyle the linens and cooking utensils that were still in the house. Needless to say, Paige was ecstatic over settling in their home for the first time.

"Frenchie, that was a delicious meal," Kyle said, pushing back from the table and patting his stomach. "One thing's for certain, your mama sure taught you how to cook good. But, I wish you had taken me up on my offer for us to eat out. With us moving and all, you must be tired."

"Thank you. I'm glad you like my cooking. But there was no way for you to pry me from my kitchen tonight. And I don't think I could ever get too tired to cook a good meal." Paige smiled to herself, pleased that Kyle had complimented her on her cooking talents.

Kyle stood rather abruptly. "I'm sure you have several things to do around here, so, unless you need me for something, I think I'll go down to the saloon and have a beer."

Fury worked its way across Paige's features that Kyle would want to go off on this, their first evening in their own home. "I can't think of a thing you'd be needed for around here!" Paige replied sharply.

Anger and rage played for control of Kyle as he twisted around to stare harshly at Paige. "I see! You have made that quite plain from the very start," he spat.

"Oh, Kyle," Paige snapped. "Don't take everything I say so seriously. I only meant I could handle everything in the line of straightening up and making the beds with fresh linens. By the way," she added sweetly, "which bedroom do you want to sleep in?"

Kyle stared at her long and hard, his spine stiffening over the hidden meaning of her words. "It doesn't matter in the least which room I get. Just pick the one you want. No . . . on second thought, I'll take the one in the back; that way, I won't disturb you in the middle of the night when I come in." He stomped over to the hall tree where he had left his coat. He yanked it on and jammed the hat on his head, nodded curtly to Paige, then slammed the door soundly behind him as he marched outside.

Paige was livid with rage. Not only did he get the last word, he had quite firmly put her in her place. To make matters worse, he acted as though he enjoyed and even welcomed their unusual arrangement. Paige was absolutely certain he was seeing another woman. After all, she reasoned to herself, Kyle is a very passionate man, and he has not tried to make love to me in a long time! Which is all the better, she thought smugly. If he doesn't try to seduce me, I won't have to refuse him again and go through another unpleasant scene. Her bottom lip trembled as she fought back the tears which suddenly sprang to her eyes. Things had become so cordial between them that this depressing scene upset Paige more than she cared to admit.

She looked at the cluttered table in dismay. She sighed wearily and stood to clear the table. When she picked up Kyle's plate, her resolve crumbled to shreds. She sat back down and wept bitterly.

Chapter Thirteen

Kyle took the horse and buggy back to the stable, turned them in, then had his own mount saddled. Under the soft glow of the winter moonlight, he rode out of town very assured of where he was going. He had to stop once and send the dog back. He did not want to be followed by anything. After an hour of endless riding, doubling back and leaving a false trail just in case someone suspected him, Kyle finally circled back around to where Seth had a small but durable cabin alongside the river. As he dismounted, he called out to Seth.

"How 'bout it, friend. Anybody home?"

A tattered curtain hanging on the window of the shack was pulled back, and in a matter of seconds, the front door flew wide open. Kyle quickly motioned with a finger to his lips for Seth to use discretion in what he said.

Seth nodded slightly, understanding what Kyle meant. "Well howdy, stranger," he said in a booming voice. "What brings you out on a cold night like this?"

Kyle threw one leg over the saddle and slid down

from his horse. "Oh, there wasn't anything else to do; besides, I ran across a fellow the other day who was looking for work, so I thought I'd ride out and tell you about him. In fact, he was supposed to meet me out here, so I could introduce you."

"Sure glad you did, 'cause I can certainly use someone." Seth held the door open. "Com'on in. Ain't no sense in us standing out here freezing when I've got a good fire going and a fresh pot of coffee." When Seth closed the door behind them, he asked anxiously, "What's the matter, were you followed?"

"No, I don't think so, but at this point there is no need in taking any unnecessary chances." He rushed on to ask, "Have you heard anything from Blinn?"

"Yeah, I saw him a couple of weeks ago. I had to ride over to Marshall for some new saw blades." Seth smiled at Kyle. "There is no need to bandy words or beat around the bush, so I'll ask straight out. How did you get roped into it?"

Kyle raised one eyebrow in mock surprise. "Get roped into what?"

"Hell, man! Don't act innocent with me. You know damn good and well what I am talking about!" Seth grinned at him. "What about this wife you have?"

Kyle told him briefly about meeting Paige in Washington, naturally he told him nothing about their personal experience, then he told him of the strange coincidence of running into her again. When he ended his story of how Oscar forced them to marry at the point of a shotgun, Seth leaned

185

back in his chair and roared with laughter.

"I always knew you would get it that way, Kyle. As many times as you've leaped out of a woman's bedroom window, it was bound to come to this sooner or later!" Seth got up and poured them a cup of coffee. "You mean her old man actually marched you to the preacher with a shotgun pressed to your back?"

Kyle nodded sheepishly.

"I'd have given ten dollars to have seen that!" Seth guffawed. "I always knew some irate father wouldn't take too kindly to you messing around with his daughter."

"Damn-it, I wasn't messing around with her, and besides," he tried to act angry but Seth saw through him immediately, "it wasn't her pa, it was a black-hearted scoundrel of an uncle."

"Aww, come on, Kyle. You would call anyone who got the drop on you black-hearted."

Kyle grinned crookedly. "Did I say black-hearted? I meant to say he was nothing but a pure-de-ole-son-of-a-bitch! In fact, you could call him worse if you could think of worse."

"Well," Seth drawled slowly, "certainly sounds like there isn't much love lost between the two of you." Then he frowned. "Seriously though, how does a wife figure into your plans?"

"I really don't know." Kyle screwed his face into a grimace. "One thing's for sure, no one is going to be suspecting me of being a union spy, not with a wife, anyway." He paused, searching for the right word to say. "As far as I'm concerned, as soon as I'm finished here, I'll be single again."

"You mean you plan on leaving her? Aren't you getting along together?"

"Hell! A damn saint couldn't get along with that woman! She beats all I ever saw." Kyle started pacing the floor, not realizing he was ranting. "One minute she is all sweet and kind, and the next, she acts like a hell cat. Shoot, it wasn't my fault her uncle had a filthy mind," he complained.

"Just take it easy, Kyle, and everything will be all right. I imagine it will work out for the best, whichever way it goes."

Kyle bit his bottom lip, thinking about what his friend said. "I guess you're right, we'll see." He slapped his leg with an open hand. "Anyway, I didn't come out here to tell you my problems, I came out to talk business."

"Go ahead, I'm listening," Seth said eagerly.

"Have you heard about someone stampeding those cattle which were supposed to be shipped up to the troopers in Mississippi?"

"No, I haven't heard a thing about it, but then, I haven't been to town in several days."

"Well, I'm the one who did it. I found out the cattle wasn't headed for the Mississippi and hungry soldiers. They were being shipped to Canada. Since the war has lasted this long, the Canadians are hurting for good beef, and whoever sold them this shipment stood to make a handsome profit . . . by selling out their cause."

"Wait a minute," Seth interrupted. "If the cattle were earmarked for Confederate soldiers, why all the fuss? Wouldn't that help us?"

"Yes, if that was all there was to it. But look at it

this way; these people are traitors. They have sold out the north and south alike. I believe it will be easier to stop them now before they become too powerful."

"Do you have any idea who they are?"

"No, not really. Most of my information came from riverfront gossip. I believe I know who a few of them are, but they are not the important ones, the brains behind all of this. The head men are who I'm after. I figure if we can disrupt enough of their deals, we can drive them out of business. It won't take long for their markets to dry up and for them to go somewhere else."

Seth asked, "Do you really think it will help that much?"

"It's bound to. At least it can't hurt us, only them. Take you, for instance, Seth. When the war is over, northerners will start flooding the area. A small few will be legitimate, but most will be bloodsuckers out to destroy the economy and to line their own pockets. You will be in a position to see who is getting and receiving shipments by wagons. And, if it is an important shipment, you could occasionally drop a box of freight."

"I see, I can be your ears and eyes on this end, Blinn will be keeping an eye on freight wagons coming from his direction, and you'll be watching the riverfront."

"That is about the size of it. But damn-it!" Kyle swore, hitting the table with his fist. "If I could only find out who is behind all of this, if I could only get a clue . . . a small piece of the puzzle . . ." Kyle stared at Seth hard. "But, that isn't all of it.

188

Someone has been lending money to farmers on their land. It's a dummy corporation, though, so that's a dead end there. I can just imagine what will happen when the farmers are unable to make their payments. If we have to wait until next fall to find out . . . then we will have failed."

"But we'll give it our best shot. That's all we can do," Seth reasoned.

"If that's the case, the president sent the wrong men." Kyle looked at Seth with injured pride. "If this mystery person is successful, he will foreclose on loans, toss everyone off their land, and turn the area into complete turmoil. You see, the people here who have been loyal to the southern cause will have to pledge allegiance back to the Union and all will be forgiven and the war forgotten. But if this person gets his way, all he'll have to do is sit tight and then when the time is right, they can just take over."

"I wonder what makes people so rotten, captain?" Seth demanded.

Kyle threw up his hands in aggravation. "Seth! I shouldn't have to caution you about calling me that! You must know how dangerous it could be."

Seth was furious with himself. "Sorry, Kyle." He emphasized the name. "You can believe it won't happen again."

Kyle nodded. "Well, guess I had better be getting back to town. Think I'll try to stir up a poker game tonight. A man can learn all sorts of things at a table."

Chapter Fourteen

A lantern was burning under the portico of Mc-Garrity's Saloon. It illuminated the wide brick steps leading to the swinging doors, which were backed with a massive solid door. Kyle entered the saloon. He quietly observed the noise and clamor that abounded in the room. His eyes trailed from the girls dancing on the stage, to the noisy men drinking at the bar, to the gaming tables where the cigar smoke hovered over them. Kyle bellied up to the bar, ordered a drink, and sized up the people who were in the saloon. The man whom Kyle had met the other night walked over to where he was.

"Well, how-do stranger. I was beginning to think you didn't like us around here."

"No, I've been too busy to come back. Been trying to get the little lady settled into a house so she won't be nagging at me. You know how they are, women are born to be natural domestic nesters."

Ryan motioned toward the back with his hand. "There's a good game going on back there. I don't know if you would be interested though, 'cause the

190

stakes are pretty high."

Kyle's brows raised with curiosity. "Oh, I don't know. What do you call high stakes?"

Ryan shrugged indifferently. "A hundred dollars with a limit of three bumps. At least that's what it was when I left. Sometimes it goes even higher."

The game sounded very appealing to Kyle. He turned his drink up, wiped his mouth with his shirt sleeve, and asked, "Do you have a house dealer or is the deck passed around?"

"In the back room, the deck is passed around the table. I wouldn't play for those stakes any other way."

"My feelings exactly, Ryan," Kyle said seriously. "Lead the way, I'm ready for a few hands, anyway." Kyle had a method that had never failed him when he gambled. He would start slow and depending on how the cards were running, gradually increase the bets, forcing some to drop out, therefore changing the run of the cards. He always sized his opponents with caution, because some were always poor losers and some poor cheaters.

When Kyle stepped into the back room, it was as though he had entered another world. The floors were heavily carpeted, the table was covered with a lush green baize covering and heavy red drapes hung over the windows in the immediate rear of the room. As always Kyle searched the room to find a means of escape just in case the need arose, but there was no doors leading to the outside other than the one they had just entered. The men sitting at the table moved over and made room for Kyle and Ryan. Soon, they were settled in for the night.

It was in the wee hours of the morning before the men finally decided to call it quits. Kyle pocketed his winnings, which consisted of only a couple of hundred dollars; however Ryan was a big winner. Only one man left the table grumbling, but he got in on the good-natured teasing. Nothing implied that anyone was very sore. That was one reason Kyle was so surprised when he left the saloon and noticed a scuffle going on down the alley. Without thinking of the consequences, when Kyle saw three men on one, he joined in the fight. In a matter of moments the three ruffians decided the fight was too even so they lit out for easier pickings. Kyle dusted off his britches and offered a hand to Ryan who had been on the bottom of the heap.

"Are you all right?" Kyle asked with concern in his voice.

"Yeah, at least I think I am, thanks to you. If you hadn't stopped, those owlhoots would have robbed me for sure," Ryan mumbled, wiping the blood from his mouth.

"Able to recognize any of them?"

"Yeah, one was that son-of-a . . . that lost all his money. I guess when he left the saloon, he went and got his friends."

Kyle examined the wound on Ryan's face. "Looks like they did a pretty good job on you. Do you live close by?"

"No, I don't," Ryan said wincing in pain. "I live about five miles out of town."

Kyle thought for a moment. "Tell you what, how 'bout us going over to my house. I'll have my wife take a look at you. That bleeding needs to be stopped."

"I couldn't put a lady out like that . . . especially at this hour of the morning."

"I don't think she would mind a bit," Kyle replied. "Besides, you're not in any kind of shape to do any riding, and the saloon has already closed. There is no where else to go."

Ryan got to his feet and to his disbelief, he could barely walk. He tried to smile through his broken lip. "I guess I don't have much of a choice. Are . . . you sure your wife won't mind?"

Kyle assured him once again it would be perfectly fine, that Paige would not object. Shortly they reached Kyle's home. They entered through the back door, making an extreme amount of noise.

"Paige," Kyle shouted. "Come here, please. I need you in the kitchen. A man is hurt."

Paige came stumbling from her bedroom, wrapping a robe around her. "What is the matter? Kyle, are you all right?" she asked, fear in her voice.

"I'm fine, but my friend has been hurt," Kyle said, reaching for the kettle to put some water on to heat. "It was lucky for him I heard the fight and helped stop it. Do you think you can get the bleeding stopped?"

Paige leaned down to examine the wound on Ryan's lip. When he tried to stand, she rebuked him. "You can remember your manners later. You need to be still or you are going to lose too much blood."

Ryan looked up at her. He tried to smile, but all he could manage was a painful grimace. "Looks like you have come to my aid again, fair lady."

"What do you mean?"

"I may look a little different out of uniform, but you should recognize me. After all you saved my life."

Paige looked at him, obviously confused. She had no idea what the man was talking about. She glanced puzzledly in Kyle's direction where he was shrugging his shoulders, not knowing what Ryan was talking about.

"I really don't know what you mean, sir," Paige said.

"Sure you do. Remember the train?" Ryan said, his eyes showing recollection of how she saved him from being captured by Union soldiers.

"You . . . ! You are the man on the train! I never expected to see you again!" Paige dropped the towel she had been cleaning his mouth with, clearly and unmistakably startled by his appearance.

Kyle's brows shot up with interest. He would definitely have to find out more about their meeting. This only proved that the world was becoming smaller and smaller with the modern ways to travel. Kyle reached under the kitchen safe and pulled a full bottle of whiskey from it. "Here, this might help kill the pain," he said, offering the bottle to Ryan.

Paige looked at his lip once the blood had been washed off. "We can tell Kyle about the train incident later." She got her sewing basket which contained some silk thread. "I think it should be sewn up while the bleeding has stopped." She dabbed some whiskey on a piece of cloth. "I think the whiskey burns more than it kills pain, but at least it will sterilize the wound." She glanced in Kyle's direction. "Do you think you should go after the sheriff?"

"I doubt if it would do any good. There are so many owlhoots who hang around the waterfront, it's impossible to keep track of them. They didn't get Ryan's money, and I seriously doubt if the sheriff would go to any trouble to look for them. If Ryan agrees, it would probably be best to just let it drop."

Ryan mumbled, "I think so too."

Kyle glanced toward Paige; he knew this next suggestion would not sit too kindly with her. "Ryan, we have an extra bedroom. I insist you stay until morning before going home. You've lost quite a bit of blood and there is no use in your trying to make it home. You should feel much better later."

"Oh I don't know," Ryan said thoughtfully. "I guess I could, that is, if you are sure I wouldn't be putting you out too much, ma'am." He looked questioningly at Paige.

"Oh no, no trouble at all," she sputtered. Politeness made her smile sweetly and go along with Kyle's suggestion, where silently her anger raged. This had to be a ploy on Kyle's part to keep her in his bed.

Kyle led Ryan to the back bedroom before

helping Paige straighten the clutter in the kitchen.

"That was certainly a sly move," she hissed.

"What do you mean?" Kyle asked in mock innocence.

"You know very well what I mean! You went out of your way to ask that man to spend the night. I wonder if you would have done that if I had not made it plain we would not be sharing bedrooms?"

Kyle's eyes were like shards of glass. "You certainly put a high price on yourself, Frenchie. For your information, I only offered a common courtesy to the man. Let me tell you something else, and you had better listen good. If I wanted you, a wall between us would be no protection." He grabbed her wrists and pulled her roughly to him, then his lips found hers, raping her mouth with his tongue as he kissed her savagely. "See? See how easy it was?" he bragged as he shoved her away. "I could have you just as easily. And it wouldn't be all nice and pretty. If I so minded, I could have your dress ripped off, and your drawers down around your knees, and in the middle of what you prize so greatly, like I did in Washington, remember?"

Paige cringed at Kyle's verbal slap in the face. "You wouldn't dare . . . !" she muttered through clenched teeth.

"Oh I wouldn't? Just try me! I'm getting damn tired of the same old story and constant bitching at me." He asked her incredibly, "Do you actually think all I have on my mind is a way to get between your legs?" his tone of voice, crude and sarcastic. "If that is so, you can take the deal we made and go straight to hell with it!" He spun on his heel. "As for me, I'm going to bed." He bowed in a low mocking gesture. "If her majesty wants, she can damn well come to bed with me or sleep standing up in the corner—I no longer care!" Kyle stomped from the room and slammed the door so hard it jarred the glasses in the cupboard.

Paige stared behind him in open mouthed surprise. She threw the dish towel to the floor and went running after Kyle, determined not to let him win the argument. She crawled into bed, and huddled on her side. She became more furious when Kyle's breathing soon turned into a soft, steady snore. It was clear that he was not too upset over their fight, which only frustrated Paige even more.

The following morning proved to be greatly subdued as Paige and Kyle tried to pretend everything was all right between them for the sake of their guest. Both had too much pride to show their anger. Although Ryan's face was terribly swollen, he managed to eat a hearty breakfast and if he noticed his hosts toying with their food, he failed to mention it.

After the strained silence of the meal, Ryan pushed his plate back and said in a grateful voice, "You don't know how much better I feel this morning." He reached across the table unexpectedly for Paige's hand. He brought it up to his lips and kissed it. "This is twice you have come to my rescue. I insist you let me repay your kindness."

Kyle interrupted. "Last night, you mentioned something about a train. I was going to ask then

197

but something came up and I forgot. What exactly happened?"

Ryan quickly filled Kyle in on what had happened. How he and his men had tried to take control of the train and how Paige had saved him from certain capture when he tried to escape. "I couldn't get medical attention for three days, that is why my leg is stiff now. But, all in all, I was very lucky. If it had not been for your wife, I would have spent the remainder of the war in some prison camp, and most probably would have lost my leg completely." He turned back to Paige, dismissing the incident. "My sister has made me promise to bring her to town Saturday for a night out on the town. I would like to invite you and Kyle to join us. We could have dinner, stop somewhere for wine, and perhaps take in the dance at the Irvine."

Paige looked to Kyle for his reaction, then defiance went through her. She simply would refuse to ask him about every minor detail and decision. "We would love to accept your invitation. But I have a better idea; why don't you and your sister come here for dinner. We could go to the dance later in the evening."

Ryan flashed her as large a smile as his swollen mouth would permit. "I think that is a charming idea. So," he looked questioningly at Paige, "is seven o'clock all right?"

"That would be fine." Paige replied with a light hearted cheerfulness tinkling through her voice.

"Since that is settled," Ryan said, standing, "I ought to be on my way home. Roz will be wondering what happened to me."

Kyle walked him outside; when he came back in he demanded: "What in the hell did you mean, inviting them here?"

Paige's eyes flew wide open. She twisted to stare at him, a chill settled in her heart when she saw the speculation which narrowed his direct gaze. "What's wrong with that?" she asked hotly.

"I saw the way you were hanging on to him last night," Kyle said, his voice tinged with jealousy. "I also noticed you put on one of your sheerest robes this morning to fix breakfast in. What were you trying to do, entice him?"

"Kyle!" Paige scolded. "You are being most unreasonable!" Although he had hurt her feelings she refused to let him know. "You have no reason to say that. You are being hateful!"

"No I'm not being hateful. I think you were flirting with him and seized the opportunity to see him again!" Paige and Kyle glared at each other like wary enemies, impatient to do battle, but dreading to win the war. They knew if the argument continued, it could lead to an irrevocable difference of opinion.

"I think you are jealous," Paige said in a half-hiss, half-sigh. "At least that is how you sound."

There was a cynical twist to Kyle's smile. "No, I'm not jealous. I simply don't trust that man, that's all."

Paige plainly couldn't understand. "But . . . why . . . did you bring him here last night if you don't trust him?"

Kyle flung his hands about in mid-air. "Because there wasn't anything else I could do. The man was obviously hurt. Just because I bring him to my home, wounded, is no reason to invite him and his old maid sister here.''

"Well, if you feel that way about it, then perhaps we can come up with some sort of an excuse," she said, disappointment breaking her voice.

"No, the damage has already been done. Besides, maybe it will give you a chance to meet some other women. And who knows, my suspicions may be wrong about Ryan."

Paige found herself wondering why Kyle was suspicious of Ryan, but she pushed those troublesome thoughts from her mind and began to dwell on their personal situation. Why was he acting so unreasonably toward her? She realized how horrible she must have sounded last night, acting like all Kyle had on his mind was sex. In a way, she did not blame him for becoming angry when she spouted off like she did. Then, the memory of his kiss came flooding back. That crushing, delicious kiss! Just the thought of it made her heart pound furiously. She couldn't understand the strange onrush of feelings which were beginning to stir whenever Kyle accidently came in contact with her. Could it be after so short a period of time, she was falling in love with him? It would be wonderful if she was, because with each passing day, she was becoming more positive she was carrying his baby. Her remaining prayer was that if she was falling in love with him, then please, please, let him feel the same way about her.

Chapter Fifteen

Paige was so excited on Saturday morning, she was up at dawn, dusting and cleaning the already spotless house. She put the coffee pot at the rear of the stove to heat and took a much needed break from cleaning.

Imagine! Never in her wildest dreams would she have thought she'd be sitting in her own kitchen when only a few weeks ago, she had been living in squalor. Now, she was anticipating the visit of a respected captain of the Confederate army and his sister. Although she had absolutely no romantic inclinations for Ryan, she could certainly understand how he could turn a woman's head. He was tall, well-built, and positively handsome, especially with his pale blond hair shining the way it did.

Paige rinsed out her cup and went in to awaken Kyle, who had been sleeping late that morning. She had no idea where he had been spending so much of his time, and apparently, he had no desire to tell her. Just as she started to open the door to the bedroom, she heard a sound that made her blood freeze. It was an owl hooting in the daytime.

Although she was not superstitious, she immediately recalled the plantation and one of the old slave's sayings. The old black man's words rang through her mind. "Anytimes child when you hear an ol' hootowl when de sun be shinin', d'en it's fo' sho', dat ill is in de wind." Paige shook off the foreboding feeling and walked over and shook Kyle lightly by the shoulder.

"Kyle, Kyle, wake up."

He turned over, stretched and yawned. "Good morning," he said, raising up and sitting on the side of the bed. "You seem to be feeling chipper this morning," he remarked. He watched as she picked up his clothes he had strewn the previous night.

"Oh I feel fine. In fact, I haven't felt this good in a long time." Her eyes danced with joy. "Kyle, I have been thinking. I noticed some of the shops selling fresh shrimp. Do you think we could afford some for supper tonight?"

Kyle replied hesitantly, "Oh, I don't know. Maybe if we couldn't get any shrimp, we could pick up some crayfish somewhere. I'm kinda hungry for some filet gumbo, myself."

Paige licked her lips as she imagined how delicious the food would taste. "Hummm, that sounds good." Giving a little laugh, she added. "I don't know if I can wait until tonight or not."

Kyle reached over and gave Paige a playful swat on her behind when she leaned over to pick up his dirty shirt. "Talking about all that food makes me hungry. I think if you were to run a fat cow through here right now, I could probably eat the whole thing.''

Paige's laughter rang through the room. "My goodness, I don't think I can provide you with a fat cow, but I do have some ham and eggs. I have even run across some of Mrs. Sanders' preserves she left here. Do you think that would satisfy you?''

Kyle smiled. "Only if it was cooked 'bout ten minutes ago.''

While Kyle dressed, he could hear Paige's voice carrying through the house as she sang a tuneless little song. He paused in the doorway, staring at her until she sensed someone was watching her.

She turned around suddenly. "Why are you looking at me like that?''

Kyle walked over to the table and sat down. He acted embarrassed at being caught. "I was only thinking . . . about how pretty you are.''

Paige blinked her eyes, obviously surprised at what he said. "Why, thank you. I believe that is the first time you have ever paid me a compliment like that.''

"Is it really?''

"Yes,'' Paige stammered. "At least it's the first time I can recall.''

"We'll have to see what we can do about that in the future, then,'' Kyle said very casually.

Paige worked around in the kitchen while Kyle ate. They didn't say much; in fact, few words were spoken until Kyle looked at her uneasily. "It means a lot to you, doesn't it?''

"What?''

"Having Ryan and his sister over for supper.''

"Yes it does,'' Paige admitted matter-of-factly.

"You see, when I was a child, people would come from miles around to visit with Uncle Silas and his family. Naturally, we were included in all the festivities. He would have grand parties and balls. It didn't matter that papa was hired help. He was such a fine man and was so well respected, it didn't matter that we were not in the same social group. In answer to the hidden meaning of your question, I guess I miss all the parties and even more, I miss my friends." She ducked her head, feeling strange at being so open with Kyle. "I think I'm trying to reach back to a more simple time, a time when there was so much happiness in my life. A time when all was right with the world." She took a deep breath and continued. "I think . . . I feel if I can get acquainted with people here, I'll feel at home."

Kyle looked oddly at her. "Paige, I don't want to start an argument with you by saying this, but how could times be so grand when people were living in bondage?"

"You are referring to the slaves?"

"Yes."

"But they really had it good. Of course, I am going by the tales we heard about how many owners treated their slaves. The ones on Uncle Silas's plantation were treated as humanely as possible. They were provided with good shelter, decent food, and warm clothes to wear in the winter, and I recall, whenever a baby was born, Uncle Silas would give its mother ten silver dollars."

Kyle snorted in disgust as he refilled his coffee

cup. "That's exactly what I am talking about. Don't you realize he was buying that newborn baby?"

"Oh no, Kyle. You have it all wrong. Uncle Silas was good to his slaves. Why, I can remember him whipping only one of the slaves all the time I was there. And that was because he tried to run away." She could still see the guarded expression on Kyle's face so she added in a trailing voice, "The slaves had it very good."

"Yeah, sure," Kyle slurred. "They probably had it good from your point of view. But, let me ask you this, how many were free to move on when they wanted to? How many husbands and wives were separated because their owner had a bad year with his crops and had to sell off his prime breeding stock? How many mothers had daughters yanked from their arms so they could be supplied for the young rake's insatiable sexual appetites, and if they struggled or resisted, the girls were sent back to the fields for a lifetime of back-breaking work." He looked at her sternly, "I want to ask you one more question. How would you like to wake up in the morning and know the only thing ahead for you was more of the same kind of misery?"

Paige glued her eyes to the floor, recalling Della's conversation with her, and how terrible the few weeks were that she spent at her uncle's house, and the helplessness she felt at the end of each day. She finally managed to tear her gaze from the floor. "I can't answer all your questions. Some were fair and some were not. But, since you brought up so many questions, I have one to ask of you. If you feel so strongly about the slave issue, why did you quit?"

"What do you mean by that?" he demanded.

Paige stopped and faced him squarely, "Don't be coy with me. You know exactly what I meant. Remember when I first met you back in Washington? You were wearing a uniform. A uniform of the Union army, and I don't believe that cock and bull story you told about wanting to start your life all over. Now, Captain Brenner, what are you doing here, your real purpose, and what are you trying to pull?"

Kyle replied tersely. "I'm not trying to pull anything as you so implied. I am only trying to make the world a better place to live in, to be more precise, to make the South a better place to live in, and another thing," he thundered, "I thought I told you to never call me by that name again!"

"You can get upset with me all you want, but somehow, I'll find out what you are doing. I don't know how I'll find out . . . but I will!" she screamed.

Kyle's eyes glittered hard in the early morning sun light. "I suggest you leave well enough alone."

Paige's eyebrows raised coyly. "Oh! Are you threatening me?"

After a strong heaviness, Kyle smiled bitterly at her. "That, Frenchie, is exactly how I feel each time I come near you. I'm not saying this to frighten you, nor will I try to bribe you. I know fancy gowns and being accepted in Jefferson society will not buy the silence of your tongue; but if you love your country, north and south alike, and if you care for the rights of all men . . . black and white alike, you'll keep your mouth shut!"

She frowned, musing over his words. "Kyle, let me ask you one thing. Are you a . . . spy?" The words, her suspicions for so long had finally been spoken, she closed her eyes tightly together, almost afraid to hear the answer.

"If you mean spy in regard to my sending information back to Union troopers, no, I am not a spy. I would not do that. But I feel I am working for a cause that is greater than that. It's not for the war or the ending of it. It is for what will happen after the war. That is all I will or can say because there could be more lives than mine which would be on the line if someone else found out about me. So there, it is, out in the open. My life is in your hands, or should I say, it is in the silence of your tongue."

Paige saw the honesty written on his face. She also remembered how he had refused to lie when Oscar threatened his life. "All right," she said slowly. "I will keep quiet about this. I believe you," she added simply.

"Thank you, Paige. I can't stress how important this is. If the wrong people got wind of this conversation, then a greater wrong and more harm would come to our country than you could imagine."

"You mean . . . it's *that* important?"

"Yes it is."

Paige nodded her head. "All right, as I said, my lips are sealed. But . . . I would like to know more about what is going on."

Kyle shook his head. "That is impossible. The less you know about my mission, the safer you will be. I don't want to jeopardize your safety or the safety of my friends."

Paige touched Kyle's shoulder very tenderly. "I understand. And if that is your wish, I will abide by it."

A veil of dread and concern lifted from Kyle's features when he saw the sincere expression on his wife's face. He breathed a deep sigh of relief. "Now that *that* is settled, I need to go. I have a few things to do." He stood and took some money from his pocket and placed it on the table. "Buy whatever you need for tonight, but if I were you, I wouldn't go messing around the waterfront. I know you want to have fresh shrimp for supper, but there are too many unsavory characters hanging around down there. In fact, I'd rather you didn't go near it. Just try to find something nice uptown." He reached over and gently brushed back a strand of hair that had fallen down in her eyes. "Take care," he added almost affectionately, "and I'll see you later this afternoon."

Paige followed him as he walked to the door. "Kyle . . . ?"

He turned to her expectantly.

"Oh, nothing," she smiled. "Just be careful and please don't forget what time Ryan and his sister are expected."

He nodded, then left wordlessly.

Paige leaned against the door, suddenly very worried and frightened. A dread gripped her heart over him. She knew a lot more was going on that he was unable to tell her about. If he were ever found out, she hated to even speculate on what would happen to him. Paige's eyes widened in surprise over the thoughts running through her mind. Every day that passed, she grew closer to Kyle. She found that she could now reason with him and he would usually respond to her kindness with a kindness of his own. All things considered, life was becoming quite pleasant!

The sun was shining brightly, falsely indicating a pretty spring day as Paige made her way around town. She went to the mercantile, then to the dress shop where she picked up the remainder of her dresses and joined Mrs. Roget in a pleasant cup of tea. She then proceeded on her way. After inquiring at several shops, she could find neither shrimp nor crayfish, so she decided to disregard Kyle's word of caution, and went down to the waterfront to purchase the delicacies.

Even though the day was bright, shadows loomed all around. After picking up some crayfish, Paige started home, her steps echoing on the board planks that lined each side of the street. Every so often, she would pause and look behind her, certain that someone was following. But, each time, the street would be clear. Apprehension filled her. Up ahead was a place where the buildings separated, leaving a huge, dark gap in between. There was no other alternative but to go ahead. She was being foolish for acting so skittish. As she stepped off the board walk, Paige screamed. Rough hands dragged her into the darkness of the alley.

"Oh no! Please let me go!" Paige screamed in horror.

A damp smelly hand pressed firmly over her mouth to prevent her from crying out again.

"Hold on, you little wild cat! Stop your fightin' and I won't hurt you none."

Paige shuddered in terror when she got a look at her would-be attacker. He was dressed in a smutty red shirt. One eye was covered with a black patch; immediately the old stories of wild pirates came flooding back. He was the spitting image of what she had been told they would be like.

He removed his hand long enough to try and press his foul, strong-scented mouth against hers. She instantly renewed her struggles again. The pirate grabbed her breast, ripping the fabric from her bosom as easily as if it had been made from sheer webbing. Paige felt utter panic over what was about to happen. "Please don't hurt me," she managed to gasp. "I'm carrying a child!"

The beast of a man laughed sardonically. "Well, well, well," he said, smacking his lips in anticipation. "That proves you are all woman!"

He threw her to the ground as easily as if he was tossing a bag of grain, then fell down on top of her, pinning her helplessly to the ground. Suddenly, Paige felt the burden on her body lighten. Opening her eyes, she saw a large black man standing over her assailant.

"Yo' git yo'r carcuss out of here an' leave dat white lady alone!"

The pirate rubbed his chin where the negro had hit him. "Git out of here, nigger and leave me be!"

A light of defiance flashed through the negro's eyes. "I might jest be a nigger to yo', but, I's tellin' yo' right now to leave dat white lady alone!" He added threateningly, "Yo' knows how strong Shem is, if'n yo' don't wants a heap o' trouble, yo' had better does as I says."

The pirate thought over what the negro had said. "Awww, you probably just want her for yourself."

"No, suh! Yo' jest be bringing a heap of trouble down on us at the waterfront. Dis lady be decent. If'n yo' finishes what yo' started, de sheriff'll be down on us 'fore nightfall!"

The pirate very hesitantly fastened his pants, realizing the black man spoke the truth. He also knew if he persisted in his attack, the black could take him if it came to a fight. Growling at Paige, he claimed, "You best thank him for saving you. But let me tell you something, lady, stay away from this part of town. If I see you again, I might show you what it's like to have a *real* man!" Before turning to run, he added, "Keep your mouth shut about what nearly happened, or I'll have to look you up some dark night." With those words, he ran down the alley as quickly as possible.

Paige slumped to the ground crying tears of relief. She finally managed to stammer. "Oh . . . thank . . . you! You saved my life!" She looked up at the black man and was surprised to see him standing with his back to her. "What are you doing?" she asked, obviously puzzled.

"Don't mean no dis'respect, ma'am, 'cause yo' are a lady, an' I's jest been freed a short while. It ain't proper fer me to look at you', 'specially with your dress all tore."

Paige gasped when she glanced down and saw the tattered remains of her dress. "Oh my!" she exclaimed. "How am I going to get home dressed like this? I can't walk through the streets half naked!"

"If'n the missus don't mind none, my shirt would be freshly washed," he stammered, "And yo' don't have to worry 'bout catchin' nothin' cause I ain't got no bugs or nuttin' like dat. Yo' can wear it home if'n yo' wants to."

Paige sighed in relief, answering quickly, "I would certainly appreciate it. This will be twice you have come to my rescue today."

The black man removed his shirt and handed it to Paige.

"My name be Shem."

"I'll see that you are handsomely rewarded, Shem," she said gratefully.

"Oh no, ma'am! I didn't mean fo' yo' to give me nothin'. 'Sides dat ol' Jake, he be meaner than a mad snake, and he'd know dat yo' told on him." Shem's eyes were wide in fright, not for himself but for others. He knew if something was said, he and his kind would be the ones to suffer.

Paige shook her head, adamantly. "No, that wouldn't be fair to you, especially after the chance you took standing up to him the way you did. I'll tell you—I have a little money left; I'll give it to you for saving me from that horrible man, although it isn't enough."

Shem toed the ground with his foot. "Yo' sho'

don't have to. But, I would be grateful 'cause it's been a while since I've had anythin' to eat."

"Why didn't you say so?" Paige asked, then realized the former slave would not have been so bold. She thought a moment then suggested, "Why don't you follow me home and I'll give you something to eat?"

Shem's face broke into a wide toothy grin. "Yes, ma'am!"

Paige gathered up her strewn packages with Shem's help and they were on their way, only Shem followed a few steps behind. Finally Paige stopped. "Shem, there isn't any need of you following behind me. I don't mind if you walk beside me."

Shem stopped short, quaking in his shoes with fright. "Oh no, ma'am. I couldn't do dat. 'Cause I knows my place, and it ain't walkin' beside no white lady! If'n a white man saw me, I'd be tarred and feathered 'fore nightfall. It's done been happenin'."

Paige nodded mutely, understanding completely. It was so hard for her to act better than other human beings because back on the plantation, the negroes were treated so well. Her mood was broken when a man rushed up to her.

"Pardon me, ma'am," the man said, tipping his hat, "but is that nigger bothering you? I saw you stop and say something to him, and I've noticed him a-following you for the past few blocks."

"Oh my no. You don't understand. You see, a . . . man down the street got a little . . . out of the way with me . . . and this nice man," she pointed to Shem, "protected me from him. He also offered to help carry my packages."

"I see," the stranger said, "But you can't blame me for thinking what I did. You can't be too careful with all the niggers roaming and looking over our women-folk."

Paige drew herself up to her fullest height. "I appreciate your concern, sir, but I am quite safe. Now, if you'll excuse me please?" she said, stepping around the man.

When they reached the house, Paige cautioned Shem to wait a moment. She ran inside and got the ham left in the kitchen cupboard. She took some money from her coin purse then rushed into her bedroom to slip into a dress so she could return his shirt. Much to her relief, he was waiting by the back gate when she went back outside.

"I want you to know how safe I felt with you there to protect me," she said when she handed him the small bundle and pressed the coins into his hand.

Shem stood a little taller under her praise. His reply was silence as Paige bent to shake a pebble from her shoe. When she straightened up, Shem had vanished as quickly as he had appeared in the alley.

She went back into the house, shaking her head and silently amused over Shem's actions. He was terribly shy and hated to stay any longer, was Paige's reaction to the matter. She heated water to wash away the dirt, the grime and unclean feeling she suffered from her near assault. After a long, lingering bath in perfumed water, Paige went about preparing a delicious meal for her highly anticipated guests with gusto. Before she realized it, the afternoon had sped by and it was time to dress for dinner.

Paige modestly admired herself in the mirror. She had every reason to do so. Her hair was arranged high on her head with a few looping curls cascading down her back. After much debate, she had decided to wear a splendid royal blue gown. Tiny, fresh-water pearls had been interwoven throughout the bodice, gleaming and sparkling as they caught the glow from the quickly fading evening sun. The waistline encircled her still small waist, but pushed her swelling breasts firmly upwards, making the neckline dangerously low and terribly revealing. Her bout with morning sickness had left her a little pale and wan, but the excitement made her cheeks glow a rosy red, adding just enough color to her face. She could hardly believe her own eyes as she stared at her reflection in the mirror. Surely the beauty staring back at her couldn't possibly be Paige Brenner! Never had she felt more desirable or beautiful. "Maybe Kyle will sit up and take notice of me now!" Paige could not believe she had uttered those words! Surprised at what she said, she burst out laughing. Things were definitely improving. She was having many pleasant thoughts about her husband, which was good.

She glanced at the hall clock apprehensively, afraid that Kyle would not arrive home in time to change for their guests. As the clock struck the half-hour, Kyle rushed through the front door. He called out, "I know I'm running late, but I'll be ready in a few minutes. I already got a shave at the barber shop." He hurried into the kitchen, carrying a small package in his arms. "I thought I had better get me something a little more fancy to wear . . ." He stopped in mid-sentence when he saw Paige, and let out a long, low whistle. "You sure are pretty tonight."

Paige blushed. "Thank you, but you had better hurry and get dressed. You are running awfully late."

Kyle started for his bedroom, then stopped and swung back around, holding on to the door facing. "Supper smells good too. I see you were able to find some crayfish."

For a brief moment the horrible man flashed through her mind, but upon remembering his warning and Kyle's caution about not going down there, she said nothing about the incident. Instead, she forced a smile. "Yes, I was able to find some." Then her voice changed to a scolding tone. "Please get ready, Kyle."

Paige busied herself by dishing up the food and placing the steaming bowls into the warming oven. She had already checked to see if the wine was properly chilled. Hearing a knock at the door, she wiped her hands on a dish towel and jerked off her apron. "Hurry, Kyle. I think they are here."

"I'll be out in a minute," he called from his room.

"All right, but bring in the wine, will you? There's also a tray of glasses already prepared and sitting on the table."

"All right. All right. I'm coming."

Paige hurried to the front door, smoothed back her hair, straightened her wide-hooped skirt, and took a deep breath.

"Good evening Mrs. Brenner," Ryan said, taking her hand and bringing it very gallantly up to his lips. "I hope we are here on time." He stepped aside to introduce his sister. "And this lovely creature is Rosalyn Ledbetter."

Paige could not help but gasp when she recognized the vivacious redhead. She stammered, "I have already had the pleasure of meeting her, Captain Ryan." She nodded politely to Rosalyn. "It's very nice to see you again." Paige's hand flew to her neck very nervously. "Oh my! I am forgetting my manners, making you stand out in the cool air. Please come in." She ushered them into the entrance hall.

She took Ryan's hat, grateful for something to help her regain her composure. Her mind raced, recalling the instant dislike and what a flirt Rosalyn was. She was rescued from this discomforting moment when Kyle came into the entrance hall and helped to greet their guests. Rosalyn seemed obviously surprised to see him, but when the woman clutched at Kyle's arm, Paige was positive she was merely acting. She must have somehow known she was to be their guest for the evening. And Kyle was so gullible. He actually beamed at Rosalyn as he took her small gloved hand and kissed it.

"It is indeed a pleasure to see you again, Miss LedBetter." Kyle nodded to Ryan who was watching him with an amused grin flirting devilishly across his face. "I had no idea this lovely lady was your sister, Ryan. You'll have to admit," he said, chuckling, "she is the one who inherited the good looks in your family."

Ryan laughed heartily. "Yes, that's for sure. I have always been told I favored our father. But," he said, confusion clouding his brows, "I didn't know the three of you had met previously."

Paige linked her arm through Ryan's as she led the way to the parlor, explaining how and where they had met. Then she scolded him. "Now Captain Ryan, don't berate yourself. I would be the first to admit how beautiful your sister is, but it is nice for a man to be ruggedly handsome, which you certainly are."

Ryan threw back his head and laughed. "Thank you, my dear, but loveliness has known none better than you."

Rosalyn's tinkling laughter came from behind. Paige turned to see what was so amusing, but what she saw only made her temper flare another degree. Rosalyn had her arm linked through Kyle's and from his vantage point, all he could see was her plunging neckline and her breasts were exposed almost to the state of being indecent! Of course, she had not been able to see Rosalyn's immodest dress until Kyle had removed her wrap. When they reached the parlor, Paige asked Kyle to pour the wine, hoping the chore would divert his attention from the flirtatious woman.

"Of course I will pour the wine. I can only hope our guests will forgive me if my hand trembles and

I spill some."

"But why would that happen?" Rosalyn asked, batting her eyelashes at him.

"Because I am so confused by your loveliness," he said teasingly.

"If that is the case," Ryan interrupted. "Please allow me to pour. It has been such a long time since I have been in the company of two lovely ladies, it will give me time for the pounding of my heart to settle a bit."

Rosalyn laughed. "I would have been surprised in Ryan if he had not suggested that. He is really a domesticated little lamb. Not at all like you, Kyle." She stared at him brazenly, almost to the point of being too suggestive.

"My, my, the claws are sharp tonight, little sister." Ryan handed a glass of wine to Rosalyn. "May I remind you Kyle already has a wife . . . and a very attractive one at that, if I may add."

Rosalyn pouted. "Of course she is pretty, Ryan." She discussed Paige as if she weren't there. "But I'm sure she won't mind sharing her husband for a short while this evening." She rattled her fan nervously. "By the way, before we go any further, I must clear the air about something. I introduced myself earlier and Ryan did the same thing tonight, when he called me Miss Ledbetter. You see, I am a married woman . . . or I should say, I was a married woman. I lost my husband at Gettysburg. Since everyone from around here knew me by my maiden name, I still use it. Naturally, when it comes to signing papers or any other legal matter, I use my full and correct one."

"That is too bad. It's a shame for such a beautiful woman to be left a widow." Kyle sympathized and offered his handkerchief to dry her misty eyes.

"Oh, I'm all right," she sniffed. "I don't know why I still get teary. We only knew each other for such a short time. In fact, we only had one week together before his call to duty touched his heart, and he went off to the war . . . never to return."

It took all of Paige's will power not to wrinkle her nose in disgust. Yeah, she thought to herself, most probably he found out what a witch you are, and joined the war effort to get away from you. If Paige had any doubts before, her mind was clearly made up! She simply hated Rosalyn! She eyed her carefully, knowing she would have to watch out for her now, and in the future.

Kyle patted Rosalyn's hand sympathetically. He changed the subject by telling amusing little stories about his life when he was a small boy back on his father's ranch. Paige was astounded. She had never heard Kyle open up about his past before. It looked very suspicious to her, especially since Kyle and Rosalyn had eyes only for each other.

She had to admit Kyle was very handsome. He had on a beige suit with a cream colored shirt and a brown satin vest. He had deliberately left a few buttons unfastened to reveal his thickly matted chest hair. His trousers also fit extremely tight. She had to admire his choice of colors he picked out. His clothes blended very well with his tanned features and dark hair. All in all, Kyle presented a very strikingly handsome figure.

Even to give the devil his due, Paige had to admit that Rosalyn looked simply charming. She was dressed in a pale pink gown and around her throat was a string of real pearls, not at all like the ones decorating Paige's dress. But the milky white complexion was enough to distract a man's view of the pearls. Paige doubted if Kyle even saw them!

Ryan sensed Paige's discomfort so he spoke. "Something sure smells good. Did you prepare dinner all by yourself?"

"Yes I did, and thank you for your compliment." She blushed demurely. "If everyone is ready to eat, I can have it on the table in just a few minutes."

Rosalyn frowned. "You mean you don't have servants?"

Paige blinked in surprise, feeling Rosalyn's tone of disapproval. "Why no, I really enjoy doing everything myself."

"My gracious!" Rosalyn fluttered her fan again. "I could have sworn you were a real southern lady and everyone knows we always have servants or at least a personal maid."

Paige flushed in anger but she replied in a soft but firm voice, "I am quite a lady. But I still like to do things for myself. I can't see why people should have someone else do chores for them simply because they are too lazy to fend for themself!" She knew she had said too much. It was unthinkable to invite someone to your home and then be rude. But everything Rosalyn said only served to gall Paige. She managed to stand gracefully and straighten her skirt. "If you will excuse me now, I'll get supper on the table." She marched staunchly from the room, leaving an embarrassed silence behind. Rosalyn being scandalized, gasped.

Ryan scowled at her. "Roz, you really should be more careful with that barbed tongue of yours. I think you hurt our hostess' feelings."

"Why, I never intended to do such a thing!" Rosalyn said, smiling dubiously.

Kyle shook his head. "Nonsense! Paige was out of line in saying what she did. I think she could come back and apologize to Rosalyn for her outburst."

"Oh no!" Rosalyn injected. "I'm sure Paige was only stating her feelings, and did not mean to be so outspoken in expressing them. As far as I'm concerned, the entire episode is finished." She paused, knowing how effective this gesture was. "I think I'll go in and make amends with Paige and see if there is anything I can do to help."

The evening meal progressed without further incident. Paige blushed under all the praise heaped upon her over how delicious the meal turned out. The rice was light and fluffy, the crayfish roux was seasoned to an excellent perfection, also the okra gumbo, and the tiny spiced apples she served with creole coffee, set the meal off.

Ryan had a look of pleasure when he asked, "Paige, where in the world did you learn to cook so well?"

"I had very good teachers. My parents were French. I can even remember Grandpapa Jean turning a hand in the kitchen. He simply refused to eat anything except French food. I'm sure his traditions had quite a bit to do with my upbringing. And," she added, "thank you for the compliment."

Ryan looked puzzled as he spoke. "I know you were brought up in the south, but your accent is very different. I suppose some of it could be from your French ancestry."

"I guess so. French was spoken most of the time when I was a small child. Although after Grandpapa died, my parents started speaking English all the time. In fact, I have forgotten many, many words and expressions."

Ryan nodded in understanding. They retired to the parlor and had a delicious brandy. The conversation drifted around the room. Ryan acted the perfect gentleman, while Kyle seemed to lap up the praise Rosalyn heaped upon him. It was as though they were going out of their way to try to make Paige jealous. The only thing that rescued the evening for Paige was Ryan's constant attention. He seemed completely enamored by her charms, which she enjoyed greatly, especially with Kyle paying so much attention to Rosalyn.

The conversation deteriorated when Ryan and Kyle started talking about the war, and who was right and who was wrong. Kyle could not use his best argument because he was cautious of saying too much to the wrong person. Finally, he managed to cool the controversy. "Ryan, I guess you'd have to say I have very mixed emotions about the war. Let me put it this way," he spoke seriously. "I feel the south is standing for a cause and also the north. But whoever said, 'a house divided cannot stand,' is correct. We cannot continue in this manner."

Ryan slapped his leg with his hand. "I agree! I'm tired of this war tearing our country apart. I can only hope the north won't expect us to grovel at their feet when they beat us." Taking in Paige's look of surprise, he added, "Yes, they'll beat us. It's only a matter of a few more months. Everything I've heard so far shows it's headed in that direction."

Kyle agreed. "What's so bad, the north is whipping the south, and some former soldiers are helping them out, and I mean confederate soldiers."

"What do you mean?" both Paige and Rosalyn asked in unison.

"It seems that some Confederate prisoners overpowered their guards, commandeered a steamship, which by the way, was carrying a Union army payroll. They were completely in the clear when a gang of men stopped the ship, murdered most of the Confederate men, and robbed them of the payroll. I should add, the payroll would have bought a lot of badly needed supplies. Anyway, to get on with my story, the few men who survived the attack swore whoever robbed them were southerners!"

Ryan's blue eyes narrowed into icy shards. "Where did you hear that?"

"I was sitting in on a card game," Kyle replied. Seeing the expression on Ryan's face, he added, "Surprised me too. I figure there is a gang operating close by. They probably see the handwriting on the wall, so to speak, and have decided to cash in and use a few devious methods to further their own needs and causes."

Paige interrupted, suddenly frightened at the way the conversation was drifting. She also was scared Kyle had said too much, and she could not help but wonder if Kyle was coloring the true story to his own benefit. "All right, you two. I think we have heard enough of this war business. I believe we should change the entire subject." She was adamant.

Rosalyn looked at Kyle, her gaze was bored, yet sultry. "I agree with Paige. The entire matter is pointless. Nothing either one of you can do will change a thing," she said. Flashing a brilliant smile at Kyle, she added, "When I was in the kitchen, I noticed a beautiful rock garden out in back. The moon is full and would provide ample light. Would you please show it to me?"

Kyle immediately leaped to his feet and escorted Rosalyn through the house. Muffled laughter drifted back through the parlor as they made their way into the brilliant moonlight. Paige sat in stunned silence. She had not figured on Kyle treating her thus. It was Ryan who broke the embarrassed lull.

"Personally, I'm glad they went for a walk. It gives me a chance to spend a few minutes alone with you."

Paige gave a nervous laugh. "You flatter me, Ryan."

He looked adoringly into her eyes. "I swear, you are the most desirable, intriguing, exciting, and yes," his voice contained delicate tremors, "you are even the most breathtaking creature I have ever met." He toyed with a curl that had come unpinned and was dangling down her neck. "In truth, I am very attracted to you. If I had a treasure such as you, there would be no way possible I would fall into the clutches of a woman like Rosalyn."

Paige didn't know what to say. She averted her gaze from Ryan's and groped for the right words. "Ryan, you know I have never given you any reason to think or to feel that way about me." Then she said in an accusing voice, "That was horrible—what you said about your own sister!"

He gave her a sidelong look and chuckled. "I know, but then I know my sister and believe me, she is no lady and deserves everything said about her." He pulled Paige's hand up to his cheek and rubbed it against his face. "I think the gods are against me. Now that I have found a woman I could truly love, she is the wife of another man."

She jerked her hand from his tender caress and edged away from him uncomfortably. "But I am a married woman!" she protested.

At that moment Kyle and Rosalyn came back into the room, laughing and giggling like school children. Paige was relieved they had broken up her confrontation with Ryan until she saw a smear of color on Kyle's lips where he had obviously been kissing Rosalyn.

Ryan, noticing Paige blanche with anger, spoke, his voice cutting through the sudden stillness like a knife. "Rosalyn, I think it is time we were leaving." He glared at her. "Put on your wrap and let's go home."

"But . . . but . . . it's early yet and besides, we were supposed to go to the Irvine and finish out the night by dancing."

"My leg is bothering me," he said curtly. "I don't feel like dancing; and Paige mentioned she had a headache." The glance he shot in Paige's direction showed her to be greatly relieved at the excuse he offered. He helped Rosalyn on with her wrap and muttered the necessary words about how much they enjoyed themselves. After they hurriedly left, Paige turned to Kyle, stared at him angrily, then stormed into the kitchen.

He followed her, knowing she was mad. "Do you need any help cleaning up?" he offered sheepishly.

Eyeing him uncertainly, Paige nervously picked at the curls which had come unwound. "I don't need anything from you!" she snapped briskly.

Kyle threw his hands in the air. "Would you please do me the honor of telling me what I have done wrong now?"

"Don't play me for a fool, Kyle." Paige's voice was hard. "You know exactly what you have done. It will do you no good to pull your act of innocence with me."

Kyle quickly slipped into a light, teasing manner, hoping to alleviate the argument which was brewing. "Innocent? Me? Honey, I haven't been innocent in many years."

Paige's lips settled into thin white lines, her nostrils flared and her eyes widened. "There is no need of getting vulgar, either!" She threw down a dish towel. "You know perfectly well why I am mad. The way you pawed that . . . that . . . red-headed hussy was shameful! And you even kissed her, Kyle! I was never so humiliated in all my life!" Tears of anger brimmed in her eyes.

"I take it you are talking about Rosalyn? Hummm, to me, she acted like the perfect lady."

"Lady my foot! I could tell you what she really is, but *I'm* too much of a lady to have such words in my mouth!" she yelled, slamming a glass on the table, breaking it into small pieces.

"My, my, aren't we touchy tonight," Kyle snipped, his teasing manner quickly turning into a fury that matched Paige's. "I didn't know if you could even see me and Rosalyn, every time I looked at you, you had mushy eyes over Ryan!"

"I knew it! I knew it!" Paige sneered. "You are trying to lay the blame on me! Just because Ryan paid me a few compliments, you are turning the circumstances around to fit your purposes." She placed her arms akimbo. "You are being very unfair, Kyle Brenner. I do not think I was out of line by paying the slightest amount of attention to Ryan. I was merely being polite, while you fell all over your feet in paying attention to that . . . that . . . creature! Now you are saying everything that happened is my fault! This is one time I will not take the blame!"

Kyle's voice turned hard, and cold as ice. "Listen, Frenchie . . ."

"Don't call me by that nickname, I hate it!"

"Listen, Frenchie," he spat, determined to have his way. "Ryan Ledbetter is a very dangerous man.

I saw the way he looks at you and with any type of encouragement from you, you'll have more on your hands than you can handle. If you lead him on and entice him the way you did tonight, there will be trouble." His voice became even more cold. "I think if I ever caught him getting out of the way with you, I'd probably kill him!"

Paige gaped at him, almost speechless. Then she sputtered, "That isn't fair Kyle. I don't believe I asked for his compliments and attention. Whereas, you fell all over that hussy sister of his, and then you say if he looks at me in an appraising way, you'll kill him! You are being unreasonable!"

"No, I didn't put it in that manner," Kyle denied, his thoughts becoming tangled. "I only wanted to caution you about the pitfalls. Ryan is used to getting what he wants, and I wouldn't take it too kindly if he decided he wanted my wife!" Kyle grabbed Paige by the arms and pulled her roughly to him. "Yes, I'll admit I was flirting with Rosalyn. But, maybe I wouldn't be enamored by another woman if the wife I have would share her bed with me!"

Paige looked up at Kyle in surprise, just in time to meet his lips as they lowered onto hers. For an instant, sheer ecstasy flooded through her entire being as his lips forced hers apart. His kiss searched, seared, and burned as he explored with an unquenchable urgency. His hand caressed her lovely throat, stroking the smooth and silken skin. Paige's mind reeled from the intoxicating heat of his passionate kiss. The trembling weakness of her knees only proved how powerful and how strong he was, and how easily she could be brought to a passionate, whimpering woman. When reality tried to reach her mind, Paige smothered a shocked gasp. Kyle, sensing her coming resistance, pushed her roughly away.

"Don't get upset, Paige. I'm not going to take you. I was merely showing you what you were missing," he said haughtily. "If you change your mind, you certainly know where my bedroom is!" He gave her one last stony look and strode from the room.

Paige stared after him, rage, humiliation, and surprise flooding through her; also some other emotions she would never be able to describe, but after she had pulled her fleeting, betraying senses back together, rage took precedence over all her feelings. "Imagine the nerve of that beast!" she thought. Using her like a rag doll and then tossing her aside like a careless child would discard a toy! Suddenly, Paige collapsed into a pool of tears. "Oh, if he only knew," she thought. "If he only knew how much I've grown to care for him. Naturally he was upset because of Ryan, but after all, I am merely a woman, and I do enjoy the attentions of a man. Perhaps the same thing is wrong with me as with Kyle. It is unnatural for a man and woman to live in the same house, and until recently, share the same bed without becoming entirely frustrated." She could not tell him the reason she tensed at the last possible moment when he was holding her in his arms. The face of that horrible man in the alley flashed through her mind, causing her to flinch in Kyle's arms. He had no idea she was about to respond to him completely. He evidently had no idea she was falling hopelessly in love with him either!

Kyle awoke the next morning to a low and distant thunder. Every so often he could see lighting stab across the dark and dreary sky. The mood he was in made the morning more depressing and wretched. He wearily sat up on the side of the bed. He had tossed and turned all night, upset and restless because of his encounter with Paige. Something was going to have to give between them. He had thought he could keep his part of their bargain and not get involved with her emotionally, but he was wrong, he had to admit. He was becoming more and more involved with her. In fact, he could almost call it love. It was practically ironic. In the past, he had became entangled with many women, beautiful women, and had always left them without a backward glance. Now, it was as if fate was laughing at him by hanging his emotions in mid-air like a puppet dangling on a string. But damn-it! That woman is so damned unpredictable it was impossible to know from one day to the next what to expect from her. Sometimes she acts so warm, then so cold, it was like two different people were inside of her. Like last night, he deliberately baited her, hoping to make her jealous, then when she responded to his advances, he had felt emotions tug at his heartstrings that he had not felt in a long time. Could it be God was deliberately punishing him for his attempt at using her for his own purpose? Or, could it be that he was afraid of loving Paige and was only trying to drive a wedge further between them?

Kyle walked to the window and stared out at the bleak day. Suddenly, he slammed his fist against the window sill. He realized what the only course was that was open to him. He would try to win his wife's love. Then the thought of his mission swept over him. What if he were caught? Would the authorities think she was in on it with him? Would they place as much blame on her? No, he would not place her in that kind of jeopardy. The best possible thing he could do for her, was try to keep things as they were, and if the war ended soon, then he would try to win her love.

He dressed as quietly as possible and slipped out of the house, being careful not to awaken his still sleeping wife. He could not face her this morning. He knew if he took one look at her, he would sweep her into his arms and never let her go.

Chapter Sixteen

Paige was happy to be out of the house at long last! For the past few weeks it had rained every day. Since Kyle was hardly ever home, time had been hanging heavily on her hands. The sun was shining beautifully and there was a balmy feel in the air that carried a hint of spring. It was a pleasure to be getting fresh air again, after being in the confines of the home she now could almost call a prison.

She walked carefully to avoid the mud puddles dotting the streets of Jefferson. She stopped at the hotel and purchased the semi-weekly newspaper called the *Jimplecute,* only to read how badly the war was going. In the newspaper was a statement by General William T. Sherman. "The Union army has cut a path to the sea." She read eagerly as she sipped a cup of tea out on the sun porch. "In all reality, Georgia has been destroyed and rendered helpless. Much of the destruction was simply a waste, and this was unfortunate. It is an unnecessary thing that happens in time of war. But if it serves to make this abominable war shorter by one day, then perhaps the price will have been worth it. But take heed. The south will fall because Georgia has had a stake driven through her heart and soul.'' Paige did not realize tears were streaming down her face until Della came over with a handkerchief.

"Now, Miz Brenner, 'tain't no heed in carryin' on so. Yo' knows how bad it could be fo' dat young'un in yo'r belly. Now hush those tears," Della scolded.

Paige tried to smile, but she could only manage a grimace. "I'm sorry. It's just . . . that it is so sad. Our homeland . . . our beloved south has been destroyed! All those poor men, they have lost so much. Some have given their lives, and some have lost their families and their homes."

"'Tis a shame, all right!" Della clucked her head in sympathy. "But look at it this-a-way, maybe it won't be too much longer 'fore it's all over with."

This time, Paige managed a weak smile and looked up at the stately black woman. "I . . . guess you are right." She took Della's well calloused hand in hers. "Thanks for being here when I needed you. I had no intention of losing control of myself like that."

"Dat's all right. Yo'd be more than surprised at how many folks have already busted into tears as soon as they read what yo' jest did."

Paige patted Della's hand. "I feel better after talking to you, Della. You have a calming, soothing effect on people. I really must go now," she said, gathering up her paper. "I had no intention of stopping here when I left the house. I was simply going for a walk to get some fresh air after being cooped up in the house for so long."

"It's been right nice seeing yo' again, Miz Brenner. I hopes . . . yo' don't think dis old woman be prying, but . . . are yo' and de Mister gettin' along all right?" Della asked, her thick eyebrows knitting together in concern.

Paige flushed, realizing this woman knew a lot about her and Kyle. In Della's simple innocence, she could inadvertently mention something to the wrong person. Paige quickly tried to soothe Della's fears. "Why, everything is just fine," Paige reassured her. In reality, Paige was very worried about Kyle. He had been spending so much time away, she was afraid he was getting in much too deeply.

"I jest wanted to make sho'," Della rattled. "I knows yo' be white folks and it ain't up to me to pry, but I sho' took a likin to both of yo'. I wants yo' to know too, when it comes time fo' dat baby to be born, yo' have Mister Brenner come see Della. I'll be right there to take good care of yo'."

"Why thank you, Della. Who knows, I may take you up on that offer." Paige started down the steps, she turned and waved. "See you later, take care now, you hear."

Even though she had just read bad news about the war, Paige's steps were light and springy as she made her way down the street. She would pause every so often and look in the shop windows. Although the Union's blockade had taken its toll on ready-made merchandise, the shops were heavily loaded with goods smuggled in from the west. She had heard southern sympathizers spirited goods west, then transported them back to the Red River where they were floated down on barges and river boats to the southern held ports. But the prices were unbelievable! Money was getting very hard to come by since the Southern government was printing more and more each day. The only true buying power was with gold. Kyle had been insistent with her, if she bought anything and paid for it with gold, then she must receive her change in gold or else buy enough goods to make up the difference. He had told her also, that when the South fell, the currency wouldn't be worth the paper it was printed on. All these thoughts filled her mind as she gazed into the shop windows. Paige was brought back to reality when she heard a small child's voice call her name.

"Paige! Paige! Is it really you?"

She turned to see who was calling her and received a pleasant surprise. It was Jessie! She was running pell-mell down the boardwalk to her. Paige swooped her up in her arms, hugging and kissing the sweet little girl.

"Oh Jessie! It's so good to see you again." She looked around anxiously. "But where are your brothers and your mama and papa?"

"Somethin' awful happened, Paige," Jessie sobbed, big tears filling her eyes. "Matthew had to bring us to this town to see if'n we can find some work. Oh Paige!" The little girl collapsed into huge racking sobs which shook her shoulders.

"There, there, Jessie," Paige whispered as she smoothed the child's hair from her eyes. "Tell me what happened?"

"Well . . . it was 'bout two weeks ago. We were eatin' supper and . . . and . . ."

"Now, now, quit crying and tell me what happened, sweetie," Paige pleaded, concern filling her.

"We were eatin' supper and mama started turnin' blue and purple. She hollered she was choking and Papa Oscar started whompin' her on the back. But it didn't do no good at all. Then, all quick like, Mama fell on the floor with her eyes staring up at the ceiling."

"Oh my poor darling!" Paige comforted and consoled her. "It must have been horrible!"

Jessie lifted her tearstained face upward, "Oh it were, Paige! It were!" Then she threw her arms around Paige's neck once again.

Paige gently pried Jessie's arms loose. "But . . . where are the boys and Oscar?"

"I don't know where Papa Oscar is. He left 'bout a week ago. He was a-drinkin' somethin' fierce. He tol' us we were nothin' but burdens 'round his neck and he had his fill of us. He jest left us there, Paige, all by ourselves. And we didn't hardly have anythin' to eat. Matthew trapped a rabbit, but then he couldn't find any more, so Matthew said we had best try to come to this here town 'fore we starved to death."

A turbulent rage spread through Paige as she gathered Jessie in her arms. It was hard to hold the child and not let her realize how angry she was by the violent shaking that consumed her by what she had heard. Finally she managed to control her emotions enough to ask again. "But where are the boys, Jessie?"

"They're here. They said fer us to all meet at that store there." She pointed to the mercantile. "They were all gonna try and find work so's we can eat." She looked at Paige so pitifully. "I'm so hungry!"

Paige's heart shattered at the beaten dejected look in Jessie's eyes. It was as though all the troubles in the world were heaped on the little girl's shoulders.

"We'll fix that up real quick!" Paige declared and lifted the child into her arms. "We'll go down and see if we can find the boys then we can go to my house and I'll cook you something nice to eat."

"Really?" The girl smiled broadly, then the smile disappeared as quickly. "I promise we won't eat too much," she said solemnly, her eyes showing far too much wisdom for her tender years.

Paige stopped. "Oh Jessie, I don't care how much you eat. I don't care how much you'll *ever* eat. I only want you to have enough just once in your young life!"

Paige hurried down the street, anxious to find the boys and take them home with her. Her wait was short. One by one, Mark and Luke came straggling back, each looking like old men, beaten and trodden. After hugging and greeting Paige, they stood silently in their vigil, waiting for their eldest brother. No one even suggested they leave without him. To leave would be deserting Matthew. Every moment which passed was a long torturous wait. Paige knew the children were starving. Finally, Luke tugged at Paige's skirt and shouted, "There he is! There he is!"

Paige turned. Matthew was the picture of defeat. His shoulders were slumped and his walk was a slow shuffle. She could tell it was a burden for him to place one foot in front of the other.

Luke hollered, "Hey, Matthew! Look who's here!"

He glanced up and a broad grin broke across his face. Then, Paige could see his bottom lip tremble ever so slightly. He hurried to meet them but stopped short as if he was afraid to say anything.

Mark piped up. "Jessie done al'ready tol' her 'bout what happened to Mama. She done tol' her that we was all hungry, and . . . and Paige is gonna take us all home with her and let us eat!" Mark added proudly.

A flicker of pride flashed through Matthew's eyes. "It sho' is good to see you again." He shyly hugged her neck. "Paige," he said, holding his back straight and haughty, "we'd be mighty beholden to you if'n you had some work fer us to do. Course, we'd be pleased to take our pay in vittles." He forced a smile. "You'll have to excuse these young'uns, they don't have too many manners, begging food from you and all."

It was all Paige could do to hold back her tears. "Oh Matthew, you don't have to work for something to eat. I don't expect any payment either."

"I beg to differ, Paige," Matthew said, his back stiffening visibly. "We're poor and times are bad. So you must be having a hard time too. Ain't no way we can come in on you and eat up your food. All we have in the world is that beat up old shack

239

and a little pride. I'm pert-near a man now, and I sho' don't intend on startin' out by accepting charity."

It took an effort of sheer will for Paige not to cry. Instead, she managed a smile. "No one said a thing about charity, Matthew. You don't offer that to people you love." She pursed her lips. "Let's make a deal with each other. I've got a cupboard filled with food, and you and the boys have a strong back. Come on to my house and after we eat, there is a pile of wood out back that needs chopping badly, and I'm almost out of wood for my cookstove. I believe that will be a fair exchange."

Matthew nodded his agreement. Without any urging, the children picked up their small bundles of clothes and followed close behind Paige.

When they reached the house, Paige ushered them inside and instructed them where they could wash up while she stoked the fire in the cookstove. Then, she turned to the kitchen safe and removed some ham and eggs. She breathed a sigh of relief that she had baked bread the previous day and had three fresh loaves on the counter. She began slicing the ham into thick pieces, and placed them in a cast iron skillet to fry. She happened to turn around and what she saw made her heart break. After Jessie had washed, she came back into the kitchen and stopped in front of the table. She was staring at a bowl full of apples. Paige watched as she leaned forward and sniffed. "What is these things, Paige? I ain't never smelled anything this good before!"

Paige put down the knife she had been slicing

the ham with and said, "Why, those are apples. Perhaps you children would like to whet your appetites with one before the meal is ready?"

Jessie's eyes lit up. "Yes, ma'am. I sure would like to have one. 'Cause if they taste as good as they smell, then, mmmummm."

"Go ahead and help yourself, but eat it slowly so it won't spoil your dinner." She knew as hungry as the children were, the words she had spoken were useless. Nothing could probably fill them up, at least for a long time. She stole sly glances from the corner of her eye to watch the expressions of delight from their faces as each one of them bit into the delicious fruit. As she started to break the eggs into a bowl, Matthew spoke.

"I know settin' the table is women's work, but I would sure be obliged to help if'n you would show me where the things are."

"Why, thank you, Matthew. The plates are up there on that shelf, and if you want some fresh milk, the glasses are beside them. I believe there is plenty of milk in the crock-jar. One thing about it," she rattled, hoping the constant chatter would make the children feel more welcome, "an old crock sure keeps the milk good and cold, especially since the weather isn't too warm yet."

With a speed unknown to her, she had the meal finished and placed on the table. The children didn't need any urging to dig in and help themselves. Before any of the children took a bite, Matthew bowed his head and the others followed suit.

"Dear Almighty: We sure thank you for sending

Paige to find us. I ask you to watch over Mama and take good care of her too, 'cause she couldn't help the way she was. And we also ask that you take pity on Oscar, wherever he is, I guess he can't help how he is either. Lord, we sure thank you for moving your hand and helping to provide this meal . . ." He was interrupted by Luke.

"Matthew, would you *please* hurry?"

"You hush up, Luke, I'm giving thanks to the Lord," Matthew said, shooting his younger brother a burning look. "And, Lord, we ask that you forgive us of all our sins . . . Amen."

Paige stood back, a grin tugging at her lips over the way the children had prayed so devoutly even though they were half starved. She was watching the children so closely, she failed to hear Kyle come in.

"Well, I guess we have guests for dinner?"

"Oh Kyle, you startled me!" Paige said, her hand flying to her chest. "I certainly didn't hear you come in. Are you hungry?"

"No, I only came back to change boots." He indicated that one had lost a heel. "If you're not busy tomorrow, could you take them to the shop and have them repaired?" He glanced curiously at the children, who had stopped eating, and were watching him almost fearfully. The last time they had seen this man, he had been tied in the back of Oscar's wagon.

Paige beckoned Kyle with her hand. "Children, I think you all remember Kyle Brenner. He is my husband now." She motioned with her head for him to join her in the other room. "You children go ahead and eat. I want to talk to Kyle alone." She called back over her shoulder, "Just call if you need anything."

Paige led Kyle into the parlor. "It's horrible! Simply horrible! Oscar ought to be horsewhipped! Those poor children are about starved to death. There is no telling when they have eaten last!" She quickly explained what had happened to Sadie and how Oscar had deserted them. "Kyle . . ." she looked up at him with pleading eyes, "please don't be angry that I brought them home with me. I simply could not leave them on the street. In fact," she added almost defiantly, "that thought didn't even cross my mind." She was so upset over the condition the children were in, and afraid Kyle would turn them away, large tears filled her eyes and her lower lip trembled.

When he wrapped his arms around her, she started crying. "There, there," Kyle soothed awkwardly. "I don't blame you a bit for bringing them home with you. It was the only thing you could have done." Kyle's lips settled into a hard line. "I only wish I could find that low-down . . ." He quit saying anything. If he had any doubts about what kind of a man Oscar was, they were promptly dismissed as he thought about how terribly those children had been treated.

"What are we going to do?" Paige asked, sobs breaking her voice.

"I don't guess there is anything left to do, except make room for them somehow," he answered.

"But Kyle—I feel as though I am already a burden on you. Besides, heaven only knows you have no legal or moral obligation toward them."

"What's the matter?" Kyle's face darkened. "Don't you want them to stay?"

"Of course I want them to stay! They are very dear to me. But, what I am trying to say is . . . well, for one thing, times are so hard right now. Can you afford to take on four more mouths to feed?"

Kyle placed his hand under Paige's chin, urging her to meet his gaze. "Now, Frenchie," he said tenderly. "I think you should leave that kind of worry to me. We can *try* to keep them with us, and if it doesn't work out, then we can find them a good home."

Paige could not believe what she had heard. Kyle sounded as if they were a normal couple living under normal conditions. She had serious doubts if the marriage would last from one day to the next, and Kyle was standing here talking about taking on a ready-made family. Her thoughts turned to the tiny life beneath her breasts, and suddenly she had a great amount of hope. Finally, she muttered, "I believe what you said has hidden meanings."

Kyle shrugged his shoulders. "I think it is entirely up to you." His eyes burned into hers with a smoldering glow.

Paige could not bring herself to speculate further on Kyle's double meanings. She ducked her head and started to turn away, but an unrelenting force made her look back up at him. Without giving any consideration to Kyle's reaction, Paige stood on her tip-toe and kissed him tenderly on the lips. Kyle was startled, blood raced through his veins, his arms started to tighten around her waist, his lips dropped close to hers in an answer, when they were interrupted by a soft but masculine voice.

"Mr. Brenner?"

Holding back a groan, Kyle turned to see Matthew standing in the doorway. Of all the times for the boy to come in, Kyle thought, as he tried to smile.

Sensing Matthew wanting to talk with Kyle, Paige said quickly. "I don't believe you two have been properly introduced as two gentlemen should. Matthew DuPree, this is my husband, Kyle Brenner."

"Not meaning no disrespect, Paige," Matthew said nervously, "but we would all rather be called by our real papa's name. It was Owens."

"Why, sure, Matthew. I understand," she said thoughtfully. "Now, if you two will excuse me, I'll see if I'm needed in the kitchen." She disappeared discreetly, leaving Matthew alone to talk with Kyle.

Kyle knew the boy felt ill at ease. He suggested they walk outside where they could talk without being interrupted. When they reached the front steps, they sat down.

Matthew started hesitantly. "Mr. Brenner . . . I sho' want you to know . . . just how much I appreciate . . . ." his voice broke.

"It's perfectly all right, Matthew. Paige has told me how kind you and the others were to her while she was living with you. I want you to know how much I appreciate that." Kyle paused for a moment, giving the boy a chance to speak, and get through what was on his mind.

"Mr. Brenner," Matthew blurted, "we ain't never accepted no charity in our lives and it's sure hard to start now. If'n you could tell me where I could possibly find some work, I'd be much obliged. I am gonna tell you straight out that I need a job to make enough money to buy staples with, things like flour, salt, and stuff like that. Also some good seeds. I figure we can go back home and plant us a crop that will carry us through next winter. By that time, I will be man enough to support us better."

Kyle fingered his chin thoughtfully. "Well, Matthew, I don't know what to tell you. I can't think of anybody needing any help now. Times are too hard, and with the war coming to an end, things are going to be much tighter. But, I will say this, you and your family are welcome to stay here with me and Paige until you can find something."

The boy's eyes visibly watered. "Well, Mr. Brenner . . ."

"Please, call me Kyle. Mr. Brenner sounds entirely too formal."

Matthew tried to smile, but he was too deeply troubled to be in a joval mood. "Okay . . . Kyle. I want to thank you for your kind offer, but I'd really feel we were imposing on you and Paige. I know people who have just gotten married kind of likes to be alone. Besides, like I said, I ain't a-hankering to take no charity."

"Now just a minute," Kyle said sternly. "Pride is an awful good thing to have, but sometimes too much of it is worse than none at all."

"That's right too, Sir, but . . ."

"Suppose we go back in the house where the children are. They are sitting there, half starved and not knowing where their next meal is coming from. I offered the hospitality of my home to you because of Paige's feelings. So, I wouldn't call that charity, I would simply call it love! So, do we sit out here and talk like men or do you go tell the children they will have to go to bed tonight with hungry bellies?"

Matthew hung his head and mumbled. "I guess we ought to talk this out." Big tears filled his eyes, as he looked up at Kyle. "I guess I am too prideful. So on behalf of me and my family, we will accept your help . . . and your love. You know what, Mr. . . . er, I mean, Kyle. It wasn't always this way." His features turned wistful as he recalled the past. "I remember back when my own papa was alive. My ma was real good to us, and we always had plenty to eat. Papa worked real hard and our house was always clean and me and Mark even got to go to school some. But when Luke was still wearing wet pants and Ma was carrying Jessie, our Pa died. Then Oscar came along. I guess Ma felt as though she had no other choice than to marry him. I reckon you know how it went after that?" he said, glancing up at Kyle. "It just seemed like Ma gave up completely."

Kyle shook his head sadly. Pity for the young man tugged at his heart. The lad was so young in years, but in time, he was an old man. Kyle patted him on the shoulder. "It's hard sometimes. But a person can only do what he can do and that's all there is to it." Kyle snapped his fingers, suddenly remembering Seth. "Say! I have an idea. I ran into a fellow who is clearing brush to build a boat landing. Perhaps he could use some help!" Kyle intended to turn Seth's excuse to see and talk to him, around to *his* purposes.

Matthew's eyes lit up. "Reckon so?"

"One thing about it," Kyle replied, "it sure won't hurt to ride out tomorrow and ask."

Impatience filled Matthew's voice. "Can't we ride out there today?"

"Nope. I've got some things to do later this evening and tonight. Before we do anything, though, we need to tell Paige our decision."

They walked inside to meet Paige who had been about to come out and get them. "Men, I need you to help me move some beds around. Matthew, I thought you and Mark could sleep in the quarters out back, and you could move a cot in for Luke. And Jessie can sleep with me."

"Oh no, Paige!" The words rushed out in an over-anxious torrent as he made his statement. "We ain't busting up you and Kyle! If we separate you in order for us to stay here, then we'll go back to the shack tonight."

Kyle flicked a nail over the top of a sulphur match and lit a cheroot. His brown eyes never wavered as he grinned slyly. "We can't have them going back to that shanty. I guess the only thing to do is, bring in the cot, put it in the largest bedroom, and Jessie and Luke can share it. That way, we can sleep together." He chuckled under his breath, knowing there was no way possible Paige could refuse the arrangements.

"But . . . but . . ." Paige tried to protest. "Maybe Jessie will be too scared to sleep by herself."

"No." Kyle fought against a smile. "Luke will be in the same room with her, remember?"

Paige knew any argument would be useless. With a flick of her petticoats, she spun on her heels and hurried out to the small building Matthew and Mark were to share.

Kyle said to Matthew, "I think I'll be able to put off what I was planning to do. I think I'll just stick around here and we can get an early start in the morning."

"That's fine, Kyle," Matthew answered, beaming. "I always wake up real early."

"Whoa now," Kyle laughed. "There is no need in getting up at the crack of dawn." He punched Matthew in the ribs with his elbow. "Let's go and and help Paige with that cot."

That night, after Paige had bathed Jessie and Matthew had taken care of the younger boys, they sat around the table having a light supper. Kyle smiled and nudged Paige and motioned in Jessie's direction. The little girl was almost nodding in her plate.

Matthew laughed. "I guess she's extra tired. It's been a while since we've had a place to get any proper rest. When we were comin' to town, we had to rest any place we could find."

Paige got up from the table and kissed each boy on his head as she passed by. "I imagine you are all tired. As soon as you're through eating, go on to bed and I'll clean up in here. Kyle?" She turned to him, whispering, "Would you please carry Jessie to bed. I'll come in a few minutes and tuck her in."

Kyle wiped his mouth on a napkin, smiled at Paige and said without thinking, "What are you trying to do? Get me in practice for later on?"

Paige blanched at his off-hand remark. "Why did you say that?" she gasped.

Kyle stopped in surprise. "Why, I don't know, I didn't mean anything by it."

Matthew piped up, a grin playing on his face. "I guess he figured it's most natural after two people marry that they have kids. Or at least that's how I always reasoned it."

Paige quickly changed the subject, not wanting any more comments from Kyle.

Before long, the kids were in bed leaving Kyle and Paige alone. She busied herself with the kitchen work, avoiding saying anything to Kyle while he sat watching her with a smile toying at his lips. Suddenly, she said to him in a muted voice, "I wish you would quit staring at me like that! You make me nervous! I feel like a . . . a mouse that is being stalked by a hungry cat."

Kyle walked over to her and drew her into his arms. "Maybe I am a hungry cat. And, I'm ready to go to bed."

Paige ducked her head, wanting to avoid the confrontation she knew was coming. These past few weeks had her heart in a turmoil. What would she do if Kyle tried to make love to her? Would she be able to respond to him? Or would she rebuff him once again? The questions presented themselves as she went to the bedroom to prepare for bed. Kyle followed close on her heels. Thankfully, he blew out the lamp before she began undressing. She settled uneasily on the far side of her bed, rigid with fright.

"You're acting as though you are afraid of me, Paige," Kyle said, deliberately baiting her.

Why! He is actually enjoying my discomfort. But how do I know what he is really feeling? Could he be toying with me as some sort of hateful revenge, or have his feelings changed about me too? After I have expressed myself so plainly, I would simply die if I turned to him now and he rebuffed me. But . . . yet, things have to improve between us. After all, even though he does not know it yet, I am carrying his child! Kyle interrupted her thoughts.

"Since you don't want to answer me, you don't have to lie over there shivering. If you want, you can snuggle up to me and I'll get you warm," he said softly, almost hopefully.

Paige hesitantly slipped closer to Kyle, hating to touch him for fear her body would betray her, yet wanting to feel his nearness so badly she was actually trembling.

She faltered a brief moment, then doubtfully edged still closer to him. He wrapped his arms around her and in a soft voice said, "Now don't you agree this is far more cozy?"

Paige could hardly speak, her heart was fluttering so. "Yes, I . . . I guess it is."

Kyle pulled her tightly to him and held her for many long moments, not even trusting himself to move. The nearness of her voluptuous body was driving him wild! But his determination not to make the first move was greater than his desire for his bride. Much to his dismay, he could feel his manhood grow with desire for her. It was all he could do to keep from crushing her in his arms and making passionate love to her. He knew it would be only a matter of minutes before she could tell the effect she was having on his faltering willpower. Reluctantly, Kyle unwound his arms from around her shoulders and turned over. Although passion choked his voice, he managed to stammer a goodnight without her detecting anything was bothering him.

Paige lay with tears spilling down her flushed face. She lamented to herself; Have I behaved so badly toward Kyle that he can not stand to hold me close? Oh Lord! If only he tried to kiss me, I think I would simply melt in his arms.

Once she started to swallow her pride and turn to Kyle, but the steady rise and fall of his chest stopped her. For hours, she lay tossing and turning; burning with desire for the man who lay beside her. Finally, she managed to drift off into a restless sleep.

The following morning Kyle and Paige were awakened by Jessie crawling into bed with them. "Why, who do we have here?" Kyle asked playfully. "Is this another beautiful woman?"

Jessie looked up at him bashfully. "Please, can I stay here for a little while? I got cold sleeping alone."

Instant love for the little girl touched Kyle's

heart as he pulled her close to him. "You can certainly crawl in with Uncle Kyle if you want to. We'll have to make sure you have more cover tonight though because I'm not going to stand for your getting cold again."

Paige propped up on one arm and watched the two of them very quietly.

Jessie turned her innocent face toward Kyle then to Paige. She broke into a huge grin. "Paige," she said in a sweet voice, "I'm sho' glad you married this nice man. Now I can pretend that you are my mommy and daddy."

Kyle said huskily, his voice choked, "Honey, you don't have to worry about anyone treating you mean again. At least while I'm around. Now, you scat back to your bed while I get up and dressed and a fire built."

"Okay!" Jessie took off running, then stopped suddenly. She looked back thoughtfully and smiled, "I love both of you." Then she scampered back to her own bed.

Paige didn't try to hide the crooked little grin tugging at her lips as she said, "I do believe that tiny little child has extended her little finger, and now you, a grown man, are very firmly coiled around it."

Kyle, very ill-at-ease at being seen in such a compassionate light, tried to smile, but did not succeed. "Well damn-it!" he growled. "That sweet little thing has known nothing but a brutal existence, and . . . if . . . there is anything I can do to give her some happiness, then I will!" he stated firmly.

"Why Kyle," Paige said teasingly, "I'm not arguing with you about keeping them, and I agree with everything you said."

"Am I that easy to see through?" he asked in all sincerity.

"In some things you are. But in others, you are a mystery. Most of the time I have no idea what you are thinking," Paige answered, more boldly than she would have under normal circumstances. But these circumstances were not normal; they possibly would never be normal again.

Kyle stared at her for a long moment. He leaned forward, lips slightly parted, certain that Paige would answer his kiss, when they heard a timid knock on the door.

"Are you up yet, Uncle Kyle?" Jessie called.

He gave Paige an exasperated look then replied, "Don't come in yet. I'm getting up and I'll build a fire." He swung his long legs over the side of the bed and hastily slipped on his clothes. Then he called for Jessie who came bouncing into the room.

Later after breakfast was over, Kyle asked Paige to join him and Matthew when they went to see about a job. She was hesitant to leave the children alone, but Mark assured her he could look after the younger ones. While Kyle went to the stables to rent a buckboard, Paige began tidying up the bedroom. Mark came into the room and told her a man was waiting at the door to talk to her.

I wonder who it could be? Paige thought as she walked to the parlor and on into the entrance hall. Standing there, hat in hand, was Ryan Ledbetter.

"It's nice to see you again, Ryan," Paige said as she extended her hand in a greeting.

Ryan brought her hand up and grazed it with his lips. "No, you are wrong. The pleasure is all mine. I'll have to beg your pardon for disturbing you so early."

"Would you like some coffee?"

"Ahhh! That would be fine." He looked around questioningly, "But hasn't your family increased?"

"Yes it has," Paige said while leading the way to the kitchen. She quickly decided not to go into any details about the children. "They are my niece and nephews. They will be staying with us for a while."

As they sat across the table from each other, Ryan gazed deeply into Paige's eyes. "My dear," Ryan said boldly, "I had to see you. I have to tell you . . . I have become completely captivated by your charms. I have not been able to sleep, eat, or go about my normal activities." He took Paige's hand. "I could not help but notice how strained things are between you and Kyle. I just . . ." he paused, searching for the right words, "want you to know if you have problems that cannot be worked out, please be assured I am here."

Paige's face reddened. "Why! Ryan, please! You are embarrassing me!" She jerked her hand away.

"I didn't mean to do that. It's . . . I've," he stammered, "to be quite truthful, I've never been so taken with a woman in all my life!" he declared.

Paige slammed down her coffee cup. "Ryan! You know I am a married woman! You shouldn't be talking this way."

"I can't help it!" His tone became almost

frantic. "I fell in love with you the first moment I saw you!" He looked relieved the truth was out in the open.

"I think you should leave." Paige stood and walked toward the back door. "And please don't come back unless my husband is here."

Ryan smiled coldly at her. He stood, bowed low and stepped forward. He took her hand and pressed it to his lips; she promptly jerked it away.

For an instant, she saw a flash of fury spring in his eyes, then he quickly regained his composure. "I'm sorry to know you feel this way, my dear." He reached out and touched her cheek. "From the way your devoted husband was captivated by my sister, I can see he has no idea what kind of a treasure he has. As I said before," Ryan placed his hat back on his head, "if you ever need me, do not hesitate to get in touch. I might add, I'm very accustomed to getting what I want, when I want it." He turned on his heel and marched staunchly from the room.

Paige slumped into a chair. She was certainly glad the children had not been in the kitchen to hear Ryan's declaration. Her mind was in a jumble over his visit. She knew Ryan liked her, but never in her wildest dreams had she even thought it went deeper than that! She was glad to push Ryan from her mind as Mark came running into the kitchen.

"Kyle is back and wants to know if you are ready to go."

Paige nervously smoothed her hair back. "Yes, tell him I'll only be a moment." She ran and grabbed her cloak and kissed the children goodbye. "Behave yourselves," she cautioned before she went out the door. "We'll be back in a little while. And don't let anyone in the house while we are gone," she warned.

When Paige climbed into the wagon, Kyle could tell she was upset. When he questioned her as to what was the matter, she simply told him that Ryan had stopped by, but had only stayed a few moments since he was not there. Kyle was not satisfied with her answer.

"Well, I'm sorry I missed him. Maybe next time," he said, giving Paige a chance to comment if she wanted to.

"I hope not!" she snapped.

Kyle looked at her strangely. It was just as he thought. Paige *was* trying to hide something from him. "I thought you were really taken with that man. Did he say something out of the way?" he asked, his temper starting to rise.

"No," Paige denied. "It wasn't anything like that. It's . . . there is something about him. I realize what you meant the other night, Kyle. I don't think he can be trusted."

Kyle's eyes narrowed. He knew from Paige's reaction something had been said, but he decided not to press the issue. Another time would do for that.

They drove through the countryside. The morning was still nippy, yet spring was bursting forth in all its splendor. The trees were starting to bud and early spring flowers were trying to turn their faces toward the sun. Even the birds sounded cheerful.

Paige pushed the unpleasant experience completely from her mind and enjoyed the ride. Matthew was very excited over possibly getting a job. He talked and prattled all the way to the river, then he settled down into a lulled silence.

Even with the episode earlier with Ryan, Paige felt more happiness and contentment than she had in a long time. Although she still felt an anxiety about telling Kyle she was carrying his child, it was no longer the formidable task she expected. It was as though Kyle had gone through a remarkable change. His hands lingered when they accidently touched hers, and he displayed an unrelenting tender gaze when he did not think she was watching. His entire manner was even softer and kinder. Perhaps in a few days, she thought, I'll be able to tell him.

Kyle reined up the horse in front of the small shack and directed Paige's and Matthew's attention to the edge of the river where Seth was standing guard over the underbrush that was burning. He waved them a welcome and came bounding up the hill.

"This is an unexpected surprise. Don't get many visitors out here, and especially didn't expect to see you again," he said, pumping Kyle's hand. He tipped his hat to Paige, apparently impressed with her wholesome beauty. "I reckon this is the little lady you were telling me about, Kyle." A slow grin spread across his rugged features. "You're right," he said matter-of-factly. "She is every bit as pretty as you said she was."

Paige laughed, immediately liking the tall

gangly man standing before them. She extended her hand in friendship.

After introductions were made, Kyle explained, "I found someone to give you a hand out here, that is if you are still needing help," indicating Matthew.

Seth walked over to the boy, gave him the quick once-over and turned back to Kyle and winked. "I don't know, he looks a little scrawny to me. But tell me, what did you have in mind?"

Paige placed her hand on Kyle's arm. "Please let me explain, Mr. Poteet. Matthew has found himself in charge of his two brothers and sister. Their mother recently died and their step-father deserted them. To be perfectly honest with you, he was my uncle." She looked hopefully at him. "To make a long story short, Matthew wants to try to keep his family . . ."

"Wait a minute, Paige," Matthew interrupted. "I sho' don't mean no disrespect. I was taught not to butt in when others were talking, but, if I'm gonna work like a man, then it appears to me I ought to speak for myself." He stood squarely in front of Seth. "Sir, I'm asking for a job. Course what Paige told you is the truth. I don't want our family to split up. I need to work for a spell and earn enough money to buy seeds to farm the land our Ma left us. I may be a bit scrawny, but I'm used to hard work and I'd make you a good hand. And I wouldn't leave you in no bind neither, I'd stay until the work was finished."

Seth rubbed his chin thoughtfully. "Since you've stood up and talked like a man, I figure you can work like one. I guess you can consider yourself hired, that is . . . if we can agree on a price."

Matthew tried to conceal the smile threatening to break across his face. "You seem like a fair man to me. I imagine you can pay me what I'm worth."

Seth and Matthew shook hands; then Seth offered, "Now that everything is settled, would you like to come in and have a cup of coffee?"

Paige glanced at Kyle and shook her head sidewise. "It sounds very nice, but we should be getting back, Kyle. I hate to leave Jessie and the boys by themselves very long."

"Hummm, I guess you are right." Kyle turned to Seth. "I think my wife wants to be getting back to town. I'll bring Matthew and his things back this afternoon and then maybe we can sit a spell and visit."

"That'll be fine with me. The blacksmith from Marshall is bringing me some iron works that I ordered a few weeks back. Do you know him?"

"I don't know. Who is he?" Kyle asked, knowing full well who Seth was referring to.

"A fellow by the name of Blinn Lansing."

Kyle eyed Paige as she watched the two of them questioningly. He realized she was highly suspicious of him and Seth so he shook his head. "No, I don't guess I do. I have heard about him though. He does real good work, or so I've heard." He glanced over to Matthew. "Would you help Paige up in the buckboard and we'll be on our way." Kyle climbed up on the seat, took the reins in his hand and said with a wave, "Adios, see you later."

On the way back to town, Matthew kept a steady

stream of chatter going. It was obvious he was thrilled about his job. But Paige watched Kyle curiously. She could have sworn Kyle and the man he called Seth Poteet had put on a very convincing act for her. She was sure Kyle had known Seth for a long time. The mystery surrounding her husband was deepening. She was positive Seth was in with Kyle on his mission, whatever that was.

Chapter Seventeen

After carrying Paige and Matthew back to town, Kyle explained he had some business to attend to before he could return to Seth's. When the horse and buckboard were returned to the stables, Kyle saddled his own horse and rode off in the opposite direction for a few miles then doubled back on a different route. He wanted to catch Blinn before he made his delivery and started back to Marshall.

When Kyle arrived back at Seth's, a wagon was standing out front. Kyle used restraint just in case the wagon belonged to someone other than Blinn.

His precautionary measures turned out to be unnecessary because the first person he saw when the door flew open was his old friend and compadre, Blinn Lansing. After greetings were exchanged, and a few good natured remarks about Kyle's marriage, they settled down to serious business.

"How are things going for you two?" Blinn asked, a worry line creasing his brow. "From what I've heard over in Marshall, there are going to be a lot more Confederate troops in this area. Seems as though they are worried that federal men infiltrated the area and are going to try to sabotage the cattle yards again. This could possibly mean the men doing the double dealing have power or at least contacts in the army."

"Well hell!" Seth swore under his breath. "That's all we need now!"

"Now settle down," Kyle said with a show of calmness. "I think we can still handle everything." He peered at both men, "That is, as long as we're not under suspicion."

Both men shook their heads no, mumbling they didn't think they were.

"I don't see where we have any problems then, that is . . . as long as we are careful," he repeated, walking over to get a drink of water from a half-filled pitcher on the water stand. "Have y'all heard how bad it's going for the south?"

Blinn spoke. "Yeah, that's why I find it curious that all those soldiers are coming here when they are needed so much in other places."

Kyle glanced at Seth. "That's because someone has been turning their cattle loose, and it's hard for hungry men to fight." Kyle spoke to Blinn. "Have you heard anything about someone buying up a lot of property down there at Marshall for back taxes?"

"Yeah I have. It's beginning to worry me."

"The same thing has been going on here. Me and Seth have been keeping an ear open as to who these people are but so far we haven't had any luck. I've got a good idea who the man is, but I have no proof."

Blinn nodded, his eyes closed slightly as he thought. "So . . . that's how they are doing it," he said slowly.

"What do you mean?" Seth asked.

"The land scheme operation must be tied in with the payroll robberies. They are using the money to buy the land."

Seth snapped his fingers. "So that's how they are financing it!"

"Yes," Kyle said. "It appears so. But there is one other thing. We should be on guard extra carefully since there is a rumor about federal men in the area. If any of us gets caught, they'll be sure to try to pin the robberies on us . . . and that would be a hangman's noose for sure."

The men sat and talked for an hour or more on what course of action they could take, and made plans to disrupt the land buying scheme as much as possible. The conversation swung around to money. Blinn and Seth said they both had plenty, while Kyle mentioned he was running a little short, but a few good nights at the poker tables would take care of that.

Seth elbowed Blinn, grinning from ear to ear. "Yeah, and he needs more money. Not only has this rascal settled down with a wife, he also has a whole passel of young'uns."

"The hell you say!" Blinn widened his eyes in exaggerated surprise.

Kyle laughed it off, knowing he had teasing coming. It was he who was the skirt chaser, and it was he who had declared time after time that no woman would pin him down to a wedding ring. Of course, neither man knew the actual truth. He let them carry on for a while, then in a bored voiced, he asked Seth: "If you can hush up for a minute, I'd like to ask a favor. Could you pick up Matthew this afternoon? I think it would be a good idea for me to stop by McGarrity's saloon and check on a fellow."

"Is this the man you suspect?" Seth asked, suddenly serious. "Who is he?"

"His name is Ryan Ledbetter."

Seth nodded. "I've heard about him. He is a mean-son-of-a-bitch, and about as ruthless as they come."

"Then our opinions of him match," Kyle said grinning. He picked up his hat and started to leave when he asked abruptly, "Could you do another favor for me?"

"Sure, go ahead, shoot."

Kyle looked sheepish. "There is an old dog that has sort of adopted me. He has been staying at the stables, but that is no place for him. He needs a place to romp and chase rabbits and tree squirrels."

Seth winked and grinned broadly at Blinn. "Talk about getting domesticated! Ol' Kyle has a wife, family, and now a dog! Wouldn't surprise me a bit to walk in at night and find an apron tied around his middle." Seth looked up at Kyle to see an expression in his eyes that told him he was on the verge of carrying a good joke too far. Seth quickly said, "I don't mind. Bring him on out here."

"All right. Think I'll ride into town now and get him. If I don't do it today, I'll be too tied up later on to do it." He grasped Blinn's hand. "You take care." Then he looked at Seth. "You both take care. We are dealing with some mighty dangerous people!"

Chapter Eighteen

Kyle was riding easy, not hurried nor rushed after delivering the dog back at Seth's. His thoughts were occupied with everything that occurred over the past few months. If his sense of duty had not been so strong, he would have turned his horse and ridden off in the opposite direction as fast as Satchel could run. There was a dread hanging over him, a feeling of impending doom. Try as he may, he could not shake it. He didn't know if it was worry about his mission, or his personal relationship with Paige. One way or the other, the hair on the back of his neck was crawling, and it never felt that way unless something was about to happen.

As he rounded the next bend in the road, he recognized Rosalyn Ledbetter examining her buggy wheel by the side of the road. He pulled up Satchel, swung his leg over the saddle and remarked, "Looks like you have a problem."

"Kyle!" she smiled. "This is a pleasant and welcome surprise. You are most definitely a knight in shining armor." She kicked the broken wagon wheel impatiently. "This horrible thing broke down, leaving me hopelessly stranded, that is," she added coyly, "until you came along."

Kyle knelt down and looked the wagon wheel over carefully. "I don't think I'll be able to fix it." He scratched his head, thinking it over. "About the only thing I can do is unhitch your horse, take you on into town and send a blacksmith back after your rig."

"But . . . couldn't you hitch your horse to my rig?" she asked, fluttering her eyelashes in a flirting manner.

"No," Kyle laughed. "Satchel has never been broke to a harness. Tried it once and he bucked and pitched until he had the whole wagon destroyed before I could get him loose." He looked at her oddly. "What are you doing out here all by yourself? Don't you know there have been a lot of robberies going on and it could be dangerous for a lady all alone."

Rosalyn agreed. "Yes. Perhaps I acted a bit impetuously, but I'll be leaving in a few weeks and I wanted to take a drive in the country and have a picnic before I left. I simply love picnics," she added.

Kyle mused, "I didn't know you were leaving."

"Yes, I am. And before you say anything, I'll tell you the way I did Ryan. After all, he did introduce me to John. I have met a man. Even if he is a northerner, and even if he is twenty-five years older than I am, I still want to marry him. There are absolutely no eligible men around here." She blinked her eyes and pouted. "After all, you are already married."

Kyle disregarded her last statement. "I can't blame you for wanting to get married and settle down. But what has his being a northerner got to do with it? After all, if you love the man . . ."

"John is simply infatuated with me. Of course, I would have preferred a much younger man, but I guess a girl can't have everything she wants." She pointed over to a grove of cypress trees which grew profusely in the area. "Look, isn't that beautiful? I know!" she exclaimed happily. "Since I have more than enough to eat, why don't you join me? We can always send for the blacksmith later."

"Oh, I don't know," Kyle debated. "I really should be getting back to town. I have some business there."

"Oh come on," she said, dragging him by the arm. "You can take care of business later. You don't always find such a beautiful spot or a beautiful day."

Kyle looked at the place she indicated. It was beautiful. Early spring grass covered the ground, blue-bonnets and wild daisies were trying to bloom. The spanish moss which trailed delicately from the cypress branches caught the false spring sun, making it shimmer and glitter in the sunlight.

Kyle started to refuse Rosalyn's offer, but the temptation was too great. He lifted the picnic basket from the back of her buggy and in a matter of moments, the blanket and food were spread on the ground.

After they had eaten, Kyle propped against one

of the large cypress knees that extended a few feet out of the ground. "That sure was good, Rosalyn." Kyle patted his stomach. "Only I ate too much!"

She edged closer to him, nestling against his shoulder. "I'm glad you appreciated my cooking. I wanted to tell you the other night that someone else can cook well too! But I thought it might sound too childish." Rosalyn had no intention of telling Kyle that her maid had prepared the meal they had just eaten.

Kyle groaned as he held his stomach. "No one could ever accuse you of not knowing your way around the kitchen."

Rosalyn chuckled and placed her dainty hand on Kyle's face. "I could probably surprise you by showing you I know how to do a lot of things," she said boldly, as she brought Kyle's lips down to meet hers.

The kiss seemed to last an eternity as it scorched and demanded more and more. Finally, it was Kyle who pulled away from the passionate embrace. His eyes locked with Rosalyn's as he stared in disbelief.

"I've been wanting a *real* kiss from you ever since the other night," she said shamelessly.

Kyle grasped both her arms and tried to unwind them from his neck. Then his control left him as he sought her lips like a thirsty man seeking heady wine. He could feel himself growing with desire for the woman in his arms. Entwining his massive hands in her long fragrant hair, he lowered her to the thick carpet of grass and showered her lips with kisses. Rosalyn was moaning with passion when Kyle suddenly pulled away, leaving them both gasping for breath.

"I can't Rosalyn. No matter how much I want to, I can't. I am a married man and I will not cheat on my wife. I can't make my wedding vows a lie!"

She slitted her eyes at him and cried angrily, "Kyle Brenner! I hate you! You're not even a man! No wonder your sweet, precious Paige has eyes for Ryan!"

"No, she doesn't, Rosalyn," Kyle said softly. "She may be flattered by him, but she isn't and hasn't been untrue to me." Kyle pulled completely from her arms, stood and dusted off his trousers.

"Go on to her, you . . . you spineless bastard!" she spat. "I hope she gets fat and has fifteen kids for you to feed!" she shouted after him as he climbed on his horse.

Kyle tipped his hat and laughed at her. "I'll send someone back for you. Perhaps you can persuade him to quench your desires!"

As Kyle rode back to town he felt like kicking himself. It had been a long time since he had had a woman, a woman to fill the need every man has. Rosalyn had freely offered herself to him, and like a fool he had refused the tempting wares. Now, his loins were aching deep inside for a woman. But the woman he ached for was his wife, Paige! That startling revelation was a surprise to him. He knew he had come within a breath to making love to Rosalyn. But, now that his head was clearer, he knew he would have regretted it. Although he and Paige had not consummated their wedding vows, he had known her. And to make love to another woman now, would be the same as adultery.

He figured his strong sense of loyalty went back to his father's teachings. He well remembered a talk he had had with him long ago.

"Son," his pa said, "you can do what you want. But I want to tell you straight off, I was an ornery cuss back when I was getting my raising. I say this, not bragging, but I had my pick of the girls and I rarely disappointed them. Now, I'm speaking about the loose girls, not the ones who went to Sunday school every week. But when I married your mother, I put all that behind me. For one thing, I quit having the urge for other women, when I stood before the preacher and promised God I would cleave only to your mother. I never went back on my word. And, son, sometimes all a man has is his word. If it ain't no good . . . then perhaps the man ain't worth too much."

Those words burned through Kyle's mind as if the old man were riding beside him speaking them. Kyle nodded to himself and thought. I hope I lived up to his expectations. But I know one thing. I've made up my mind. I know now how much I love my wife. We are just going to have to clear the air between us. The way we've been living has not been natural. If she wants to be my wife in *all* respects, I'll cherish her until the day I die!

Kyle looked around feeling foolish. He realized he had been speaking aloud. But he meant what he had said. He loved her and she would have to accept him as her husband, or else they would have to forget this preposterous existence. He knew he could not live another day with this unnatural life!

When Kyle reached the outskirts of Jefferson, he had to wait in line to pass on the toll bridge leading into the bustling city. Jefferson reminded him of the busy seaport city of New Orleans. It wasn't as fancy, but if things continued, it wouldn't be long before Jefferson would be second to none.

Kyle stopped at the stables and told them about a woman's carriage breaking down and instructed them where to find her. For an instant he wavered. He felt an overpowering urge to go home and confront Paige, but he knew Ryan would be getting to the saloon soon. Against his better judgment, he turned Satchel toward McGarrity's boisterous saloon.

Chapter Nineteen

It was not surprising that only a few men were in the saloon when Kyle entered and bellied up to the bar. He ordered a beer, and commented to Zeke the bartender about business being slow.

"Yeah, but it'll be picking up as soon as those troopers get here."

Kyle nodded his agreement, then looked questioningly toward the back room.

"Yep. There's a game going on in the back room," Zeke said, as he polished the already clean glass he was holding.

"Reckon there would be room for me?"

"Now you know better than that, Mr. Brenner," he chided. "If the table is full, then I would imagine they'll make room for you. They all like to play with you, even though you usually walk away a winner, 'cause you ain't no hot head."

Kyle picked up his beer mug and started toward the back room, stopping for a moment to speak to one of the girls who entertained the men nightly.

"What are you doing here so early, handsome? Decide to come and sample some of my wares?"

She fluttered her heavily made-up eyes at him. "Or would you like to have your back rubbed?"

Kyle laughed and swatted her on her well rounded bottom. "Honey, it's for sure if I needed my back rubbed, I'd certainly know where to come."

Norma chuckled a bawdy laugh. "Anytime, honey, anytime."

Kyle placed a coin in her hand and said, "Be sweet and bring me something to drink in about an hour." The woman promptly dropped Kyle's generosity down the front of her dress.

Kyle knocked on the door and was admitted into the back room. He pulled up a chair and was dealt in. Kyle started winning a few and losing a few, and after a while he started pulling pots on a regular basis. He stayed ahead enough to enable him to play for the bigger stakes that would be available later that night. Finally, Ryan came in and took a seat beside him. As usual, he had a large bankroll.

"Damn!" a man called Rylie exclaimed. "What bank did you rob? I ain't never seen that much money at one time in all my life!"

"My man," Ryan boasted, "I just sold off a lot of cattle. I figured the way things are going, I'd sooner sell them for a cheap price than to have them confiscated by them damn Yankees!"

Kyle tried to appear as objective as he could by saying lightly, "From the size of your roll, it looks like you might have stumbled onto that buried silver I've been hearing about."

"Nope! But I sure would like to find it. In fact,

I've been looking for it some in my spare time."

Rylie asked, "What in the hell are you talking about?"

"You tell him, Ryan," Kyle said as he dealt the cards. "You probably know a lot more about the legend than I do."

Ryan cleared his throat and began the tale that caused men's hearts to race, their imaginations to run wild, and their dreams to soar to new-found heights.

"In the early spring of 1816, King Ferdinand the VII, of Spain sent a ship called the *Santa Rosa* down to Mexico and back to the Texas coast close to Galveston. It was run afoul by corsair Jean Lafitte in the Matagorda Bay. I might add, Jean Lafitte is the same who fought with Andy Jackson during the battle of New Orleans on January 8, 1815. There were two more men who played a part in this treasure legend. One was known by the name of Thomas Beale and the other's name was Gaspar 'Hot Horse' Trammel. Now, anyone who knows anything about local history will know that old Gaspar blazed a trail up from Galveston all the way to St. Louis, and in fact, that trail is still known by his name which we call it Trammel's Trace. I might also add, old Gaspar got his nickname, Hot Horse, honestly." That statement received many chuckles from around the table.

Ryan continued with the story. "To try to link all of this together, I have to go back and pick up the story with the ship, the *Santa Rosa*, that Jean Lafitte and his men plundered. Now," Ryan said doubtfully, "whether they got three million in gold, silver, and precious jewels, is only hearsay. But legend has it that it took six loads of wagons to carry away all that bounty. I've heard tell Gasper Trammel was the best damn freight hauler there ever was, and apparently so, because Lafitte gave him the job of transporting that treasure. They brought it up Trammel's Trace." Ryan took a sip of his drink and went on with the story. "The men got as far as, some folks say, Hendrick's Lake, while others say they camped on the Sabine River during a heavy rain and *thought* it was a lake. Anyway, Gaspar had sent out some scouts to make sure they weren't being followed. His men came riding back to camp hot and heavy. It seems that a whole Mexican cavalry unit was coming up on them pretty fast." Ryan paused for effect, clearly enjoying all the attention he was getting. "That meant two hundred soldiers on their tail. Legend has it that Gasper had the men pull the wagons up on top of a hill, unhitch them, and push them down the hill and into the lake. By the time the soldiers arrived, the treasure had settled safely on the bottom. Then, all hell broke loose and only a few men survived."

Ryan looked at all the men closely. "I realize that some of this story is simply rumor and legend. But it is a documented fact that Mexican soldiers searched this area for over five years for treasure that came off the *Santa Rosa*. Some folks say that this Beale fellow came back when it was safe and raised several of the wagons and recovered some of the loot. But the rest is still supposed to be under water."

Ryan sat for a moment, then gestured with his hands. "Now this part is pure speculation. The fact is, around Hendrick's Lake, there aren't any hills tall enough that would enable wagons to be pushed off them . . . and anything in the water to be completely concealed. I know personally of people staying at the remains of the old Tatum plantation and searching the entire area. Then too, it's been speculated on that the Sabine River gets out of its banks quite often, and the shore line could have changed over the years, and it could be there." Ryan looked at the men carefully. "Do you want to know what I actually think?"

Kyle asked slowly, "No, what, Ryan."

"I think Trammel's men were camped on the river, and they probably dumped the wagons off onto a sandy shoal and they sunk deep in the mud." Ryan leaned back in his chair, his eyes half closed. "As I said before, the Sabine is notorious for getting out of its banks. I think that treasure is probably setting somewhere in the riverbottom under a few feet of plain old dirt . . . dirt that use to be under water fifty years ago."

The room was extremely quiet as each man sat and speculated about the untold wealth and all the wonders it could bring, all the pleasures it could buy, and even all the heartache it could cause.

Finally, the silence was broken by Rylie as he said in a sarcastic manner, "Aww, bull! I think all of you are touched in the head to believe in that crap! Did you come here to play cards or to sit around the table like a limp peckered old man who has nothing better to do than talk about that lost pirate's treasure?'' As he looked around the table, the men broke out in laughter, each a little embarrassed at being caught up in an old wive's tale.

Kyle cleared his throat and coughed. "You know men, he's right. Come on, let's play cards.''

The afternoon passed into night. Some men went broke and some grew too tired to play any more. There was a steady stream of men to take their places when one fell out of the game. By night, the entire table had changed except for Kyle and Ryan.

Kyle leaned wearily back into his chair and said, "It looks as though I'm about four hundred ahead. If you gents don't mind, after a few more hands, think I'll call it quits for the night.'' He had found out all he needed to know when Ryan had come in with a huge sum of money.

At that moment, Kyle heard a voice over his shoulder that made his hair stand on end. A voice he swore he would never forget.

"Don't reckon you gents would care if I were to sit in fer a spell, would you?''

It was Oscar DuPree! Kyle leaned forward and edged his gun out of its holster without anyone noticing. He nodded in Ryan's direction, and sniffed. "The air suddenly stinks in here. Looks like a pole cat is trying to join us.''

Oscar had just started to sit down. Then it was as if he stopped in mid-air: he had recognized Kyle. "Well I'll jest be damned!'' he said, slumping in the chair. "If it ain't the man who spirited my own blood niece away!''

The men in the room realized there was bad

blood between Kyle and the man who had suddenly appeared. They watched in silence, waiting for Kyle to make the next move.

Oscar mistook Kyle's silence for fear and grew much braver. "What's the matter? Didn'tja like being trotted off to the preacher's 'cause I caught you and my niece out in the barn?"

Kyle did nothing but stare coldly at him.

Oscar grew much bolder in his accusations. "By the way, soldier, where in the hell is all them men you said you had, now?"

At those words, Ryan jerked his head sidewise to Kyle, wondering what Oscar meant. Kyle knew he had to say something clever and fast!

"Why you mangy son-of-a-bitch! I really didn't think you were so stupid as to believe that cock-and-bull story I fed you . . . and me without a uniform!" Kyle shamed him. "If I hadn't said I was a soldier and had some men camped near by, I'd be face down with a bullet hole in my back right now. As for me spiriting away your niece . . . my wife has already told me how you tried to . . . let's say you didn't act like a gentleman around her." Kyle clicked his tongue against the roof of his mouth. "And you are her own uncle!"

Oscar started to look nervous. "But . . . I caught you in the barn with her."

"Sure you did. I'll be the first one to admit it. But you are neglecting to tell about the welts on her back. Welts you and your wife put there! She was trying to run away from you and I caught her. I was going to take her back in the house and make her face up to running away when she told me the truth about you and showed me the welts. That's when you came in. And naturally your mind took off in the only direction it knew where to go." He laughed sardonically. "I'm glad you marched us to the preacher. Because she is one hell of a woman!" He glared at Oscar who was now quivering with fear. "Oh, I might add, those kids you left to starve after your wife died are safe and sound. They are at my home, and for a change they have food in their bellies. And that's where they will stay!" Kyle growled.

Oscar wet his lips which had suddenly gone very dry. "If you gents don't want me to sit down with you, why didn't you say so in the first place?" He picked up the money he had placed on the table. "I think I'll leave and try to find a friendlier place," he muttered, and started to rise.

"Oh, no you're not!" Kyle said coldly. "You are not going anywhere." He placed his revolver on the table. "You came in here to play poker . . . so I think you and I will deal a few hands. Ryan," he said, looking briefly in his direction, "would you mind dealing the cards?"

"Hell no! I don't mind a bit. Don't particularly care to deal to a man who would desert little kids, but I think I'll make an exception in this case." Ryan started passing the cards to the two men. Oscar clearly understood the meaning of Kyle's gun pointing at him and called every hand and every card dealt whether he had a call coming or not. It wasn't long until he was broke.

"I'm wiped out. I have to leave now, don't even have the money to buy a beer." Oscar stood and shuffled toward the door. Then in a rush of anger he turned and shouted, "I guess y'all know that this is the same as highway robbery!"

Kyle sat there for a moment as the men watched what he was going to do. He moved slowly and easily. "Oscar, I can overlook the fact you came in here and bad-mouthed me in front of my friends. I was even going to overlook how you mistreated my wife when she was in your care . . . and I guess I was going to do the same about your deserting those children. But I damn sure ain't going to stand for you to call me a thief! Unbuckle your gunbelt, now!" he shouted angrily.

"No! No!" Oscar whined. "If I take off my gun holster, you'll shoot me down!"

"No, I wouldn't do that," Kyle said and started unfastening his holster. "In fact, I'm going to give you a better chance than your kind would give me. We are going to have a fair fight. But you had better be prepared, because I intend on whipping the hell out of you!"

When Kyle dropped his gunbelt, Oscar saw the opening he needed. He picked up a chair and cracked it across Kyle's shoulder, temporarily stunning him. Ryan started for Oscar but Kyle shook his head. "No, this fight is between us."

Oscar backed into the corner. One of the men had walked over and stood in front of the door, barring his way. Fear was written on his face. He knew Kyle was going to beat him to within an inch of his life. Being a coward, Oscar fell to his knees and pleaded, "No, no! Please don't hit me!"

Kyle grabbed him up by the front of his shirt and

shook him. "You sniffling bastard! Come on and fight like a man!"

"No! I can't fight you!" Oscar whimpered.

Kyle looked at him in disgust and shoved him to the floor. "I can't hit a coward," he snarled. He grabbed Oscar again. "All right you sorry . . . I will say this only once so listen good. Get out of here and if I ever see you again, I won't show any mercy!"

Oscar fell to the floor once again. Then as quick as he could possibly move, he had his gear gathered and was running out the door much to the delight of the men who were laughing at him.

Ryan slapped Kyle on his back. "There's nothing I'd like better than to buy you a drink. You certainly got rid of that low-down vermin."

Kyle declined the drink. "Maybe next time," he said. "I think I ought to get on home just in case he decides to pay a visit to Paige and those kids. He is the type to try to cause trouble."

"I know what you mean," Ryan agreed. "Seriously, Kyle, if you have any more trouble with him, let me know, and I'll help you get rid of him once and for all."

"Sure thing, friend!" Kyle said, emphasizing the last word.

After Kyle had left, Ryan motioned for one of his friends to come outside with him. "What in the hell did Oscar mean by coming in here flashing all that money?"

"I don't know, Ryan," the man said.

"Listen, I want you to go find him for me and tell him to meet me down at the old deserted warehouse on the riverfront about midnight. You can tell that son-of-a-bitch, he had better show up. I have a job I want him to do for me. I want him to remove a thorn from my side . . . by having him get rid of a soldier-boy. You can also tell him there will be plenty of money in it for him."

Chapter Twenty

Kyle walked out to the hitching post, mounted Satchel and rode off. He was anxious to get home. It was still fairly early, the sun had set and it was twilight; dark, but not as black as the night would soon become.

He dared to plan ahead. If Paige would accept him as a husband in every sense of the word, perhaps as soon as the war was over, they could go back to the land that was waiting for him . . . to the ranch he and his father had worked and built and poured their dreams into. Just the thought of working the ranch again, feeling a working horse under him and the taste of cattle dust parching his throat, brought back a longing and a sense of anticipation. Somehow, he would convince Paige this could be the life for them. A life they could build together, have babies and raise their sons with a legacy that could be passed on from generation to generation. Kyle spurred Satchel on; he was very anxious to see Paige and hopefully, set things right between them.

Kyle was met at the door by Jessie as soon as he

entered the house.

"Shhh," she said, her finger pressed to her lips. "Paige is mad at you!"

Kyle had to refrain from laughing at the little girl's concern. "What have I done?" he asked in mock seriousness, kneeling down on one knee in front of the child.

"You forgot to fetch Matthew to his job. But a real nice man came by and got him, but Paige is still mad 'cause you never did show up. She's been slammin' pots and pans around somethin' fierce." Her eyes were wide from fright.

"Matthew did leave with a man, though?"

She nodded.

Kyle looked around, and asked in a hushed voice, "Where are the boys?"

"Mark and Luke are out back choppin' some kitchen wood."

Kyle whispered in her ear. "Tell the boys to get the jar of sugar out in the shed, and feed some of it to Satchel. Tell them to be sure and feed him the sugar though, or Satchel will rear up and maybe hurt them. When they have made friends with him, Mark can lead him back to the shed and put him in the stall." He looked at her closely. "Do you understand?"

Jessie nodded, her eyes shining at the idea of doing something for Kyle. "I'll tell 'em, sir. But," her bottom lip quivered, "you didn't notice I had on a new dress."

"I sure did, honey," Kyle said, patting her hand. "In fact, I was thinking to myself if I wasn't already married, and since you look so doggone pretty, I would be tempted to wait for you to grow up so I could marry you myself!"

Jessie smiled brightly, her face turning the color of a fresh spring rose. "Awww, you're just funnin' me."

Kyle tried to look as solemn as possible. "No I'm not. I swear it." He raised his hand.

Ducking her head shyly, Jessie said, "I had better go and do what you asked me to." She looked up at him. "Can I give Satchel a lump of sugar?"

He smoothed her hair. "Of course you can. Only don't give him too much." He watched, amused as Jessie ran out the front door. Kyle looked around to see Paige standing in the hallway, tapping her foot impatiently and her hands were planted firmly on her hips.

"So! That's how you get all the females to swoon around you! You simply turn on your charm and they can't resist you," she snapped peevishly.

Kyle smiled as he stood up. "There is one lady I know who seems to resist my charms very well."

Paige ignored his remark and said bluntly, "Matthew was very disappointed when you didn't come back for him as you promised."

"You don't have to be mad about that. Seth came for him, didn't he?"

"Yes," Paige admitted. "But still, the boy was disappointed. He was scared you wouldn't get back in time and Seth wouldn't go ahead and hire him. He was scared Seth would think he was undependable."

"I'm sorry I disappointed the boy. But everything worked out all right." Kyle shrugged.

Paige changed the subject. "There is some fresh coffee. That is . . . if you can spare the time to drink it!" She spun on her heel and marched into the kitchen. She sarcastically mumbled over her shoulder, "Or do you have to take Rosalyn on another picnic?"

Kyle followed close behind. "If I didn't know better, I'd swear you were jealous."

"Jealous my foot!" she exploded. "What makes you think I would be jealous of a redheaded floozy like her?"

Kyle ignored her question. "How did you know I joined Rosalyn on a picnic?"

Paige slammed a skillet on the stove, she turned, her eyes blazing. "I went down to Austin's Mercantile to buy some dress material for Jessie and she was there! She had to rub it in how you took her up on an invitation to a picnic and spent practically the entire afternoon together." Paige continued her ranting. "And to think, I had lunch fixed here, but do you think my husband had the common courtesy to come home and share lunch with his wife? Heavens no! He'd rather escort that redheaded floozy all over the countryside!"

In spite of Paige's ranting and raving, Kyle was very amused, in fact, he was almost happy because she *was* so angry. That meant she had some feeling for him. He placed his hands on her arms. "Look," he said seriously, "I can explain, that is . . . if you will listen?"

"Well," Paige wavered, "I'll listen, but your

explanation had better be good."

Kyle explained how he had a chance happening, coming upon her with her wagon broken down, and how she had invited him to share her lunch. He told her truthfully about Rosalyn flirting with him but he had spurned her advances. Naturally, he did not tell her how much Rosalyn had flirted.

"I suppose there was nothing else you could have done," Paige said slowly after considering how helpful Kyle's manner actually was. "But . . . I feel that Rosalyn somehow senses the problems we are having and she has set her cap for you."

Kyle pulled Paige closer to him. In a husky voice he said, "Things could be right between us, Paige. All you would have to do is say the word and I'd forget a redheaded woman by the name of Rosalyn ever existed."

For an instant, Paige felt her resistance grow weak. Her lips were but a short distance from him. She could feel his warm breath on her cheek. Then suddenly, the back door slammed and Luke came running in.

"Mr. Brenner! You ought to see that big ol' black horse eat right out of our hands! I ain't seen nothing like it before!"

Kyle slowly released Paige, after giving a deep, disappointed sigh. He had been so close to kissing her . . . and to having her kissing him. He gave Paige a weak grin then followed Luke outside. They stayed until Paige called them back in for a late supper.

*   *   *

The house was very quiet. The children had been asleep for over an hour and there was no danger of their interrupting. Kyle lay in bed, watching as Paige timidly undressed in the corner of the bedroom. Unknowing to her, her shadow cast a reflection onto the wall, revealing a seductive, tempting silhouette. After slipping on her nightgown, she sat at the dressing table and brushed her beautiful long black hair. It was as though the moonbeams cast a bewitching, almost enchanting spell over Kyle, as desire for his lovely wife increased with each minute that passed slowly by. He could feel his loins tightening while his blood pulsated through his veins. At long last, he felt the rustling of the covers as she lay down beside him. It was now or never, Kyle felt. He took a deep breath then asked in a hushed voice, "I'd like to know exactly how you feel about me, Frenchie?"

Paige raised up on one elbow and stared at him in the darkness. "I really don't know what you mean."

Kyle scowled, his features darkened. This was not going as he had planned. "Oh hell!" he swore. "You know damn well what I meant. I'm tired of the silly games. I am serious and I want to know!"

Paige looked at him. Sudden tears gathered and threatened to spill. Then she averted her head to stare at a shaft of moonlight flooding one large spot on the wall. His words had cut into her deeply. Her thoughts had been the same as Kyle had openly voiced.

"You didn't answer my question," he demanded,

pulling her roughly into his arms. Then he looked at her strangely, a glimmer of dread went through him. "Then too, perhaps you are answering my question by remaining silent." His gaze penetrated hers.

Paige turned her face; she was uncomfortable. She tried to struggle free from his grasp, but he would not release her. Suddenly it dawned on her. This was the confrontation she had long awaited. She was a fool for resisting!

"Really, Kyle, I'm not trying to be difficult. I simply did not understand what you meant," she said softly.

Kyle took a deep ragged breath. "I'm tired of the games we have been playing with each other's emotions," he blurted. "I'm tired of this senseless charade we have been putting on for everyone else's benefit."

"*You're* tired of the games!" Paige interrupted. "How on earth do you think I feel? It's like I'm trapped in some . . . sort of a void, a vacuum, a darkness, and not even a glow of light can be seen ahead. Oh, Kyle," she moaned, "all my life I've wanted to be nothing more than a wife and mother. But, that also means I have to have love, both given and received freely . . ." Her voice trailed off as she realized what Kyle had said. Suddenly, it was as though a giant hand reached deep inside her bosom and wrung her heart as tightly as possible. "Wait a moment. You . . . are tired of this arrangement?" She lowered her eyes refusing to even look at the man she loved. "Does this mean you want out of our bargain?" she asked softly.

"You silly ninny! Don't you understand?" Kyle asked wretchedly. He raised up on one elbow and pressed Paige against the pillow. "I know I made a vow to you that I would not seek you out, that I would not touch you, and if you ever wanted more, then you would have to come to me." His gaze bore into her. "I'm breaking my promise to some extent. I refuse to force you into anything, but the choice is yours to make now. I cannot take this living hell of seeing you everyday, sleeping with you each night, and not having you. My darling, I love you very much. But, if you think life with me would be intolerable, I'll get up from here and walk through that door and you'll never have to worry about me again." He paused and looked at her, silently imploring her not to reject him again. "Everything is entirely up to you," he added tenderly.

Paige gazed at Kyle in openmouthed astonishment. Her heart began to race frantically. "You mean you really love me?"

"Yes," Kyle answered simply.

"Oh, Kyle . . . my darling, I love you too!"

Kyle looked at her, his eyes burning into hers like two glowing coals of fire, capturing and returning her gaze of tenderness. The room was completely silent except for the faint ticking of the hall clock and the outside sounds which crept quietly inside. The shadows danced throughout the room as Kyle's lips came closer and closer to Paige's rosebud lips. His hand left a searing trail as it sought the bottom of her chin, lifting it upward to meet his demands. His lips parted as they met hers. Time had no meaning as his mouth leisurely sought and found the treasure of sweet nectar. His hand trailed downwards, finding the pleasurable mounds of her breasts and the valley dipping deftly between them. His lips parted from hers and edged slowly to the path his hand had taken. Cupping one firm, taut breast in his massive hand, he plied the peak with his mouth. First one then the other until it was as though liquid fire threatened to consume them both. With a ragged, bated breath, he managed to say:

"My darling, I do love you. I want and need you so much."

"Oh, Kyle," Paige muttered in a passion-muffled voice. "I want and need you too. Take me! Take me now! Make me completely yours again!"

A moan surfaced from deep in his throat. Only with a strong show of willpower did he restrain from crushing her brutally into his arms and taking her immediately. Instead, he gently took the precious vintage that was now so willingly offered. Their lips met and met again. Each kiss became more searing than the one just past. He curled his arm around one of her shoulders and the other hand strayed to the small of her back, pressing her hips firmly upward to meet his demanding thrusts. Then . . . the winds howled with the mighty force of a killer hurricane, waves crashed upon the beaches, the seas parted and the heavens opened up their arms to accept the two, but for a moment, the earth, time, and all eternity was stilled. Then the turbulent onslaught of a thousand molten volcanoes unleashed their fury . . . as the two came together, blending into God's master plan of oneness.

"If you think you would like to, we can go back to my old home and make a fresh start, just as soon as this war is over," Kyle said.

His words went on and on as Paige nestled snugly in Kyle's arms. One of her legs was wedged firmly between his muscular thighs. Her fingertips toyed with the matted carpet of hair which grew profusely on his chest. His words had no direct meaning, as she was much more interested in being in the arms of the man she loved. All the while, her thoughts were racing. Imagine, all this time we wasted arguing with each other when we could have been so blissfully happy. Thank you, God, for answering my prayers. All this time, you had given me the man of my dreams and I never realized it. I swear to you this night, I'll make it up to him for cheating us out of many happy moments. I swear, I'll follow him to the ends of the earth and back if he so asks. At that moment, Paige felt a slight quickening in her belly. Her hand flew to her stomach as she realized the child she was carrying beneath her heart, moved in agreement. She smiled and envisioned the expression of joy on her beloved's face when she told him about the child she was carrying. Paige took one slender finger and placed it over Kyle's lips, then raised her body over his.

He laughed and said when he felt her naked body against his. "Guess I'm going to have to change your nickname to chubby, if you keep gaining weight."

Paige bit her lips to hold back the chuckle threatening to break loose. She wanted to tell him about the child, but for now, she didn't want to share the moment with anyone. "Would you hush your silly prattlings?" she asked teasingly. "We have all the time in the world to plan our future." She snuggled her arm around Kyle's waist. "At this moment, I want you to take me back in your arms. I want to feel you next to me . . . completely." Her voice settled into a soft, delicate whisper. "I want you to make love to me and make me forget what a fool I've been all this time."

With a groan, Kyle scooped her into his arms, then he chuckled slightly. "I knew I would make a wanton woman out of you if given a chance."

Paige grinned back at him. "Husband, I do believe you are trying to punish me for being so hateful." Then her voice mellowed as the fiery flames of love engulfed her heart. "Oh, Kyle . . . love me . . . love me . . . !"

Chapter Twenty-One

Paige awoke to a still darkened morning. Outside, in the distance, a rooster was crowing for the fast approaching daylight. Although the temptation to snuggle back under the covers was overpowering, she knew the children would be awakening soon and would be demanding to be fed.

Not wanting to wake her sleeping husband, Paige eased out from underneath the covers as quietly as possible and dressed. She would have liked to stay in the bedroom to watch and admire Kyle's sleeping figure, but she knew her unrelenting gaze would disturb his restful sleep. After brushing her hair, she crept silently from the room to start the morning fires. As she entered the hallway, she was startled by furious pounding on the front door.

"What is the meaning of all this noise so early in the morning?" Paige demanded in a harsh whisper as she threw open the front door. Her voice trailed off when she saw the uniform figures of Confederate soldiers. "What . . . what do you want?"

"Sorry to disturb you, ma'am," one of the soldiers snapped., "Is this the home of a . . . a Kyle Brenner?"

Concern gripped Paige's voice. "Yes, yes it is. What do you want with my husband?"

At that time, Kyle padded from the bedroom after hastily donning his pants. "What's going on in here?" he asked, sleep and confusion obviously muddling his mind.

Instantly, four of the soldiers surrounded him, bayonets fixed.

"Is your name Kyle Brenner?" one of the soldiers asked gruffly.

"Yes it is," he answered puzzedly as his eyes swept Paige's fully clothed figure.

"By the order of the Confederate States of America, you are now under arrest!"

Kyle drew back indignantly. "On what charge may I ask?"

One of the soldiers stepped up to Kyle's face. "On what charge, he asks! Huh! Listen to me, you yellow bellied dog, and listen good! You are charged with being a Union spy!" The soldier laughed in Kyle's face. "It'll be our pleasure to take you over to Camp Ford and stand guard over you until you have a fair trial. See, yellow dog, we treat our prisoners fairly, not like you Yankees do." The man walked slowly around Kyle, teasing, and taunting him. "But you won't be a prisoner of war 'cause you're a spy, and they ain't nothing but scum! Yank, I'm sure gonna enjoy hearing them pass judgment on you at your trial. But I'm gonna enjoy it a hell of a lot more when you're hung by your sorry neck until you are good and dead!''

Paige's hand flew to her mouth in a horrified gasp. "Oh no! Please Kyle, don't let them take you!''

As she tried to run into his arms, one of the soldiers grabbed her, but not before Kyle pushed her roughly away.

"Leave me alone, woman!" Kyle shouted. "Isn't it enough I'm being accused of this crime because of you?''

Paige blanched. "No . . . no! What are you saying? It isn't my fault!''

Kyle looked at her coldly. "The hell it wasn't! I wondered why you were fully dressed this morning. You usually slip on a robe. I guess it was too nippy to go outside and get these soldiers in your nightgown." He looked at her with venom in his eyes. "I had no idea you hated me enough to turn me in, especially after last night. I can say one thing, you certainly are a damn good actress!''

"I didn't, Kyle!" Paige sobbed.

"Shut up!" he thundered. "Lies! Lies! I'll not hear them anymore!" he said, covering his ears.

The soldier broke in. "Look, y'all. As much as we are all enjoying this cozy little domestic scene, we've got orders to have you back at the captain's office by a certain time. So, Yankee spy, I would suggest you get your butt on the move!''

Kyle looked him straight in the eye, knowing to fight would be useless. "All right. I'll go with you, but first, let me slip on my boots and shirt.''

The soldier shook his head sideways. "Hell no! I ain't gonna let you get dressed. My brother froze to death in a Yankee prison, so I damn sure ain't gonna pay you no favors."

Kyle stared at him.

Paige touched the soldier's arm. "Please, let him slip on some clothes. This February morning air is too cold for a man to go outside undressed," she pleaded.

The soldier who seemed to be in charge, spoke to Paige coldly. "Ma'am, and I use my ma's good teachings by calling you that, I think it would be best if you were to stand aside. I don't cotton much to a woman who would turn in her own husband," he said, taking Kyle's accusations as the truth. "And I even cotton less to a woman who would turn against her own kind by even sleeping in the same bed with a low-down-yellow-bellied-Yankee spy! So, I'll say this one more time and one time only, kindly remove your hand from my arm and step aside."

Paige's hand fell limply down to her side. Her face paled as her world crashed into heaps around her. She called out to Kyle as they put wrist manacles on him. "I'll do something! I'll get a lawyer," she cried frantically.

He glared at her. "Leave it be, Paige. Haven't you done enough already? Just stay out of my sight!" His mouth clinched into a thin white line as he uttered, "Frenchie, damn you to hell for what you have done!"

After the soldiers had taken Kyle away, Paige leaned against the door, pounding on it in anger, then finally collapsing into hysterical tears. She did not know how long she remained huddled against the door before a small hand touched her shoulder.

"Paige . . . Paige . . . ? Did you really turn him in?"

She whirled around to see three accusing faces staring at her. "Mark! How could you ask such a thing? Of course I didn't turn him in!"

Jessie spoke up in a thin voice. "Paige, are they really gonna hang him . . . till he's dead?" Tears spilled down her tiny, drawn face.

"No! They won't lay a hand on him!" Paige tried to fight for control of her emotions, not wanting the children alarmed more than they already were. "Mark, run down to the stables and get the buggy Kyle has been using. I've got to go for help. You other kids stay here and don't let anyone, and I mean anyone, in the house. Do you understand?"

Mark said, "Don't worry none. I'll take good care of everyone until you get back. I jest hope you can find Mister Kyle some help!"

Paige tried to smile but only managed what appeared to be a grimace. "Don't worry. I know at this point, not worrying is awfully hard to do, but children," she hugged them close to her, "we have to have faith that right will prevail." Tears threatened to spill from her eyes. "We have to believe that!" She sounded as though she was trying to convince herself, not only the children. "We just have to have faith!"

The morning dawned gray and gloomy with occasional stabs of lightning streaking the sky on the distant horizon.

The memory of Kyle's horrible accusations were permanently etched in her mind as she frantically urged the horse onward with an almost frenzied fury. All she could see was the hatred blazing on Kyle's face as the soldiers led him, shackled, from their home. She could still hear his curses as he swore his vengeance at her. How in God's name could he possibly believe she was the one who had reported him to the Confederate soldiers?

She pressed the horse on, even faster than before through the pine-dotted countryside. The lightning flashes came closer and closer. Tiny droplets of rain settled over the area in a fine mist, producing a crisp, sharp chill in the air. Paige couldn't help but worry about the way Kyle was dressed when he was taken away. Only a thin pair of trousers stood between him and the elements.

After several wrong turns, Paige finally turned the buggy into Ryan's yard.

"Why, Paige! What in the world brings you out here?" Ryan exclaimed, opening the front door and inviting her inside.

"Oh, Ryan!" Paige sobbed as she stumbled through the front door and collapsed on his shoulder. "I need your help, desperately!"

"What's happened, Paige?" Ryan held her at arm's length, his brows dipping in worry.

"It's Kyle. Before daylight, Confederate soldiers came to our house and arrested him! They accused him of being a spy!"

"Oh my God!" Ryan muttered under his breath. Then he asked, "Do you know where they have taken him?"

"Yes," she mumbled, rubbing her brow with her hand. "I think one of the soldiers mentioned a . . . a Camp Ford."

"Oh good heavens! I certainly know where it is. Paige . . . I know I am alarming you by saying this, but it is a stinking hellhole!"

"Wait a moment," Paige said as she recalled a long ago conversation. "I met someone once, who said her husband was a guard there." Paige looked up at Ryan, "Isn't it about sixty or seventy miles west of here?"

"Yes, it's about that."

Paige implored, "Is there anything you can do to help him, Ryan? Please!"

Ryan grasped her shoulders. "I'll do what I can . . . but first, I have to ask you this question. And Paige, I must caution you to be completely honest with me." Ryan took a deep breath. "Is Kyle guilty of what they are charging him with?"

Paige withdrew from his grasp and walked over to the window. She stared for a moment at the rain that was now peppering down. "Do I have to answer that question, Ryan?" she asked as she spun abruptly around.

Shaking his head, Ryan said slowly, "I think you answered it by your reply. Paige, you have to tell me the truth if I am to help him."

Paige hesitated for a minute then spoke in a dejected voice. "All right. I'll tell you what I know, which is very little actually. I also want you to know I am breaking a vow to him by telling you this."

"You can trust me, Paige. You know you can."

Paige sincerely believed him. She knew she had to turn to someone if Kyle was to be saved. Since Ryan and Kyle were in a sense, friends, he was the only person to whom she could turn.

She started slowly. "I believe he was here trying to prepare things for when the war is over. Now mind you," she was quick to add, "he wasn't looking for information to send back to his commanding officer. I think it had something to do with keeping big business from taking over." She buried her face in her hands. "Oh dear! It's no use. I'm not much help. She looked pleadingly at Ryan. "I really don't know that much about it. I do know that he wasn't on a military assignment, and was not sending back any information pertaining to military whereabouts."

Ryan nodded. "This is very important, Paige. Do you know if there were any men working with him, and if there were, what were their names?" he asked, his breathing suddenly becoming very rapid.

"I don't know," she answered. She started to mention her suspicions about Seth, but decided against it. Looking hopefully at Ryan, she said, "Have I been any help? Do you think you will be able to come to his aid?"

He nodded. "I think so. At least I can certainly try."

"Oh, thank you!" she cried. "Let me go back to town and pack a small bag, then I'll be ready to go."

"Whoa!" Ryan said and grabbed Paige by her arm as she started for the door. "I didn't say a thing about your coming with me. I think I had better go by myself. A prison camp is no place for a woman." His words rang out loud and clear. "If you trusted me enough to ask for my assistance, then please trust my judgment in the matter."

Paige canted her head, her nails digging deeply into the palms of her hand. She knew what he was saying was right. She dropped her head and muttered. "You're right. Kyle wouldn't want me there anyway. He thinks I'm the one who turned him in."

"He what?"

"Yes," she sobbed. "He actually believes I was the one who betrayed him. I guess I would think the same thing if I were he, because I guess I am the only one he confided in."

Ryan solemnly patted her shoulder. "Now, now, I'm sure he will come to his senses as soon as all this is cleared up. After all, there was probably an information leak somewhere and he was understandably upset. I wouldn't worry if I were you."

"That's easy for you to say. What frightens me was the expression on his face . . . the way he looked at me . . ."

"It will all work out, you'll see," he said confidently. He walked over to the hall tree and removed his coat. "If I'm going to do him any good, I had best be on my way. I will have one of my men drive you back to town. You are in no shape to be by yourself right now," he said, noticing her trembling hands. "I don't know how long it will be before they will have his trial, but I would imagine it will be as soon as possible."

Paige placed a restraining hand on Ryan's arm. "Do you believe he will receive a fair trial?"

"I honestly don't know," Ryan replied, shaking his head sadly. "We have to hope I can talk to them on Kyle's behalf. After all, I feel the word and integrity of a former Confederate officer should pull some weight. It looks to me that it'll be hard for them to prove anything, especially if all he has been doing is what you told me." He called a young boy who had been waiting expectantly. "Go out to the barn and tell Thomas to saddle my horse." He addressed his next remark to Paige. "I can make faster time riding than taking the buggy." He toed the floor with his shoe; something else was definitely on his mind. "Paige?" he asked questioningly.

"Yes, Ryan?"

"I think there is something I need to set right with you."

Paige sighed. "Ryan, if you are referring to the scene at the house, yesterday, I hope we can both forget about it."

"I'm pleased you feel that way," Ryan smiled. "I would like to say that I am truly sorry."

Paige nodded. "Apology accepted. It's hard to even think about such an insignificant matter in the face of what has happened."

"I certainly agree." Ryan rubbed his hands together. "Well, if I'm going to be on my way, I had better go." He turned and added, "Since I need to go into town and pick up a few supplies, I'll escort you in, instead of having one of my men take you."

The trip back into town was a nightmare for Paige. The temperature had taken a nosedive as a bad norther blew in, bringing with it intermittent snow and sleet. The heavy gray clouds threatened to produce much more bad weather before the storm was over. Ryan had tied his horse behind the buggy and drove it in himself since Paige was not accustomed to handling a rig.

She could not shake the heavy burden of worry she had for Kyle. She could only hope the soldiers had sought shelter before the storm became too bad. Ryan finally pulled the buggy to a stop in front of her home. The children all peered anxiously out the window as Paige bid Ryan farewell and wished him luck before making her way into the house.

"Is he gonna get Kyle turned loose?" Jessie asked worriedly.

Paige hugged the child close to her and said, "He is certainly going to try, honey. Ryan is on his way now, even though the storm is very bad." Paige tried to smile but only succeeded in making a poor attempt. "If all goes well, Kyle will be back here in no time at all."

"Do you want me to take the buggy back to the stables?" Mark asked as he watched through the window at the horse stamping his feet against the cold.

Paige went to the window and looked up at the low hanging sky. She shook her head. "No, I think I had better take the buggy to the mercantile and replenish some of our supplies. There is no telling how long this storm will last, and I am running awfully low on some things. I shall stop back by the stables and have one of the boys bring me home so he can take the rig back."

"I don't mind watching Luke and Jessie, but if you think you'll be needing some help, I can come along," Mark offered.

Paige smiled at his eagerness to help. "That's all right, Mark," she said, tousling Mark's hair. "You don't need to be out in this bad weather. Take care and I'll be back as soon as possible."

The snow and rain had stopped as Paige hurried through the doors of Garrison's Mercantile. Even though the store was but a short distance from her house, she was glad to be inside where it was warm. Her hands were nearly frozen in the short time they had been exposed to the cold. She silently hoped there would be enough gold on deposit at the store to take care of her purchases. She was almost positive Kyle had mentioned he had put some more money up recently on their account.

Other townspeople and folks living in outlying areas apparently had the same idea she had, because the store was quite crowded. She paid no attention to the muted whispers and stares that came her direction as she fished in her handbag for a piece of paper to prepare a shopping list. When it was her turn to be served, Paige stepped up to the counter and said, "I would like this order filled, please," and handed the paper to the clerk.

The store clerk peered over his glasses at the list for a brief moment then handed it sullenly back to

Paige. "Can't fill this until I see that you got the money to pay for it."

"Pay for it? Why, we have money on deposit here!" Paige exclaimed, suddenly becoming aware that the store was deathly quiet.

"Don't recall having a Yankee spy's money on deposit here," the clerk snapped.

"Why that's not true. You are being terribly unfair and downright dishonest!"

The clerk's eyes hardened. "Lady, I sure don't take kindly to them words. I'd suggest unless you got the hard, cold cash to buy this stuff on the list, then you can turn around and go back to your den of spies. Fact is, you may be a spy too!"

Paige shrank back in horror before regaining her composure. "But, sir, I am not a spy and my husband has not been proven a spy either! I say one more time, either you fill my food order or return the gold that was placed on deposit here. There are three children at home who are depending on this food."

A soft but firm voice behind Paige asked. "What seems to be the problem here, Mrs. Brenner?"

Paige whirled around to see Seth Poteet standing with a worried crease on his brow.

The store clerk intervened. "This ain't no concern of yours. That is . . . unless you've started taking up with spies?"

"Spies? Who has been accused of spying?"

The clerk's eyes bulged. "Why, that Brenner fellow. I figured right from the start something was fishy 'bout that man. Didn't work or have any visible means, yet he always had a pocket full of money!"

"Wait a minute," Seth said, shaking his head in disbelief, while in actuality, he was trying to find out what had happened to his friend and captain. "Am I to understand that Kyle Brenner was arrested for being a spy?"

"He sure 'nough was. The soldiers arrested him this morning."

Seth gave a low whistle as he said, "That's kinda hard to believe. I met that Brenner fellow and he seemed like a right nice man."

The clerk laughed crudely. "Just goes to show that a body can never tell."

Seth frowned. "But what's this argument about?" he asked Paige.

"This man," she answered, glaring at the clerk, "refuses to give me credit for the money Kyle placed on deposit here."

The store clerk threw his hands in the air. "I done already told her, she don't have no credit!"

"I most certainly do," Paige argued, "and there are three children at home depending on the food I've rightly got coming!"

At that time, a fat lady with wispy gray hair stepped forward and wagged her finger in Paige's face. "I wouldn't be so sure about that, young lady!"

"What do you mean?" Paige asked, her heart gripped in terror.

"Humm! I'll have you know, the sheriff is on his way right now with the clergy from our church to take those poor babies out of that wicked house. Ain't no telling what those poor young'uns have gone through since they have been with the likes of you!"

Paige blanched and her hand flew to her mouth in horror. "Oh no!" she muttered, turning on her heel and fleeing from the store and hostile people as quickly as possible.

Seth tried to stop her but to no avail. He went back in the store and said to the store clerk angrily, "Go ahead and fill Mrs. Brenner's order and I'll pay for it myself. I don't know if her husband is a spy or not, but there is no excuse for taking it out on a poor, defenseless woman. She is certainly no spy, because I was told they were newly married when they arrived here."

The clerk looked at him suspiciously. "It appears to me that you are coming to their defense real quick like. Since you're new around here, perhaps we ought to be checking you out!"

"Go ahead," Seth replied coldly. "I am only trying to rebuild a life for myself." He thought quickly and decided to tell a convincing lie. "My wife and children were murdered by Yankees and I have no love for any of them. But I also like justice. Maybe it's best that I found out exactly how this town is before my roots took hold very good. I'm not fond of living in a place that will condemn a woman because her husband has been accused, and I stress the word *accused*, of a crime!" He turned to leave, then walked back and grabbed the grocery list from the counter. "I know for a fact that they had money on account here, because I was here the other day when he gave it to you!" Seth gave the now quiet crowd a piercing glance.

"I know everyone here has probably been touched one way or the other by this war, and you certainly can't be blamed for being suspicious. But to take your fears out on a defenseless woman who is just barely more than a child herself, and three little children is downright shameful! As for you," he snarled at the store clerk, "I'm changing all my business down to Austin's Mercantile. At least it's run by honest folks!" He then strode out the door.

As Seth rode toward Kyle's home, he was deep in thought. He had been afraid of this moment the first day Kyle had told them about the mission. He had no idea what could have gone wrong to cause Kyle's cover to be blown. He didn't know if someone had caught him in the act, recognized him from his past, or what. He would make some discreet inquiries, and try not to place his own mission in jeopardy. The most important thing right now was to try to find out what happened and to let Blinn know the situation here in Jefferson. If there were any way possible, perhaps they could do something to help their comrade without blowing their own cover.

He pulled up in front of the Brenner's house in time to see the sheriff lead away a crying little girl and two young boys trying desperately to act like men. Seth was quick to note sympathetically that the tallest of the boys was struggling to keep tears from sliding down his drawn face.

Seth rushed through the house and into the kitchen to find Paige sitting at the table with her head lying on her arms and crying bitterly.

He sat down beside her, cleared his throat and

said uneasily, "I'm sorry about the kids being taken away." He paused, unsure of what to say next. "Is there anything I can do at all to help?"

She looked up at him with tears streaking her cheeks. "No, not unless you are a magician and can turn the clock back to yesterday when I had all my dreams and was living in my own safe little world." She shook her head and fought for control. "I am so worried about Kyle . . . and I feel so helpless because I don't know what to do." She gazed at Seth intently. "How can they put him on trial for his life when all he was trying to do was make this country a better place to live?"

Paige's words clearly startled him. He didn't know how much Kyle had told her. He could feel the blood pound through his temples when he asked, "Mrs. Brenner, do you actually know what Kyle's business was?"

"No . . . not really. He never would say anything definite. I . . . I only know he was not a spy! Not the way they mean it!"

Seth asked hesitantly, "I take it, he was on some sort of government business?"

Paige looked at him suspiciously. Her eyes narrowed until tiny furrows appeared on her brow. "You sound as though you are cross-examining me. What are you? A Confederate agent?"

Seth laughed but obviously was not amused as he replied, "No ma'am, I'm not."

Paige sighed deeply. "I'm sorry. I know I'm sounding suspicious about everything. But I have no idea who I can trust and who I cannot!"

"I'm not so thick-skinned as not to understand."

He licked his lips, trying to get the dry feeling from his mouth. "Were the children the sheriff took away Matthew's brothers and sister?"

Paige nodded, not trusting her voice to speak.

"Do you know where he was taking them and how long they will be in his custody?"

Paige winced visibly as she recalled the sheriff's biting words. "No," she mumbled. "He only said that I was a scarlet woman to have been living with a Yankee spy and he was using his authority by removing them from such a bad environment."

Seth consoled her as much as possible. "Try not to worry about them. They will be all right. I think our main concern should be with your husband."

Paige tried to smile. "I think I've been able to send him some help. We are friends with a former officer in the Confederate army and he is on his way this very minute to Camp Ford to offer his assistance."

"Would this man be Ryan Ledbetter?"

"Yes . . . why are you looking so concerned?"

"I didn't realize I appeared to be concerned," he said off-handedly. "I was merely trying to recall if Kyle had mentioned him to me, or if it were somebody else."

"Oh, I see," Paige said as she nodded.

Seth stood, twisting his hat in his hands. He could imagine the help Ryan Ledbetter would be to his friend. He could not afford for Kyle's wife to know how upset he was, hearing that bit of news. Finally, Seth spoke. "I guess I had better be on my way. I don't think it would do your reputation any good for me to be here for very long. especially after what's happened." He looked at her questioningly. "You were trying to get a grocery list filled. Are you out of food?"

Her lips pressed into a thin white line. "No, not entirely. With the children gone, I will probably have enough to last until I can work something out. But," she exploded loudly, "that man was lying! I know Kyle had placed money on deposit there!"

Seth shook his head in agreement. "I know, but you would have a hard time proving it." He walked toward the door, turned and said, "Don't worry about Matthew. I'll take care of him, and we will get this mess about the kids straightened out, I promise you that." He added sympathetically, "Let me know if there is anything else I can do."

Seth glanced back through the kitchen window in time to see Paige drop her head back onto her hands and resume crying. He shook his head sadly, knowing there was little he could do. He turned his collar up against the wind and went down to Austin's Mercantile to make arrangements for them to send some supplies out to Paige. Then he made his way home.

Seth welcomed the roaring fire and bubbling stew Matthew had waiting for him. Although his appetite was poor, he tried to eat but only managed to push the food back and forth on his plate. At last, he told Matthew what happened.

"You mean they arrested Kyle for being a spy!" Matthew said in astonishment.

"Yep, they did," Seth stated firmly. He went on to explain what had happened to the children but assured him they would be all right. As he talked to the boy, a plan began to form in his mind. "Matthew, I'm going to tell you something . . . something that will prove I have complete faith and confidence in you."

"Yes, sir, Mr. Seth. There's one thing you can do and that's trust me," the boy said earnestly.

"You know . . ." Seth spoke with extreme caution, "Kyle is guilty as hell . . . and so am I!"

"W . . . what?" Matthew asked unbelievingly. "That cain't be true! There is no way you and Kyle can actually be spies!"

"Yes, there can. I want you to know there are many different kinds of spies." He went on to explain exactly what his and Kyle's mission was.

"If'n y'all were sent here to do all them kind of good things, then why are they want'n to hang Kyle?"

"I don't know," Seth said seriously, "unless the Confederacy feels they are losing the war so badly, they think they have to do something. I guess I should make this plain; Kyle hasn't been sentenced to hang, yet. But it is very possible they will try to do it. After all, who knows what they have been told about Kyle. Now, Matthew," he added cautiously, "I don't think I have to tell you if you reported this conversation we've had tonight, my life would be in danger also."

"Oh no, Mr. Seth," Matthew said solemnly. "You don't have to worry 'bout me tellin' none. None t'all."

"That pleases me, Matthew. Now, I'm going to ask you something. And it could place your life in peril." He looked expectantly at the boy then continued. "If I went to Camp Ford, I would probably be an immediate suspect, so this is what I am asking of you. I need you to go over there and keep your eyes and ears peeled to the gossip and rumors. If possible, try and sit in the spectator's section when they have his trial. That way, we'll know what the verdict is and if worse comes to worst . . . we'll know when he is to hang and where." He looked directly into Matthew's eyes. "But the decision is yours, and there would be no hard feelings if you were to refuse."

Matthew looked down at the floor, thinking over Seth's request. Then he glanced up. "If they caught me, then I'd be in bad trouble, wouldn't I?"

Seth nodded. "Yes, I imagine you would."

A slow and easy grin broke across Matthew's face. "Shoot fire! I don't reckon a little bit of trouble will bother me none." He stood. "When do you want me to leave?"

Seth smiled. "Oh, I think you should wait until tomorrow. Perhaps the weather will have cleared up by then. But I think you ought to take that ol' mule we've been using to pull brush with. I would let you take my riding horse, but he might be a little too fancy for a poor ol' farmboy to come riding in on." Seth breathed a sigh of relief that Matthew had agreed to his request. "Yep," he said as if talking to himself, "ol' Slink might be an old scotch-eyed mule, but he will be a lot more convincing, and he will get Matthew there in plenty of time."

Chapter Twenty-Two

Kyle was thrown roughly into the cold, dark, damp cell. After the iron door slammed, the keys rattled, and the faint echo of fading footsteps filtered into the cell. A pall of stillness settled over the corridors of the prison. Kyle pressed his ear to the door, listening for a sound to reassure him; he was not alone. He pulled his threadbare blanket tighter around his shoulders to help ward off the cold. Kyle sat down dejectedly, and scooped the straw strewn about the floor over his bare feet to warm them.

On the trip over, one of the soldiers, over the objections of the man who had done most of the talking at the house, gave Kyle a blanket for protection against the cold.

How he hated the man called Turner! Every chance that soldier got, he taunted Kyle about how he would personally like to hold the rope that would be used at his hanging.

As Kyle stared off into a sea of nothingness, an overpowering bitterness filled him. Damn that treacherous bitch to hell! She had to be the one who turned him in to the authorities. She had to be! How she must have hated him to do what she had done. Kyle knew he had not been watched, and he hadn't done anything in the past few days which would throw suspicion on his actions. Paige was the only possible one who even had a glimmer of knowledge of what he had been doing in Jefferson.

Kyle's thoughts raced back to the previous night when they had at long last gotten together. Could it be that Paige deliberately set out to seduce him? Kyle, in his muddled state of mind, completely forgot about who made the advances. Perhaps she had formed a plan of revenge from the moment they had been forced to marry. Maybe she hated him so desperately, hurting him was her intention all the time. These thoughts tormented him as he sat there in the ever-increasing darkness.

It finally became so cold, Kyle had to start walking back and forth across the short length of the cell to try to warm himself. Somehow . . . someway . . . he had to formulate a plan to escape. He knew he would not be able to rely on Seth or Blinn. If they tried to secure his release, they would only be placing their own lives in jeopardy. He could only hope his friends did not try to break him out of prison.

He immediately began checking the walls for some show of weakness or decay in the mortar. He silently cursed the fact that not even a barred window was in his cell. If not for a tiny bit of light seeping underneath the door, the entire room would have been in complete darkness. He scoured the walls, but to no avail. Upon hearing keys rattling against the locked door, Kyle hastily sat down, not knowing who would be entering.

Turner threw open the door and waited a moment for his eyes to adjust to the darkness. He waved a pair of leg manacles while he growled to Kyle.

"Get your butt over here in the light where I can see you. Seems as though the lieutenant didn't fancy the idea too much because you didn't have leg-irons on. In fact, he didn't like it 'cause they weren't chained on the way over here." Turner chuckled sardonically, "Only thing, I was kinda hoping you would have been itchy enough to try to run. You had better believe I kept my rifle handy at all times." He fastened the manacles on Kyle's legs and laughed again. "With these ankle bracelets on, you won't be gettin' a chance no more."

Turner stood with his arms folded, staring down at Kyle, an evil gleam shining from his eyes. He dropped his weight on one foot as if starting to turn, but then, he swung savagely with his other foot and sent Kyle sprawling across the floor. Like an animal, Turner was on his prisoner, hitting him in the stomach, side, and a few well aimed punches to his kidneys. But still, Kyle remained silent. He refused to admit to the pain and declined the temptation to cry out in agony. He knew to do so, would only make the beating worse. When it finally was over, Kyle was barely conscious enough to feel Turner's piercing eyes stab him like daggers.

"That's for them poor souls who are left in those

Yankee hell holes!" Then Turner spit on Kyle and marched outside, slamming the iron door soundly behind him.

One day was just like the next. Beatings, mushy gruel, and the ever present cold eventually took its toll on even Kyle's healthy body. By the time the weather cleared, the lack of proper clothing and nourishment had weakened Kyle considerably. A nagging cough developed and a low-grade fever sapped his strength even more.

Kyle judged he had been in his cell more than two weeks the day Turner brought him a pail of water to wash with, and a ragged but clean shirt to cover his grimy body.

"Get yourself cleaned up, Yank," Turner ordered. "You are fixin' to get your fair trial today!"

Kyle stared at him hard, a cold hatred filling his eyes. He glanced at the pail of water, and crawled over to it on unsteady limbs. He hated to give Turner the satisfaction of knowing how good the water felt to him as he splashed it over his face and chest. Kyle relished the refreshing bath, make-shift as it was, and was surprised at how much better it made him feel.

"That's enough, Yank," Turner said tersely. "You only needed enough to get the stench off. Fact t'is, this ain't no fancy tea party you're going to." Turner unlocked one of the wrist bands, enabling Kyle to slip the shirt on. Seeing the sudden gleam which flashed through Kyle's eyes made the guard back nervously away.

"I wouldn't try nothing stupid if I were you," he sneered. "You don't really think I come down here everyday by myself, do you?" Turner called back over his shoulder to another guard who was waiting outside the door, just out of Kyle's sight. "Doyle, you might stick your head in the door just to show this fool he ought not to try anything."

When the guard called Doyle showed himself in the doorway, Kyle looked at one, then the other as he weighed the odds against the chance he would have to escape. He knew he might never get another one, so he sprang into action. He whirled around, slamming the dangling wrist manacle against Turner and sent him sprawling face down onto the floor. Kyle dove for the other soldier's legs, causing them to buckle. The two men scuffled; Kyle getting the upper hand. Suddenly Kyle felt a sharp rap against the back of his head. Exploding pain crashed and burned red-hot as Kyle felt himself slowly sinking into unconsciousness.

Kyle became aware of reality as sheets of water splashed against his face. Shaking his head to clear away the red fog of agony, Kyle was able to focus on the two soldiers towering over him.

Turner roared in a maddening rage, "Now that was a damn foolhardy stunt. You bastard, what were you trying to do to me, anyway?" he asked as he rubbed his throbbing shoulder.

Kyle's head snapped up with such force that his hair fell tousled on his brow. "By God, you were lucky! I was aiming for your head instead of your shoulder." He couldn't resist adding, "And if I get another chance, I'll do it again!"

Doyle stepped forward, bringing one foot

backward as if to kick him. Surprisingly, Turner stopped him. He said in a brusque voice, "No, leave him alone. We wouldn't want the officers at the trial to think we have been mistreating our prisoner." He shook his finger in Kyle's face threateningly. "But just remember one thing, Yank. When you walk up the steps to the scaffold, I'm gonna be there . . . right on the top step waiting on you!"

Kyle was led into the courtroom and was placed at a small table well away from the main body of the room. A Confederate flag was hanging above the long oak table that was to serve as the officers bench. He eyed the officers warily as they walked in single file and took their chairs. The senior officer glared impatiently at Kyle when a fit of wracking coughing momentarily stopped the proceedings. When his coughing subsided, the officer in charge cleared his throat and addressed the sergeant who was in charge of keeping the records of the trial.

"Sergeant Elerick, would you please note that this trial has been delayed for the past eighteen days because the commander of this post had been called to the front lines. It has taken this long to assemble the five officers necessary to hear and pass judgment on the charges against this man."

"Yes, sir, Captain Beaumont," said the sergeant. "I will so note."

Captain Beaumont picked up the gavel and brought the proceedings to order. "Kyle Brenner, would you please rise and hear the charges against you."

Kyle stood, proud and straight.

"You have been charged with the crime of spying, without the benefit of uniform, against the Confederate States of America, sending the Union army information on the positions of our troops, and disrupting and robbing Confederate payrolls." He looked solemnly at Kyle. "How do you plead?"

Kyle spoke in a clear and steady voice. "To these charges, sir, I plead not guilty. I also have to protest my arrest, and my treatment since I have been arrested."

Immediately, muted whispers broke out in the back of the courtroom.

Captain Beaumont pounded the table with his gavel and demanded order. He took a deep breath and said, "It is my duty to inform you of the gravity of these charges." He ignored Kyle's protest of bad treatment. "If you are found guilty of these charges, this court will have no other recourse or alternative than to sentence you to hang. Is this clear to you?"

Again Kyle spoke in a clear voice. "Yes, sir, I understand. But I have noticed no one is here to represent me and I have had not a chance to confer with council. Is this legal?"

Captain Beaumont spoke sternly. "Mr. Brenner, most men who have been accused of being spies seldom make it as far as a courtroom. If you are indeed a member of the Union army or service, you will know this is true. You can rest assured that myself and the officers who are sitting on the bench with me have no desire to send an innocent man to the gallows. We fully realize how in the course of war, people's imagination can and does run rampant. You stated that there is no one to represent you, that's true. But if this board sees the evidence against you does not warrant the charges, you will be released." He addressed the court clerk. "Sergeant Elerick, would you please call the first witness?"

The sergeant stood. In a loud booming voice, he called, "Oscar DuPree, would you please take the stand?"

Kyle kept his eyes to the front of the room. He refused to turn and look for his wife.

Oscar shuffled toward the witness chair. As he passed by Kyle, he stopped and smiled sardonically at him. After he was placed under oath, the captain asked him to tell what he knew about Kyle Brenner.

"Well, you see, it was like this," Oscar said in a whining, high-pitched voice. "This man rode up to my place 'bout two . . . three months ago. I offered him the hospitality of my home, 'cause I really thought he was jest a good-ol'-boy passing through."

"Did he say or do anything to make you change your mind?"

"Yeah, he sho' did. He enticed my niece to meet up with him out in the barn. When I caught them together, naturally I was mad and made some threats and tried to defend her honor. He tol' me if I tried to stop him from cartin' her off, then he'd run his Yankee troops in on me and burn me plumb out!" Oscar ducked his head acting very ashamed. "I guess I ain't got no complaints about

324

the way he's treated her. I heard tell that he treats her right nice and buys a lot of clothes and stuff for her. But I feel I didn't do my duty by that girl. Just as soon as he carted her off, I should have gone right then and reported about him and his soldiers, but, sir," large tears brimmed in his eyes, "I had a whole passel of kids to think about and we were just getting in the last of the crops. Then my wife took sick and died, leaving me all her young'uns to care for. But . . . I guess you don't want to hear about my problems." He twisted his hat in his hands and continued. "Then I guess it was 'bout the same time he was arrested that I was over in Jefferson. I had stopped in a place to have a beer, and he was in the saloon too. He was bragging and throwing his weight around. He threatened to whip me if I even tried to see my niece. He even went on to boast about as soon as the war was over, he was gonna be a rich man 'cause he had a lot of Confederate silver stashed somewhere . . . silver that he had gotten by ill found means!"

Captain Beaumont asked sharply, "Mr. DuPree, are you positive Kyle Brenner said he had some Yankee troops camped close to your home?"

"Yes, sir! As sure as shootin' I'm positive that's what he said."

Captain Beaumont glared over at Kyle, he then glanced up and down the table to see what impression Oscar's testimony had made on the other officers. Each one looked thoughtful, as if they were engrossed in the treacherous deed they had just heard. The captain dismissed Oscar and instructed Sergeant Elerick to call the next witness.

"The court now calls the honorable Captain Ryan Ledbetter to the stand."

Kyle watched as Ryan limped to the stand. It was strange, Kyle thought to himself, how Ryan used a small limp to his advantage when he wanted. Ryan Ledbetter taking the witness stand only proved to Kyle that his suspicions were correct all along.

Captain Beaumont asked, "Sir, will you please tell the court why you are not actively engaged in the war effort at this time?"

"Yes sir, I sure will. I was wounded a short while ago." He made a fist and hit his leg lightly. "I really haven't recovered enough to go back and do battle, but I have offered my experience to the local soldiers stationed in my immediate area. I might add, I have hired three men to help fill in for me on the front lines," he stated matter-of-factly. "As you know, this practice has become very widespread."

The captain snapped, "Yes, I know it has . . . unfortunately," he added. "Would you please state your knowledge of the defendant?"

Ryan batted his eyes, glanced around the room, and was very careful to glare coldly in Kyle's direction. "I have personal knowledge this man is a spy. I can tell you what I know for a fact, and if you will accept hearsay evidence, I will also tell you what his wife had to say about the matter. Truth is, she was the one who informed me about these proceedings and sent me over."

One of the lieutenants on the board interrupted. "You mean to say that this man's wife would testify against him?"

"Yes, sir! At least she would if she had been able to make the journey over here. You see, this entire situation has made her very sick." He leaned forward in his chair. "I will also add, if it had not been for Mrs. Brenner, I would have never suspected him."

"Go on, Captain Ledbetter, continue. We find this line of information very interesting," Captain Beaumont said.

"Mrs. Brenner came to me and said Kyle was responsible for all the silver shipments being robbed and looted around Jefferson. I can handily admit to knowing the defendant always has plenty of money; he has been known to flash it around a lot. I might add, he refused several offers of jobs. Always said he didn't have to work. But I guess what really iced the cake so to speak, Mrs. Brenner said her husband admitted it! He admitted that he was working for the Union and he'd see the South fall before too much longer."

The lieutenant asked tiredly, "Captain, is there anything you can tell us that you know personally?"

"Yes there is. One night I saw Kyle sneaking around the stock pens there in Jefferson and the next morning I found out that the cattle had been turned loose." Even though Ryan was deliberately lying, he had no idea how close to the truth he actually came. "I did some quiet checking, and even had one of my men follow him. We found out that Kyle did a whole lot of bragging. He said that as long as he was in Jefferson, not too many Johnny Rebs would be eating beef!"

Kyle leaped to his feet, unable to take any more of the accusations. "Ryan, you are a liar and a thief, and my wife is also lying!"

Sergeant Elerick rushed over and shoved him roughly back into the chair.

"Mr. Brenner," Captain Beaumont shouted as he pounded the table with his gavel and tried to regain order. "You are in serious trouble! I would suggest you refrain from any more outbursts like this, or I will have you removed and placed back in your cell!"

"Yes, sir," Kyle mumbled, knowing it was useless to argue.

Ryan stood. "Captain Beaumont, I would like to approach the bench and make a personal request."

The captain nodded his permission. "Yes, what is it?" he asked as Ryan stood nervously before him.

"It's about Mrs. Brenner. She told me the same thing as her uncle testified to. About how she was forced into this marriage with the prisoner. You see, she fully realizes the stigma that will be attached to her for the rest of her life. All of us here are reasonable men; unless some kind of miracle happens, we will lose the war. Even though this area will be under martial law, Mrs. Brenner will have to face and live with the knowledge she was married to a spy. The folks around here could make it hard on her. She really loves the South and what it stands for, and hates her husband for what part he has played in helping to destroy it. She wishes for this court to grant her an annulment so she won't have to go through life with a spy's name. She feels she will be branded wherever she goes or whatever she tries to do." Ryan walked the length of the bench, staring deeply into each man's eyes, trying to gain their sympathy for Paige. "Right now, all Mrs. Brenner wants to do is raise the orphaned children Oscar DuPree entrusted in her care. But the good citizens of Jefferson, because she is married to a man they believe is a traitor and a spy, have deemed it necessary to take the children from her custody. The children would be returned to her if she were no longer associated with that man." He pointed to Kyle. "So I beg you, if you have any mercy, any compassion, please allow this fine woman to regain her sense of pride."

While Ryan stood watching them, the officers exchanged glances, then scribbled notes to each other, and passed them back and forth. The captain finally announced, "Captain Ledbetter, this court will provide a statement revealing our findings. You can take this document to Judge Hastings and I'm sure he will issue a decree of annulment."

Ryan snapped to attention and saluted pertly. "I thank you for your fair and just decision in this matter."

As Ryan passed by Kyle, he paused, but seeing the black glowering look Kyle was giving him, he decided not to say anything; he just smirked and left as quickly as possible.

Kyle stood wearily to receive the sentence the court had reached. The decision had been swift.

The officers had filed out of the room only a few minutes before, and Kyle had not even been taken back to his cell. Kyle was not surprised when he heard the sentence being pronounced that he was to hang on the fifth day of April.

Kyle knew his hearing had not been conducted in accordance with his legal rights, but when he had accepted Mr. Lincoln's proposal, in a sense he had given up all his legal rights, and would be placing his life in jeopardy. But as long as he had breath in his body, he would still have hope. Fortunately, his sentence would not be carried out for nearly a month. A month in which he would devote every ounce of strength, and every waking moment to try to find some means of escape. To Kyle, who was filled with so much bitterness and hatred, escaping did not mean his freedom, but a means to seek revenge on the treacherous bitch who had betrayed him! He swore to have her begging for mercy!

Matthew, who had not been allowed into the courtroom, staggered out of the compound to where the mule was tied. He had been camping a few miles from Camp Ford for days. When he had arrived, days earlier, he had found out Kyle's trial had been delayed, but had not gone back to Jefferson to report to Seth his findings, for fear of the trial being held while he was gone. He had pressed an ear to a crack in the wall of the building to hear what had gone on. He had missed very little of the proceedings. It was hard to believe Paige had betrayed Kyle. He thought he knew her better. True, they had said many things he did not understand, but they were also well-learned men, and they believed what she had said. His lips curled in distaste over the thought of the lies Oscar had told. If he had lied, perhaps the other man lied too. Matthew knew he was too young to question an adult, but as soon as he was able, he would confront Paige about what had been said. He would have to hear it from her own lips, before he would ever believe she had betrayed Kyle. If she had said all those things, then Matthew knew he would never want to see her again, and would do everything in his power to keep her and her evil influence away from his brothers and sister. But now, the most important task which lay ahead was to make it back to Jefferson and tell Seth about Kyle's sentence.

Chapter Twenty-Three

Paige paced the floor aimlessly. One of Ryan's men had just left after bringing her a message saying he would be there to see her in a short while. For the past weeks, he had kept her informed with messages, but this note was different. It said Ryan would soon return. Nothing was said about Kyle! The long wait had been an endless hell for her, now knowing if Kyle was well, if he was being mistreated, beaten, or if he was even still alive! She felt so helpless, so utterly helpless.

She stopped her restless pacing and stood at the window searching frantically for Ryan. Her hand automatically smoothed the loose fitting dressing gown over her rapidly thickening figure. Since the near three weeks that Kyle had been taken away, her stomach had become quite rounded. Paige had been reduced to wearing loose fitting garments to conceal the fact she was carrying a baby. She wanted so much to climb the tallest rooftop and shout to the world she was carrying the child of the man she dearly loved, but common sense told her it would be unwise at this time. Reluctantly, Paige decided she had better try to hide the pregnancy for as long as possible. It was strange, she thought, since the moment she knew she had conceived, the baby and any declaration of the baby had been kept a secret. But this time, it was for far different reasons.

Was it only a week ago that Mark had slipped away from the small orphanage to see her? He had only wanted to tell her they were being treated well, but missed her and Matthew terribly. She recalled the poorly masked misery in his eyes when he asked about Kyle. In his innocence he had no idea how he made her heart wrench when he mentioned Jessie crying herself to sleep each night in grief over Kyle's being arrested and taken away.

She was unaware of tears trickling down her face as she remembered the expression on the boy's face when the sheriff appeared at her door demanding she release the boy immediately. Then how Mark had walked proudly away, refusing to even let the sheriff touch him. Paige was at least grateful Mark had not created a scene. She strongly doubted if her emotions could have withstood it if he had cried.

Paige snapped back to the present as Ryan stepped up behind her and touched her shoulder. Whirling around, Paige's throat tightened, constricting the words she knew she had to ask. Ryan stood, hesitantly clearing his throat, while she asked the unspoken question with her eyes, searching, silently imploring, for an answer. Her heart almost burst through her chest when she saw the sorrow that was written on his features as he lowered his eyes, unable to even look at her. She grasped his arms, shaking him as she cried.

"No! No! It can't be! Please tell me it isn't true!" she pleaded as tears fell freely down her lovely, drawn face.

Ryan gently pried her hold loose and took her tenderly into his arms.

"I'm sorry, Paige. I did everything I could do. I hated for it to end this way," he soothed. "Go ahead and cry, cry and get it out of your system."

She looked up at him bitterly. "How in the world can I get him out of my system? I love him more than life itself." She leaned her head against his shoulder. "Tell me exactly what happened."

Ryan patted her compassionately. "I really don't think you should hear all the details. They would upset you too badly."

Paige jerked back wildly. "I happen to be Kyle's wife, and if it concerns him, it also concerns me. I have the right to know what has happened to him!"

"Now, now," Ryan soothed, not wanting her upset any more than possible. "Come on over here and sit down and I'll tell you about it."

Paige let herself be led over to the stuffed chair and sank gratefully onto the softness. Ryan knelt down on his good leg and took her hand in his. Looking deeply into her eyes, he said, "I will tell you what happened as long as you remain calm. If I see the news is upsetting you too much, I will stop and send for the doctor. Do you understand?"

Paige nodded.

"They had a good case against him, reliable witnesses, the whole bit. He was found guilty . . .

and he was sentenced to hang. He . . . will . . . be executed on the fifth day of April." He watched her expectantly, fearful that she would go into hysterics.

Paige could only sit there, feeling as though someone had hit her in the chest with a mighty blow. All color drained from her face and the room spun around, or so appearing. She felt herself slipping . . . sliding into the dark realms of unconsciousness.

"Paige! Paige! Are you all right?" Ryan asked anxiously as he placed a wet cloth across her brow.

"Oh no! Please, God, no! Don't take him away from me!" she wailed.

Ryan scooped her easily into his arms and carried her to the bedroom. He placed her gently on the bed. Smoothing her hair back, he said, "Stay here for a moment and rest. I'll go fix you a cup of tea, and leave you alone to collect your thoughts and perhaps calm down a little." He drew the drapes tightly shut and left the room.

Paige lay in the darkness, silently cursing God for deserting her and Kyle. Just when happiness was within their grasp, the fates drew their mighty sword, cutting them apart until eternity. She felt her baby stir beneath her heart and for a brief moment she had hope, hope that their love would survive. At least the child she carried would show the world that a man by the name of Kyle Brenner existed! Eventually, Paige could no longer hold back the tears of grief as they consumed her being. She cried.

Ryan wisely left her alone in her hour of darkness. He knew she would have to have time to face the reality of the situation, but he also knew his next bit of news might send her over the edge of sanity, but he had to take the chance if he was to have her, if all of his well-laid plans were to succeed.

"Drink this, Paige," Ryan commanded. "It will make you feel better," he said as he offered her a cup of steaming hot tea.

Paige sat up and gratefully accepted the cup. She put it to her lips and drank greedily, then she sputtered and coughed. The contents was not tea, but liquor as well. In a moment, the drink warmed her, and consoled the cold, hard feeling in the bottom of her stomach. Finally, she said, "Thank you, Ryan. I guess I needed something that strong." She briefly cast her eyes upward as if seeking some divine help from the God she had just cursed. "I'm sorry I fell apart, Ryan."

"That's perfectly all right. I understand. I know how much you love him." He was extra careful not to speak of Kyle in the past-tense. He took a deep breath, and Paige could tell he had something else on his mind.

"What is it, Ryan?"

He shook his head slowly, "I don't think I ought to tell you anything else at this time. You've gone through enough for one day."

"No, Ryan." A startled look had come in her eyes and she demanded, "If there is something else, I need to know. No, I *have* to know!"

"All right, all right," Ryan conceded. "You see . . . I had a chance to talk to Kyle after the trial." He looked her straight in the eye. "Now, I want to say this without any interruptions because it is Kyle's wishes and instructions. Do you understand?" he asked mercifully.

Paige was solemn as she nodded.

"The guards let me in his cell because of the respect they have for my rank, otherwise, I might not have been able to see him. But what I want . . . no, excuse me, I don't *want* to tell you this," he lied, "but I have to do as Kyle wished."

"What is it?" Paige asked impatiently, clinging to every word he said.

"He asked me to go before the court and tell them that you had absolutely no idea . . . no knowledge of what he was doing, and to see if the court would annul your marriage," Ryan said in a rush of words.

"What?"

Ryan gestured with his hands. "Now hear me out before you go getting upset again. I'm merely repeating Kyle's wishes. He was afraid you would be faced with the stigma that would be attached to his name, that you would never have any chance for happiness as long as your name was Paige Brenner. He knew the people would talk, and hold it against you. Even if you moved to another part of the country, nasty rumors have a way of following a person, and you would always be known as the woman who was married to a spy. He also figured that you would be blamed as much as he was. But . . . if an annulment was granted, the folks around here would think you were innocent and weren't aware of what he was doing, therefore, not hold anything against you."

"But I can't get an annulment! I just can't!" Paige's voice rose to the edge of hysteria.

Ryan tried to smile as he patted her hand. "Kyle and I figured this would be your reaction, that's why I went ahead and did it."

"Did what?" Paige asked with a calmness she did not feel.

"I have already gone to the judge." He handed a paper to her. "And the annulment has already been granted."

Paige's eyes quickly searched the paper; finally in a weak voice she asked, "Is there any way it can be undone?" She searched Ryan's face for an affirmative answer.

"No. There is absolutely no way." Then Ryan watched, totally confused when Paige burst out in laughter. His confusion ended when the laughter quickly turned into hysterics. He let her regain control before speaking. "You do understand why this was done, don't you?" he asked searchingly.

"Oh yes! I understand very well! I understand many things . . . things you can not possibly know about." She looked wildly about. "I understand I will lose the husband I love to a hangman's noose. And regardless of what you and Kyle did for me, there will still be whispers behind my back when I walk down the street." Paige glared at him proudly. "But, I would have carried his name with pride. The protection you and he sought has turned into a cruel act. You see . . . now when I walk down the street, people will be able to turn and say," she mimicked in a terse voice, "there goes that spy's woman and look! She even has her bastard child with her!"

Ryan swallowed hard, then he asked incredibly, "You mean you're going to have a baby?"

Paige pulled her gown tightly around her stomach, revealing the roundness of it. "What does it look like? That I'm getting fat? Oh, I'm getting fat all right . . . the only thing is, in a few month's time, my round belly will have shifted to my arms! Oh Ryan!" she wailed. "Kyle's baby deserves more than what's ahead for him. I know you and Kyle were trying to be kind, and to think of me and my feelings, but the only thing you have managed to do is break my heart once more and to turn an innocent baby into a fatherless bastard!" She collapsed back into a pool of hysterical tears.

Ryan swore under his breath. "A brat!" The one thing he had not counted on. He had to be careful or he would blow his entire plan. He began to pace back and forth across the room while his mind raced and plotted. Then a sly wicked grin flirted on his lips as he thought, Why, this may be the very excuse I needed to get her! As soon as the brat is born, I can get a wet nurse for it. Then whenever it gets a litle older, it can always be shipped off to a military or finishing school. I know as long as Kyle's bastard is around, I'll never be able to make her forget him. I swore I would have her, and damn-it, I've come too far to be defeated now. Ryan walked over to Paige and knelt down. "Sweet Paige, if I had only known . . ." Then he asked almost hesitantly, "Was Kyle aware of the child?"

"No, no, he didn't know. I was going to tell him the day he was arrested."

Inwardly, Ryan sighed from relief. "Then there is only one thing that can be done!" he said boldly. "And since I had a part to play in this disastrous situation, I am the only one who can do anything about it!"

Paige looked up eagerly. "You mean . . . there is a possibility of having the annulment reversed?" she asked breathlessly.

"No, my dear," he said sympathetically. "I didn't mean to revive your hopes. But there is something I can do! I can marry you myself and give the child a name!" he said in a blurt of words.

"What?" Paige's cry was a chorus of incomprehension. "No! I . . . I can't marry you! I love Kyle . . . and . . ." Her words trailed off as she looked at Ryan, not believing what he had said. She rose to her feet and stepped over to the window, pulled back the curtain and stood staring out it into the damp, cloudy twilight. She turned, and spoke softly. "Ryan, I realize why you made the offer. You feel guilty." She shook her head gently. "Please don't. I understand why you and Kyle did what you did. I truly respect you for the part you played and if anything . . . I love Kyle even more for thinking of me, especially with no future ahead of him." Her voice caught in a sob. "But I couldn't marry you just to give the child a name." She placed one hand on her arm and rubbed nervously. "You can see why I love Kyle so much. Even with all the tribulations he is suffering, his thoughts are still with me." A frenzied expression suddenly crossed her face. "I've got to see him! Ryan, will you take me there?"

"No," he said gently. "Kyle made me promise to keep you away." Ryan took a calculated risk when he added, "He said for you to remember him as he was, and to remember your last night together and how he held you in his arms the night before he was arrested. He explicitly requested that you try not to see him . . . before . . . the date . . . he is to be . . . executed."

"But he has to know about his child!" Paige cried wildly.

"Paige, get a grip on yourself!" Ryan grabbed her arms a bit too roughly. "Think woman! Think what that news could do to the man! It would drive him crazy, knowing you were going to have a child, and he wouldn't be here to share the baby with you, to help raise it . . . to love it!"

"Stop it! Stop it!" Paige cried, clasping her hands over her ears to keep from hearing the words Ryan was saying. "Don't you realize how much you are torturing me!"

"I'm sorry," Ryan replied gingerly. "That was terribly callous of me. I was only trying to make you see how much it would hurt Kyle," he explained.

Paige ran her fingers through her hair. "I know . . . I know. It's . . ." She looked over at the bed, the bed she and Kyle had so blissfully shared. "I need to lie down for a while, this is . . . simply too much for me to handle."

"That's right, my dear. You have to rest and conserve your energy. But I do wish you would

341

reconsider my offer; no! I don't want you to consider my offer, I want you to consider the baby . . . the baby you love so much." He said compassionately, "These may be biting words, but I feel I have to speak to you in this manner for you to understand how serious it is. I'm offering you a name for your baby. I realize you don't love me. But maybe someday . . . we could share some happiness." He looked at her through pleading eyes. "I think you know how I feel about you. I promise to be kind and not make any demands." Tenderly Ryan took her in his arms. "I'll leave now, but I will return in the morning for your decision."

The night passed slowly as Paige lay in bed unable to sleep. Although her heart was broken at the thought of Kyle and what he had suffered, she had to give consideration to the child she was carrying. She at least had the consolation that Kyle had come to his senses and realized she had not betrayed him.

It was true, she could move away after the baby came, but someone, somewhere, would always appear, knowing the sordid story of her life. Then what kind of a future would her child have? Nameless . . . the child of a convicted spy. No! No! She could not do that to an innocent child . . . Kyle's child. But the thought of accepting Ryan's proposal was amost more than she could bear. There would come a time when he would take her into his arms . . . and she knew Kyle's face would never escape her memory. No matter how much time passed, she would never forget the feel of his arms around her. She did not want Ryan. Her soul screamed for Kyle, the man she deeply loved. Deep inside she had known they would never be able to live a happy life together. She had known when they took him away that dark cold morning, that they were taking him away to hang!

Throughout the night, Paige lay in torment and anguish. Several times she rose from the bed and paced the floor aimlessly, lamenting over the decision that was staring her in the face. A decision she had to make from the bottom of her broken heart. And deep inside her shattered soul, she knew what it would have to be!

Chapter Twenty-Four

To Paige, the morning dawned colorless. She sat at her dressing table and carefully brushed her hair until it gleamed. Then she painstakingly dressed. Not because of vanity, but because she didn't want Ryan to know what an agonizing time she had had in reaching her decision. When she heard someone knocking at the door, her feet felt heavily laden as she went to answer it.

Ryan looked at her darkly circled eyes. "You must not have slept any last night," he stated.

"No, not much," then she admitted, "none at all, in fact. But," Paige added with determination, "I have made up my mind. I have made my decision." She looked at him straight forward. "I will tell you now, I will marry you, but, I cannot promise to love you. I will respect you and your feelings, and . . . I also have one condition to make."

Ryan could barely conceal the happiness in his voice. "Yes, Paige. What is your condition?"

She searched his eyes for understanding. "I want to go away. And I don't mean next week, tomorrow, I mean today! I don't believe I can stand to be here in this town for another minute longer than necessary. I don't care if we have to walk a thousand miles with nothing but the clothes on our back. I want to go now!"

Ryan looked at her for a moment, staring into her beautiful but aching green eyes. "All right, my dear," he said slowly. "I think I can manage your request. I can . . . leave my plantation in charge of the overseer, and I have a considerable amount of cash on hand." He nodded firmly, anxious to make the final arrangements. "As luck would have it, there is a small steamer that will leave for the Gulf today. We can go to Houston, then later, maybe on to Mexico, or someplace like that. But," he took her into his arms and gazed at her tenderly, "we will go somewhere far away, and I'll make you forget this tragic moment in your life. I'll make you happy, Paige . . . this I swear! I know I will never be able to make you forget Kyle, and I wouldn't try to do that. But someday, you will grow to feel the same way about me as I do you." He brought her hand up to his lips and kissed it, although he wanted to take her into his arms and make passionate love to her, he knew he had to control his feelings . . . at least for a while, until he won her love.

Feeling uncomfortable, Paige pulled away from him. "I suppose I should be getting my things together?"

He gave a wave of his hand. "Leave it. I'll buy you new things . . . much prettier," he boasted.

"Oh Ryan, please . . . don't say things like

that," Paige said as she turned so Ryan couldn't see the sudden burst of tears.

"I'm sorry, my darling. That was callous of me." He took her back in his arms. "Can you forgive me? I was simply carried away by my enthusiasm."

Paige pulled her eyes from his piercing stare. "Of course, Ryan," she said hesitantly.

"Now that everything is settled, there is a small amount of business I must attend to." He hurried to the door; calling back over his shoulder, he said, "I'll be back before you know it." Then, he disappeared out the door.

Paige walked through the house, stopping and picking up small items, examining them closely, then laying them down. She knew she would have to get busy if she was to be finished by the time Ryan came for her. Finally, her bag was packed, and she was ready to go. She walked over to the desk and picked up a pen, intending to write a letter to the children, but after much deliberation, decided against it. The children would receive good care, perhaps not the loving kind, but at least they would not go hungry. But, she should sever all ties with them, since it was impossible to have a relationship with them any longer. Suddenly, she was very anxious for Ryan to return. The temptation to change her mind was almost overpowering. But she knew she could not do that. The only way she would ever have any peace of mind would be to leave this town far behind her, and quickly!

Chapter Twenty-Five

Paige stood on the deck of the steamship and watched as the muddy water swirled in small eddies, forming whirlpools, then drifting effortlessly away as if they were on a journey all their own. They had left Jefferson the day before, but in reality, it seemed like a lifetime ago. She had no idea how Ryan had completed his business arrangements so quickly, but he had moved with incredible swiftness.

Ryan had convinced her that the sooner they were married, the better off they would be. He told her he would confide to the captain the reason why they were in a hurry to marry. It would imply the child she was carrying was his, and the war raging had prevented them from doing the honorable thing.

They were to meet within a short time in the captain's cabin to be secretly wed. Paige cried to herself, "Why, Lord, why? Am I doomed to be unhappy? Why do my weddings always have to be so sorrowful? What have I done to find such displeasure in your eyes? Her thoughts were broken by Ryan when he touched her shoulder. "Come my dear, the captain is waiting for us."

Ryan escorted her gently through the small crowd of people mingling on the deck, but she was oblivious to everyone. It was as though she were in a frozen stupor, and numbed by her personal tragedy.

They were married in the captain's quarters. If Paige had been aware of the room, she would have been enchanted by its beauty. The captain had painted Irish murals on the walls to remind him of his homeland. She would have even admired the Irish captain. He had sandy red hair, and wore a thick, but neatly trimmed mustache, and spoke with a thick Irish brogue. Yes, under normal circumstances, Paige would have been highly impressed with Captain Edward Baker and his ship, the *Helene*.

When the ceremony was over, wine was poured and toasts were made. Paige could only remember she had glued a smile on her face, and it did not disappear until she reached the privacy and sanctity of her room.

For days, Ryan was patient with his bride. Each morning, he would dress her, brush her hair, then lead her outside where she could get fresh air by sitting in the deck chairs lining the ship. He knew patience and gentleness were the key to Paige's survival, because of the traumatic shock she had received. One thing was certain. Ryan knew she had plenty of time to get over her shock. But he was getting extremely worried about her. She simply was not responding to their life. Even when the

Helene docked at the small ports dotting the river, Paige did not acknowledge she knew where they were or what they were doing there. By the time they had ridden the overland coach to Houston, and checked into one of the city's finest hotels, Ryan's patience was finally drawing to a close.

He walked into the parlor, expecting to find Paige dressed and ready for dinner. When he saw her sitting just as he had left her, clutching that stupid green cloak to her as if it had some magical power, he exploded.

"Damn-it! There is no reason for you to carry on so!" he thundered in her face. "I happen to have feelings too! I know you are grieving for Kyle, but he died four days ago. They hung him and nobody can ever bring him back!" He stabbed his chest with his finger. "I'm alive and I'm standing here, and I happen to be your husband." He stared at her for a long moment, watching as her tears threatened to spill but didn't. As quickly as he had become angered, his voice softened. "Paige, my darling, I don't expect you to be a wife to me in every sense of the word. But I have watched you grieve until I cannot stand it any longer. I have reached the end of my endurance." He stood wearily. "I'm going downstairs to the bar and order a bottle of wine. Then I shall return. We will then drink the wine and go to dinner, and by God, we are going to enjoy ourselves!" He spun on his heel and marched to the door, slamming it loudly behind him.

Paige stared after him. She dropped her head into her hands and tried to cry but the tears would not come. It was as though someone else was inside her body, commanding it to eat, to sleep, even to breathe! She knew she had to snap out of her depression; it was not good for the baby. The baby! Just the thought of the tiny precious bit of humanity should have been enough to pull her out of this morbidly depressing feeling. Paige rose from the couch and walked over to the window where she stared at the far off ships sailing to and from tropical places of paradise. Maybe when the baby is born, she thought, we could take a long trip. Maybe a trip to France, where I could see my homeland and look up relatives who have long since forgotten me. She shook her head, as if trying to clear it from a dense fog. Before she could even think about anything like that, she had to feel better about her life. Suddenly, she saw the anguish on Ryan's face and then, like a cold hand twisting her heart, she remembered another time when another man had begged her to use reason. That night in the small cabin, the first night she and Kyle had been married. If only she had relented, they would have had at least a few months of happiness. But no! She had been stubborn and hateful!

Paige walked through the parlor to the opposite side of the bedroom where the wardrobe was standing. She removed a filmy chiffon gown and put it on. Then, she rushed to the bureau, sat down and began to brush her long black raven hair, vigorously. After she had finished, Paige stepped back and surveyed the results critically. Her face was much thinner, but the loss of weight only made her cheekbones more prominent, more alluring. The immodest cut of the gown and her fully rounded breasts only served to heighten her femininity. She appraised the gown, and silently appreciated Ryan's taste in clothing. It was a pale green which made the green of her eyes stand out like jade emeralds. The long flowing sleeves made her appear much more graceful. For how long she stood, she did not know. Then she heard the front door open cautiously.

"I'm in here, Ryan," she called out in a surprisingly clear voice.

When Ryan stepped into the room, his mouth flew open in astonishment. Never had he seen her so beautiful. "What . . . I . . . don't understand," he muttered as he sat the bottle of wine on the bureau.

"There is nothing to understand. I guess I finally grasped what you have been trying to tell me." She stood, twisting and wringing her hands nervously. "Ryan," she said slowly and walked back to the window, "I want you to know how much I appreciate what you've done for me and my unborn child. I also want you to know that a portion of my heart can never be touched and I'm asking you to not even try. But . . . I think I'm ready to . . . become your wife. By my similarly foolish actions, I deprived Kyle and myself out of many happy days, weeks, and even months." She looked at him sincerely. "I vow never to do that again. I also realize every time Kyle's name is mentioned, I see you flinch. I will try not to speak his name in your presence again." Ryan rushed to her,

351

but she waved him aside momentarily. "Wait," she cautioned, "I'm not finished yet. I will speak honestly and from my heart. I can have no idea when I will become a loving wife, but from this moment on, I will try to be a faithful wife to you. Don't get me wrong," she rushed to say, "I shall always be faithful, but I am speaking in mind as well as body. But, I can't promise I'll never think of him." She touched her stomach gently. "You and I both know that is impossible. But . . . I can say from now on . . . I'll try and I'll try really hard."

"Oh my darling!" Ryan whispered crushing her into his arms. "I love you and I guess I've loved you since the moment I first laid eyes on you. I'll make you forget! I promise I will!" He lifted her up into his arms and carried her lovingly to the bed. Then he stopped motionlessly. "Wait! Is it . . . will it . . . since you are pregnant . . ."

Paige managed a weak smile. "No, Ryan it won't hurt for us to have relations."

Ryan breathed a sigh of relief and started kissing her. His mouth sought hers, passionate, searing, demanding.

Paige shuddered involuntarily, then quickly hoped Ryan did not sense her distaste. Try as she might, Paige could not respond to his urgent demands. She could only cringe in horror as his hands sought and touched places only one other man had known before.

Suddenly, Ryan leaped from her shouting, "Damn-it Paige! Don't torture me this way. Do you have any idea how it makes me feel when you . . . treat me like . . . like . . ." His words trailed off as he bowed his head and his shoulders shook with deep rasping sobs.

"I'm sorry!" Paige cried. "You have to give me time!"

Ryan cast her a sidelong glance, then strode over to the bureau and poured a hefty portion of wine into the glass. With a defeated slump to his shoulders, he walked over to the window and stared out at the blackness of the night. Finally, he turned and looked at her curled into a tight little ball on the huge bed. "I wonder . . ." he pondered slowly, "if there will be enough time left in the world to make you forget Kyle Brenner?"

For hours the cheerless scene continued. Ryan kept staring out the window, lost in his remorseful depression.

"May I have a glass of wine?" Paige asked. "I think it may help me to relax."

Ryan spun quickly around. He had not heard Paige's approach.

"Why sure!" Ryan told her and rushed to pour his bride a glass of the amber liquid.

Together they sat, not speaking but each deep in their own heart wrenching thoughts. After a short while, Paige's terrible trembling stopped and after a few more glasses of wine, she was even able to smile at Ryan. She took a deep breath, knowing what must be done should not be delayed any longer or a rift would form between them that might never heal.

She called softly, "Ryan?"

He looked at her with longing in his eyes.

"I want you to make love to me. I want you to make me your wife," she spoke hesitantly.

"Are you sure?" he demanded. "I don't think I could take your rejection again." He turned her fae directly toward him so she could not avoid his piercing eyes.

Her voice faltered then carried strong as she replied, "No . . . I'm sure."

Ryan stifled a moan, then scooped her easily into his arms once again. This time, he did not spend as much time fondling and kissing her. It was as if he was afraid she would change her mind and again deny him what he wanted most in the world. He did not realize she had been able to accept his love making because she had drunk enough wine to numb her senses, and to block out her true feelings. And even though she had earlier said she would remain faithful to him, the man making love to her was Kyle . . . her own love . . . her only love!

Paige awoke early the following morning. In Ryan's sleep, he had pulled her tightly to him, one arm possessively entwined around her shoulders and the other hand closed firmly around her breast. She studied him thoughtfully as he slept. You deserve so much more than I can give. I know I promised to block Kyle from my mind. I also know I'll never be able to do as I have promised. After Kyle having me, even though you have now put your brand on me . . . I know he will be the only man I can ever love. Her thoughts were interrupted by someone running through the halls shouting.

"It's over! It's over!"

Ryan instantly awoke. He leaped to his feet, grabbed a robe and rushed to the door to see what the commotion was all about. He caught a young lad by his collar and demanded, "What is all this ruckus about?"

The boy's eyes gleamed in happiness as he shouted, "The hotel manager told me to run up here and spread the good word. To wake everyone up if necessary."

"What?"

"The war's over! The war's over! It ended yesterday! General Lee surrendered to Grant at Appomattox!" The boy paused, disbelief written on his face as the news gradually sank in. He walked off muttering under his breath, "I can't believe it. The war is finally over!"

Ryan rushed back to Paige with a wide grin on his face. No one would have been able to tell his was the losing side. "Did you hear what the boy said?" he asked excitedly. When he saw Paige just sitting there, his smile dwindled.

She looked sorrowfully around the room, torment on her face as she said in a bitter, quaking voice, "It ended yesterday. Four days too late! A lifetime too late!"

Discretion playing the better part of valor, Ryan backed away from the bedroom to leave her alone for a few moments. He closed the massive French doors and breathed a huge sigh of relief. Imagine! If the war had ended a few days earlier, then Kyle would be alive at this very moment and there could be no place on earth where he could hide from his wrath and vengeance. Ryan smiled to himself almost sardonically. Now, he would make his wife fall in love with him. There would be nothing to stand in his way now . . . except for the bastard she was carrying! But . . . all he had to do was wait and bide his time, and he would rid them of that obstacle too!

The passing days turned into weeks. Paige gradually began to accept what had happened. She even took the news of President Lincoln's assassination gracefully. Neither one said a word for or against it, only registering shock that humanity was sinking to this low form by such animal action. Ryan wisely left her alone in her understandable sorrow. He realized if he placed undue demands on her, she could have wilted like a spring flower on a cold day. Then news began to filter in about the northern carpetbaggers taking control of the south. Ryan was worried about his holdings, but upon receiving messages from his men, everything seemed to be going smoothly. When Paige read of the account of the carpetbaggers in the newspapers, she discovered Kyle had died for nothing. What he had been sent to stop before it started was completely destroyed by a madman at the theater.

Ryan decided they would take a tour of Europe as soon as the baby was born. He would go for as long as possible without making sexual demands on Paige, but when his overpowering need for her consumed him, he took her. As always, she plied her senses with wine which only served to anger Ryan, but he held his silence. He could not live without her, and if the only way she could accept him was with the numbing qualities of liquor, then for the time being, he would accept that. But he vowed to himself, he would not tolerate it forever.

On Independence Day, a blistering hot day in July, a son was born to Paige. She knew it would be a boy. Over Ryan's quiet objections, Paige named her child Jason Brenner Ledbetter, giving him Kyle's middle and last name. She wanted to call him Bren, but Ryan absolutely refused her request.

Days passed into weeks, weeks into months, and the months into years as they toured the world. They saw sights unfold before their eyes that would remain treasured in their hearts for all the days of their lives. France, England, Europe, and the Far East unfolded before them. Paige's life with Ryan settled into a comfortable one, but the one bright ray of sunshine in her life was the tow-headed little boy she worshipped. Ryan accepted the small amount of feelings Paige let herself give without complaint.

The only thing that Ryan insisted upon was securing a nurse for Jason. He was bitterly jealous of the child. He refused to share Paige with the boy and was constantly arranging things to keep them apart. Paige realized why Ryan did the things he did, and she went along with his demands as long as he was not too strict with Jason.

The years passed, and they were good years. Life went by at a leisurely pace. Then the day came when Ryan received news that he had suffered severe financial setbacks in the States and they required his personal and immediate attention. He refused to leave Paige in England, and over her objections, he made arrangements for the return trip by way of Boston, then the railroad, then overland stage to St. Louis. It was with a heavy heart that Paige allowed herself to be returned to the place where her life was completely turned around and in a strange sense of the word, destroyed.

Chapter Twenty-Six

July 1, 1868

Jason stood at the rail jumping excitedly up and down when the great paddleboat rounded the last turn on their journey home. Paige glanced fondly down at her son and smiled at the enthusiasm he showed. She only wished she could be as happy to be returning to Jefferson. From where she was standing, she could see the Irvine Hotel, Austin's Mercantile, and other shops she used to patronize. But surprisingly, the crushing, painful memories did not return as she had expected, although the memories were there . . . plenty of them.

The blast of the steam whistle jarred her from her reminiscence. She hurriedly began the time consuming tasks of preparations to leave the ship. It seemed as if the past three years were spent either boarding or leaving a ship from far distant places.

"Sara, Sara," Paige called to her Negro maid. "Be sure and don't forget Jason's stuffed toy he left in the stateroom. You know as well as I do, there would be no sleep for anyone tonight if he didn't have it."

"Sho' 'nough, ma'am. I be on my way to pick it up now."

"Sara!" Ryan shouted. Then he started scolding her in front of the amused onlookers. "How many times have I told you to use correct English. You know as well as I do that you can speak correctly. I will not tolerate having my wife's personal maid sounding as if she just came out of the jungles!" he spat.

Sara bowed her eyes. "Yes, sir, Mr. Ledbetter. I . . . I guess I forgot."

"Well see that it doesn't happen again!" Ryan spun on his heel and strode angrily down the gangplank.

Paige patted Sara's hand. "Don't fret about it, Sara. Mr. Ledbetter has a lot of pressing things on his mind lately and has been crosser than usual. He will simmer down in a few days and his tongue won't be so sharp."

"Yes, ma'am. I know he gets a might too touchy when we've been traveling for too long a spell." The woman added sincerely, "I wish he wouldn't take his short temper out on the little boy though." She picked Jason up in her arms.

Paige reached over and tousled his hair. "Now, Sara," she chided. "You know Mr. Ledbetter loves him. He is just a little too strict sometimes."

"Yes, ma'am, that would be the truth," Sarah muttered as she walked away with the boy. Inside she was steaming over the way Mr. Ledbetter inflicted cruel punishment on him, not that he ever whipped or beat the child, but sending him to bed hungry just because he happened to turn over a glass of milk or was out of line by simply acting like the small child he was. Lately, he had refused to even allow Jason to dine with him and the Missus except when they took breakfast in their stateroom. How Mrs. Paige never saw the looks of hatred whenever the boy's Papa looked at him, Sara couldn't understand. But she had seen them . . . plenty of times!

Ryan waited impatiently at the foot of the gang-plank for Paige. "Come on, hurry! The wire I received from my men said they would have a carriage waiting for us."

Paige was standing at the top of the deck, astonished. In fact, she was intrigued at the sight of all the Union soldiers milling quite freely about. When she reached Ryan's side, she asked rather breathlessly, "Doesn't it seem strange to see all these blue coats walking around as if they owned the place?"

"Damn right, it does seem strange. But I should remind you that they do own it! They bought it the day Lee surrendered to Grant!" He searched the crowd for the carriage that had been promised. "Aha! There it is." He guided Paige through the milling crowd toward the carriage waiting for them at the end of the walkway.

"But . . . but . . . shouldn't we wait for Sara and Jason?" Paige asked as worry touched her voice.

"Paige," Ryan's voice was subdued and only Paige knew the threat behind the calm. "How many times have I told you that people of our stature do not make their entrance with all their servants and luggage? We may be a little financially embarrassed at the present time, but we certainly don't have to act like sharecroppers on our first visit to the big city!"

"And whose fault is it that we're financially embarrassed?" Paige hissed. "I never wanted all those fancy jewels in the first place!"

Ryan chuckled unpleasantly. "It's a damn good thing we had all those jewels, my dear, or we might have had to work for our passage back to the States. Now would you please be quiet," he muttered, "we are attracting attention from the other passengers."

Paige seethed quietly in her anger as Ryan greeted the man who was driving the carriage, and introduced him to his wife. Paige couldn't help but compare his biased opinion of who was hired help. She supposed it made all the difference in the world if the help's skin was white.

To her dismay, they turned up the street and stopped in front of the Irvine Hotel. "What are we doing here?" she demanded.

"Now darling," Ryan chuckled, but Paige knew he was angry at being questioned in front of his driver. "I don't think the plantation will be ready for occupancy for several days. After all, the main house has been empty for over three years. Besides, there will be a lot of parties and dances coming up in the next few days. Everyone will be celebrating the fourth. I am sure you will want to be where we can join in all the festivities."

"If you wanted my honest opinion, I had much

rather have an extended rest, and not have to worry if my hair is fixed just so, or if my dress is hanging properly."

Ryan looked at her sharply. "Now I'm sure you don't mean that. Surely after a good night's rest, you'll see things differently."

Paige sighed, knowing it was useless to argue with Ryan once his mind was made up. She followed passively behind him as he strode up to the hotel desk and registered for a room. She forced herself not to remember a time long ago with Kyle. But as the bellman led them down the hall, she couldn't help but to reminisce, especially when a tall, dark headed man stepped from the room she once shared with Kyle. Over the period of years, the hurt had subsided. But whenever she saw a tall stranger swagger down a flight of stairs, or caught a certain glance across a crowded room, her memories came crashing back.

She studied Ryan solemnly. How she wished she could have grown to love him. Oh, through the years a fondness had developed because he was so devoted to her. She also knew Ryan was afraid the trip back here would cause them to drift apart. This town could rekindle too many memories for both of them.

Ryan saw to it that they were settled comfortably in their suite before he left for their plantation. Since he would be gone for hours, Paige allowed Jason to lie down with her for a nap, which was something Ryan strictly forbade. But when Jason had asked with his little-boy charm, she simply could not refuse. Lately, he had been having terrible nightmares that his mother was leaving him behind. Even with her constant reassurance, he continued to have the dreams. Paige blamed it on their constant traveling, and never being anywhere permanently. She had expressed her wish to settle somewhere, but Ryan was seeking an ambassadorship appointment in France or in England. He had told her earlier, the only way of securing one was to be seen in the right places with the right kind of people. She was happy to be away from the hectic life on the continent, but was not particularly pleased to have returned to Jefferson. Her only consolation was they at least would be in a permanent place for a while.

That day and the next passed without Paige leaving the room. But on the following morning, she decided to go shopping for Jason's third birthday present. Sara offered to keep the boy with her, but Paige insisted he needed the fresh air.

As they walked down the street, she was simply amazed at the way the town had withstood the reconstruction. They had received accounts of how the entire south had been plundered of its wealth and how the cities and towns were rapidly deteriorating. But Jefferson apparently had suffered none of this.

Paige stopped to look in a shop window and Jason tugged at her skirts.

"Look, Momma!" Jason exclaimed as excitement danced on his face.

Paige laughed aloud at his childish delight at seeing a beautiful multi-colored butterfly perched on the window sill. "Yes darling, isn't it pretty?"

She went on about her business of looking at the merchandise in the window, unaware that Jason had followed the butterfly as it flew away. In a few minutes, she reached for his hand, and to her horror, Jason was nowhere to be seen. She searched for him inside the shop, thinking he might have wandered in there, but she saw no sign of him. She then began a frantic search, first in one store then another. Paige rushed around trying to find him. She became very frightened. The town was so busy with the influx of extra people coming in for the celebration on Independence Day, she was terrified he had wandered off and someone had picked him up. She had almost reached the state of hysteria when she saw Jason's head bobbing up and down. Someone was obviously giving him a ride on his shoulder. She heard Jason squeal when he saw her and pointed in her direction.

"There's my Momma!"

"Oh, Jason! You scared me half to death!" Paige scolded, holding out her arms for her son as the soldier lifted him off his shoulders.

"Appears this little fellar slipped away . . ." His voice trailed off as he recognized Paige.

"Why, Seth! Seth Poteet!" Paige spoke in astonishment. "How in the world are you?"

He tipped his hat. "I'm fine, ma'am, and you?" he asked politely.

"Oh I'm all right I guess. We only arrived back in town a few days ago, and we were shopping and Jason slipped away from me." Paige knew she was rattling almost incoherently, but she was so upset by seeing one of Kyle's friends, she really didn't know what to do or to say. She was relieved of that dilemma when Seth spoke.

"Ma'am, I thought I would never see you again, and quite frankly, seeing you again has taken me by surprise. Would . . . would you mind stepping in here and maybe have a glass of lemonade to refresh yourself?" he asked, gesturing toward a small cafe.

Paige opened her mouth to refuse his request, but then her overwhelming curiosity of what happened to Matthew and the other children overcame her reluctance to discuss Kyle or anything pertaining to his memory.

"All right, Mr. Poteet, or should I say, Captain Poteet?" she said, noticing the bars on his uniform.

Seth escorted Paige into the cafe, helped her and Jason with their chairs and then stared intently at her before speaking.

"You know, you stirred up quite a stink around here, disappearing the way you did."

She looked at him boldly. "Frankly, Captain Poteet, I really doubted if anyone cared."

Seth nodded slowly. "Yeah . . . there were a lot of people who cared. Matthew, his brothers and sister for starters."

Paige flinched visibly. "I know . . . but I cared for them deeply. You have no idea how I've wondered about them over these past few years. Do you know what happened to them?"

Seth snorted indignantly. "Now is a mighty fine time to start trying to find out about them. It would appear to me that you are about three years too late!''

Paige replied angrily. "Look, Captain Poteet! I know I should have left them some word, but you have no idea the mental state I was in. The authorities had taken the children away, I had just received word that Kyle had been sentenced to hang, and I could not stay here and face it. I just couldn't!'' Paige looked around sheepishly when she realized her voice had carried and people were staring at her.

Seth spoke in a brusque voice. "No I guess you couldn't. And I would also wager your conscience has been a little hard to live with these past few years too!''

Paige took Jason's hand and started to rise. "Sir, I do not have to sit here and listen to your insinuations. But, I really don't know why you are so hostile toward me!''

"Because, lady, and believe me, I use that word loosely, Kyle Brenner was the best friend I ever had!''

Paige sank gradually back onto her chair. "I . . . thought . . . so," she said slowly. "You seemed to get along too well to have just met.''

"Then I was lucky I didn't end up in prison with him, wasn't I?''

Paige's mouth gaped in surprise. "You mean . . . you actually think I had something to do with his being in prison?'' she questioned in a tight voice.

"You're damn right I do!'' Seth replied tersely. "It looked strange to me as soon as you heard how Kyle was going to hang, you got an annulment and high-tailed it out of here with Ryan Ledbetter. I figured you were running to save your treacherous neck." He stared at her long and hard. "I'll tell you one more thing. I know you are married to Ryan. And I just happen to be the commander here, and just in case you don't know, Jefferson is still under military law, and if I even hear that you or that son-of-a-bitch you are married to, even spits on the street, then I'll have your hides nailed to the nearest wall! And lady, that is no idle threat, it is a promise!" He stood and roughly shoved his chair from the table and strode off.

Paige sat there for a moment, then she proceeded to chase after him, dragging Jason along.

She caught up with him on the teeming busy street. Oblivious to the curious stares, she grabbed Seth by the arm, and with strength she didn't know she possessed, she spun him around.

"Now let me tell you something, Captain Poteet!" She shook her finger in his face. "Don't you dare question how I felt about Kyle! I loved him more than life itself! You claim to have been such a good friend . . . well, apparently you weren't as good a friend as you thought you were. And furthermore, you certainly have a few facts wrong!" She happened to glance down and see her son staring up at her with his huge brown eyes . . . eyes much like his father's, she covered his ears with her hand and spoke in an angry whisper. "Kyle was the one who insisted upon an annulment! No one asked me a thing about it, and it was done before I had a chance to protest, or anything. If I had been asked or consulted, I would have refused." She planted one arm akimbo. "As for Ryan, he is a kind and decent man. Apparently he was more of a friend to Kyle than you thought, because he at least cared enough to give Kyle's son a name!"

Seth's eyes widened in surprise. "You mean . . . you mean . . . !"

"Yes, Jason is Kyle's son and I am proud of it!" She picked her son up and cradled him to her breast. "I'll say this, I believe what Kyle was doing for our country was good! And when Jason is older, he will be told why and how his father gave his life for our country!" She then spat in the dust. "There!" she said hotly. "I just spit in your damn street! Are you going to arrest me?"

Seth looked at her strangely, then he shook his head slowly. "No . . . I won't arrest you."

"Then step aside, sir, and let us pass."

Seth moved to let her by and stood staring thoughtfully after them as she marched stiffly down the sidewalk.

Chapter Twenty-Seven

Seth was deep in thought as he trudged slowly back to his office. He stepped inside, walked over to his desk, poured a stiff drink, then sat down and propped his feet up on the desk. He sipped his whiskey slowly, then rested his brow on his hand as he watched the man sleeping on the cot with his hat pulled snugly down over his face.

"Kyle . . . wake up. I've got something to tell you."

Kyle stirred on the cot, rose his head groggily, then asked, "Have you heard from Blinn?"

"No I haven't. What I want to talk to you about, concerns a different matter."

Upon hearing that, Kyle settled back down, disinterested, into a much needed slumber.

Seth quickly made up his mind. He would not mention that Kyle had a son. The decision was an agonizing one. It could harvest irreconcilable hard feelings between them if Kyle ever found out he had kept the truth from him. That was, if indeed Paige was telling the truth about Jason belonging to Kyle. But for now, silence was best. If later on

Kyle found out the boy actually belonged to him, he could handle the situation any way he wanted.

"Damn-it, Kyle, wake up! I need to talk to you, *now!*" Seth demanded.

"Hell, man," Kyle snapped, swinging his long legs over the edge of the cot. "I have ridden over four hundred miles withouth much rest and I'm completely done in. If the news isn't about Blinn, then what in the hell could be so important?"

Seth chuckled. "You always were cross as a bear when you had lost a lot of sleep." Instantly his smile dropped into a frown. "Do you have any idea who I just saw?"

Kyle lit a slim cigar then went over to Seth's desk and poured a drink of whiskey, all the while studying his friend intently. "I realize you know how tired I am and I really don't think you would wake me up to play a cat and mouse game if it wasn't important. So . . . I'll bite. Who did you see?"

"Paige."

The silence hung heavy in the room. Neither man spoke as Seth watched Kyle's reaction. Kyle's face blanched and his lips pressed into a thin white line. After a short pause, he managed to choke out bitterly, "So . . . the treacherous bitch is back. I wonder who else she's playing for a sucker?"

"That's right, Kyle. She is back. And I'll tell you something I was not aware of, and you probably weren't either. She thinks you are dead." Seth let those words sink in before he added, "You want to know what I think after talking to her? I don't believe she is the one who turned you in, and fur-

371

thermore, she is still very much in love with you, or at least in love with your memory."

Kyle opened his mouth to speak, but no words came. He walked back to his cot and sat down, then he leaped to his feet and started pacing the floor back and forth like a caged animal. He stepped over to Seth's desk, snatched the whiskey bottle up and poured another drink. After he downed that one, he took a pull directly from the bottle. "What in the hell is the matter with you?" he finally sputtered. "Have you completely lost your mind?" He started pacing the floor again, this time swinging his arms wildly about. He stopped in front of the desk, leaned over and shouted in Seth's face, "Man! What kind of a snow job did she pull on you? This is Kyle you are talking to, *remember!*" He jabbed himself in the chest with his thumb. "I had to sit over there during that damned trial and hear everything . . . including all the things she had to say about me!" He glared at Seth and muttered, "You've gone crazy . . . absolutely crazy!"

Seth jumped to his feet. "Now settle down, Kyle. Before you start ranting and raving, listen to me." He mocked Kyle's gesture by pointing to his chest with his thumb. "This is Seth you're talking to, remember? And friend, I've known you too long without being able to tell when you are hurting inside. You can't fool me. I well recall how you ran around here like a madman looking for her after me and Blinn busted you out of that prison in the nick of time. You searched high and low for that girl until you found out she had married Ryan and had left for places unknown." Seth paused and said belligerently, "In fact, you ran around here so much we were afraid the Rebs would recapture you." Seth leaned back in his chair. "I know another thing. Perhaps you don't even love her anymore, but I doubt that. I will say that you have not been the same since you've lost her."

Kyle slammed his fist against the top of the desk. "No, I'm not the same man, but did you ever stop to consider that I had a different reason to want to find her? I planned on finding her and twisting her rotten little neck for what she did to me and for what she said at my trial."

Seth shook his head in disgust, then said in a somber voice, "Kyle . . . that is my point. She wasn't even at the trial. Have you ever stopped to consider it was Ryan who was on the stand; it was he who said all those things, and it was he who stood to profit by your hanging. After all, it was also Ryan who took Paige off and married her!"

Kyle looked at him for a moment then slumped dejectedly onto a nearby chair. He dropped his head into his hands and mumbled in a somewhat confused voice, "Sometimes in the past three years, my hatred of her was the only thing that kept me going. I've lost her, and I really don't know what I would do if I found out she is innocent." He looked over at Seth. "She must have really said something worthwhile to convince you we've been wrong all this time."

Seth shook his head. "No, actually it was *how* she said it. And, Kyle, there is one way we can possibly find out the truth."

"How's that?" Kyle asked, a ray of hope shining in his eyes.

Seth rubbed his chin thoughtfully. "Think, Kyle. Camp Ford has been locked up all these years. When the Union army took over, that place was in such disrepair, it wasn't worth the trouble to fix up. The records should be intact, that is, except for the ones that were used to find out the identity of the men who died there. We could probably ride over and look through all those old records until we find something."

Kyle walked aimlessly around the room as he thought. *What if we do go over there and still not find anything? It will do little good. But on the other hand, it might prove her guilt or innocence one way or the other.* He poured another short drink and stared moodily out the window. *Why did she have to come back after all this time? Why couldn't she have stayed in the past where he had firmly placed her? But, how could he ever have a moment's peace when he could have tried to find out the truth but didn't? After all,* he reasoned, *Paige has convinced Seth she loved me,* and he knew from past experiences his friend's opinions had always been hard to crumble. Kyle ran a work-calloused hand over his whiskered face. Having made up his mind, he wanted to act quickly. "Before we go off half-cocked, is Blinn in any danger?"

"No, not any more than he has been subjected to for the past three years since he's gone completely undercover."

Kyle nodded. "All right. Let's go get some

leather. We're gonna have to hurry if we are to meet with Blinn tomorrow night.''

Kyle's thoughts raced back to the beginning as they rode over the brushy and rugged terrain toward Camp Ford. He remembered lying in his cell the night before he was to hang. How that sorry old dog had held the guards at bay while Seth and Blinn had rescued him from his doom. And how much he had enjoyed twisting Turner's neck until he was dead. He had laid low at the deserted cabin where he and Paige had spent their wedding night deep in the tall pines. Once he received word that Lee had surrendered to Grant and the war had ended, he had thrown caution to the wind and ridden brazenly into town each night looking for his wife, even though the streets were still being patrolled by a few straggling soldiers who had refused to give up on their cause. It was only after the Union soldiers arrived that he was able to openly search for her. But by this time, President Lincoln had long since been assassinated and his plans for reconstruction had been cast carelessly aside, sending the country even further into the pits of hell. When the steamer, the *Helene* returned from a trip to the Gulf, Kyle had discovered the truth, or at least what appeared to be the truth.

Kyle had felt as though his life were over. He knew the only place that would offer any solace would be his ranch in far West Texas. He and Matthew had gone there and worked from sunup to sundown. They got the old homeplace in shape, before sending for Mark, Luke and Jessie. Kyle had not seen nor heard a word about Oscar, so he had absolutely no qualms about building his new life around the children he had grown to love. And Matthew . . . after he had gotten over the shock of hearing what he did at the trial, never wavered in his faith in Paige. He insisted she was innocent and someday some kind of proof would surface. Kyle couldn't help but think about that as they rode all day and into the night. Perhaps soon we'll see if his faith was justified, thought Kyle.

It was late that night before Kyle and Seth reached Camp Ford. They pried loose enough boards from the windows to gain entrance. Even though the courtroom was musty and dust covered, Kyle was transported back in time. It was almost as if he could hear the Southern officers pass judgment on him again.

The men went into the room where the records were kept, lit some candles and stared around the room in disbelief. Rats had chewed through the boxes holding the papers, and pilings were every-where!

"Hell!" Kyle swore. "We may be here too late to find anything salvageable."

Seth managed a weak smile. "I guess we can give it a good try though."

The silence in the room was broken as the men dug through each box of records. They found some totally intact, and some were completely destroyed. Finally, Seth called excitedly across the room. "Wait a minute, Kyle! I think I've found something!"

In a flash Kyle rushed across the room and took

the papers from Seth. He knelt down by the candle light to see better, all the while devouring the words written on the papers. Thankfully, the rats had not chewed or nested in that particular box of papers. Seth could feel the tension while Kyle shuffled through them. A short time later, Kyle exhaled a deep, withered breath and slumped onto the floor. He sat with his legs straight out in front of him. He rubbed his whiskered face with a shaking hand and said, "Well I'll be damned! It was Oscar all along! But Ryan was the one who took the stand and told the damaging lies. He had to be the ringleader of that trouble for him to know what to lie about! And it must have been his idea to get the annulment!" He looked at Seth with hurt and frustration shining from his eyes. He choked, "All these years I've hated and blamed her." He looked squarely at Seth. "I haven't asked . . . I've almost been afraid to, but . . . is she still married to him?"

Seth nodded, not trusting himself to speak.

Kyle's features turned sadistic. "I'll get even with him if it's the last thing I ever do!"

Seth cautioned, "Now wait a minute, Kyle. Let's not go off half-cocked. We have a mission to do first before any personal vendetta can be . . ."

"To hell with that!" Kyle exploded. "I'm going back with my gun strapped low, and I swear when I find them, I'll kill both Oscar and Ryan!"

In a hard voice, Seth spoke. "Oh no, you're not, my friend. You are not going to do a damn thing!" Although it hurt Seth to talk to his old friend in this manner, he knew he must. With squinted eyes, he said, "You owe me one, Kyle, and I'm calling in the debt!"

Kyle's eyes narrowed dangerously. "What do you mean, I owe you one? Did you mark it down that you and Blinn saved my life?"

Seth rolled his eyes toward the ceiling. "Hell no, Kyle! Just stop and think a moment." He gestured with his hands. "Think about why you were contacted and asked to come and help."

Kyle sat back and blinked. It was all slowly adding together. Blinn had been working undercover ever since the war had ended, and Seth had told him Blinn had slipped into his office about two months prior with important news. He had heard someone *big* was coming in to lead a rebellion, a rebellion that could possibly plunge them back into another civil war. Also this person could lead his band of men to a huge cache of silver, to finance their uprising. Blinn had reported that the situation was extremely dangerous to the entire country. That if the whipped southerners got a taste of victory, a lot of bloodshed was in store for the future.

Kyle looked slowly at Seth. "It makes sense. We suspected Ryan a long time ago. Blinn hears a rumor and suddenly Ryan is back in the picture, and we've got one hell of a mess on our hands." His lips clenched tightly together. "And the hell of it is, Paige will be caught right in the middle." Kyle shook his head sheepishly. "Sorry I lost control of my temper . . . but I still mean it. I'll kill them both!"

Seth smiled. "Now you are sounding like the Kyle I've always known. As far as I'm concerned . . . you can have that pleasure. Only thing, we need to be getting back to Jefferson. Blinn might be in over his head. And we have no idea when all this hell is going to break loose!"

Chapter Twenty-Eight

Paige sat in the hotel courtyard and fluttered her fan listlessly. She had no idea how stifling and humid the summers could be in the piney woods of East Texas. Sitting there, it was as though she were transported back to the summers she spent as a child in South Carolina . . . the only difference being the palmetto trees growing profusely there, and the occasional breeze from the ocean blowing its fresh washed breath over the plantation.

Sara had put Jason down for a much-needed nap. They had all been up late the night before; Jason being thrilled by his birthday, somehow got the idea all the fireworks had been for his benefit, and Paige had not told him differently. Later on, after he had fallen asleep, she had been forced to sit through and endure another senseless ball of artificial people tittering, discussing who was wearing what, and who was being seen where.

Paige knew she did not want this sort of life. She wanted more than the feigned, fradulent, tinsel relationships with the people Ryan encouraged her to associate and be seen with.

Her heart longed for a home of her own. She wanted a yard in which to grow rows upon rows of pretty flowers, and perhaps a tall oak tree to hang a swing on so Jason could play to his heart's content, instead of being cooped up in some cheerless hotel room. She needed a place where Jason could run and play and get dirty like any other normal little boy. Instead, he was gradually turning into a sad and somber child that stared wistfully through the window at the other children frolicking in the street.

Thunderation! she thought, leaping to her feet. There was no excuse for them to stay in a crowded hotel room when Ryan owned a fabulously large plantation. So what if it needed a few minor repairs! She certainly didn't have to have all the finery Ryan thought she needed.

Paige marched determinedly through the hotel looking for Ryan. She found her husband in the lobby talking with some other men. She waited impatiently for Ryan to finish his conversation before disturbing him.

Ryan glanced up and when he saw Paige waiting for him, a slight frown appeared on his brow. "Did you want to see me, Paige?"

She nodded. "Yes. But if you are too busy discussing business, I can wait until you are finished."

"No, that isn't necessary. I'm through here," he said, dismissing the men. Ryan took Paige's arm and escorted her down the hallway to their room.

"Now, what do you want to talk to me about?" He leaned over and kissed her cheek lightly.

Deep creases of anguish marked her brow when

she replied, "Ryan, I simply can not exist like this another day."

Alarm echoed in Ryan's voice. "What is the matter? Are you sick? Is there anything you want?"

"Yes! There is something I want very much!" Paige walked over to the French windows rubbing her arm in a nervous gesture. "I want to leave here! Surely your plantation isn't so bad and in such disrepair that we couldn't live there while the carpenters are working on it."

Ryan chuckled in relief. "Is that all it is? For a moment I thought it was something serious."

"But it is serious, Ryan. You have no idea how much I detest living in endless hotel rooms and having absolutely no privacy. And this heat is horrible! The buildings are pressed together so tightly, there is not fresh air to breathe. Ryan . . ." tears misted her eyes, "I want a home I can call my own." She searched his eyes. "You know how much I hated to return here, so, please, get me out of this hotel!"

He gazed at her thoughtfully. "It actually means this much to you?"

"Yes, it does," she said softly, yet apprehension made her voice break.

Ryan threw up his hands in mock disgust. "All right! You know I can't refuse you . . . especially when you look at me that way."

"Oooh Ryan!" she squealed in excitement. "Can we move in today? Please?"

A wide smile flashed across Ryan's face as he nodded. "All right. We can move today."

Paige flew into his outstretched arms, showering him with kisses. "You are so good to me," she whispered. "So deliciously good!" For a brief moment, sadness passed through Paige. She felt that Ryan was too good for her. She wished she could return the love he showered upon her. Instead, she was haunted by a ghost from her past.

The next few hours sped by rapidly. Paige woke Sara and Jason, and they all pitched in to help with the packing. She sent Sara down to Austin's Mercantile with a list of supplies to be delivered later on in the day. Eagerly anticipating the thought of a new home, even Jason's usual solemn expression disappeared from his pinched little face.

Oh! How they enjoyed the ride to the plantation! Even the merciless sun and the humid air relented as billowing white thunderclouds drifted aimlessly overhead, blocking the sun's daggers of heat. Ryan rode alongside the wagon chuckling at how Paige, Sara, and Jason were carrying on like carefree children.

Soon they reached the plantation. While Jason scurried around and investigated the house, Paige admonished Ryan. "Why this house isn't as rundown as you led me to believe."

"I know it isn't too bad, but I only wanted you to have the best. Now that I've come back here, I have been able to secure a release of some of my holdings and money is no longer a problem." He smiled at her. "We can do just about whatever we want to do."

Paige smiled at Ryan, amused that he placed such value on material things. Then she said, "I'm happy for your sake that your financial problems are over. But," she paused accusingly, "there is absolutely no sense in your spending a small fortune on something I do not need or want." She broke away from his embrace and asked, obviously puzzled, "Why are so many men here? I would imagine there are at least a hundred or so men stirring around outside."

"Now there you go! Worrying your pretty little head over things that shouldn't concern you. But if you must know, the men are gathering here to start a trail drive in a few days."

"Oh, I see," Paige said, not realizing well over a hundred men was an absurd number to do what Ryan had suggested.

Their conversation was interrupted by a deep voice. "Where does you wants me to put dis here trunk, Mr. Ryan?"

Paige turned around to see a huge black man stooped slightly under the weight of a huge trunk on his back.

"Shem? Is that you?" she asked incredulously.

"Why sho' 'nough ma'am," he said as recognition crept into his eyes. "And I 'members you too!"

Paige smiled at the Negro's stammering. "I'm pleased you are looking so well. Have you been here long?"

"No ma'am, I hasn't." He ducked his head low as he backed out the door. "Pleasure to see you all safe and sound, ma'am."

"Paige!" Ryan admonished in a scolding voice. "You shouldn't lower yourself by speaking to each and every field hand you meet!"

"But he isn't a field hand! In fact . . . he practically saved my life once."

Ryan's attention perked up. "Yeah . . . how's that?"

Paige told him in halting words how the giant Negro had pulled the pirate from his attack and how he had made the man back down.

"I understand what you mean, but still, you ought to watch it a little closer."

As Ryan strode away, Paige watched him sadly. They were so different. Their personalities clashed so much. She could not help but compare Ryan to how Kyle used to be. She strongly doubted if Ryan was faced with the same set of circumstances, he would have never taken in the children like Kyle did so long ago. Paige thought with a dejected shrug, they could be so much happier if only Ryan wasn't so ambitious.

The rest of the afternoon was spent settling in and unpacking their trunks and baggage. Paige took a much-needed break by walking around the yard just as the sun was setting. It was so pleasant, Paige felt like clasping her arms to her breast and spinning around, squealing at the top of her lungs.

"Mama! Mama!" Jason shrieked as he came running from around the house. "It's fun here!"

Paige stopped to see her son in all his splendor. His face was streaked with dirt and his knee was skinned, but his face beamed and radiated happiness.

Paige laughed cheerfully and lifted him high in her arms. To his dismay, he was carried into the house for a sorely needed bath. He was so tired by the time they sat down to their light but delicious supper, his head was nodding in his plate.

Paige took a leisurely bath, then threw back the heavily draped window after blowing out the candles so she could stand, dressed in only a thin chemise, out on the alcove. She savored the cool breeze in the privacy of the darkness. This was the first time she allowed her mind to wander . . . back to a few days ago when she saw Seth. Seeing him again had reopened an old wound. She thought she had firmly placed Kyle's memory to the back of her mind. He had rarely surfaced in a long while except for a few smattering glimpses into the past. She shook her head remorsefully, knowing she must push these torturous memories aside. She knew she should never compare Kyle to Ryan again. It was something that put her through unnecessary misery.

Somehow, her attention drew away from these heart wrenching thoughts as she noticed a faint glow of a cigar flickering in the darkness, then she heard muted voices carrying through the stillness. Not wanting to eavesdrop, Paige turned to go back inside. Then . . . a name . . . caused her to stop suddenly. Kyle! The men were speaking about Kyle. She leaned forward, eagerly grasping each word. She gripped the rail of the bannister for support when she recognized the voices.

"What in the hell do you mean, saying I owe you more money?" Ryan demanded, outraged.

Oscar whined sarcastically. "Well now, Mr.

386

High-n-mighty Ryan Ledbetter, if'n I hadn't tol' them soldier boys 'bout that Brenner fellar, then I've got a notion you would never have got my niece that you had the hots fer.''

"Keep a civil tongue in your mouth when you speak of my wife!" Ryan shouted angrily.

Paige's hand flew to her mouth in horror as their words faded away. She tried to silence her cry of consternation. "Oh God no!" It was Ryan and Oscar who turned Kyle in! They were the ones responsible for her beloved's death!

She whirled around and raced back inside. She lit a candle and began throwing clothes in a bag. She could not and would not stay under the same roof with that man for another night. She would go far away where she would never have to see him again. The dress Paige was holding fell to the floor as she recalled bitter words that Ryan spoke such a long time ago. If he wanted something badly enough . . . he would figure out how to get it, regardless of what means he had to use. Now Paige had discovered what means he had used to get her. He had murdered Kyle as sure as if he had pulled the latch loose on the gallows!

Paige threw the bag on the floor. She wanted nothing that belonged to Ryan. She ran down to the room where Jason was sleeping and picked him up.

"Wha . . . what's the matter, Mama?" he asked sleepily.

"Nothing, son," she whispered, hoping not to alarm him. "I've decided we should go for a ride. I

387

want you to be very quiet and lie still until I come back for you. I'm going down to the barn and harness a rig." Paige silently cursed herself for waking the boy until she was completely ready to go. But she had been angry, and had acted on the spur of the moment. "Will you be very quiet?" she asked.

His large brown eyes grew very solemn. "Yes, Mama, but please hurry . . . 'cause I'm scared!"

Paige reassured him everything would be all right, then she slipped down the stairs and out of the house. What she saw confused her. Down by the former slaves' quarters, all the men had clustered under burning torches and Ryan was at the front giving them instructions. He was shouting something about an uprising and they would be successful! Paige slipped quietly into the barn. Speed was of the utmost importance. Not only must she escape from Ryan's house, she had to warn Seth about Ryan! Everything had come together and all the pieces closely fit. Ryan had been the ringleader in all the trouble and it was he whom Kyle had been investigating! In some way unknown to her, Ryan was the cause of all the trouble in the area!

She had just finished hitching the horse to the carriage when a voice caused her to spin around.

"Where in the hell are you going?" Ryan spoke in a voice she was not accustomed to hearing.

"I'm . . . leaving!" she spat. "I've found you out! I overheard you and Oscar talking." She glared at him with a bitter hatred. "Just how much did I cost, Ryan? How much was Kyle's death worth to you?"

The truth was written all over Ryan's face as he looked at Paige in awe. It seemed to him all his hopes and dreams came crashing down on him in the last minute. When he was finally able to speak, he muttered, "Paige . . . my darling, you don't understand. I loved you! I had to have you! Anyway, anyhow . . . I had to possess you. Don't you understand?" he pleaded.

"No," she spat in a voice filled with venom. "I can't understand any of this . . . except how much I hate you!"

Ryan ran and grabbed Paige by her shoulders. "You are not leaving me now! I've worked too hard and planned too long for this moment." Ryan implored her. "Everything I've done has been for you and for our life together."

"Oh no, Ryan!" she accused. "The evil deeds have been for the glory of Ryan Ledbetter and no other!"

A look of fury crossed Ryan's features. He had one high card he could play. "All right! Leave! But Kyle Brenner's bastard will stay with me!" He hurried over to the barn doors, threw them open and shouted across the yard to one of his men. "Bart, take your shotgun and go in the house. Go up stairs and stand guard in my son's room. If anyone . . . and I mean anyone other than myself tries to enter, blow their heads off!"

Fear gripped Paige's heart. She had not figured on this. She ran to Ryan and grabbed his arm.

"No! No! You are not keeping my son! I won't let you have him!"

Ryan pushed her roughly back on a pile of hay. His laughter had a ring of insanity to it. "I don't think you have a choice in the matter!" He swaggered cockily over to where she was lying. "In fact, I've got you where I want you. In fact," he rubbed a finger nail on his hand, "a lot of things are going to be different around here from now on." He started removing his gunbelt and unbuttoning his shirt. "I'm going to make love to you right here on the barn floor, and *this time,* you are going to enjoy it! You will sink your claws into my back and moan with pleasure when I take you. And," his eyes blazed with madness, "it will be my name you mutter in passion!" He started walking slowly toward her, paying no mind to her cringing in terror.

"I don't think you are going to hurt de lady."

Paige's glance flew to the door where Shem, the large Negro, was standing menacingly in the doorway, brandishing a gun.

"I said to back away from de lady!" Shem growled. "You ain't gonna hurt her any. Missus Paige," he glanced at her but still kept one eye on Ryan, "I cain't help you none with your little boy, but I can hold him back while you gets in that rig and goes fer help."

Paige didn't have to be told twice. She scrambled for the carriage, taking the whip in hand, she flicked it over the horses' heads and she was off, driving the rig as fast as she could. She could only hope Shem hadn't endangered his life for hers.

Terror mounted with each pounding hoofbeat. Paige prayed for a miracle, that she would be able to reach Seth in time for them to rescue her son from that madman, and also that the reign of terror could be stopped that was about to swoop down on them all!

Chapter Twenty-Nine

Paige, thankful that a light was shining in Seth's office window, leaped down from the carriage and raced breathlessly inside.

"Seth! Seth! Thank God you are here!"

Seth looked up from the papers that were scattered all over his desk. He was surprised to see Paige standing in front of him with dirt streaking her face, wearing a torn dress and obviously distraught.

"What in the world is the matter?" he asked in alarm as he rushed around the desk and helped her to a chair.

She sputtered out the story in a gasping, breathless voice, and after she finished, Seth slumped on the corner of his desk, his face ashen.

"Please!" she begged after telling Seth the story. "You have to save Jason and stop this madness that is taking place!"

Seth worriedly paced the floor. This was happening too quickly. They had not been expecting the uprising to take place for several more days. They would have to move very fast! He ran outside and had his guard sound the alert. Then he came back inside to see if he could get any additional information from Paige. He was questioning her when another man ran into the room.

Kyle asked in alarm, "What is going on? Why the alert? Have you heard . . ." His voice trailed off to nothing when he saw Paige sitting there. All the feelings he had hoped had disappeared came springing back to life when he saw her before him.

Paige looked up at Kyle in shocked disbelief. She felt herself swaying . . . sinking into blackness.

Kyle rushed to her side. He momentarily forgot she was now the wife of his enemy as he gently took her in his arms and held her as he had held her in his dreams. He murmured tenderly, "Oh my darling, thank God I've found you again!"

Paige felt her eyelids flutter as she opened her eyes to gaze at the man she had always loved, but thought dead. To actually see him before her was almost more than her mind could comprehend.

"Kyle . . . my love, is it really you?" she asked incredulously.

"Shhh, my darling. Questions can be answered later. Right now, the most important thing is, I'm holding you in my arms."

"Oh Kyle, I love you and always have." She spoke tenderly, and reached up to gently touch his face.

Seth cleared his throat and quickly brushed away a tear. "Kyle, Paige, I hate to bust this up, and God only knows you both deserve a moment aone right now, but it'll have to wait, because, Kyle, all hell has broken loose."

Kyle's embrace did not waver as he asked, "What's happened?"

"It was Ryan all along . . . just as we figured. Only problem is, sounds like something has snapped in his mind. I believe he's on his way now to get that silver." Seth threw Paige a cautious look. "There is one other thing . . . Ryan is holding Paige's little boy hostage out there on that plantation."

Seth could see the startled expression on his friend's face when the child was mentioned. Kyle had no idea Paige had a son, nor did he know the child was his.

"Kyle . . . Seth," Paige said as she looked from one to the other. "Please . . . I know stopping . . . Ryan is what is important. But . . . I'm so afraid he will hurt Jason." A confused frown crossed Kyle's brow when he heard Paige had named her son after him. Paige continued, as she turned to her beloved. "Kyle, I only found out tonight that it was Ryan and Oscar who betrayed you. All these years . . . I had no . . . idea that you were still . . . alive." She glanced back toward Seth. "I can now understand why you were so hostile toward me the other day. But please, please, try to save my little boy!"

Kyle cradled her head to his chest. "Hush, my love. Don't cry. I'll save your son for you." He pulled away from her enough for her to see the words he was speaking were the truth. "I can see how everything was twisted by Ryan's lies . . . and

Paige, he has to be stopped." He was silently telling her Ryan's life might hang in the balance.

"I know. You do what you have to," she said softly.

"Kyle," Seth spoke up. "I've got plenty of men. You go ahead to the plantation and take a couple of my men with you. I think we can manage Ryan and his band of cut throats all right." Seth caught Paige's fullest attention. "Paige, when we met the other day, you had the boy with you . . . well, I didn't tell Kyle *nothing* about him. I figured it would be better if you were the one to explain." He walked slowly outside leaving the reunited lovers together while he got things organized.

"So you have a son," Kyle stated slowly, taking a deep breath. He gazed adoringly at Paige and tried to smile. "You know me, I love kids. Regardless of who his father is, he is still a part of you, and I'll love him as much as his mama." He spoke of the future when everything would be right again.

Paige looked up at Kyle. Even though she was under a terrible amount of pressure, she had to stifle a smile. "I believe you will have no problem loving Jason. He is a darling child. In fact, he is exactly like his father. He looks just like *you!*"

It took a moment for her words to sink in. When they finally did, Kyle blinked in surprise. "What!" he exclaimed.

Paige giggled as she explained further about Jason. When she finished, she was greatly touched to see a trickle of a tear seep from Kyle's eyes.

"He cheated us out of a lot, didn't he?" Kyle asked in a gruff voice.

"Yes, he did. But we'll have to put it all behind us," she said softly, wondering if it were possible.

Kyle walked determinedly to the door. "Time is wasting. I'll take a few men with me, and we'll go after the boy. You stay here where it's safe," he said with a deadly gleam in his eye.

"Oh no! I'm going too! We have been through too much for us to be parted now!" she said adamantly.

Kyle looked at her deeply, then kissed her with tenderness. "All right, but you'll have to promise to stay low and well out of the way."

"I will."

The ride to the plantation hadn't lasted long, but a great deal of time had passed while Kyle and his men crept as close to the house as possible. Paige drew back in alarm when suddenly Ryan ran out of the house and shouted something to a few of the men still standing in the yard. Ryan looked and acted insane. He was yelling and thrashing his arms wildly about. The men rode off quickly and Kyle motioned for his men to follow them. He felt he could take Ryan by himself. He inched closer to the house, cautioning Paige to stay low when Sara, her maid, came running out of the house screaming to the top of her lungs.

"He's gonna kill him! Lord, please send help 'fore he beats poor little Jason to death!"

Kyle leaped from his crouching position and started running as fast as he could. He ran past Sara with pistol drawn as she stared after him, her mouth agape as if she couldn't quite believe her prayer had been answered so promptly.

Kyle kicked open the front door in time to see Ryan raise a thick leather strap over the child huddled in the corner.

"Hey, bastard!" Kyle shouted enraged. "How about picking on someone your own size?"

Ryan turned around and stared at Kyle as if he was seeing a ghost. Then he overturned a table which held a burning lamp to try to stop Kyle's advance.

Instantly, flames leaped everywhere, feeding on the sheet-draped furniture, as the two men fought. Kyle hit Ryan, then Ryan punched and gouged at Kyle. For endless minutes, the battle continued as the fire raged out of control.

Paige and Sara stood in the front yard, watching in panic as the flames crept higher through the house. Paige began screaming for Kyle and Jason to get out of there before it was too late. Then Paige took off running for the house; she knew she had to get inside and save her child. Somehow, she had to have faith that Kyle could fend for himself. They had to be reached before the raging inferno became worse, or no one would escape alive. Paige felt herself being pulled down from behind and Sara pinned her mistress to the ground.

"No! You can't go in there! You'll die too!" Sara shouted.

Then suddenly, the women stopped their struggles as they watched in terrifying horror as the roof of the house came crashing down, forever trapping the ones inside in its burning hell.

Paige started to rise, then she slumped back to the earth. Tears of anguish were running down her face as the flames shot up into the sky. She stared at the blazing spectacle with a searing pain of anguish. Falling forward, Paige beat the ground with her fists, as she screamed hysterically. Her world was gone. It had been utterly destroyed. Fate had played a cruel trick on her, giving her a beautiful son, then giving her back her lost love, then tragically taking them both away. As Paige was crying in torment, she looked up, dazed and confused when she vaguely heard Sara cry out. "Look! Look, Miz Paige!"

Through her tear-laden lashes, she saw Kyle coming around what used to be the corner of the house. He was carrying Jason in his strong arms.

Kyle knew they had a great and glorious future ahead of them when he saw Paige's tear-streaked face break into a bright, beautiful smile, and when he felt his son's arm clutching him tightly around the neck. He knew everything would be all right for them again. He also knew that Seth would be successful in stopping Ryan's men and their ill-formed plans. He imagined Paige's joy when she discovered the children were living with him on his ranch and how their faith in her had never wavered. But his greatest joy was in knowing he would hold his love tightly in his arms under the star-filled West Texas sky.